Crossing the Lines

Crossing the Lines

MELVYN BRAGG

SCEPTRE

Copyright © 2003 Melvyn Bragg

First published in Great Britain in 2003 by Hodder and Stoughton
A division of Hodder Headline

The right of Melvyn Bragg to be identified as the
Author of the Work has been asserted by him in accordance
with the Copyright, Designs and Patents Act 1988.

A Sceptre Book

3 5 7 9 10 8 6 4 2

A CIP catalogue record for this title is available from the British Library.

ISBN 0 340 82965 6

Typeset by Hewer Text Ltd, Edinburgh
Printed and bound by Clays Ltd, St Ives plc

Hodder and Stoughton
A division of Hodder Headline
338 Euston Road
London NW1 3BH

‒⁓⁓‒

PART ONE
EASTER, 1955

‒⁓⁓‒

CHAPTER ONE

'Joe! Want a ride, Joe? I'll show you something.'

The words had to be repeated. The boy was deeply sucked into the shop's display. He was not, as might seem, fastened there by the footballs and cricket balls, the tennis racquets and cricket bats. They furnished the best window-excuse in the town, but it was himself who held his hungry gazing, his own reflection, transparently imposed on the armoury of sporting objects. His own face challenged him as he tested how long he could hang on without flinching, without his mind or was it the soul abandoning him, hovering outside him, leaving him a mere body, paralysed by this unnameable affliction that he had to face out in secret and alone.

He was winning these days, but not always. He knew he had to construct something untouchable inside himself and that could only be done by tests and dares, however often they misfired. But on this morning, this spring morning, this day when his dad had pointed out some returning swallows and the northern sun had a shine of warmth in it, he was winning. He was not divided. He half hummed, half sang to himself, in private cautious celebration, 'Dem bones, dem bones, dem dry bones, now hear the word of the Lord.'

The second shout, more imperative, hooked him and slowly, as if

3

afraid he would spill something brim full, he turned and smiled because it was Diddler and Lizzie. It would be worth it. He crossed the street and sat on the flat cart beside Lizzie.

'The time has come,' Diddler announced, 'to break in that young fella at the back. He's been wild long enough, Joe, and Lizzie's going to help me make a man of him.'

Joe tried to look appraisingly at the glossy piebald unbroken colt whose lead had been tied to the back of the cart. He knew that it was the best Diddler had ever bought at Wigton Horse Sales. Everybody knew. 'More than fifteen hands already. See the stamp of him,' boasted the man whose tinker neckerchiefs and gaudy waistcoats were envied by the dully dressed schoolboy. 'Never had an animal as just so. The breeding in him would satisfy the Queen of England.' Now was the time for the breaking in and Joe was invited, accidentally. No matter. He would be there. 'Lizzie here,' Diddler continued, 'is the best hand at breaking in a horse you could meet any place on God's earth and I'll swear to that!' He gave the bold-looking girl a doting smile, which showed off all his gums.

Lizzie laughed loudly then put her hand to her open mouth repeatedly as she let loose a continuous note which the slapping punctuated into an Indian war cry. Whenever Joe saw Lizzie – who had grown up in the yard next to his when they both lived in the slums in the nucleus of the old town – he felt a pang of grief that he was not older so that he could go with her. Lizzie had just left school, about to join the two hundred or so other Wigton girls at the clothing factory. Passing out of girlhood, she would be eternally out of reach.

'She came to Vinegar Hill on the dot!' said Diddler as his old ginger mare plodded up towards the Memorial Monument known as the Fountain. 'On the dot. She loves Vinegar Hill now – don't you, Lizzie?'

4

Again the doting smile, again Lizzie's challenging laugh. Joe felt left out.

'My dad lived in Vinegar Hill when he was little.'

'So he did,' said Diddler. 'And a game cock he was, the same boy. Afraid of nothing. We sort them out on Vinegar Hill.' He sized up the boy: blue-eyed like his father but without the bite of copper hair, more sandy, gentler, like his face, more his mother's boy, her wariness.

Joe was pleased by the 'game cock' and he tried to picture his father as a boy in that ramshackle heap of buildings called Vinegar Hill, fortressed in age and squalor, moated by wisps of field though plumb in the gut of the town. 'Afraid of nothing.' That brought the shadow: unlike himself, afraid of everything. He concentrated on the piebald roped behind him, at the white star on its forehead, and tried to work out how they measured the fifteen hands.

'Look at her now,' said Diddler, aloud but to himself. 'Isn't she the one?' It was not to Lizzie he referred but to a middle-aged woman hanging above him, as still as a portrait. There was puzzlement but more admiration in his tone, a tone which in some measure reflected the generous part of the town who respected Mrs. Stanford's daily vigil at the window. The scandalised part despised her for it, saying it ruined dignity, dissolved sympathy, made an exhibition of her: and that this vanity excused her husband's crime.

'So what are you thinking?' Diddler murmured, weighing her up. He was more than ordinarily entranced by her. There she sat this Maundy Thursday morning, as on every morning, framed in the central window on the first floor in the fine rooms above her brazen husband's ambitious business. She was dressed for a visit, hair strictly parted in the old style, fine antique necklace and brooches well displayed. She looked down on the town, staring it out.

'If you could turn your looks into your revenge, Mrs. Stanford, I

5

know where they would take you. They would fly across the Fountain, up the High Street, up to the bell tower on the great house on the hill where you come from, but you'd fly over that too, wouldn't you, missus, and find out the little bungalow he built for the other one, the one he spends all his nights with, and keeps without shame. But she'd disappoint you, missus, because I know the woman, I find the bits and pieces he gives her, the bird baths, the gnomes with fishing rods over a small pond, bits of statues he brings her for her little front garden, and she's just a pleasant, soft, easy body, Mrs. Stanford, nowhere near what you want her to be. Nowhere near your weight.'

For a moment or two the thought yet again flared up that one day he might contrive to steal that still figure from its frame. Diddler was seduced by her remoteness, that stillness, elegance of dress, just waiting, he thought, to be taken and despite his rock realism, there was in the silence of the man some voice that whispered, 'But why not by me?' What style the woman had, he thought! 'It's revenge you dream of, isn't it?' he said to himself. 'You'll take it one day, missus, I'd bet the piebald on it.'

On the day she did take her revenge, the tinker was deep in the country, trading, and he did not witness the prime town taxi, the polished old funereal Daimler, take her up the Hill, past the great house of her early childhood, park outside the bungalow and wait. After, it was reported, looking with contempt at the garden, she went in, straight-backed, and stayed for almost an hour. News of the encounter was merely gossip and rumour and all that fed it was the hunted look which replaced Mr. Stanford's brazen air and the end of his quaint ornamental gifts.

Diddler tipped his cap to her as he always did and Mrs. Stanford ignored him as she ignored all of them.

A cluck, a flick of the reins and the mare grudgingly moved into a trot, taking them out of the old town, past fields in the direction of one of the new council estates, down West Hill to the field of the famed copper beech, still stripped for winter, buds not visible on the immense and complex brain of branches that spanned the River Wiza. Joe opened the gate and Diddler drove down to a place that sloped sweetly into a rare straight stretch of the compulsively wending river.

'Now then,' he said, 'say farewell to your careless youth, my beauty.'

He undid the lead and walked gently into the stream. The two-year-old followed, already wary. 'He's been handled carefully, you see,' he said, partly to himself, partly to Joe and Lizzie, but mostly to have the sound of his familiar warm voice beguile the suspicious animal. 'He's got used to the bit. You can't do anything with a horse until it is comfortable in the mouth, so.' Joe had seen cowboys breaking horses – bucking, high-rearing, head-dipped, bow-backed frenzy – and he looked fearfully at Lizzie, who was wholly absorbed in studying the apprehensive colt.

'Now then, young fella, we'll just slip this on,' and the tinker's hand smoothed the slightly shivering neck and tracked down the right leg to the hoof, lifted gently, a loose figure of eight loop of thick twine slipped on, tightened but still some slack in it. His wide, rather Mongolian face turned to them and split into a smile. 'He can't rear up now, you see, Lizzie, they can only rear with one leg going up in front of the other. I'll take him in a bit deeper, then he won't be able to buck either – he has to put his head right down for that and he won't put his head under the water.'

Joe was impressed that Diddler walked into the river as if the water did not matter. His boots, the bottoms of his trousers, soaked in an instant. But all impressions – the sense of trespass in this private

7

field, the vague consciousness of wrongdoing to be at this on Holy Thursday, the pride in being included – were wiped out when Lizzie, barefooted, walked forward, slim, erect, tucking her skirt into her knicker bottoms. For some moments she simply stood beside the colt and then, slowly and tenderly, laid herself over the now restless straining animal, draped herself with sure care over its back, just below the tensed black neck, her slim white legs dangling, her upper body and head hidden from Joe's sight, and the boy stared with unacknowledged lust at the bottom half of her, supine, passive, acting dead on the trembling, shuddering body of the violated animal which could not rear or buck, could not lift his front legs but tried to kick out the back, twisted and humped with all his powers to throw off this terrible invasion, straitjacketed in panic which pushed the blood violently through his near bursting heart. He neighed shrilly, thrilling Joe with the high screaming sound of it, wrenched against this clamp, swivelled his head to bite at Lizzie, but she was well placed, just too far away, lying without moving, seeming light, while Diddler stood in the river holding the lead, murmuring, 'Now then. Now then . . .' at the young horse, sweating with fear and fury, but water-bound, maddened, trapped under the stripped network grandeur of the copper beech. Joe was swept up in a force of short-breathed excitement which had to be wordless, choked-on, he knew, not to make a sound.

'Straddle him over, Lizzie. Nice and quiet.'

Not immediately, waiting for her own guiding pulse, Lizzie swung one leg over the broad back; it seemed lazy, the way she moved, sat up, patted and soothed the sweating pelt, held onto the mane. The man let the colt calm itself, gave it full time, and then in a rapid move, plunged his hand into the water and released the front legs, ready for anything. 'Now then,' he repeated, his eyes fixed on those of the terrified piebald, 'we'll walk him in the river for a while, Lizzie.'

8

She tapped its flanks with her bare heels, taking it into water a couple of feet deep, water which submerged all its forces of attack. For some time Lizzie kept it in that narrow stretch, under the open roof of bare branches, slowly backwards and forwards, her long white legs nudging, guiding, her hair covering her face as she leaned forward on its neck and talked and stroked and brought the broken colt into its new world.

On the bank beside Joe and as lost as the boy in watching them, the man said,

'She's some girl, eh Joe?' He took a stump of a cigarette from behind his ear. 'She's stopping being a girl now, Joe, she'll be bringing out the itch in a man soon enough, but that's not for you, not yet.' He lit up, his eyes fixed on the pair of them.

She was out of the water and in the field now, sure of the horse and looking round at them, knowing they were looking at her, excited.

Joe's friend Speed had gone with her on his last leave. Smart in his army uniform, toughened, clipped, but still friendly enough to the younger Joe, whose father had stood in for Speed's own. Speed had said she was a sex-pot, but Joe could tell, jealousy a sure analyst, that he really liked her as well. He looked at her, bare-backed, bare-legged, in the spring meadow, the northern sun finally this late morning shifting the heavy dew, and knew that it was hopeless, even prayer would not help, 'dem bones, dem bones' crept across his mind once more as he willingly let himself be seduced by the sight and thought of her, 'now hear the word of the Lord'. Helpless with longing.

A fine animal, Diddler thought, broken in the old way, the way it had been done as long as you could think back, a kindly sure way, two beautiful creatures out there in the field, the girl the master now.

'I suppose you'll want to be paid,' he said when eventually she brought the horse back to them. Joe drew away from the power of the creature: the rage was still in the eyes, the force of breath through pink enlarged nostrils.

'You said half a crown.' The smile slid from the slim, success-flushed face and the lean jaw lifted just a fraction, giving her, Diddler thought, the look of a woman you desired. He fished in his trouser pocket, drew out the large silvery coin, spat on it, gave it a rub on his sleeve, and placed it on the thick crinkled yellow nail of his thumb.

'Double or quits, Lizzie?'

She held out her hand.

'You're a good girl, Lizzie,' he said and slapped the coin onto her slender palm.

CHAPTER TWO

Sam went up the street although there was no need. True he had his day's bets worked out and would call in and place them, but they could have waited until the bookie's runner ducked into his pub for the usual illegal transactions at midday. True it was good business practice to be out, to be seen and greet, but in mid morning with most spenders at the factories or on the farms the male encounters would be with that unyielding core of Wigton men who preferred to pass their days philosophically, broke, leaning against the railings around the Fountain, honing their local intelligence.

But on these quiet streets, after the army, after the factory, he felt acutely, and at last, that he was his own man.

Sam relished that he could stroll so pointlessly on the knuckle of a working day. No matter he had been up and working since eight, no matter he would be behind the bar until after ten in the evening, this was true liberty.

He smoked as he walked and every so often he would stop for a crack. It was as if, for a few minutes, he had slid out of his own skin and put on the workless, untied, feathered world of P.G. Wodehouse, who could always cast a spell on him, Bertie Wooster golfing down Piccadilly to his club, the grind of the world buried, out of mind.

There was the lightly sentimental song that had come in a few months back – 'Softly, softly turn the key that opens up my heart'. Sam liked the title, could hear Ruby Murray sing it, liked to use the phrase. 'Softly, softly' up peaceful sun-washed King Street. Ruby Murray and Maureen O'Hara both had a look of Ellen: she was in the song for Sam. When Joe was younger, the boy had said once or twice that his mam looked 'just like a film star' – a passing, childish remark that Sam kept.

Ellen, left to guard the pub, knelt on the recently installed padded bench in the darts room and looked out at Market Hill, arena of her childhood, now taken over by the bus company whose red double and single deckers claimed a space once – as Mr. Hawesley pointed out – designated as solely for the use of the people of Wigton. Designated, he had used the word more than once, in the deeds of a trust, which should have been inviolable. You have to employ eternal vigilance. Ellen liked the high talk of this new chairman of the Labour Party, which held its weekly committee meeting in the kitchen of the pub.

She had to stay in until Sam returned because Joe also was out and there had been no cleaner for a week and the notion that the pub could be left unguarded even on a sunny innocent spring morning was unacceptable.

Because there was no one to help, Ellen had got up earlier every morning that week, and employed Joe more than usual. That morning, after he had chopped the kindling for the weekend she had asked him to lay the fires – kitchen, darts room, bar, singing room – before helping Sam carry up the crates of beer. All three of them had hurried their work and now she was beached in unaccustomed idleness.

So she knelt on the leatherette bench and gazed across towards the house where her Uncle Leonard and Aunt Grace had taken her in as a child. To most observers it would seem an ordinary, monotone prospect, with the sun lighting up the high row of big early Victorian terraced houses that crested the top of the hill and acted like a wall of the old town. For Ellen this small patch was a space of histories, hers, Joe's, their friends, of adventures, fears and games that endlessly filled the lengthy light of summer evenings, of growing, of weddings, deaths, new generations. She could pluck away the façades of those houses and know something, often more than was comfortable, of the lives and ways of every one of those whose refuge and shelter they were.

Beyond the Hill, past the steps leading up to Birdcage Walk, and the woodyard, beyond the Swimming Baths and the Auction Fields, beyond even the great Georgian house surmounted by that unlikely Italianate bell tower, were the lapping, undulating fields, winding rivers, unnoticed hamlets, remote cottages, lonely copses, remains of mediaeval forest, scars of ancient occupation and battlefield which she knew from country walks with her girl friends and bike rides with Sam and their gang before the war.

There would be daffodils everywhere now, you came across them in the lanes to farmyards, clusters bending over a stream, their meek heads nodding or shaking in a gentle wind or tossing their heads as it said in the poem she had by heart from school, wild but well secured, the yellows in the petals and trumpet always making her smile to herself, such a golden gift of colour in the sombre browns and greens of the dour Cumbrian land. She could see now, summon up, many places of daffodils.

Once upon a time such a dip into the reservoir of her past would have been more than enough to occupy her, would have been welcomed, as would this rare chance to be utterly alone in the crowded world of pub and customers, opening times, meal times and cleaning, but not now. Not quite enough. New purposes were budding: one almost immediate and open and backed by Sam; another, soon, he did not know about; and under all, a tidal pull which she herself could not clarify, an ache, even a hunger.

'Sam Richardson standing there sunning himself in all his glory! Good morning to you, Sam.'

Sam turned and shook his head at Sister Francis, his favourite of all the Irish nuns in the convent attached to St. Cuthbert's, just down from his pub. Her putty glasses were most of what could be seen of the playful pure fat little face peeping out of the periscope of rigid snow-white wimple.

'I see you won,' said Sam.

'Only just.' She shook her head. 'We'll never catch St. Aidan's.'

'Second again?'

'Second for the second season running.' She was vexed. 'We need a strong centre forward, Sam.'

'They all say that.'

'But they're good lads. They behave themselves when they come into the pub, don't they now?'

'Good as gold, Sister Francis.' He halted. His eyes had swung to the markedly slighter, younger nun beside Sister Francis.

'Sister Philomena. She's just over from Cork. Very young. Untried. And much to learn. This is Sam Richardson, the landlord of the Blackamoor pub, and very generous he is when we go collecting at Christmas.'

'Just out of Ireland, eh?' For Sam, Ireland was a heaven of fine horses, of men as mad on sport as he was, of fellows like Diddler he had grown up with, of long stories that could keep the night at bay. 'I've always fancied Ireland.'

'There you are now,' said Sister Francis.

'What do you make of Wigton?'

The slight, enwrapped figure who had seemed shy and girlishly subservient first looked at Sister Francis, took the nod, then lifted up startlingly bold eyes to Sam, eyes with an expression that shed all the bondage of confined apparel and said, 'It's a terrible disappointment, Mr. Richardson, it is. In Ireland we were told about this great place, England, the palaces, the castles, the big streets, that ruled half the world and lords and ladies and such and I land up in Wigton! Give me Cork any day!' Eyes, angry now, swept up and down the High Street, ignoring, unaware, uncaring of its Roman and Anglo-Saxon roots, its unquiet persistent history, finding only a place to scorn in its meagre putter of small and few motor cars, its more numerous bicycles and now Diddler's little cavalcade trotting contentedly back towards Vinegar Hill. 'And horses!' she said. 'Nobody said you'd still have horses!'

'You see, Sam,' said Sister Francis, 'there's work to be done.' Firmly. 'We must visit Mr. Nicholls now, the tumour's as big as a football.'

Without waiting for a response, indeed blocking it, she shepherded her younger colleague away, leaving Sam to scratch his head with the hand that held the cigarette while he followed them, darkly exotic, wearing robes from remote, pre-Christian Eastern deserts and coiffed in a style perfected in the legendary and jewelled courts of mediaeval Europe, come to this temperate post-war plain northern town as Sisters of Mercy, and yet he also saw them on patrol, one guarding the other's back, forever on the lookout for the enemy. He followed them until the light wind billowed them around the corner. How, he wondered, could a startling feisty young girl like that so bind and crib herself for the whole of her life? A pure impulse from childhood now straitjacketed. How would she cope with such an imprisonment?

15

Henry Allen was standing outside his betting shop, pale consumptive face tilted into the weak sun.

'Take advantage, Sam, every drop.'

Sam handed over his bets. Henry glanced at them.

'Will you be at Carlisle on Monday? We used to have good days there, eh, Sam?'

Sam nodded: he had worked part-time for Henry before getting the pub and Carlisle Races had always been a highlight.

'We had our times,' said Sam, absently.

'They were good times,' Henry urged. 'We always ended up at the Crown and Mitre. Still do.' The barest pause. 'Here comes trouble.'

It was only Joe, flattered by Henry's accusation. He was fingering one of his last three boils, suddenly becoming active on the back of his neck. He stopped at a look from Sam and stretched himself to catch up to his father's height.

The men talked on, clocking the town. A slow time of day. Women ferrying the shopping for the next meal when the men came back. Clothes and shops still drab, still weary, after the second great bloodletting of the century. The men looked on names that had survived. Topping the Butcher, Redmayne Gentlemen's Outfitters, Parks for Shoes, McMechan for Stationery and Papers, Snaith for Clocks and Jewellery, Studholmes, Ismays, two Johnstons, and others, all surmounted by flats to which the owners would soon retreat for Thursday Early Closing and keep their watch over the shop-shut streets.

The vicar drove by in his old-fashioned open topped car: Joe saw that Edward's mother was beside him, long blonde hair loose. He did not know where to look. Surely he should have been doing something more Christian on Maundy Thursday: but the vicar waved, while Edward's mother looked straight ahead.

'Off to the woods we go.' Henry's wasted face followed them enviously.

'Softly, softly . . .'

—◊—

Ellen had her coat on, not for warmth but for respectability, and she went out the minute they returned.

Determined though she was, it was not an easy task she had set herself, not for someone whose will had been so self-restrained, so resolute in courting ordinariness, aspiring to anonymity.

'S-S-Sadie's up street.'

The two women had planned it so.

'It's you I want to see, George. It won't take a minute.'

George opened the door of the semi-basement more widely and Ellen stepped into the damp bleak room. She could not remember it looking so bare and poor but she had only been there before with Sadie, whose character warmed the space around her.

She was uncomfortable to be alone in a room with a man and on his territory even though she knew George well, had been at school with him. She wondered, as did the rest of the town, how this mild, slight, stammering figure could turn into the monster who beat his wife, and the thought clouded her purpose. How could anyone beat Sadie? Drink did it, they said, but other people took drink. 'W-w-well?' He made no gesture that she should sit down, as alien to a social visit as she was to such a potential confrontation. She swallowed at her nervousness.

'I've come about Sadie. Doreen can't do the cleaning any more and I want Sadie to come back.' It was harder than she thought.

George registered nothing and in that twilit mouldering basement she began to be afraid.

She paused. It was his turn, surely. It was he who had forbidden Sadie to work in the pub after rumour had wrongly convinced him that she was having a fling with Colin, Ellen's half-brother: the beating he had given her now re-appeared in Ellen's imagination and she took a step back, back towards the door. 'Sam won't let Colin in the pub now.' He had done odd jobs there for a few years but finally Sam had banned him for persistent theft.

'Colin comes nowhere near it now.' This was not strictly accurate. After the final thefts, Sam had let Colin keep on the loft above the old stable for his prize budgerigars. But he came and went by a separate door and surely that did not count.

'The money's good,' Ellen added, wildly, surprising herself.

'How m-m-much?'

She told him.

He seemed to be making a calculation and making it carefully. She had time to notice how big his nose was in that pinched face. The black curly hair uncombed, braces over a tieless shirt; not a scrap of fire. She felt cold.

Then he smiled.

'You never ch-change, Ellen,' he said. 'You were always the b-b-bonniest lass at school.' He stared at her, greedily enjoying the thick black hair, the rather pale slim face, the nervous, exciting, he thought, brown eyes.

Ellen nodded, now truly afraid. Her lips parted, she passed her tongue over their inner skin.

'Remember when Joe Willie t-t-tickled Miss Ivinson's bare b-bum with a bunch of n-nettles when he made a hole in that c-c-corrugated lavatory?'

George laughed, a gurgling sound, a laugh stuck, not happily, in the throat. 'There was hell to pay,' he said and shook his head relishing the memory.

'Let her come back, George. I miss her, you see.'

'Do you?' He looked amazed. 'M-m-miss Sadie?'

'I do.'

And she did. Gypsy-faced Sadie, childless, moneyless, cheaply dressed, dancing Sadie, coarse-toned Sadie, bottom of the heap Sadie, but to Ellen a conduit into wholly unexpected gusts of happiness, sudden songs, trivial moments charged with life, life never let by, let down, cold-shouldered, resented: a friend.

'And you'd be doing me a favour, George.'

That was the line she had rehearsed. She felt rather a cheat saying it.

Almost imperceptibly in that crepuscular, damp-moulded room, he nodded.

———⟋⟍———

'Sadie's coming back.'

'Joe's going to give up training.' Sam delivered his own news in a tone that punctured Ellen's announcement.

'I didn't say for certain.' The boy kept his head down.

It was rare that the three of them sat down for a meal together. Ellen had saved up her news as a treat. She had not anticipated no interest.

'He can give up training if he wants.' Ellen was more vehement than necessary and knew she should not have added, 'He gave up the piano. Money wasted.'

'They told me you were in line for county trials.'

Joe bent his sodden head to the half-slice of white bread well covered in jam. He should have said nothing. Whenever you told parents anything they made something of it. They took it the wrong way. They turned it back on you. They found a way to make you wish you had said nothing. It was only because he and his father had been laughing over bits they liked in *Lucky Jim* that he had dropped his guard. It never paid. Proof: she'd brought up the piano again.

'Maybe he wants to concentrate on other things. Swimming does take a lot of time.' She was back on his side.

And she was right. She was often right about him but he would not admit it aloud. Even admitting things gave them a chance to get in to you. He reached out for more bread.

'So Sadie's coming back.'

Sam looked at Joe for a common and companionable response but the boy's head was still down. A few minutes before they had been laughing together and Sam had felt warmth between them, a sense of equality, the same book read, the same passages hitting the funny bone, now gone, so suddenly.

'I like Sadie,' Joe said, through crumbs and jam, and Ellen was satisfied. Then he added:

'Does that mean Colin will be coming back?'

Ellen looked away so they could not see the blush of shame.

'No.' Sam looked towards his wife's averted face. 'Colin's not coming back.'

'Choir practice,' said Joe, grabbing a biscuit. 'Early tonight.'

And he was out of the room.

To do something, Ellen began to clear up although neither she nor Sam had finished.

'So it's only Saturday afternoon I can go then, is it?' It was imperative for her to go on Saturday afternoon. Yet she wanted to provoke Sam.

Her tone was brittle, but Sam thought he understood: she was a lioness with a cub over Colin, even now when she could see through him.

'With one thing and another.'

'With Carlisle Races on Monday.'

'Why do you have to go so far on one of our busiest weekends?'

'I want to go over Easter.'

'But it takes so long to get there, Ellen; there and back.'

She took a breath: this was the second test.

'Mr. Hawesley's said he'd give me a lift. He visits an aunt near there. He says it would be no trouble and I could be back by six, seven at the very latest. I'll leave you your tea. Joe could get fish and chips for your dinner.'

Sam pulled out a cigarette and said nothing, wondering why such a helpful, friendly offer from a man for whom he had respect, certainly trusted, a man of education . . . He lit up and drew to the bottom of his lungs . . . Why was he a little unnerved?

'You seem to have it all sorted out,' he said.

Ellen was stung by the softly uttered truth.

'It is my father's grave,' she said.

Sam drew again and poured himself another cup of tea.

'Well then,' he said, 'you must go.'

Ellen cleared the table in silence. They heard the door slam as Joe heaved his bike out and set off for St. Mary's. It would be opening time in less than half an hour.

'I'm glad Sadie's coming back,' Sam said and Ellen nodded, but still felt, unaccountably, shaky.

She went upstairs to get ready and Sam tried not to think of the two of them together, in the car.

Ellen had baulked at the big revelation. Her Aunt Grace had told her of a letter received by Colin, a letter from his mother, the woman her father had married after running away from her own mother. Grace had made Colin show her the letter, in which she informed him that she planned to go to his father's grave at about four o'clock on Easter Saturday.

Colin said he would not reply, just turn up or not as he felt like. Ellen had seized the moment and written, saying that she too would be there that day, that time. She was distressed at concealing this from everyone, even Sam. It would have been a relief to talk it over with him. But something in her wanted to hold it to herself alone.

She just had time for a quick bath. She was still cold from that meeting with George – so mild a man he seemed and yet she had come out of that cellar scared cold.

She heard the front door being opened for custom. Not a day it did not open.

CHAPTER THREE

Joe stayed because Alfred stayed. The vicar's son needed to be reminded of the invitation to tea delivered by Joe the previous Sunday and instantly, graciously accepted by Alfred, on holiday from his public school: but Joe wanted to be sure.

Alan, his best friend, and Edward, another of the gang, had hurried away after the choir practice to Edward's house for pontoon and maybe for Edna. It had been hard not to go with them but he had to be certain of Alfred and at this climactic time in the Christian story, his own faith, now at full stretch, demanded he resist all temptation. This could count.

The organist had stayed, two tenors, one bass, a soprano and two altos: Alfred and he were the only trebles. The vicar entered the vestry. Slowly, burdened, Joe could tell, by what in the Palm Sunday sermon he had called 'the gravity of Christ's Passion'. Immediately Joe himself felt more solemn. He set himself to try to capture a worthy Christian image from the flicker of pictures that moved like shadows in his mind, a worthy thought from the tumult scurry of almost words. If he was to be a true Christian he must learn to arrest thought and concentrate solely on Jesus Christ. 'These paintings,' the vicar's beautifully bred, rich voice was low, dramatic, 'show Christ crucified as depicted by artists of the past. I want you to look at them, in silence, I want you to dwell on them, leave singly, and nurse them in your minds through this night of betrayal.'

Joe was overcome with significance. He felt he ought to recite to himself 'Jesu Joy of Man's Desiring' which they had just been practising.

They shuffled up, one by one, as for communion, or as pilgrims to a holy well, and the vicar, on the other side of the vestry table, announced, almost chanted, the names of the artists as he pointed to one garishly coloured print after the other. 'Masaccio, Fra Angelico, Antonello da Messina,' the pronunciation was round, lingering, 'Raphael, Titian, el Greco, Rubens, Anthony van Dyck, Velasquez, Delacroix. All these great and religious painters drawn as we are to the Passion, a Passion that belongs to each one of us, a death that brought life to the world.'

Joe was intoxicated by the names and wanted to ask about them but he said nothing. He was fearful before the vicar and still ashamed that he had been barred from serving at the altar: a rejection, a fault he could never forget. For a while the depleted choir stood in solemn silence; only at an indication from the vicar – a hand barely raised – did they steal away. Alfred stayed and so did Joe. 'Which is your favourite?' Alfred's voice was light but utterly confident, clean of dialect, foreign to Joe's ears, cast from a different mould of diction.

'This.' The vicar pointed to the van Dyck.

Joe was disappointed. He would have bet on the Messina, with the two thieves racked, buckled, writhing on their common tree trunks, suffering every bit as much as they should while Christ just hung there, dead, on a proper cross, waiting to be resurrected. But he must be wrong and so he concentrated on the van Dyck. 'We see the resignation of Christ,' the vicar said, 'we see it in the grace and surrender of that broken body. He is not dead but he is beyond pain.'

What about the blood? Joe wanted to ask. That waterfall of blood coming from the wound the Roman soldier had made in his side with the sword, the blood coming out from the holes made by the nails. Didn't that hurt?

But he suppressed these thoughts and tried to see it from the vicar's point of view. 'The sun is obscured although it was the middle of the day. Jerusalem just seen in the distance, see? – he was crucified "Without a City Wall" as the hymn says, "where our dear Lord was crucified" . . .'

'Who died to save us all,' Joe whispered, to finish it off. 'Who's that woman at the bottom?' Joe's question was unpremeditated and too loud. The woman was dressed in gold, she was kneeling, her arms around the feet of Christ, her lips very near the nail on the left foot, Joe observed. He liked her long, loose golden hair.

'We think she is Mary Magdalene,' said the vicar, not quite prepared. He collected the prints together and walked out.

'I shouldn't have spoken,' Joe said, miserably. 'He said be silent.'

'I wasn't.' Alfred smiled.

'So I'll see you on Sunday, then? Four o'clock.'

'Spiffing.'

Alfred hurried after his father. Impatient though he was, Joe let him get a start, not wanting to seem to be cadging proximity to the vicar, cautious, even afraid of the commanding man of God. He counted to a hundred, then he sped out of the vestry, slung himself over the wall, down the twists and turns of Church Street, King Street, New Street. Edward's house.

Edna was there. So was Edward's mother, glowing in an obscurely exciting way that Joe could not fathom. She was a young woman and though she had mothered Edward and a younger sister she could still look even girlish, as she had that morning in the vicar's car. The woman at the foot of the cross, nearly kissing the nail! Edward's mother to a T. The same flowing hair! He would tell the vicar when he got the chance, just slip it in, show he took notice.

They made a place for him around the table and gave him his stack of matches. Edward's mother looked on from a fine armchair next to the fire. Alan and Edward flanked Edna but by stretching out his legs under the table, Joe managed to make contact with one of her feet. Should he tell Edward's mother she looked like the woman at the foot of the cross? He wanted to please her, both for herself and for this place, this haven, this kitchen.

In the pub, the kitchen would be filling up. Sometimes he would be drawn into the talk, even initiate it; it could be good. But it was not a real kitchen in a real house like this. Not a place for just the family and their friends. Not a kitchen barred to all but those belonging or those invited. This was a kitchen you all ate in together and at the same time. Just you. You did not have to go to your bedroom for peace and quiet or feel driven there by adult indifference. This was a kitchen a family lived in as they should.

They tried to let Edna win. She was not very clever at pontoon. She could have been utterly and disruptively hopeless and the three boys would not have given a hoot. Each was in a state of agitation about this well-developed girl, orphaned and just arrived from out of the country to live in Edward's house. Edward's father had been cousin to her father and in his typical Christian fashion – Edward's father, much older than his mother, was a scrupulous church warden – he had volunteered to take her in. The older woman watched eagerly, even greedily, as the three boys posed and played for the handsome, rather plump young girl's favours. The sadness about her won their sympathy, touched their sense of gallantry, increased their desire.

'I can see what your feet are doing, Joe Richardson,' said Edward's mother, lashing a blush onto his face, provoking a lie in his denial, and, 'Edward! I saw you give her that king!' Alan, the most careful, the solid to Joe's liquid, the polite to Edward's familiar, eluded her criticism, playing more stealthily, and winning her, Joe could see it from the glances.

Frustrated at merely commenting, Edward's mother said, 'Why don't you have a kissing contest?'

They stopped playing. It was as if she had become one of them.

'We did. When I was your age. Mind you,' her tone darkened, 'that wasn't long before they married me off.'

The pontoon school waited for more.

'There would be two or three lads. You would find a wood. I lived near woods just like you, Edna. I loved those woods. Deer came there in winter, big stags with antlers. The lads would be given five or ten minutes each or just until the lass,' she smiled proudly, and jutted her right thumb in the direction of her breasts, 'got sick of it. Best kisser got to go with me.'

That was fair, Joe thought. He had studied kissing at the Palace. As a younger boy, kissing on the screen had made him squirm, shut his eyes, groan, bend his head, feel horribly self-conscious, and it always held up the picture. Recently he had begun to take notice: there was a progression – pecking, first embrace, a decent one, a smacker, then all the way to torrid.

'I wouldn't like that.' Edna spoke firmly. 'I don't want them all just kissing over me.'

'Suit yourself.' The older woman was put out: her manner was more girlish than that of Edna: even a pout.

Nobody followed up. The game was suspended. The charge

which had been introduced by the kissing contest was replaced by general embarrassment.

'We had great times when I was a girl,' the tone was defiant, 'I should never have been made to leave.' Her expression became sullen. 'I was far too young to be brought to Wigton to marry anybody.' Edward's father had been represented as a good catch: money had changed hands but in the way of kindness, help for her parents with a large family, a good man, could even be spoken of as a gentleman. 'You could walk anywhere you wanted in the country without anybody spying on you! Everybody spies in Wigton.'

'I saw you in the vicar's car this morning,' said Joe.

'What of it?'

Edward looked frightened. Joe's tongue thickened. All the pleasant, stirring urges and incipient fantasies about Edna were blown out like a candle at those three hard words.

'He takes me back into the country to see my brothers and sisters. That's what vicars does.'

'The vicar showed us some pictures of the Crucifixion after choir practice and in the one he liked best there was a woman who looked like you.'

'Did she? On a picture?'

'Kissing His feet. *Nearly* kissing His feet.'

'He said he liked that one best?'

'He did, missus, honest.'

Her smile lit up the room.

'Come on, Edna. Let's get these lazy men something for their stomachs.'

They went into the tiny back kitchen – a luxury in its way – where meals could be prepared discreetly. Left alone, the three friends looked at each other with relief.

Edward took over.

'Let's divide her matches up between us,' he said. He handed the cards to Alan. 'Do a new shuffle.'

But the game soon petered out after the jam sandwiches. Joe saw Alan home, hoping to be invited in to the flat above their shop, but Alan just said, 'So long,' and went up the stairs alone. Just as well. Alan's mother seemed to hate him and would have found any excuse not to let him in.

It felt too early to go home. He decided to use the time. There was still some warmth in the air and Joe let himself drift around the honeycombed middle of the town, looking in the alleyways and the gaps which led to the old yards, seeking out passages slit narrowly between buildings. The lighting was poor, the darkness thick. 'Bible-black,' he said to himself. That was what he wanted. The English teacher had read out parts of a new play, saying it reminded him of Wigton. 'Bible-black.'

The two words seemed to guide him along Proctor's Row, which faced the churchyard. He went into the churchyard, its headstones made paving stones by the vicar, only three or four grandiose tombs remaining upright, the rest underfoot or down to grass. Even so, even though it was now supposed to be more like a park, even though Joe was long trousered and intimately acquainted with the geography of the place, there was apprehension, a prickling more demanding than the boil whose itch he had forced himself to ignore all day as an act of self-denial. But it was this apprehension turning to fear that he sought out.

He went behind the east window in the niche he had first found as a boy when they played hide and seek on choir practice nights. It was as well he knew the lie of it. There was no moon. He was bible-black.

It was, in its juvenile but purposeful way, a calling up of his demons. The dislocation of what might be his mind, or soul – that which made him know he was the boy he was – had tormented him for more than a year now. It was difficult to remember a time without it, without being scared to be alone or panicked totally by a scooping out of self which could not be resisted and left him helpless with terror until he was joined up to himself again. In desperation – no one to tell, nothing to refer to – he had begun to seek for ways to face it down. To let music drown him in its sensations. To engulf himself in reading so hard and fast that his head seemed to sweat with the cram of words: to look into mirrors and windows and let himself divide and wait, knowing he must not move until there was a reunion. Forcing it.

Now he stood, pressed shoulders against the east wall of the church, facing the black mass of the slaughterhouse. He was already flaring with anticipated fear at the mere sound of his breath. That it drew in. That it panted out. How did it keep on going on? What if he forgot how to suck it in? The sound of it was so dominating. No churchyard noises to distract: no owl hooting, no sudden flurry of wind. Just the breath. Panted out. Heaved in this time to make sure, a filling of his lungs. Why did that begin to unnerve him so much? An every day, every hour, every minute sound: living, dying, living, dying.

The fear gathered itself in the darkness, in the black holly tree, rising at him from the stricken headstones, from the tombs. He wanted it to come, the darkness to mix into his mind so that he could take it in, take it on and still not be split from himself. It was like being under water too long, swimming for a record underwater span, but you could reach for the surface in water. Here the dark just pushed in and his breath trembled, he saw the trembling of the horse's nostrils after Lizzie had broken it in, the skin on him grew clammy and oh! he wished he had not started this. He wished he had not dared this,

30

pinned below the east window which inside, in ruby and yellow and blue glass, showed and said, 'Suffer little children to come unto me and forbid them not.' 'Our Father,' he said, but not out loud, 'which art in Heaven.' He shut his eyes. There was Christ on the cross and the woman nearly kissing the nails. Just stay. As it rolled through him, just stay, as it rolled through him.

Eventually, weak-kneed, he walked away, not exulting in a victory but knowing that he had endured it and that not very long ago he would have fled before putting himself in such danger.

He was too shaky to face the pub but he needed a refuge. He made for the house in which he had been brought up with his mother during the war, his mother's Aunt Grace and Uncle Leonard's house, a big but familiar house, once given over to lodging rooms but lately reduced to one tenant, the schoolmaster Mr. Kneale, installed permanently it seemed in quaint space and comfort on the top floor. And Colin. Nothing would shake off Colin. Aunt Grace's failing health had prompted the running down of the business: Mr. Kneale was no trouble, a respected schoolmaster and by now a close friend of Leonard.

Joe deliberately took the darker route back, where he was unlikely to meet anyone, and he forced himself to stroll despite a drilling urgency, that he had to get at the boil. He had denied it long enough: a whole day surely proof enough that he could subdue the flesh.

He went straight to the bathroom, locked the door, flung off his jacket, tie, unbuttoned shirt and fingered it tenderly. Perhaps not quite perfectly ripe. Not that soft truly cushioned ripeness that gave at the base which told you that the core of it was ready to be squeezed out. But ripe enough. He could not resist: he had to evacuate that boil, that livid eruption gathering in its poison just below the collar line. He unpicked the scab with some skill: at one stage there had been nineteen boils. Down to three. There were still eight pock marks on his legs.

He pressed gently, from the base, wiping away the ooze with the flannel. The relief made him sigh contentedly, steadily working it out. By twisting his neck he could see it in the mirror. He surrounded the base and felt that central core, it slid under his fingertips as if trying to escape them: the fingertips cornered it, pressed, it slid away, pursued, encircled, held steady, then Joe applied sudden violent pressure. It began to rise, forcing out more yellow pus and the boy felt a thrill of pain as he struggled to break the core from its moorings deep in his neck: and succeeded. It hurt but he was jubilant! He wiped with the flannel and dabbed until nothing was left but the puckered tip, the wrinkled collapsed walls of skin no longer alive, no longer shiny and stretched by the poison. Two to go: still maturing.

'You took long enough. Your tea's nearly cold.'

Grace's complaint was a comfort. Joe blinked into the company of people he had known all his life. Leonard and Mr. Kneale were involved in a game of chess, which both professed to have played much better in their youth and, now re-stimulated by the teacher's purchase of a fine set at a knockdown price, was more an excuse for a conversation than a battle of wits. Grace was reading the local paper and she went back to it as soon as she saw Joe take up a biscuit.

Leonard parked his knight in a spot that signalled an interlude.

'So what's new, Joe? What's the little town up to tonight?'

Joe swallowed the tea without pleasure: it was cold but he had to swallow it.

'The vicar showed us pictures of Jesus Christ on the cross.'

'Did he now?' Mr. Kneale chimed in, encouraging, wanting more. Joe remembered that expectation. As always he tried to respond

32

to it, all but seeking out his absent mother whose glance would have told him to be respectful to Mr. Kneale, who had been so good to them while his father was away in the war, take notice of the helpful schoolteacher, such personal attention is a privilege.

'Different painters.' No names had registered. 'Long ago. With the two thieves, some of them, and Mary, Joseph,' faltering, 'disciples . . . God was in one of them – and there was one of a woman kneeling, hugging his feet.'

'That would be Mary Magdalene,' said Mr. Kneale.

Grace lifted her eyes in warning.

'It must have hurt.' Joe sensed that the subject was acceptable. He felt free. 'The vicar said he was beyond pain but it must have hurt before he got beyond it.'

'They do say being the Son of God he didn't feel pain like you and me.' Leonard wore his atheism discreetly. It was a religious town dominated by a dozen demanding denominations and his reputation as a solicitor's chief clerk and rent collector rested on being above suspicion.

'That Son of God business . . .' Mr. Kneale paused. Joe after all was still a boy: a boy on the way to being a youth, but more boy still: rather a late developer, Mr. Kneale thought, and all the better for it. He himself had been the same.

'There's many suffered worse,' Leonard pitched this in the tone of one musing, a statement that could be ignored, one presented in such a way as to deny direct confrontation.

'I'm inclined to agree with you,' said the schoolteacher.

'But he did it to save us all,' said Joe, taking the last sandwich.

'That's true,' Mr. Kneale was judicious. 'But that doesn't mean your Uncle Leonard's altogether wrong. I've gone right into the war business for this book and I would even go so far as to say that there's

33

Wigton men – and by extension men from all over – who have indeed suffered, who did suffer worse.'

'Worse than being nailed to a cross?'

Mr. Kneale pursed his lips – he had gone too far. But truth would out – and he nodded. *Wigton Men at War*, begun to celebrate the heroism, the epic courage of ordinary men, the sacrifice and joy of righteous battle, was taking him into darker areas than he had anticipated.

'And he rose again, you see.' Leonard pulled out a cigarette as he completed that sentence. Had he gone too far? He wanted some smoke between Grace and himself.

'He didn't know he would rise again!' Joe was heated. ' "My God, my God, why hast thou forsaken me?" he said. What about that?'

'Don't get him excited.' Grace would not be obscured. 'It's near his bedtime.' This was more than a hint: it was a ruling.

Mr. Kneale picked up the moment.

'I think this bishop will do the job nicely,' he said.

Joe lingered, wanting the argument to go on, happy in the companionship of these men. He sat beside Grace, reading the paper over her shoulder.

'Don't listen to your Uncle Leonard,' she whispered, 'he's been like this all week, since Mr. Churchill resigned.'

Grace had come to admire Leonard for being able to feel so deeply about someone he did not know. The more dependent on him she grew, the more she let her appreciation show. Leonard's involvement with the evils of socialism, the foolish doings of people half way across the world, trades unions on strike, America taking over, but above all with Mr. Churchill, had finally impressed her. She saw it as his hobby – some men kept pigeons, others had allotments; Leonard had a touch of the gentleman about him and so he had Public Affairs. And there was pride in having Winston Churchill in the family.

'End of an era,' said Leonard, scarcely acknowledging her. 'Downhill all the way from now on. Mark my words. How about that?' He moved a castle.

'Everybody has to retire at some time.' Mr Kneale spoke without lifting his gaze from the board. Leonard's move had surprised him.

'Hell-o! Now then! What's this, stranger?'

Colin's entry disturbed them all. Grace could see her nephew rather the worse for drink: she hated the coarseness it brought out, and feared drink would weaken him still further, as it had her brother, his father. Mr. Kneale regretted that an unusually interesting game would now be interrupted. Leonard detested him.

'I never see you nowadays, Joe.' There was genuine regret, even anguish, in Colin's tone and Joe's guilt flooded in.

'He's busy,' said Leonard.

'You mean I'm not?'

'I'll get you some tea,' said Grace, extricating herself with difficulty from the deep armchair. The second stroke had weakened her noticeably.

'I'm off,' said Joe.

'As soon as his Uncle Colin comes in, he's off.'

When Joe was younger, Colin had insisted he call him Colin. Now that his split with Sam had proved to be irreparable, he insisted on Uncle Colin. Joe no longer felt at ease in his company.

'He's gone off his Uncle Colin.'

He was a thin, even spindly young man, lank hair over-greased in a failed D.A. style, jacket draped like the much younger Teddy Boys, pasty-faced, a smoker of cigarettes to the smallest butt, in permanent

35

impermanent employment, but with a look sometimes exactly like Joe's mother.

'No I haven't,' Joe lied hotly.

'Have a walk up street with us, then.'

'I've got to get back.'

'Who says?'

Joe had no answer.

'Goodnight, then, Joe,' said Leonard, looking at Colin. 'Tell your dad we'll see him for the quiz as per usual.'

'The quiz I can't go to? In my own sister's pub!'

Colin slammed himself in Grace's armchair, crushing the news-paper.

The air was fresh and Joe did not rush across Market Hill. He looked down Burnfoot and beyond in the direction, he had been told, his dad had come from, after the war, walking the last few miles home. He could not remember the return but he had been told more than once that it had happened here, on the steps beside him.

The moon up now. Almost full. It would be shining on Jerusalem too. Jerusalem the Golden. The Last Supper would have finished. Judas would be off to betray him. Joe tried to settle into the story now, at the end of the day.

Before he went fully into the pub he stared at the glass middle door which portrayed the little black boy, the Blackamoor, who gave the pub its name and whom Joe had been told, years before, had been kicked to death by a horse in the stables and left his spirit in the pub itself, in the unbroached loft. Joe had heard him there, and been frightened many times. He stared him down.

There were too many people in the kitchen. The boy made himself some cocoa, took a packet of crisps, went through the small wicket gate up the stairs to his room and after eating and drinking he practised kneeling.

On newsreels at the pictures he had seen women in other countries walking on their knees at Easter, walking for miles on their knees, crying with the pain of it, even going up stone steps to a church. They set the standard. He was nowhere near. The vicar had said that the finest response to those three hours of total silence from noon onwards that they would share with Christ on Good Friday would be to kneel throughout. Joe had so far managed no more than twenty-five minutes before self-consciousness, or cramp, levered him from his vigil and ushered him into bed to gnaw on his failure. Perhaps it would be better when there were prayers because although everybody else was to be silent, and try to kneel, the vicar had explained that he had to stand from time to time and say prayers, recite psalms. The previous year, not to universal approval, he had spoken some poems from the First World War.

Joe's prayers ran out after a couple of minutes. He thought of other things to pray for but the most insistent was that he should pass his O levels so that he could stay on in the Sixth Form. He would start swotting again on Tuesday. People did not know that his father was paying him a wage – in return for jobs about the pub – a wage that would enable him to keep up with Alan. He wanted to declare it so that people would know he was not showing off by going on into the Sixth Form. But why should God be concerned with his O levels especially on a night such as this when all over the world millions of Christians were at one, as the vicar said, with the Passion of His Son?

In bed he was ready to take on the terror that took him out of his body, but he sensed that it would not come this night, was ebbing, driven back, perhaps retreating.

He could even risk another test. 'When I survey the wondrous

37

cross,' he sang, 'on which the Prince of Glory died, my richest gain I count but loss, and pour contempt on all my pride.' The sound! He knew that the choirmaster had been eyeing him for weeks. Sometimes he mimed – you could get away with that in a choir, for a while. He guessed that they were letting him stay until after Easter to keep up the numbers. After that he would be asked to leave, exiled in a way, only allowed back with a new deeper sound, a man's sound. He had tried to duck the truth for a few months, but it was no longer possible. His voice had broken.

Maybe there would be a miracle.

To summon sleep he counted through the day, let his mind drift, saw Lizzie, Lizzie lying across, Lizzie strongly straddling, Lizzie on the fine young horse. Her long hair loose over her face as she leaned down to whisper in its ear. It was Lizzie who was more like the woman at the foot of the cross, he thought. Of course it was. Her arms embracing his feet, bleeding from the nails.

He reached down in the dark, turned on the wireless, scanned the stations with the tuner, searched for music that would take him safely out of himself, possess him body and spirit.

CHAPTER FOUR

They were behind the bar, the two of them, father and son. Sam enjoyed the feel of it, working together. Work as a boy with his own father had often been cold, founded on necessity, hard. There was give here. Joe was on his knees, wiping and regimenting the bottles on the half-hidden shelves, labels to the front, daily filled, daily drained; Sam was pulling fresh water through the pumps, twice weekly, purifying the passage of the beer. Sadie, in the darts room with Ellen, was singing to herself; Sam realised he had missed her. Busy, the four of them, preparing the old trade of hospitality, cleaning, burnishing, the polished bar glossy under the morning sun, a few dust motes freckling the space before the window frame. Outside the town too was about its work and Sam experienced the rare realisation that in this moment, these moments, he could count himself happy.

'If you don't go to communion at Easter,' Joe said, 'you won't be saved, you know.'

'Who told you that?' Sam kept a straight face.

'The vicar. You have to partake of the body and blood of Christ especially now when He's being crucified and resurrected.'

'I'll see what I can manage.' He wanted to dampen the boy's excessive ardour.

'No you won't.' Joe's tone was matter of fact. He put the dark bottles of Guinness in neat lines, a dozen a line.

'It's one of our busiest times of year.'

'What does that count against spending eternity in Hell?' Joe did not look up. He meant it. As he spoke it he imagined it and felt it and saw Ellen and Sam in the perpetual flames, tortured by demons, forever lost. He too might be lost, he knew that, often he felt there was no hope for him but at least he had not given up. He had to try to save them.

'You've just given up, haven't you? How could you?'

Sam checked himself and took it seriously. The boy's tone moved him more than the words.

'I've got my own religion, Joe,' he said. Like his son he did not let the talk stop his work.

'What's that?'

'It's a private matter,' Sam said, eventually, truthfully, 'between me and myself. Maybe when we've got some time, when you're a bit older . . .'

'I knew you wouldn't go.' The boy sounded desolate.

He piled three empty wooden crates one on top of the other and steered himself out of the bar and back down the cellar. Sam turned to look at him after he had passed by, saw the back tensed at the over-ambitious load, saw the remains of the boil on the open-collared neck, wanted to say more.

What was his own religion? Before the war, going to church had been relaxed, acceptable. Since his return, the idea of organised praying and singing, ordered responses, communal confessions and credos, had seemed altogether foreign, a strange even an alien thing and he recollected with puzzlement that once and not long ago he had fitted in with its ways and meanings in such a docile manner, never as

40

fundamentalist as Joe, but he would have nodded at being asked if he were a believer. His religion now? Something about sharing a cigarette before or after an encounter with the Japs, or securing an interval of solitude out there to lie flat on his back and look at stars, or feeling a blood surge of unnameable affection for the men walking into certain danger beside him.

But what did that add up to? Hell – he could say, though only to himself – he had seen something of: Hell in those children bayoneted, strapped with barbed wire onto trunks of trees, left hanging there by the Japs as an example, that and the gut spillage from slaughtered men, sights more hellish than any Hell described in scripture, he thought. Heaven he could not fathom. The best he could do was to think of it as one of those moments of recognised happiness frozen for ever: like Joe and himself in the bar just then.

He looked in the bucket. The water was clear. He swilled it away and opened a fresh packet of cigarettes. In the war the Sally Army always turned up with cigarettes – why did the Salvation Army come into his mind? He leaned on the counter, pretending to look out. Joe? Softly.

'There's thousands going to Glasgow from Carlisle.' Sadie held a tin of polish and rags. Small mahogany tables glittered around her, dust had been vanquished from leatherette seats, work nearly done. Ellen was wiping down the scoreboard, rearranging the sticks of chalk, taking more time than the job deserved to be with Sadie on her maiden morning. 'Billy Graham would be the boy for me if I wasn't what I am.'

'Can Catholics never change?'

'No fear.' Sadie wiped the last gloss on the table. 'Not even a bad 'un like me. They keep tight hold of the lot of us. But that Billy Graham.' She struck a pose, extended her arms, dustcloths in both fists. 'If you believe, come to Christ. Come and be saved.' Her American accent was strong. 'And they all do, don't they? Marching up – Come to Christ! Here's Joe!' She put the cloths on the table, wiped her hands on the long pinny and said-sang, 'Cha cha. Cha-cha-cha. Come on, Joe. Take your specs off. You can't cha-cha-cha in specs.'

She sashayed towards him and the boy took her in his arms. He was just taller than Sadie now and so he could lead without feeling patronised. Sadie brought in all the new dances: Ellen had taught him the old.

'One, two, hitch, pause, one-two-three – and cha cha, stop a bit – cha-cha-cha – swivel your hips, see, like this, like film stars the way they wiggle their bums, cha cha cha-cha-cha . . .' Criss-crossing in the narrow room, its eight feet of rubber matting marking out the compulsory distance from the darts board. 'Swivel your hips!' Sadie cried. 'It's Latin-American!'

Joe thought he might be getting the hang of it when Ellen left the room. He had to follow her. She had gone into the kitchen.

'Have you decided then?'

'Oh Joe, I'm busy.'

'You said you would make up your mind nearer the time. It can't be much nearer.'

He pointed to the wall clock which was crested by the carving of a rearing stallion. 'Five past eleven.'

'I can tell the clock!'

'Well? If you can't make communion on Sunday because – why can't you?'

His tone, his persistence, wearied Ellen yet she did not know whether her truer feeling was to send him packing or to be moved that he so desperately wanted to save her.

'Because Saturday's so busy and there's always such a mess to clear up on Sundays – you know that, Joe, you know that. Sundays are our hardest mornings. You know that.'

He did not reveal his agreement but he recognised the truth of what had been said.

'But not even once. Just this once.'

'Joe. Please.'

'Well, today then. Sometime, any time, the vicar says people's supposed to just pop in and out between twelve and three, only some of us have to be there all the time – can't you just come for half an hour? Or an hour would be better.'

'I'll try.' Ellen saw a film of relief appear on his expression. So more firmly she said, 'I really will try my best.'

'If you can just pop in and out,' Sam said, at the door, standing behind Joe, 'why don't you pop out at two o'clock?' he suggested to Joe. 'We'll be closing then – I'll take you down to see Carlisle.'

'I can't.'

'They'll be fighting for a win. Tranmere's a good side.'

'I can't, Dad.' To turn down the temptation of a football match and with his dad! That had to count.

'I won't push it.'

Sam was not wholly successful in keeping the disappointment out of his voice. The idea had just come to him and felt perfect for both of them – a treat, an exclusive time, just the two of them. He left; Ellen went into the back kitchen; Joe was alone.

'I'm Ready, Willing, and Able.' Sadie's voice was a call to arms.

Joe went upstairs for a final prayer before the service.

The day was quieter than a Sunday. Even the smattering who came out of the meagrely patronised pubs looked around, taking care on this day. Muffled bells from St. Mary's Anglican Church, muffled from St. Cuthbert's Roman Catholic, silence at Nonconformist Congregational, Methodist, Primitive, Quaker and the others, as Wigton's religious sects called in their flocks, and they came, singly or in small family groups, steadily, walking the twisting alleys and narrow streets to contemplate the crucifixion of a young Jewish teacher whom many truly believed had become divine, through this death pointing the way to life everlasting for all those who sinned no more.

Joe had not reckoned on being part of the congregation. Only the vicar was in his usual place. Joe sat between Edward and Alan as he did in the choir, but this time no whispering, no noughts and crosses, no singing messages to the tune of the hymns. No hymns, neither psalms nor anthems; no music at all. People just knelt or they sat. The three friends knelt. Joe noticed that across the nave Alfred, with his mother and sisters, was sitting. But sitting very still. He beat his twenty-five-minute record but then he had to get up: cramp and showing off. Alan and Edward had given up earlier. So they sat and, intermittently, Joe did manage to find a few seconds here and there to be steady in seeing Christ on the cross, the sun covered over, the piteous cry to His Heavenly Father, the sponge of vinegar pushed in His face, the Roman's wounding sword, the taunts, the eternal shame of Judas, the lesser shame of Peter, John the favourite comforting Mary His mother at the foot of the cross.

The three hours went very slowly. Many times he thought his watch might have gone wrong, sitting became as uneasy as kneeling, so once more he knelt, but only Edward came down with him and they did not stay for long.

From time to time the vicar stood and read, or just talked. He told the story as it had happened at just this time on just this day. Joe prayed that he was taking it all in.

He liked Joseph of Arimathaea who let the body of Christ be put in his unused tomb, or was it a sepulchre? The words 'Arimathaea' and 'sepulchre' – a cave made into the rock, the vicar said – took him into a dream somehow to do with Sinbad and Aladdin, but it was the name, Joseph, his own, which allowed him pride in a sometimes burdensome connection. Joseph and his coat of many colours, Joseph the husband of Mary – it was a name to live up to. He was glad people called him Joe.

He was almost too stiff to stand when the vicar made a final deep bow to the altar and walked, black-cassocked, no other redeeming robes, head bowed and very deliberately not to the vestry but the length of the nave, making straight for the west door to stand between the two urns of daffodils where everyone would have to pass him on their way out.

The choir boys had been told they must be the last to leave in case any help was needed. It was difficult to think what it was you were supposed to be thinking now He was finally dead on the cross. Eventually Edward's father waved them on.

The vicar was outside the church, a few of the congregation still there, unwilling yet to quit the pull of the church or dawdling with intent. Joe was embarrassed to see that the vicar was talking to his mother. Although he could not have defined it, he could tell that she was not at ease, wishing she was not in such conspicuous company. The boy's embarrassment was, in its first flush, so intense that he turned away and saw, at the corner gate, that the vicar's wife was talking to Edward's mother. He knew the vicar's wife disapproved of him, had done since he had gone to that tea at the vicarage when the vicar had told him he would never make a server at the altar. So his look, though brief, was keen. He was sure Edward's mother was almost crying or trying not to cry, he could not tell. The vicar's wife stood well apart from her, head back, her hands in the pockets of her coat, looking severe. Then Edward's mother turned away, ran through the gate, ran like a girl into Proctor's Row and only slowed to a walk when she was well distant. It was the wrong way for her to get home, Joe thought. The vicar's wife waited. Her husband had his back to her.

Joe felt that he had to join his mother.

'Well, Joe,' the vicar's smile was unusually warm. 'You were very good. I had my eye on you. The Church needs disciples like you and we are lucky to have them.'

Ellen smiled stiffly. She had still not forgiven the man for turning Joe down as a server and she never would. The boy had been heartbroken. Joe was confused by this praise.

'Billy Graham gets thousands of disciples,' he said, diluting and deflecting the compliment.

'Billy Graham's way is not our way.' And Joe's timid flicker of gratitude was snuffed out.

Ellen, who like others had drunk in all that had gone on between the two women while having quite enough left over to cope with the vicar's convenient manoeuvre of conversation, nodded across his shoulder to indicate the solitary figure at the small side gate. His face tightened but he turned away and all but marched across to his wife.

'Take my arm, Joe.'

They walked down the High Street, step for step.

Why did Edward's mother run away? he asked his mother. Maybe there was a bus to catch, was the reply he got, and all he got.

'This is Jackie Cassidy,' said Sam. Joe came into the bar, too full of the day to want to shut himself away in his bedroom yet.

'The seven stone weakling,' said Jackie.

'More like the "ghost with the hammer in his hand".'

'That wasnae me, landlord.'

'I know. But not far off. British Bantamweight Champion!' Sam's delight in having the man as a customer was contagious.

Joe shook the man's hand. It was smaller than his own. The boxer was little, sadly thin, the skin on his face a dry parchment stretched so tight across the bones you feared it might snap if he should laugh, but there was no laughter in him. His raincoat was too big and stained with oil.

He was the sole customer in the bar.

'I saw this man fight,' Sam said. 'Gamest little fella on two feet. They were frightened of him at his own weight.'

'Bantam,' he explained. 'I had to fight above my weight to get contests.'

'They were frightened of you.'

'Makes no difference now, landlord.' He looked sadly but with transparent cunning at his two empty glasses, the whisky and the half-pint chaser.

'On me,' Sam said. 'I saw you once in Newcastle – Jimmy Fletcher – how much did you give him?'

Jackie waved his hand – dismissing the punishing disadvantage.

'He was good,' he said, reaching out for the half-pint, 'Fletcher was good.'

He sipped, several rather dainty sips.

'It was a hell of a fight.' Sam turned to Joe. 'Jackie had him down twice.'

'It's no life,' he said to Joe. 'Stick to your father's trade.'

'And they gave the decision against you!'

'Changed my luck, that fight.' Jackie smiled. 'I was up for anything 'til then.'

'They avoided you.'

47

Jackie did not disagree.

Joe felt obliged to contribute.

'Who's the best world champion, do you think?'

The man grimaced, as if caught by pain.

'World champion,' he said. 'They thought I . . .' He swallowed the whisky, eyes closed, face white, hollowed, ill.

'There's a fella I'm meeting in Carlisle,' he said. He looked at the clock. 'Got to get there. We're setting something up.'

Joe saw his father's exuberance suddenly drain away. His tone was now consoling.

'There'll be a bus in a couple of minutes,' he said. 'Just across the road.'

The ex-boxer guzzled the rest of the half-pint.

'I'll be away then.'

Sam wanted to ask a question but he did not want to impose on the man. Yet it was not intrusive and the odds against him meeting another contender for a world championship were very long.

'How do you know when you've – you've really nailed some-body?'

The man drained the very last drops of the whisky.

'It goes right up the arm,' he said. 'To the shoulder. You always know. Then you move in.'

Sam nodded, satisfied, and almost as an afterthought, said:

'You'd nailed Fletcher that night, hadn't you?'

The little fighter went to the door, looked back at Sam.

'There was big money on Fletcher that night,' he said.

Sam was so silent that Joe felt he ought to leave him alone with it, but as he made to go, his father said, 'Poor little beggar, eh? What is there left for him? He'll be – thirty-five? Look at him. But what a fighter in his day, Joe: the real thing. Jackie Cassidy.'

48

Joe could see that his father was moved by the encounter but no more was offered and so he went through into the kitchen where his grandfather now parked himself on Friday evenings, happy with the two bottles of Guinness per evening courtesy of the house, enjoying a late sociability in his son's pub, pleased to have Joe to talk to at this empty early hour. Joe liked him being there. He liked his dad calling his grandad dad.

I know what'll happen to that poor little beggar, Sam thought. He'll be bought drink. He lives on it now. All that wasting'll have turned him off food. Forced starvation. Anyway he's skint. Not the type a pro gym would take on. Not the type to do anything but labouring and look at the size of him for a shovel and pick job. He'll have come from nothing and he'll go back to nothing. Found in some cheap digs or in an alley, pushed under, not a friend to help him.

From then on for some years, Sam watched the papers for news of Jackie Cassidy, hoping that his sentimental prophecy would be confounded. It was not. He was given very few lines in the news-papers. Age, thirty-nine. 'A tragic end.' 'British Bantamweight cham-pion found dead.' No details.

Sam had gone back to fan-childhood at the sight of Jackie but the thought of what he saw as a certain desolate end to such a game life, a life which had held out glory, depressed him. The feeling clung to him through the evening, the pub less full than usual on this Good Friday. No hound trails, no dog men in.

Ellen, he thought, was rather distant, no doubt dwelling on her trip with William Hawesley the following day. That, unjustly, and knowing he was being unjust, was how Sam chose to see it. And what sort of man was it who insisted on the William – no Will, Willie, Bill, Billy – the formal William? Nothing fitted. Joe over-earnest with this overheated adolescent piety, even asking, as they were counting up the

49

takings, if he could go to Glasgow the next day to take part in a Billy Graham rally, be one of the thousands 'being saved'. At least that had been easy to say no to.

Yet again, as at the beginning of the day, the boy had turned his back on his father. This time, though, he had let him go.

Later, as he followed Ellen to bed, he remembered the spent boil on the boy's neck and saw himself in a long queue in India when they were on their way to Burma. Women were promised at the end of the queue and despite the shocking films on sexual diseases which had been shown them, Sam had for the first time joined the queue and shuffled silently forward for a few minutes until he focused on the neck of the man in front, and the boil, large, angry, a red sore ready to burst. He had pulled out.

That first time had been the last time and he smiled to himself as he went into the bathroom. Thank God for boils! What would Joe make of that?

CHAPTER FIVE

Joe was sweeping the front of the pub when Colin came over. He had brushed all the dirt into the gutter and was about to push it down towards the drain where he had placed the shovel ready to take it through the back to the dustbin. It was not such a bad job when the school buses were not running. When they swirled onto the hill and caught him the embarrassment was like prickly heat.

Colin gave him an envelope.

'This is for Sis.' He gave the Blackamoor a glance meant to be contempt, but Joe saw the hurt in it and felt for him. 'I can't go in to give a message to my own sis, thanks to you-know-who! But it's important. Comprendez?'

'I'll just finish the front.'

'He has everybody working for him!'

Colin hesitated, wanting to express more bile, to wound the son for want of the father, but Sam might come out any time.

'You and me was pals once.'

His bitterness could never be consumed. Hurt never drained from the surface.

Joe finished the job rapidly.

'Come across,' the message said. 'Right now.' And as soon as she could, Ellen obeyed.

'He'll be up in his own room,' said Leonard.

Because he knows he's not welcome down here, Ellen thought, resenting her uncle's dislike for her half-brother even though she understood it.

'If he wants one of his summit conferences,' Leonard peered above the racing pages of the local paper, 'use the sitting room. Grace isn't herself. I've made her stay in bed. She's sleeping.'

'It's not serious?'

Leonard shook his head and returned to study the form.

She padded up the stairs, nervously. Yet she had to get to him. It was not usual for Colin to write.

'Ellen!'

Mr. Kneale spied her on her way past the sitting room. His moon face, spectacled, his pate rising balder by the year through whitening hair, his eyes fond on the young woman.

'Mr. Kneale.'

So many years, he thought, companions through a war, some sort of parent to Joe, never a wrong move or word or slip of his feelings for her, feelings well buried, and still she called him Mr. Kneale.

'I am usurping the Royal Quarters.' The ornate over-furnished space with its controlling view across Market Hill and beyond was Grace's throne room.

'Is she bad?'

'I don't think so,' said Mr. Kneale, carefully considering his words in the way which had always reassured her. 'Anno Domini, Ellen. And Leonard is coming into his own. She listens to him nowadays.'

52

Both of them smiled and both felt warm in the snap spontaneity of that rather conspiratorial smile.

'Sometimes quite a modest change of location can . . .' Was he holding her up? She was outside the door, stood rather politely, as if she were something of a stranger. 'Are you . . . ?'

'No, no.' She stepped over the threshold. There was, there always had been, a compliance before Mr. Kneale, respect, gratitude, more than that even. He took her for what was best in her.

'Same old mess,' he said, pointing to the neat stacks of notes on the table beside the window.

'You're the tidiest man I know, Mr. Kneale.'

The warmth of tone far exceeded the modesty of the compliment and Mr. Kneale responded in his usual way, by diving for cover.

'I've been looking up the early settlements in Wigton,' he said. 'The first we have any real evidence for after the Romans were called back to defend Rome. Except for King Arthur – now there's a book! I feel in my bones he came from these parts, Ellen, and Carlisle was his Camelot, but bones are no good for historians, we must leave them to the medicine men – there's nothing until the Anglo-Saxon – the High Street, the Crofts, still there today, you know' – as she did; as he had recited her to her many, many times, as she never tired of hearing, it gave her town a deep root, a long engagement with the past, a sense of being securely moored in time – 'and these men worshipped Warrior Gods – Thor, Odin – you can see what I'm getting at, can't you? The men who marched off to war had these warrior ancestors inside them somewhere. But the mystery is, how do they keep it going when they're now supposed to worship a God who tells them to turn the other cheek and think not of this world but the next? How do you think they square that when they go off to war?'

He wanted an audience, not an answer, Ellen knew that. For

fifteen years now she had been his most trusted audience. He waited for her arrivals, she knew that also, to pounce on her: and his assault was always like this – an expression of present affection by way of his love of the past, a romancing devoid of all display, all softness self-denied, love which could express itself fully only wholly masked, a passionate declaration by way of local history.

'Ellen!'

The raucous shout ripped through the tender cord between them.

Ellen went upstairs.

Colin had fixed up his small room, inspired by Do-It-Yourself, so that it was more than a bedroom. She sat in one of the two chairs, feeling on trial: Colin could still do that to her.

'So what's this about meeting my mother today without telling me anything about it, then?'

He crossed his legs, cocked his cigarette, triumphant.

'Auntie Grace told you?'

'I got it out of her,' Colin conceded.

'Well,' Ellen tried to hold his look steadily, 'it's true.'

'So why wasn't I told? She's my mother, you know. Not yours.'

'I know. I should have said.'

'So why didn't you?'

Because I wanted time alone with someone who knew my father and would not make me grovel for every scrap of information about him. Because you would have wrecked all that. Because I have asked you more than once to come to his grave and you have always found excuses. Because I wanted time alone with him, and with her.

'I don't know,' she said.

'You didn't want me there,' Colin said. 'That was it.'

'You must come along then. After all it was you she told she was coming.' Ellen was firm. 'Mr. Hawesley's driving me down. He has an aunt nearby. We're leaving at one-thirty.'

'What if I've got something else to do?'

'Couldn't you put it off?'

'Typical! What Colin does doesn't matter enough to count, does it? He can just come to heel whenever there's a shout. And "put it off". He's got no life, Colin.'

Ellen winced.

'You'll be very welcome.'

'Not welcome enough to give notice to.'

'I'm sorry about that.'

'I never thought you were a sneak, Sis. Our dad would never have thought he'd had a sneak.'

Ellen pulled back her face, as if hit.

'I'm sorry, Colin. I don't know what got into me.'

'I do!'

'What, then?'

'I'll keep it to myself. I know you. I know more than you think.'

'One-thirty.'

'I'll make up my own mind in my own time, Ellen. I have business this afternoon. Sneak!'

He looked out of the window at the row of old cottages across the cobbled yard, indicating that the meeting was over. Ellen was too ashamed to protract it.

Mr. Kneale watched her from the bay window and noted that she walked carefully, looking at her feet as if afraid of stumbling.

Joe wandered up street after he had finished his set jobs, partly to avoid being given more. Alan would be working in his father's shop. Edward was not in: his mother had taken him away with Edna to stay with a relative in the country. He knew that Malcolm did things with his father on Saturdays, enviable things, cleaning the car, going to Carlisle to a record shop, and John spent these mornings with his father too, scavenging in the fields and copses beyond their damp little cottage on the western edge of the town.

Perhaps he would meet one of the others in the gang just by drifting up the busy street, an Easter gift to trade, chocolate eggs returning to the sweet shops, Easter bonnets, new suits for some, new shoes, something new for Easter: Joe had been bought a new pair of grey flannel trousers.

He met Alistair. Alistair stood on the lip of the pavement opposite Meeting House Lane. Hands in pockets, pepper-and-salt drape jacket, black shirt, no tie, fag in gangster corner of mouth. His pose was defiant. Law-abiding shoppers who passed by thought he should never have been let out of Borstal, and the sooner he was packed off to the army the better. But the men who leaned against the Fountain railings could be provoked into embattled pride in him.

'Joe!'

The greeting was a demand. Alistair's younger brother, Speed, had been Joe's hero and in some manner, though two or three years older, a friend. Alistair's mother was certainly a friend of Sam and Ellen. They used to be neighbours in the long-condemned Victorian congestion of Water Street. She still lived there. They said even she was scared of Alistair.

'I was looking for somebody for a walk.'

Joe fell into step as Alistair moved smartly up the street, ignoring the numerous short cuts offered by the alleyways, keen to be seen, nodding at passers-by, greeting people by name, undoubtedly legitimised by the company of Joe. For Joe, to be with this much older boy – he might even be nineteen – and a boy of such a terrible reputation for violence, was thrilling. He basked in reflected danger, tough by association.

Alistair was not tall. His force came from the power of his shoulders and a taste for brutality. You felt muscle there, and a constant readiness to use it. He was deeply chested, strong thighed, but his best feature, the men said, was that he was fast, quick with his feet. The head was large, nose even classical, lips thin, skin pale and the hair, which fascinated Joe most, was being perfected into an enviable D.A. with the front tuft bouncing onto his broad fine forehead.

Joe wanted to ask about Alistair's father who had gone on the tramp after suffering 'a breakdown' when he came back with Sam after the war. It was the word 'breakdown' that drew the boy in. When people asked Speed about his father he would ask them if they were looking for trouble. Alistair, Joe sensed, would not be as courteous as his brother. Everyone had heard of the last fight, the one which had finally sent him to Borstal. Alistair had badly bashed up three of them. How could you be sent away for bashing up three of them, Joe thought, indignantly. Winning against three deserved a medal. And after all, the boy thought, they had come from another town.

They moved swiftly out of the old town, up to the Syke Road.

'See that house?' Alistair jabbed out his finger. Joe nodded: it was on his paper round. 'There's a boy came there – years ago, years. Them's his grandparents live there. He only came for his holidays. Never been let back. They just keep him. Wouldn't let him go to school, nothing. Just keep him for themselves.'

Joe had seen the boy occasionally, hugely fat, always between the two grandparents, always near the front door, gazing myopically at the outside world.

'Just keep him?'

57

'He's in prison in a back room. There's nothing I don't know about what goes on in this town. Dead hole.'

'I like Wigton,' Joe replied, 'there's always plenty to do.'

'For kids maybe.' Alistair's walk was a fast march: his expression was grim. 'They're in the Dark Ages, man. When I can get away, you won't see me back.'

They swung down towards Old Carlisle, the large unexcavated Roman camp to which Mr. Braddock had taken them for a local history outing. Before then, Joe had loved it as a unique place of huddled little hillocks, paths winding between beehive mounds, corrugated with turf ridges to hide behind or gather your forces in stone fights. After the history outing the magic of the place had diminished but the description of what lay under the surface partly compensated.

'The Roman Cavalry used to be there,' Joe said, to break the silence: he spoke with considerable local pride – look, this is what Wigton has behind it. 'A thousand of them. Crack troops, Mr. Braddock said – ready to go up to the Roman Wall or down to the coast to get the Picts. There's a theatre there, under that grass – he showed us an aerial photograph – there's temples, and stables, even baths: it was a smart spot then.'

Alistair, who like his brother Speed would have been far more at home in the Roman world of sword and shield, of face to face combat, of naked courage, than in a world where technology was making such warrior virtues obsolescent, gave it about two seconds of his consideration and said,

'What I want is a bit of legover, Joe.'

Joe's throat went dry.

'I need dosh,' he said, stopped in his tracks and turned to face the younger boy. 'Shekels. This jacket – not full drape but there isn't one like it in Wigton. But no drainpipes, no bootlace tie – not that they'd know the difference here!' He smoothed back his hair with the palms of his hands. 'D.A. coming on, still a bit short. But I need dosh.'

The boy's obliging, earnest mind raced to help.

'Dad might need somebody else to wait on.'

'Real dosh. Teddy Boys spend hundreds. Hundreds! The real cases. The Rock and Roll lads down in London.' He grinned. 'Know what Rock 'n' Roll means, Joe?'

'Music? Bill Haley?'

Shaking his head and still grinning, Alistair had made a circle of the thumb and index finger of his left hand and was energetically poking his right index finger in and out of it. Joe looked on rather mystified.

'In – out. In – out, in – out – Rock 'n' Roll – get it?'

Suddenly, Joe got it. For a moment he felt as he had done a year ago when the prefect in charge of his table in the canteen had informed all six younger boys that everybody's mother and father 'did it'. Joe had dissolved in disbelief and tremulously mounted a defence based on Eve having millions of eggs inside eggs inside her insides.

'Lads would dance with lads,' he said. 'Some lads where I've been at. To teach you Rock 'n' Roll. Big City lads.'

Alistair suddenly resumed his rapid pace.

'Scottish lassies is the best when their husbands is away in the forces,' he said. 'I've met lads in the building trade, thirty bob for their keep, another ten bob and marriage rights – the lot – thrown in.'

Joe nodded, trying to keep up. What marriage rights? What was 'the lot'?

'Always carry a French letter,' Alistair said, and produced an example from deep in the drape pocket of his jacket. 'Two if you're feeling lucky.' Eyes front, on they walked, wheeling right to Red Dial, onto the road the cavalry had once taken to patrol the Empire's furthest border. 'The Four "F"s, Joe. Find 'em, Feel 'em, Fuck 'em and Forget 'em.' Joe's throat was dry. He was dizzy from this battering. He began to watch the bounce of the front tuft. 'If she gives it to you first time, she's a tart. If she holds back, she's a bitch.' On he strode: Alistair was angry now, another right turn wheel and back on track for the town, Highmoor Bell Tower to guide them in. 'Never admit responsibility. If she's let you at her there's been others at her before.' What did this mean? At her what? 'It's when she starts playing with your old man that the fun starts, Joe.' What fun? What sort of playing? But he wanted this. Another bounce; how did it stay like that? The boy was adrift. 'There's only one woman worth fighting for, Joe – that's your mother. You have a beautiful mother. Remember it was me what told you that.' Up the final hill into the town. 'You can swing for your mother,' he concluded and waved Joe goodbye as he slewed into the Brindlefield Estate to which some of his childhood friends from Water Street had been transplanted in the recent old town clearances.

Joe reeled slowly down Southend Road, thoughtful, scattered in confused lusts, believing he was now much older.

He wanted to look like Alistair.

In the bathroom, he dipped freely in his dad's Brylcreem and attempted to mould his school haircut, with the regulation parting on the left, into a D.A. Sides swept back: the heap on top just tumbling down a touch onto the forehead, the back converging like a duck's . . . He found it difficult to swear even to himself in his own house. His mother was very hard on it.

The hair was reluctant to abandon the school regulation but Joe tried, mixed soap and water to thicken the texture, found some Vaseline and rubbed that in, lost himself in the doomed effort at transformation.

'Fancy yourself?'

His mother had come into the bathroom. He feared that she had been there for some time. He blushed at being caught red-handed, preparing to show off. His self-confidence crawled into a miserable corner and curled up. His mother could always strip him down. Had she watched him twirl his fingers in the front bit to get the tumble effect?

'You're pleasant-looking, Joe,' she spoke calmly, even normally, he noticed. 'Nothing more. Run across and tell Colin we have to go: it's nearly quarter to two.'

Maybe this would wipe out the offence.

'Tell her,' Colin said, trying to drawl, holding his cigarette in a new dandified way, 'I'll come if and when I'm good and ready and not a minute before. If and when. Got it?'

Joe reported verbatim. It was an answer guaranteed to upset her.

'We have to set off now.' Mr. Hawesley took his lightweight pipe out of his mouth to smile more becomingly.

'Go without him,' said Sam, who was on the steps waiting to witness the departure.

'Maybe I should run across and try to persuade him.'

'That'll make his day.'

'We really must set off, Ellen.'

Ellen looked from Sam to Joe, across the hill to the home of Colin, then to Mr. Hawesley. The woman would be waiting for her at the graveside.

'Tell him we waited,' she said to Joe, who nodded.

'I'll look after her,' Mr. Hawesley said to Sam as he held open the door for Ellen and offered her a blanket to tuck around her knees.

Sam did not respond to that. He gave a nod to Ellen and went back into the pub before the small car pulled away.

Joe ran up to the bathroom to try again

CHAPTER SIX

'Please call me William,' he said, when they were well on their way.

Ellen's discomfort at sitting so close to Mr. Hawesley was intensified by this request even though the Labour Party chairman had taken care to couch it in a neutral tone.

'After all,' he continued, filling the gap, 'I call you Ellen.'

The fairness of this explanation appealed to her but she knew that she would devise many ways to avoid calling him William.

In thrall as he was, Mr. Hawesley knew he might have gone a little too far, but he had planned carefully to say that to her on this trip and at about this distance on the outward journey from Wigton. It had been put on his List For Today. Later, it could be ticked. But tread softly, he thought, softly . . . he must not escalate this further, not now, not for months, years, perhaps never. It was enough to be with her, side by side close in the shared little portable house steering carefully along the winding roads to Lancashire.

'Do you like Paul Robeson?'

Ellen nodded.

'I'm referring to his singing,' he said. 'Although you can't think about that without thinking about his acting and you can't discuss his acting without reference to his politics. He is the whole man, I think,

Paul Robeson. And being black, on top of it all! Racial discrimination is proof positive of the union of ignorance and prejudice. Paul Robeson settles all of that!'

He did not seek out pauses intended for her contribution as Mr. Kneale did. That was a relief.

'I heard him on the wireless this morning, singing Russian songs. I tell you, Ellen, the hair on my neck stood up – the feeling the man brings to those songs. Any man would want that strength of feeling. They are the songs of the Russian people, Ellen, songs of resignation redeemed by the dignity of labour. I don't mind telling you I stood stock still in the middle of the kitchen, a cup in one hand, the tea towel in the other, stock still while those songs went right through me . . . The power of true feeling, Ellen, feeling which is right for its time, that is irresistible, that is why it has this physical effect, strange though it seems, just a song can make the hair on your neck move and a sort of rush of goosepimples shiver over you and stop you right in your tracks.'

As his confidence developed, the voice of this unimpressive, rather short man, spectacled, moustached like his hero Clement Attlee, recently removed brown trilby hat revealing an unbecoming red rim around his forehead, accreted authority and Ellen was drawn in by it.

But the image which stuck was that of Mr. Hawesley in his kitchen, tea towel in one hand, cup in the other . . .

Even before he had become a widower, Mr. Hawesley's domesticity had been exceptional. Admittedly his wife had been bedridden for her last two or three years and described as 'never a well woman' but few men would so openly have done the shopping, puffing at the lightweight pipe as he considered his neat lists, and admitted to dusting and cleaning, washing, even ironing, even cooking. Yet there was about him something which checked derision. People recognised a decent man.

Ellen could never see Sam doing woman's work but her fairness made her attend to the other side of the scales – he worked hard enough at what he did and what was made they shared.

Yet this man's unselfconscious tea towel and cup lingered and she found it unaccountably touching.

'I'll be back in an hour and a half,' he said, scrutinising his watch. 'Three thirty-five,' he said. 'Just after five o'clock.'

'I'll be here,' Ellen promised.

'Till later then, Ellen.'

The woman nodded, wincing that she so obviously resisted his too obvious attempt to bring out 'William'.

There was confetti around the church gate and on the path and Ellen smiled as at a sentimental secret. Weddings warmed her. No wedding in Wigton escaped her. Here, even on the way to her father's grave, even with the imminence of a meeting with his wife, she paused to looked at the confetti, the dots of coloured paper peppering the slate-grey flagstones, fragile remains of the day's showering of hopes. There was a penny lodged between flagstones, overlooked by the children who would have scurried to claim the throw of small change. She left it there, maybe it would bring luck.

The grave was against the cold north wall of the churchyard but the cemetery itself had surprised her. Rather than the expected grimy Victorian graveyard of the industrial interred, she had found a pre-conquest church miles beyond the city in a village next to Morecambe Bay, with a view to the Lake District. For that alone she felt grateful to this woman she would meet.

The woman was almost half an hour late.

'You must be Ellen,' she said. 'I would recognise that look anywhere.'

Ellen took her hand and received a strong handshake.

'You must call me Marjorie.' The plump, rather fashionable woman, gloved, hatted, smartly fitted, dark blue two-piece suit, seen beneath the well-cut, unbuttoned tweed coat, ushered her to a nearby bench. It overlooked the Bay.

'Beautiful, isn't it?' she said. 'People come here just for the sunsets.' She took out a cigarette from a gold-looking case, offered, made no comment when Ellen shook her head, lit up, sighed out the first deep puff. 'I got him in here because it was my church. I wanted somewhere nice for him. I grew up just over there.' She waved the cigarette towards the village which crept up hesitantly from the shore to the lichened and salt-scoured little pinnacle of worship. 'It's a wonderful viewpoint.'

Her handbag matched her shoes, Ellen noticed, and her purple silk neckscarf matched her gloves. Ellen felt lumpily underdressed.

'Silly we haven't met before, when you think,' she said, looked carefully at Ellen and then added, suddenly thoughtful, with a switch of tone which made Ellen realise that the woman, Marjorie, was probably nervous too, 'but that wouldn't have been possible with him alive.'

'Why not?' Ellen's firm voice took her by surprise.

'God! You have such a look of him.' Again she drew deeply on the useful cigarette. 'Why not? He wanted to put it all behind him. At the same time,' she threw the half-smoked cigarette away, unnipped, 'he was obstinate.'

Clearly it was Ellen's turn but her mind was accelerating into turmoil already at the mass attack of impressions, information and speculation released by the arrival of this open, direct woman. To ease the weight of it, Ellen asked her about her journey and was rewarded by a similar question from Marjorie which led to polite exchanges enabling Ellen to steady herself. Marjorie relaxed and was more friendly when Ellen said,

'He never came back to see us.'

'I didn't know you existed.' The smile was rueful rather than bitter; later good fortune had overlaid that. 'Not until I was pregnant did I know you existed – can you imagine? – and then we were all stuck. Are you sure?'

Again she held out the opened cigarette case. 'You don't take a drink either, do you?' Ellen shook her head.

'I can always tell. Sensible.' She took the cigarette and lit up with a leaping flame from a slim silver lighter. 'And abortion was out as far as I was concerned.' Ellen's mind began to list. 'Religion. But he wouldn't get a divorce. We had to move to another town. Pretend we were married. It was very hard on me, Ellen. It was very hard.'

'Why did he . . . ?'

'Not get on with it? He was weak. He had that weakness. But there was so much else about him.' She paused and for the first time looked directly at Ellen, honestly. 'He was just livelier, there was just more to him, he lit up the room – you know that saying? – more than anybody else I'd ever met.' She nodded, confirming even now the justification for her fidelity. 'Earned good money and handed it over. I told my parents we'd got married a little quickly, quietly, in the other town. Better the little lies. Not until your mother died did we tie the knot.'

Marjorie stopped, looked out at the sea which was now sweeping swiftly into the Bay, seemed set to pause for a while but then said, 'Well. I've got that off my chest. What about you?'

And suddenly in the middle of that comfortably clad, comfortably layered, comfortably sensible woman, Ellen saw the flint.

66

'I want to know more about him. And,' this she had not prepared, 'something about Colin.'

'Your father,' Marjorie said, after a conspicuous look at her tiny watch, 'was a charmer. He was a looker. He danced like a film star. He was lazy but always clever enough to hold down a good job. And I brought a bit of money to the table. But,' she turned rather tenderly to the younger woman, 'he was a ruthless man. A selfish man.' Her voice dropped. There was nothing of blame in the tone. 'But he was mine, you see, and I knew how to keep him.'

Ellen knew that there was little if any chance that she would see Marjorie again.

'Did he talk of me, of my mother, of us?'

Marjorie nodded.

'I knew you would ask that, and why not? I won't lie to you, Ellen. It's too late for lies. I forced a few things out of him regarding your mother. And – now I'll say this just the once – there's no doubt that he thought about you and felt terrible that he had cut himself off from you.'

Ellen's feelings, her mind, spirit, soared; for a moment she was breathless, eyes prickling with gratitude at this healing revelation.

'Did he?' It was a whisper. It was a plea to have the message from the other side repeated, stamped indelibly.

'Oh yes, Ellen. But he reckoned just turning up out of the blue would do you more harm than good. Right or wrong that was his decision and he stuck with it but he suffered for it. "I have to starve myself of her," he said and it took me some time to work out what that meant.'

'What did it mean?' More, Ellen's eyes pleaded, more, more, more about him and me, my dead father now for the first time alive.

'I think he meant that if he saw you, or wrote, or sent any

67

messages, then something would start up that he wouldn't be able to cope with. And he thought you might not be able to cope with it either. That's the best I can do.'

Ellen nodded. Marjorie relented on her schedule, stayed for a few minutes more.

'And Colin? Do you mind talking about him, Marjorie?'

Ellen could sense, even see the woman shrinking away as the name was uttered. Her rather high-pitched, well-spoken voice grew harsh.

'I should never have told him he was born before we got married. Some stupid – maybe I was getting back at your father – he wanted Colin to be kept in the dark – I don't know what possessed me . . . I can't understand that, Ellen, except to say I thought he would be bound to find out one day and better he found out from me. But it backfired! Believe me, it backfired, Ellen. Colin grabbed it, you see. It was his excuse. It was his great get-out. He wouldn't let go of it.' She took a deep breath. 'We most likely won't see each other again, Ellen, so I'll tell you the truth. Your father could see this but I never put it into words.' One more breath. 'It got so I couldn't stand him. My own son. So what sort of mother, what sort of woman does that make me? But I couldn't. I tried, I pretended, I made up for it, I lied – but he could see through me. He said he was like an X-ray machine as far as I was concerned and he was right.'

Ellen kept very still.

'And Gerald, my new husband,' she looked hard at Ellen, 'I don't know whether this is going to help you, but Colin won't be any easier on you than he was on me – Gerald was – well, let's put the best light on it we can – Gerald was very happy that Colin went his own way, and "kept his distance", he said, after they'd had one or two brushes. I send him money, not much but about once a month. I'm lucky if I get a card.' She puffed out her cheeks and expelled the air forcefully. 'So there it is, Ellen. Some good, some bad. But life's for the living. Gerald and I are off to Spain in June.'

She stood up and held out her hand. This time the clasp was warm.

'Life is for the living, Ellen,' she repeated and glanced over to the grave. 'You've made a very good job of it. Goodbye now.'

Ellen watched her go across and lay a bunch of white trumpet lilies beside the daffodils brought by her. She stood there for a few moments, turned, gave Ellen a small, purple-gloved wave and then walked briskly to the lych-gate.

Poor Colin, Ellen thought. Poor Colin.

But that was only one of the thoughts which thronged in her mind, an inrush of questions, answers, insights, longings for more. Had he really thought so deeply about her? Why had he let Colin be born – like that? Starved himself? 'He was mine. I knew how to keep him.' She could always write to Marjorie and ask for another meeting. She must be quite rich. Brought money to the table. Why didn't he come back to see them? Her poor mother, waiting, abandoned, in full public view and forced to hide in Grace and Leonard's house where she skivvied as Ellen had done as a child and been grateful for the refuge as Ellen still was. Did it kill her mother young? Ellen was now older than her mother had been at her death.

—⁓—

William opened her door and helped her out. She stood outside the Blackamoor, uncertain of everything.

'I've been rather quiet.'

'You've been totally silent, Ellen,' he smiled, 'but I understand.'

He did not know about Marjorie. 'There are some things in life which demand all we can give to them.'

With some effort she imagined the life of giving endured by the man before her as his wife perished slowly and painfully before his eyes.

'I've been a bit selfish,' she said.

'You couldn't be selfish if you tried.'

'I'd best go in, Mr. Hawesley. I'm late as it is.'

'But of course. And any time, Ellen, any time. And it's William.'

He watched her until she was well inside the pub, just beginning to throb with Saturday business. She goes in to life, he thought, as he got back into the car, she encounters it and deals with it, and I go to an empty house, cold now, boiled eggs and toast. He indulged in an uncharacteristic burst of speed past St. Cuthbert's, where young Sister Philomena was spread-eagled on the floor, not in Wigton, not even in Cork, but in Jerusalem outside the sealed sepulchre of her Lord and bridegroom, exalted, ecstatic.

It had been a good day, he decided, as he went into the house and turned on both bars of the electric fire in the old sitting room, now his study. He knew her so much better from feeling her grief on the way home. Such depth of grief: such depth of feeling, he thought, and wondered at the quality of her. He did not take off his coat until he had made his supper, which he brought to the fire, set the tray on his knees, turned on the wireless to wait for the news, took his time over the choice of book he would read. There was always reading to soothe the pain of it. He decided on *Antic Hay*.

After *Seven Brides for Seven Brothers* Joe and Alan walked the two sisters to their home on Greenacres. They had tried before and failed. Now they struck lucky. Alan was reluctant: he had received a message that Edna had picked him but immediately afterwards she had been taken off into the country with Edward and his mother. Alan did not want rumour of this escorting of the sisters to damage his chances with Edna, so he tried to keep a distance from his one: Joe tried to get as close as possible to his.

They passed under the copper beech and over the bridge up to the new estate where Joe had once lived for a while. At the house the girls parted: pre-arranged. Alan trailed after his. Joe was eager and they found a dark wall.

She let him kiss her right away. It was somewhere between a peck and a first embrace although the embrace did not really count as she kept her arms by her sides. Joe did not know how to proceed to torrid and the awful truth was that he liked her no more than she seemed to like him. But the idea of escorting back home and being escorted back home and being seen had a great deal going for it. With a leap of dangerous enthusiasm, he planted his right hand on her left breast. What were you supposed to do with a breast? The pictures never showed you. Just keep your hand there? That was very nice but surely there was more. Squeeze? Rub around? Sort of pump it? What was it Alistair had said? 'Feel 'em and forget 'em.' He squeezed, quite hard. She yelped, and a hitherto limp hand rocketed up to rip his grip loose. They went back to just kissing, but the excitement had gone out of it.

As they walked up the hill into the old town, Alan blamed Joe for getting him into what could prove to be a mess. There was some truth in this – Joe had needed to persuade Alan, even pressurise him – but that caused Joe to resent his friend's accusation all the more. He was not too unhappy when Alan sulked off home alone.

It was the tilting time of a Saturday night. The pubs were as full as they would get but the roaring for drink before the 10 p.m. closing time had not yet begun to gather volume. The nine o'clock news was being used as the prompt to send people and hot water bottles to bed.

71

The cinema was packed for the second house. The first percolation of the crowd was beginning to seep into the Market Hall for the dance. Joe was too young to go but he let himself wander up High Street to breathe it in from the brightly bulbed doorway.

Lizzie was there and the way she looked sent an uncomfortable jolt through the boy. Her hair was stacked in a reckless tangle, the dress followed the boyish body so closely that it revealed a slender but voluptuous contour, a cigarette dangled from painted fingernails, uneasy lipstick, unsteady shoes, to Joe more glamorous than Rita Hayworth, whom she imitated. But there was no comparison, he thought, as she spotted him and beckoned him to the bright mouth of the cave which led to grown-up life and feverishly anticipated pleasures. Rita Hayworth was just in the pictures. Lizzie was real. He went across the road as helplessly and despite all odds as hopefully as any convert in Kelvin Hall on that night going to God via Billy Graham.

Lizzie's friends were late. She wanted company.

'How's Joe?'

'How's Lizzie?'

This emergent woman, daring, shimmering, sexually electrifying, but still perhaps, because he had known her when she ran with the gangs long ago in Water Street, just within reach: all he had to do was find the key. What had Alistair said?

'Fag?' She held out a packet.

He shook his head. She looked down the street, peering through the yellow blobs of the street lights, searching for her friends.

'I've just been to the pictures.' Joe's real message was: 'Can I take you to the pictures?'

'We went last night,' she said. 'What dancers!'

We? Who was his competition?

'Great dancers,' he agreed. Meaning: I like dancing and although I'm not quite as tall as you, even smaller now you have those shoes on, I'm good enough to dance with you; I could give you a good dance. One would be enough to show you.

'Come on in, then.' She smiled and nodded to the bare-walled, green-painted brick passage leading to the doors beyond which the band was playing a quickstep. 'I've seen you dance. I'll give you the first one, Joe.'

It was as if the boy turned into a pillar of salt. What he longed for was before him, but he could make no move. He would have to run back home for the money. He would have to change. He would have to explain this to his mother. He would have to lie to the doorman and say he was sixteen. He would have to ignore the necessary preparation for the most important communion of all the next morning. He would have to be somebody else.

'Next time,' she said, kindly, and her smile which promised the world seemed tailored for him alone. She knew: but he was just a boy. It was, though, a tribute and her smile regretted that life could not be different or multiple. He truly loved Lizzie: the scar would never quite go nor the nag of what might have been, but in the end he had been too afraid; being too young was an excuse.

'Wigton's crap.'

Lizzie's two friends had arrived, behind him, two girls from the same estate as Lizzie, both dressed to the nines. Arms linked. They ignored him. The one who spoke had flat peroxide-blonde hair, famous in Wigton, 'got out of a bottle'.

'Crap.' The commonplace condemnation was echoed with a vengeful spitting emphasis by her friend.

'I went up street this afternoon,' said the peroxide. 'No knickers on. What happened?' She took a fag from Lizzie. 'Not a sniff.'

'Wigton's crap.'

'So long, Joe.'

'So long.'

'Next time.'

He watched them all the way to the door, stayed for a moment to let the possibilities play out a few more chords of fantasy and then turned to go.

He was bumped into the gutter, deliberately, by one of three men walking abreast, filling the pavement. They did not break step, for which the boy was very grateful. It could have been much worse. They were bad men. His father had long ago barred them for life from the Blackamoor and more than once they had threatened him on the streets. Now, intent on drink, tanking up for the dance, urgently focused on the next pub, one of the minority from which they were not barred, they merely, but with menace, ignored him.

Joe sought the comfort of chips. Josie was on, which meant that when he asked for scrams she put a heap of the shards of batter on the vinegar-soaked chips and the boy went into the glimmering night streets with a feast, which he ate at his leisure.

Safe now, he could bring out a secret he would not confess to anyone. He was fascinated by the bad men. By their badness. Badness was the biggest dare. Maybe bad men were the bravest. Not just the fighting, others did that, nor just the thieving, breaking into the St. Dunstan's Blind box in the pub which had justified the ban for life, nor their language, their regular appearances in court, spells in Durham gaol – it was something other which provoked the boy's fascination. They were a law unto themselves. Mr. Kneale had said that, shaking his head, but Joe stole the phrase and prized it. A law unto themselves. He leaned against the railings of the Fountain, clocking the town as the men did: Lizzie, the bad men, the darkening streets, the chips sliding down his throat, time enough to get in the right mood for eight o'clock communion in the morning, the pang at missing the dance comfortably transformed into resisting temptation.

The noise in the pub below was heavy but he read through it. When it became too threatening he turned up the music. Time was called. He decided not to go down and help his father count the takings. He had stolen a march on his swotting and was well into another reading of one of his O-level set books, *The Cloister and the Hearth*. He put it aside. He needed all his energy to concentrate on the Resurrection.

Outside his window the customers went into the night. Joe knelt by his bed and read the account of the Passion in the Gospel according to St. Matthew. He was calm: there was no room for fear. Even Lizzie, he believed, could be forced to the outer edges of his mind. A law unto themselves? He stared at the bible to drive out everything else.

Sam was disappointed that Joe had not come down. He would have welcomed his company. He was still out of sorts. Ellen, it seemed to him, had done her best to avoid him since her late and flustered return with 'I'll look after her' William.

All that Ellen wanted was to be alone. The hours in the crowded pub, greetings, orders, chatter, prices, news, drink, noise, noise, had been a torment. The noise was louder than ever before, she was sure. The Milburns more threatening. The singing rowdier. The whole place without that coat of cosiness which made it tolerable. Just another raucous drinking den on a Saturday spree. She wanted to go upstairs and sit in the dark in the unused parlour but how could that be explained away? She wanted even more to get out and walk, beat the boundaries of the old town, recall the words of Marjorie, revise them, commit them to eternal memory. But instead she opened the bottles which foamed a little at the neck, gently poured the drink into an inclined glass, made the many little journeys to and from the till, expressed delight, surprise, and regret, made promises which she would keep, kept her sense of the flow of the place, its cohering mood as closing time approached, suffered others as best she could.

But she could not stay for the final drinks and round-up chat in the kitchen when the last customer had gone and the initial mopping up had been done. Wished goodnight to them all, said she had a headache after the journey in the car, 'She's not used to cars,' said Alfrieda, whose waitress wage more than covered the petrol on her own car, 'Cars can make you feel sick,' said Jack Ack, still fresh after three hours on the accordion. Tom Armstrong just nodded. She wished she could have stayed to have a word with Tom, who had brought a chair leg wrapped in brown paper to 'see him back home', he said, now that his brothers and the Milburns had fallen out again. She liked Tom and knew he was looking for a bit of support but there was nothing she could do about the force which drew her upstairs and to solitude.

Sam saw them out and stood on the steps, the final cigarette, still a little warmth in the evening, the town seemingly peaceful before him. He considered a stroll up to Howrigg Bank where Mr. Hawesley lived – but Ellen would hear the door shut and ask where he had been and he would be ashamed to tell her.

William stayed up later than usual, listening to Gilbert and Sullivan, playing the records softly to spare the neighbours, yet again unpicking the hours he had spent so privately confined with Ellen, feeling for the first time in his life a pleasure of longing, obsessive, which disturbed but also impressed him – that he was a man of such strong feeling. That it was wholly unrequited and certainly hopeless in some measure made it more romantic. Though was it entirely hopeless? A rogue whisper would not be completely stilled. It made him a new man. But what to do with it? She was totally loyal to Sam and the loyalty was part of her desirability – he put it high on his list. He would go to the Congregational Church, but in the evening. He had difficulties with the Resurrection. She would be asleep now, he imagined, calm, untroubled, at one with the tranquil and decent little town.

—⁓—

The three men had given Lizzie rum and detached her from her friends. They strolled up towards the estate on which all of them lived but took the less familiar route. There was a house along the way, standing on its own, empty for months. They had more rum. They dared her to break in with them.

CHAPTER SEVEN

'And the third day He rose again according to the Scriptures. And ascended into Heaven. And sitteth on the right hand of God the Father. By whom all things are made. For us men and for our salvation.'

Joe chanted the words, subdued by his broken voice but no less passionate. Nothing mattered but this. He could see it all clearly. Christ coming out of the sepulchre, become divine, no longer a man, coming back from beyond death to gather in His flock. Joe, on his knees waiting for communion, driving out with all his might all thoughts, even sights, jealously watching Alfred and Malcolm, servers at the altar, above the altar the Pre-Raphaelite Christ shepherding the little children, the whole congregation now His children, people shuffling to the altar as he had seen them do for years, years of devotion, centuries the vicar said, but most of all his mother, earlier spotted, miraculously there about to take communion – but all of this had to be ignored as he prepared to drink the blood and eat the body which would raise him from the dead and make him, too, divine. Why did the words of Alistair, the tangled hair of Lizzie, the fear of the shuddering colt, still breach his concentration on such a morning in such a place? He was not worthy.

'I am not worthy, Holy Lord, so much as to gather up the crumbs from under thy table . . .' He had to be! 'My soul doth magnify the Lord.' What was his soul if he could not be undistracted? He had confessed his sins. The vicar had absolved him: he had absolved the whole congregation. Struck dead now he would go up to Heaven as fast as the good thief on the cross. But already he was thinking about swear words and seeing Lizzie lying across the horse, his belly pinching hunger after fasting that morning. He stood in line to go to the altar rails, his hands tight in fists of effort but it was no good. He was no good. He could not be wholly given over to Christ, not even when God had changed his mother's mind, which was surely a sign. The waxy rather plastic communion wafer stuck on his tongue and he coughed too loudly as he forced it down. He did not like the taste of wine.

But after the service the choir, fully robed, spilled gaily out of the vestry into the churchyard where Mr. Kneale took photographs, first of the whole choir, then groups – tenors, basses, sopranos, trebles – and finally, disrobed, of clutches of them, chattering and smiling on the benches, the women and girls newly bonneted, some of the boys in new suits, Joe wearing his new grey flannels and a blazer and, like all the other boys and men, a white shirt, tie, polished black shoes, hair flattened into short back and sides. The burden of the communion lifted by the gigglings before the lens.

The photographs in the churchyard cheered him up so much that he would have skipped down the streets had he been younger. The town itself seemed reborn: strong, sure, clean, purified. His mother had not waited for him but the full significance of her attendance at communion elated him. He was unable to imagine that she might have come for reasons other than his evangelising. She said nothing when he got back to the pub, hell bent on catching up to meet opening time, noon on Sunday. Joe changed into his old clothes and went down the cellar. His father seemed less open than usual: Joe could tell he regretted missing communion. Sadie had shut herself in the singing room which, she announced, needed a real seeing to. She had not been to communion either and Joe knew that for Roman Catholics this could be fatal to your chances. She was not singing.

'It's the best I could manage.'

Less than half an hour to opening time, the three of them discordant in the kitchen. There were half a dozen thin slices of cold ham, bread and butter, pickled onions, tea and a bowl full of the excessively hardboiled dyed eggs, called pasce eggs, which Ellen had put on before she went to church, letting them solidify. Now the eggs were as tradition demanded, the white meat rubbery, the pale shells shot with many colours, streaked, gaudy, two bucketsful in the scullery, ready to be sold in the evening for sixpence each and to be fought with – bashed or dumped against each other until an unbroken champion emerged who would receive half the takings.

'Mr. Kneale said if we wanted a family photo he could do it this afternoon,' Joe reported. 'But Alfred's coming for tea.'

'Ah.' Sam gave Joe a look he could not read. 'Clear all decks. We are to be hidden away.'

Sam crunched the egg onto his plate, podded off the shell, leaned forward and took two slices of ham with his fingers, ate deliberately grossly.

'We used to go down to Pasce Egg Hill – where you sledge – when I was a little girl,' Ellen began.

'You've told me,' Joe said. 'You always tell me. To roll the eggs down the hill.'

'We could break into one of your chocolate eggs for pudding.'

'He'll be keeping them,' Sam said, mouth full. There were two resplendent chocolate eggs, luridly wrapped, on public display on the window sill alongside humble pasce eggs brought as gifts. 'They'll be for this Alfred.'

Ellen stopped eating and poured the tea.

The clock struck louder than usual, Joe thought.

'We really are being unfair to Colin,' Ellen said, intent on the pouring.

'It's good ham.' Sam held up a wadded forkful and stuffed it all into his mouth. He added a pickled onion.

'I'll dump with you.' Joe held out a heavily guarded egg to his mother. Too casually, she tapped it, hoping to let Joe win. His was the egg that cracked.

'You can't beat your mother's luck,' said Sam. He burped.

'Sam!'

Joe looked from one to the other, at sea. He could tell they were angry.

'Grandad does great eggs.' The boy pointed to three eggs dyed a wash of yellow and then painted, miniature scenes of lakes and mountains.

'I'll tell you something about your grandad.'

Ellen nibbled at the food, knowing she must eat something, wanting to be out of this vortex of other people, jobs to be done, customers to prepare for, the world to obey; wanting to go over yet again, and again, what she had heard beside her father's grave.

'This was when he worked in the pits at Siddick.'

'The mines that went under the sea,' said Joe, as he always did, always thrilled with fright at that image, men hacking black rock under the deep waters of the sea. It was the most important thing he knew about his grandfather: the first World War, in which the old man had served throughout, was hardly mentioned.

'He came up from his shift this day and then he set off, the seven miles to where one of his sisters lived. He had heard that her husband was knocking her about. He got there, called him out and gave him a terrible hammering.' He could see that the word got home to the boy and excited him. 'A real hammering. Lay one finger on her again, he said, and next time I won't answer for it.' Sam took a deep mouthful of tea. 'Then he walked back home.'

Joe glowed. He had been included, he was grateful. Yet his father's anger made him afraid. It always would.

'What did you want to tell him that for?' Ellen asked, although both of them knew he had told it to her.

Sam looked at her almost cockily. He reached for the Capstan.

'You haven't time for that,' she said. 'Joe, help me clear up.'

The boy fell in, further elated by a man-to-man wink. He hurried with the dishes because part of the deal was that on Sundays he helped his dad behind the bar for the first hour, to give his mother a rest. It was never a busy hour.

Afterwards he mooched up street, but all he saw of interest was Colin on his motorbike with Paul proudly clinging onto the pillion seat. Paul had once been in Joe's gang but lately had fallen away. He had heard that Colin had taken him up but this was the first time he had seen them together. A shot of jealousy surprised him because only fear would have persuaded him to take Paul's place. Colin had turned against him and Joe was nervous of the consequences. Colin did not wave and Joe was hurt.

'I've put everything upstairs,' Ellen said when he returned. 'That's how you wanted it? There's lemonade but if you want tea – just make it.'

They stood in the kitchen, his parents, side by side, both wearing coats even though the day was warm. Coats looked smarter.

'You'll not be broken-hearted that we're out for a walk.' Sam's mood was a little more amiable, but still carried the edge he'd shown when Joe insisted that he and Alfred had tea together upstairs in the parlour. He and Alfred alone.

'Your dad wants to go for a walk.' Ellen did not look too happy. What she wanted above all else was time alone to gather up every last drop. Why had Marjorie said she knew how to hold onto him? Why could her own mother not do that? Colin was a good dancer too. And Joe. She should have made a list: Mr. Hawesley would have loaned her pencil and paper.

'The Easter Parade,' said Sam, and put on his trilby with a little flourish, tapped the brim.

Joe took the stairs two at a time. Everything was perfect. Egg sandwiches. Jam sandwiches. Four iced cakes from McGuffie's. Two packets of crisps. Four pasce eggs. Two bottles of lemonade. One chocolate egg. The boy nodded to them. This was something like a tea, far and away better than the amateur effort they put on at the vicarage.

Alfred was prompt. He was reluctant to go upstairs. Joe gave him an unplanned guided tour of the pub. Alfred was very taken with the singing room. 'You mean people just come in and sing? Do you pay them? What do they sing?' The kitchen baffled him. 'You're having supper and people just walk in and order a pint! Do they have supper with you?' To divert ever-increasing embarrassment and upgrade the place, Joe pointed to a shelf in the corner which would soon support a new television set. 'Father says television will end all conversation,' said Alfred and Joe wished he'd kept his mouth shut. Eventually Joe levered his guest upstairs into the parlour, neat, shining with polish, tea laid out on the table, dead smart, Joe thought. Alfred ignored the room.

'Are those cakes from a shop?'
'McGuffie's.'

'We're not allowed shop cakes.'

'We could start with them.'

Joe held back and ate one cake to Alfred's three. Then the chocolate egg. The crisps, the lemonade. Joe went downstairs for another two bottles.

'You can just go downstairs and nick bottles of pop?'

'I'll offer to pay.'

'Are those dumping eggs?' Joe nodded. 'Can I try?'

This was not as Joe had planned it but Alfred's good humour was flattering. The accent of the vicar's son was so far above his own, the way he carried himself, the gesture and poise of him. Joe was fascinated by someone who had walked off the pages of the public school stories which dominated boyhood reading material. Alfred was a specimen.

He explained the holds on the egg, the very simple rules, demonstrated the short tap, the point to point butt, the cruncher, discussed the separate virtues of round end and pointed end, told him all he knew.

'Right.' Alfred clutched his egg tightly.

'I have to see some of it. Otherwise how can I dump it?'

Alfred revealed a coy crescent of shell. He would never have got away with it in a real competition, Joe thought, but he was a guest. He tapped quite gently. As he did so, Alfred pulled back the egg. That was cheating.

'Your turn,' said Joe, showing a generous rump. Alfred failed to crack it.

Joe hit hard. Both eggshells broke.

'What happens now?'

'We can use other bits until it's all knackered.'

'My turn.'

'You have to eat it,' said Joe, after a disappointing draw. Alfred took it in two bites and picked up a second egg.

Bored, Joe went for a quick win and lost.

'Do you think,' Joe said, as they munched through egg number two, spiced with salt, lubricated with cherryade, 'that Jesus got divine in that sepulchre or did He go up to Heaven and change up there and come down again different?'

'They're jolly good eggs. Don't know. I expect he went up.'

'Do you think,' Joe was hoping for a proper discussion with this public school boy, 'that He felt no pain on the cross and if He didn't how can we say He suffered?'

'I just go along with it,' Alfred said and reached for a jam sandwich.

'What's it like sleeping in a dormitory?'

'Hell at first,' Alfred's reply was instant and heated. 'But you get used to it.'

'Do you escape at night?'

'What for?'

'I thought you had adventures.'

'Could we play darts?'

When Sam and Ellen returned they were on a marathon – who would be first to reach one thousand. Alfred immediately broke off the game and extended his right hand. 'Good afternoon, Mr. Richardson.' And again, this time with a little nod. 'Good afternoon, Mrs. Richardson. The tea was spiffing.'

Both Ellen and Sam noticeably stiffened at the formality. But they were calmer, Joe observed: the row had blown over.

'We had an extra bottle of pop,' Joe said. 'Each.'

'What's this you're playing?' Sam referred to the crush of numbers chalked on the scoreboard.

85

'First to a thousand.' Joe muttered his reply.

'What sort of game is that?'

'Sam!' But Ellen was not really cross. There was in Sam's tone a banter which brought the boys out. Her role, she saw, was to dust away all awkwardness. 'I'll put the kettle on.'

'Could we play a proper game, Mr. Richardson?'

Sam glanced at Joe, who shrugged. Nothing else had worked.

'Two hundred and one then,' Sam said and wiped the scoreboard clean with the rag. 'Middle for diddle.'

'Middle for diddle!' Alfred's voice rose half an octave, near enough a scream of delight. For the first time, it grated on Joe. Sam was tickled.

'Nearest the bull starts off. You throw.'

Alfred hurled the dart like a javelin.

'Good God,' said Sam, 'is that what you've been playing at? Here. This is how you hold a dart. Stand here, twist a little bit sideways, fix your target, bring your arm up smoothly as if you're going to brush the sides of your hair, then throw, firm but not hard, and follow through, the follow through is what makes it. Now then. Try again.'

I could have taught him that, Joe thought: why didn't I?

<hr />

'Not a bad lad at all,' Sam said, later.

They were in the kitchen, sitting over the tea Alfred had very politely refused.

'They have beautiful manners, you have to give them that.' Ellen was thankful for the harmony, however temporary it might prove. 'They turn out some big smart well-spoken fellas.'

'I met plenty in the army.'

'The officer who came to see you once. He was a beautiful speaker.'

'Colonel Oliphant.' He drank his tea now without slurping, Ellen noticed. 'But there were others every bit as bad as he was good.'

'There's bad and good wherever you go. They'll turn him into a well-turned-out, good-mannered man.'

'What about Joe? What'll they turn him into?'

'You needn't bring Joe into it. Isn't it about time you got washed for evensong?'

'So your friend wasn't afraid of the Big Bad Wolf after all, Joe? And what do you know? We didn't embarrass you a bit.'

The boy was ashamed. He knew his father had realised from the first what was behind the manoeuvre to get the tea upstairs. He looked at him, fearful, deserving punishment. And yet, coiled inside him was the unforgivable knowledge that he would do the same again.

'He's a nice decent lad,' Sam said. 'But I'd back you against him any day. Away you go.'

The boy went out on a rush of gratitude at such undeserved support.

Alfred was not at evensong. After the service when the vicar had given the choir the final blessing, Joe sidled up and asked why not.

'He felt rather sick.' The vicar's smile was too obviously strained. 'His mother thought it was something he'd eaten.' People were listening. 'The cakes, I think she mentioned cakes.' Listening closely. 'Alfred isn't used to – rich – food. But you were very kind.'

Joe slunk to his corner to hang up the surplice and cassock without daring to look anybody in the eye. The organist decided to postpone telling Joe that he would have to leave the choir. The boy walked through the dark Sunday streets feeling worthless.

'How can cakes make you sick?'

He was alone with his Auntie Grace. She had soon winkled out the cause of his hurt.

'It's what you're used to. When I was in service none of the family would have tolerated bought food – they didn't have to. We cooked and baked the lot – but it's only what you're used to. That's all. Don't take it on yourself, Joe.'

They were in her room. Leonard had lit a fire despite the warmth over Easter. Grace had turned off the main light, leaving only a side lamp as she had intended to drowse and liked firelight, lamp glow, a domesticated dusk. But Joe was no disruption, especially a Joe in need, a perturbed, deflated Joe, a Joe whom she had watched over from the cradle.

'I was second cook!' said Grace, and laughed – quietly, but she laughed, not a common sound, and the boy who was sitting at her feet, between her rocking chair and the fire, felt favoured, felt complicit. 'That was how your Uncle Leonard found me. But a second cook was somebody then, Joe, and for all his money I made him wait. His mother was against it, of course, but I soon had her sized up. If you can keep a man waiting, Joe, then he's yours for life.' Again the laugh, more of a chuckle this time, a warming embrace of sound which did what it was meant to do and calmed down the demons wounding the boy's spirit.

'You had to do everything for them,' Grace said, 'they were such babies!' Her scorn made Joe feel stronger. 'You dressed them, you washed and ironed for them, you drew their baths and made their food, you polished their shoes, laid the fires, you saw to the men's drinks, the women's creams and oils, the car was buffed up every morning, the dogs were to be brushed down, a speck of dust was a crime. They were babies but they had a grip on you and you always knew your place. You had to. Most of that went in the war, Joe, and

I've met some who miss it – but not the cleverer ones. We knew we were well out of it. However nice some of them were and some were. There were big smart men among them and some lovely-looking tall women. But when all was said and done, you were only a servant. You were treated like one and you had to think like one. Once you do that, Joe, you're a goner. Remember that.'

Her voice was low, the strokes had softened and slurred it. But there was that in it which lulled the boy, an undemonstrative urgency as if the failing woman sensed that there would be few times for them to be close like this, few occasions when he would welcome help, or when she could give it. 'Remember that,' she repeated and reached out to stroke his hair.

When he saw Alistair outside the pub, just to the side of the steps, Joe hesitated. Alistair was drunk. Joe had seen many drunken men and some women over the years and Alistair was drunk. Dead drunk. When he got close, Joe saw that he was rocking on his heels, his hands in his trouser pockets, his glazed eyes focused nowhere.

'Joe!'

The boy had to stop. Alistair tossed his head, the tuft, and Joe moved close to him.

'Your father,' he said, 'is a good man, Joe. Even if he's just said I can't drink in his house tonight. He won't serve me. I went to Carlisle dance yesterday, Joe, and just got back tonight. That's some dance, eh? A twenty-four-hour dance, Joe, eh? I'm not banned, Joe, just not tonight.' He reached out, rocked a little, took Joe's shoulder and pulled him close. 'You tell your dad I'll cause no trouble for Sam Richardson.' His face was riveted with fatigue, the words came emphatically through a desperation of drink. 'Sam Richardson's been good to my mother, see? So tell him no trouble. And . . .' Joe had used the full stop as an excuse to move off: Alistair pulled him back. 'And tell him that if he wants anybody taken care of just send me a message. Tell him that. Anybody taken care of. Send for me. I won't have trouble in Sam Richardson's pub, I'll clear it out for him, O.K., pal? Tell him that.'

'I will.'

'You do.' He released him, stumbled.

'I will.'

'You do.'

'Goodnight then, Alistair.'

'You tell him.'

Joe turned at the top of the steps.

'I will,' he promised. Alistair nodded, hugely, and then began his slow ascent of King Street.

In the pub the dumping competition drew everyone into a party battle and the gaudy eggshells littered the floor, one after another cracked and broken, some of the whites stained by the dye, Sam the judge for the semi-finals between the winners in the kitchen, the singing room, the darts room and the bar, and then for the Final. Joe, moving among these adults at play, drinking, talking too loudly, warm now, far from the strictures and ceremonies of the church which had begun his day, the inflamed sense of failure which would never go, found ease and distraction here and comfort, hope, energy, in what was so ordinary, so common. He felt a happiness, immersed in and being fed by this pagan celebration, a gratitude that there was this life also.

—m—

Later, after the pubs had closed, after the stragglers had made it back, when the only noise in the town was the shuddering of old machines in the sleepless factory, no cars on the street, last trains long gone, Lizzie looked fearfully out of the dank abandoned house.

It was too light. The moon was just past full and the near glowing orb of it made shining rivulets of the streets, pooled into light the yards and lanes, silvered the railway tracks, made visible the fields which circled and penetrated the old town. You could have read by that strong light. She stood as if paralysed for a while but she had to move. She would find the shadows. She was aching so badly now, thirsty, hungry, stunned. They had finally left her only in the middle of the day.

Her face was bruised, cut, set in a terror that made her look intently into the silent town before taking the first step. Her dress had been ripped – her mother would kill her – the shoes were ruined, no coat. Barefoot, licking her swollen lips, panting little straining breaths, Lizzie crept up the hill, making for the only place she could, the last place she wanted to be seen.

CHAPTER EIGHT

When Sadie learned on Easter Monday morning that Ruth Ellis had been charged with murder for shooting her faithless boyfriend outside the Magdala pub in London, she felt guilty. She admired the blonde, glamorous-looking young woman. She would have bet everything that the playboy type who messed her about deserved the bullets. She could see herself doing it – she could see that too clearly. That was the guilt. But the pain of her unabsolved soul, the burden of her private despair, forced her to deny her true opinion, and by the time she had worked the first hour in the pub, she had changed sides.

'He deserved it but they'll have to hang her,' she said.

'She has to be found guilty first of all,' said Ellen.

'What does Joe think?'

The three of them were having a morning break in the kitchen. Sam had been up hours before, done his work and joined the coach party to Carlisle Races.

'Mr. Braddock wanted us to have a debate on capital punishment after O levels,' he said, 'so Ruth Ellis fits in.'

'But you think they shouldn't hang her.' Sadie smiled coquettishly at Joe. 'It's them vital statistics. She's like a film star, isn't she? But she's still murdered him, Joe, whatever he did.'

'Outside a pub,' Joe said, seeking a kinship.

'She must have been driven to it.' Ellen's voice was the most thoughtful of the three. 'They said she loved him. How can you love somebody and shoot them unless you're driven to it? How could she turn into a murderer?'

'Murderess,' corrected Sadie. 'It said on the wireless. Ruth Ellis, Murder*ess*. Ruth isn't much of a film star name. Joe would let her off, wouldn't you, Joe – like all men?'

'It says "Thou shalt not kill". That's what it says.'

'That's daft.' Sadie smiled at the easy victory. 'You can't have wars without killing and then where would you be?'

'Ruth's a nice name,' Ellen said.

'She must have just stood there outside that pub in cold blood, just waiting for him to finish his drink and she sees him when he comes out and bang, bang, he's dead. But she's got to hang, Ellen, whatever drove her to it. We can all say that. There's not enough hangs. That's what I think.' Sadie got up abruptly. She was angry. Joe had never seen her anger and he flinched. 'I'm off to do them Ladies' toilets.'

'What's the matter?' he whispered, after Sadie had quit the room. Ellen shook her head.

'I'll need you on tap 'til your dad comes back,' she said.

—◊—

Mid morning and the curtains were still drawn in the front bedroom where Lizzie and her sister slept. It was noticed. One or two of the neighbours went round to the back but the door was locked. The knocking was in vain.

—◊—

Sam had done unusually badly. He had behaved like a novice. First in putting too much on an outsider because he fancied his chances against the bookies: then in putting everything on a hot tip – genuine, from the stable – which pulled up with less than a furlong to run.

There were two races to go and he would have to bluff his way through. He seemed to meet everybody he had travelled with from Wigton, all of them asking, 'How's it going?' His reply was, 'Holding my own.' As this was the reply habitually given it carried conviction, but he felt redundant – a gambler with no stake. Watching a race was nothing like watching a race when you had a bet on it. He kept away from Henry Allen's board.

'Long face, Sam.' Diddler was rather bleary-eyed but steady on his feet. 'Given it all to the bookies?'

There was long intimacy with Diddler.

'I'm skint.'

'With two to go. Bad job.'

The tinker pulled some notes out of his trouser pockets.

'Can't see a man from Vinegar Hill skint with two races to go, Sam.'

He licked his thumb.

'One for you. One for me. Yours. Mine. Sam's. Diddler's.'

'This'll do, Diddler.'

'We'll split the lot, Sam. Not far to go. Yours. Mine. And again. I'm told Bold Simon's been saved for this one, Sam. But there's a fella from Newcastle I have to see first.'

Sam smiled to himself as Diddler lumbered away, cutting off all chance of thanks and by his swift departure courteously ensuring that the younger man did not give offence by promising to pay the money back.

'It's a gift,' said Sam, watching him nose through the open-necked sunny crowd.

It was about this time in the afternoon that the first serious rumours of Lizzie's ordeal began to percolate into the town. There had been no gossip on the bus though one or two had been nudged by the first thin drizzle of comment, too little to go on, nothing to work on. But now, from that high new estate, Brindlefield, standing like an encampment to guard the town against the south, came the first whispers, door to door, pavement encounters, excited appalled rumours.

'It's Robert Carter.' Sam's naming spun the man around.

'I was hoping I'd see you, Sam.'

They shook hands and went over to sit on a couple of beer crates outside the big tent.

'When was it last? Leeds?'

'What a Test!'

'Seven years. I thought I'd bump into you again. Up here,' said Sam, and offered a cigarette to the man, once a comrade in arms in Burma. 'Remember the Sally Army?'

'I don't mind if I do,' Robert quoted as he reached out for one. Sam tried his best not to notice the frayed cuffs of the stained and shiny jacket. 'I lost that job soon after you came down. In a dead-end hole now. So I thought, any sun on Easter Monday and I'll off to Carlisle Races to bump into Sam.'

Sam lit them both up. When Robert thrust his face forward, Sam saw all he needed to see in that blotched, glazed, flaking skin. Robert was on the booze, heavily.

'Good day?'

'Average.' Robert looked away, a sudden self-consciousness possessing him which touched Sam.

'Can't be worse than mine. Tamburlaine's going to retrieve my fortune.'

'I'll let this one go,' said Robert. 'You put on your bet. And wait for your winnings. I'm happy to stay here.'

He wanted what money he had for drink, Sam knew, and didn't look back as he went to the bookies so Robert wouldn't think he was being spied on as he slipped into the beer tent.

The horse was second but the each way bet meant that he had held his own and a little more, on the race if not on the day.

'I have a busload with me,' said Sam. 'Why don't you come back with us?'

'I've a train to catch from Carlisle.' Robert smiled, sadly, and pulled the last quarter from his pint. 'We met up too late, Sam. Some other time.'

But what other time would that be? And Robert's first words had been that he was hoping to see him. Perhaps he had come from Leeds especially.

'The bus goes through Carlisle,' he said. 'I'll give you a lift down. We can have a drink or two and I'll catch a service bus later.'

'Don't let me put you out, Sam.'

'I can't stay long. I don't want Ellen on her own for too long.'

'My train's just after seven.' It was a plea.

They went to the large bar at the back of the Station Hotel. There was space enough for them to be isolated. Robert brought the two pints of bitter from the bar, and a whisky for himself.

'Are you sure, Sam?' He raised the whisky.

'This is my limit, Robert. Good health!' He raised the glass.

'Good health.' Robert threw back the whisky and took a good mouthful of the beer before he sat down. This time it was he who offered the cigarettes.

As Robert tacked about the subject he might never reach, Sam reassured himself that the pub would be manageable for the first hour or two on an Easter Monday evening; coach trips would be out in force but with such sunny weather they would take the benefit and if the expected two or three stopped on Market Hill to give the trippers their last chance for a drink, it would be later in the evening. Joe could always help out. He waited for Robert to say what he had come to say.

Sadie came across to bring the rumours to Ellen. She knew that Ellen had not intended to go out that afternoon, seemed relieved at the opportunity to be alone for a few hours. Joe had gone off on his bike somewhere as soon as the pub closed. It was only rumour, but Sadie was sure there was something in it. Three of them at her. Kept her prisoner. Infiltrating the town now, gathering pace, gathering material: they had brought others in, all of them were at her, they did things to that girl, there'll be murder over this.

'It's just somebody to talk to about it.' Robert looked away. He was well into his third pint, second whisky downed. Sam, feeling rather prissy sticking to the one pint, excused as business, patient but caught looking at the clock. 'Not so much answers.' Still looking away. 'It still comes back to me, Sam. By now I thought it would have gone, nearly ten years, Sam, ten years but it's like yesterday to me.' He stubbed out a cigarette, immediately lit another and lowered his voice further, even though they had found a secluded spot. 'Not just through the night. In the day. I remember things. That retreat when we couldn't slow down, not even for our own. There was a lad walking on bits of tyres. I can still see his feet, Sam. You couldn't call them feet – just big swollen

97

things full of pus covered in sores, and the poor lad couldn't walk, Sam. I tried to carry him a bit, but the Sergeant. He was under orders. Fair enough. Then he just peels off and falls down. I'm looking at him. Our lads go past trying not to look – who can blame them? Who? Not me. Then I'm told: move! And you know, Sam,' his expression, weakened by drink, turned towards tears, 'you know, I thought best to shoot the lad there and then. Better than Tojo. Torture. Buried alive. Skin him. Head off last. I should've shot him, Sam. I should've done it. What happened to him, eh? What happened to him? We should have given the lad a grave, Sam. He was our own.' Robert gave way to the tears and silently they irrigated the dry ruined skin of his face. 'And there's other things, Sam.' He breathed in very deeply. His next words were spoken in a forced normal voice, almost rapped out. 'Do you get that? Does it still bother you? Or is it just me that's going crackers, Sam?'

'I try to keep it in,' said Sam.

He wished Robert would stop.

He did not want to think about it. The bayoneted children barbed-wire bound to the trees. Ian cradling his guts in his hands. Killing in mad fear-fury the Japs in that wood and the sudden flash of awful joy in the killing. He did not want to think about it. Self-consume the nightmares. They would come back harder again now. Ellen and Joe would feel his nightmares even though he said nothing. How much worse it would be if he talked. He wished Robert would stop. He listened.

'Still the wife?'

Sam nodded.

'I never remarried. The kids just drifted away.' He looked at the beer. 'Can't say I blame them.'

'There's a lot feel like you do,' Sam offered. 'I'm sure of that.'

'Yes.'

'Another?'

'Thanks.'

The men stood side by side on the platform. The train was already in, a Races special.

'I was always glad I saw young Neil Harvey make that century,' Robert said.

'The boy still talks about it, now and then.'

'I'll be on my way, then.'

He held out his hand. They shook. Sam walked away.

—◊—

Almost exactly two years later, Sam received a letter from solicitors in Leeds. The message was brief. Robert Carter had died, sadly at his own hand. He had asked for this letter to be forwarded. Enclosed.

'Dear Sam,' he read,

'It all got too much. I know it's the coward's way out but there's nothing for me here. I've no hope in anything anywhere else either. The memories got worse, Sam, and there's no living with them. Not for me. I wish I'd – no point in wishing now.

'You were a good pal, Sam. Thanks for that. There are two photographs you might like to have. Maybe your boy will get something out of them. I like to think that a fond gaze will look on them and they'll mean nothing to anybody else.

'So long. Sorry.

'Yours very sincerely

Robert Carter'

One photograph was of the football team in India. Both he and Robert had been in it. On the back, Robert had printed all the names.

The other was just the two of them, in uniform, wearing their Bush hats. On the back it said: 'Me with Sam Richardson, my pal, Burma 1945.'

—m—

The first trip had arrived just before seven o'clock and about thirty people crashed into the Blackamoor for drinks, crisps, lavatories and cigarettes. Joe flew to Sadie for help. Even though the crowd was good-humoured and many happily sunburned from the day on the coast, there was impatience to be served and Ellen was struggling when William Hawesley arrived. He stood in the corridor gazing into the bar, relaxed, amused. Ellen felt that the lather she was in made her look like the red-faced flustered landlady in seaside comic postcards. William looked on her as a symbol of loveliness made more glorious by work.

'Yes?' She wrenched herself from the pumps, from the packed, singing crowd, keeping her eye on Joe coping valiantly with orders from the darts room and the kitchen. Sadie was at the sink.

'I just thought I'd drop in,' Mr. Hawesley said, in a well-prepared, easy, chatty tone, 'to let you know that this being Easter Holiday Monday we won't be holding our usual meeting here to-night.'

Ellen's rather bewildered look was interpreted by him as lack of clarity.

'The Labour Party meeting.'

'Yes, I'd worked that out, Mr. Hawesley.'

'So we'll just skip that one.' his voice had to rise: the trippers were launching into 'Davy Crockett'.

'That's very good, nice, yes, Mr. Hawesley.'

How could she get back into the bar? You could not turn your
back on Mr. Hawesley and she had not the capacity to send him off.

'Can I help?'

'Sorry?'

'Can I help? You seem very busy. I'm in no hurry. Can I help?'

'You can wash up,' Ellen spoke before she had thought about it.
'Then Sadie could help Joe wait on in the other rooms.'

'I'm good at washing up,' said William.

He walked into the bar and nodded when Ellen had the nerve to
add,

'We need the bottle glasses quickest.'

For Sadie to wait on in the rooms was a dream at last fulfilled. Joe
liked the speed and excitement of it, remembering a long list of orders,
totting up the prices. Almost instantly the pressure was relieved and
Ellen too began to enjoy this rush and push, this fervent outpouring of
determined enjoyment, this furious spending of hoarded leisure and
cash, this day out. But of all of them it was William who bloomed.
Deft at the sink. Fast on the rinse. Meticulous with the tea towels.
Made a bit of a show of it even. And still time to look around, feel he
was part of the crowd, the heave of people, salt of the earth, singing,
some even dancing in the corridor, 'King of the Wild Frontier'.

This was how Sam found it, but just moments after his arrival a
whistle was blown, drinks were downed and the regiment of pleasure
seekers made for the bus to travel to pastures new.

'Don't worry, Sam,' William called out, popping in his unlit pipe
for comfort, 'all under control.' He flapped the sopping wet tea towel.
'Need another of these.'

Ellen took care to avoid looking at Sam.

'I met Robert, from Leeds,' Sam's tone was apologetic.

'We managed very well,' said Ellen and meant it.

101

'I suppose I'll have to go now.' Sadie made a play.

'Sadie was a real help,' Ellen said. 'It was no trouble, was it, Sadie?'

'As long as somebody does the adding up I'll do it for buttons.'

'Customers ahoy!' William had spotted another coach tour swing onto the hill. 'All hands on deck!'

Ellen laughed. To this man it was like being let loose in a fairground. Perhaps it was.

Once again the day trippers funnelled in through the door and thirty orders filled the pub with what William later described as 'an exhilarating cacophony'. Sadie, who had hung around hopefully, seized her moment once more.

Like all air going out of an antique organ, this trip soon drank up its twenty minutes' break and left the pub near empty, near silent.

'I could do this all night, me,' said Sadie.

'So could I!' William's endorsement was hearty, earnest, some-how funny.

Again Ellen found herself smiling at this male, finding attractive his unfaked, almost boyish enthusiasm for what, to her, was a chore. The pub had closed. They were in the kitchen for the postscript of the day. Jack Ack had turned up for a drink and stayed to help. He was waiting to talk, Ellen sensed that, and she knew the reason: but he would not talk in front of the stranger William was to him. Sam, too, more open about it, was ready to welcome William's departure. This was made impolitely clear, Ellen thought, and his expression brigh-tened when William announced,

'Well. I must be off.'

Sam was on his feet.

'I'll see you to the door.'

Goodnight, goodnight, thank you, goodnight.

On the step William made an offer it was extremely difficult for Sam to refuse.

'I'd like to help more often,' he said. 'On a Saturday. That's your busy time, isn't it? You can call on me on other nights. Just the washing-up. I know my place! It would release Ellen from a bit of drudgery and frankly, Sam, now I'm on my own I would enjoy it.' He paused. Sam's silence was taken to be consent. 'No payment, Sam. Strictly friendly terms. We accountants are well enough off.' A second, and as it proved, a final pause with Sam unable to focus on a courteous, plausible, firm objection. And why should he object? 'Being with the People,' said William, and breathed in very deeply. 'Well then.' He held out his hand. Sam found that he had taken it. 'And whenever Ellen wants to go down to her father's grave, any weekend, I can easily fit it in. There's so much time on my hands, since.'

He put on his hat and walked across to his car. Sam watched him go, dissatisfied with his unease. He lit a cigarette before going back. He wanted to avoid sleep, avoid the consequences of Robert's talk. He wanted Ellen.

Jack Ack used Sam's re-entry into the kitchen to let loose the news about Lizzie.

'She looked as if she'd been run over.' Sadie had added to her intelligence since last talking to Ellen and more than any of them she had picked up the whisperings in the pub.

'I like Lizzie,' Ellen was distressed. 'It's an awful thing. Are you sure?' It was a plea for hope. There was a rush of memories of Lizzie in her earlier childhood; Lizzie collecting pebbles for ammunition for the boys' stone fights; Lizzie trying to help Joe when the bigger boys set on him after their move to Water Street; Lizzie loud in infinite pride when they got a house on the new estate with an inside lavatory; Lizzie around the streets, the smile, the wave, the instant vital friendliness of Lizzie, the pinched face and thick plaits turning towards handsome, towards luxuriant, the just niceness of a girl from a big family who was taking life on and winning. She did not want to talk about it. And by men she knew. How could they? How could they do this thing?

'They were all at her,' Jack Ack said, excited despite his disgust that men he had worked with could do this.

'Some say she egged them on!' Sadie was affronted. 'She wouldn't do that, would she, Ellen?'

'Oh no. No. Not Lizzie. She's a good girl.' Ellen felt short of breath as the certainty of what had happened now forced her to imagine it. She wished they would stop. 'Joe. It's past your bedtime.'

He had hoped that by keeping very very quiet and not moving – 'Now!'

The boy walked out slowly, accompanied by silence, as if he were in disgrace.

'They know who it was, then?'

'She wouldn't tell.' Sadie, who was experiencing all this to the point of acting a part in it, spoke defiantly, proud that the girl had not split despite everything. 'But they know who it was. We all know them.'

'They denied it. They've denied it all day.'

'Like St. Peter,' said Sadie.

'Where did Kathleen think she'd got to?'

'Sometimes she'll stay at Jean's house.' Sadie had almost the complete version of the timetable. 'So she didn't bother till about dinner time. Sean is on the morning shift.'

'When he got home he went on the warpath.'

'Lizzie, though.' Ellen did not want more story. She was increasingly upset by thoughts of Lizzie and those men, that great dark house,

104

the girl who always gave her a smile and a wave in the street. Something in her pulled away from all of them. She felt cold.

'I'm going to bed,' she said, abruptly.

Joe heard her come upstairs but was too ashamed to call out. He wanted to hear more. All at her?

―∭―

Ellen lay at the edge of the bed, eyes clenched, wide awake. Sam undressed quickly, needing comfort, but she aped sleep when he reached out for her. He turned to his side of the bed. William was of no account, he told himself. In what state was Robert now? He set himself against the memories. Ellen was too tense to be asleep. He knew that.

CHAPTER NINE

Kathleen had said that she would murder Lizzie when she got her hands on her, but at the sight of her – 'What have they done to you? Sweet Jesus. What have they done?' – she led her to the bathroom, bathed the uncontrollably sobbing child, threw the sullied clothes on the fire, stood before Sean when he got back from the shift in the afternoon and told him he could not see the girl until she had told him what had happened.

It took a great deal for him not to bring his fury down on Lizzie herself, but Kathleen faced him down and he had never hit her. When he did go and see Lizzie and saw her so frightened, fragile, swollen-faced, blemished, cowering against the wall, 'I'm sorry, Da. I'm sorry. I'm sorry, Da, I'm so sorry,' he nodded, pushed his anger down.

'You'll be all right now. Just you do what your mother says. You'll be all right, so.'

'She's a good girl.' The sentence was Kathleen's shield.

—⚬—

Sean sent word to two of his brothers who were in the building trade on the West Coast. They came with the sons who were of age. Lizzie's

106

older brother, Michael, was determined to be included although he was only seventeen.

Lizzie's father had no compunction about loading the odds. These three men were feared and now they were on the lookout. Everyone knew they had done it. Still they walked down to the pubs together and back together, swearing innocence, supported by no one.

They fell on them near the estate after the pubs had closed. The O'Connells had stayed in Sean's house for the evening, drinking steadily but not mad for it, Lizzie unseen upstairs, unseen and not referred to. They let their rage grow. When they went out and stood in the shadows of the high gates to the long driveway which led to the great house, they were ready for murder: fear had been driven out.

Like his two brothers, Sean was a big man. Brought up to heavy work on his father's meagre holding in Donegal, continuing with shovel and pick work daily at the factory, heavy-muscled, gentle in movement, devoted, a man who attracted no trouble. It was he, though, and his brothers, whose fury sustained itself longest, despite the recklessness of their sons, it was these three whose terrible purpose finally gave the men a brutal hammering.

As they lay, blood, fractures, the sound of breath harsh, grabbing for air, the few spectators across the road, more in the houses, shaken with the savagery of it, Sean, whose big face was split, blood-raked, his chest in agony, lifted one by the hair as if he would have his head: 'I'll tell you only the once.' He breathed in with difficulty. 'You get out of this town by the weekend or by Jesus Christ Himself I swear next time I will swing for you.'

—✺—

They took her to Kathleen's sister's family in Liverpool. She would be looked after there.

Lizzie cried all the way, remembering, re-living it, seeing them, the men, helplessly trying to force forgetfulness, the cold empty house, the darkness, the dank smell of it, the scream that would burst her head but not be let loose for fear she would be found, and what the men had done, what they had done that night, what they had done to her.

CHAPTER TEN

Joe liked to take the short cut home from school by way of Vinegar Hill. His satchel was slung on one shoulder. His cap was stuffed in his school blazer pocket.

Diddler was there which was always a bonus. The boy went over to him. He was studying the piebald which was cropping the poor grass in the small patch of field.

'How's Joe?'

'Fine. How's yourself?'

'There's been better days, Joe. There's been worse.' A perfectly straight jet of spit flew from his mouth. 'Want to get on his back?'

Joe shook his head.

'School uniform.' But both of them knew the boy was afraid of the powerful young horse. Joe felt a blush of shame.

'So what's the crack, Joe?'

'Got to go and do my homework.'

'Homework is it? Now that's a thing.' The man looked out at the piebald and clicked his tongue gently, rhythmically, against his palate. The horse began to move towards him. 'Well now,' he said. 'Homework it is, Joe.'

PART TWO
LESSONS, 1956

CHAPTER ELEVEN

Rachel watched him. Morning break, upper school, lounging packs of green-blazered adolescents occupying the grounds of the wisteria-bedecked old town house, extended by an assembly hall with minstrels' gallery, a new wing of green-tiled classrooms and two tennis courts, but still essentially the rather grand Georgian town house, quietly centred near St. Mary's. A century earlier it had been philanthropically bestowed for the improvement of the girls in the town. It was now home to the older half of the mixed grammar school, rustily returned after the freedom of the long summer holiday, catching a breath of the golden September morning before being penned in again, independence forfeited, the uniformed green flock herded back for yet more schooling. Joe knew he was being watched.

He wanted to go out with her. So did Richard Armstrong. Word was that Richard had fixed up to see her on Saturday night. Joe had not been prepared for that. He had thought he was nearly there with the build-up of obvious glances during the last weeks of the previous term, craftily engineered accidental encounters in the holidays, the coded encouragement of her two best friends, Linda and Jennie. Richard had just crashed in.

Richard was repeating a year in Upper Sixth Science. He was

rugby captain, an under-eighteen county player, an England school-boy trialist, fine-jawed, good bones the girls said – like Gregory Peck – and as widely admired as, Joe feared, he himself was widely disliked. Joe was one of his warmest admirers. He would have traded a lot to be as brilliant a sportsman, a natural they all said, as popular, easy going, unafraid. He had never quite succeeded in becoming Richard's friend. Now he was competition. By rights Richard should have her. He knew that Richard's friends thought he should back off. Richard was better, older, nearly a man. Richard was It.

So was Rachel, Joe thought. Two years younger, entering her O level year as he was entering his A level one. Deep black hair, eyes almost as jet, a yielding promise in her body that Joe could only have described in words he wanted to avoid, the nose strong as her will, reported on respectfully by Linda, very fat, closest friend. Rachel's face, so expressive, already Joe believed he was an expert on her thoughts, her complexion dark after the summer, intense but with that almost smile galling, teasing, watching him.

Once she went with Richard that would be that. As he stood there pretending to listen to Malcolm's mirthless analysis of 'The Ying Tong Song' a familiar mist of panic closed on his mind. Nowadays it was nowhere near as terrifying as the previous blank-outs. He could even go for long walks in the country, face them, steep himself in the comforting undulations of the copsed and river-runnelled Solway Plain. But panic could still seize him, threaten him, force action to throw it off.

He stared across at her. Oh yes, she was so lovely. Not to go with her could not be imagined. Richard was leaning against a wall of the old Rose Garden, full face in the sun, around him a court. Joe went across.

'How's Joe?'

'Fine.'

Richard's smile seduced the slighter, younger boy, so charming that you wanted to please it, so confident you wanted to surrender, so honest. Joe wanted the others to peel away so that he could ask the question, but they stuck by their leader and when the bell was rung they accompanied him like a guard about him and there was no chance.

He managed to catch Linda. Held her back until they were at the very tail of the queue. Richard had already gone in: was this manoeuvre some sort of betrayal of Richard's smile?

'Ask her could she come to the pictures tomorrow. Second house.'

'What's on?' Linda's gaze was very steady.

'*On the Waterfront*. Marlon Brando. They say he's great.'

'Isn't it about a boxer?'

'I don't know.' Joe lied. He had to get back in to school.

'Would you book? Saturday second house gets crowded.'

'I'll book.' Upstairs, he thought. Lash out. Back seats.

'I'll ask her then.'

'I'll see you after dinner?'

'I'll tell you what she says.'

Joe hurried in. Linda took her time.

In his agitation he risked being even later and veered off to the Notice Board outside the hall. Promptly after Friday morning break the first fifteen rugby team was put up. He had to know. He had trained alone in the holidays, he had practised kicking, literally for hours, he had tried to drill himself into the conviction that he was not, not really, frightened of tackling and being tackled. He had to be on the sheet. Not to be picked would expose his cowardice for everyone to note. He would be the only rugby-playing male in the Upper Sixth not in the team. Not to be picked would be public shame, condemned as a mere swot.

He was in! He was blind side loose forward. He could conceal most of his weaknesses in that position. Richard Armstrong stand-off half and Captain. Joe Richardson, first first-fifteen game! Blind side loose forward! That would do. The relief made him feel giddy for a moment or two.

He was late for English but Mr. Tillotson rarely made a fuss.

—◆—

'Nice of you to drop in, Richardson. We're on "The Tables Turned". Brenda?' Brenda read the verse beginning: 'The sun above the mountain's head . . .'

Arthur took up the next verse. There were only seven of them in Upper Sixth English and the lesson was held in what had been a handsome bedroom overlooking the gardens. It was deeply quiet, their gentle locally accented reading echoed the tones of Wordsworth's flat Cumbrian drawl, which could sound like the murmuring of bees, Mr. Tillotson had observed, several times. He kept bees.

Five girls, two boys, together for a year now under Mr. Tillotson, Yorkshireman, hardly moved his lips but a strong voice, black hair plastered flat on his head, long pale face, supposed to have been in military intelligence in the war, Eastern Europe, mentioned it now and then, last day of term just the brief lifting of a curtain, mad on cricket. Alison. 'One impulse from a vernal wood,' she read, 'May teach you more of man, Of moral evil and of good, Than all the sages can.' There was a peace here, in the double lesson ending Friday morning, in the former Georgian bedroom, fireplace intact, windows floor to ceiling, cornicing not entirely gone. Mr. Tillotson himself took the next verse, powerfully read through the tight lips, especially the last line, 'We murder to dissect.'

'Richardson.' So he had not been left out.

'Enough of science and of art, Close up these barren leaves; Come forth, and bring with you a heart/That watches and receives.' He knew it by heart. All of them did.

'Now then, Richardson, last in first in, what is the poet telling us?'

'He says Nature can tell us things books can't, do you believe that, sir?'

'It makes no matter whether I believe it, Richardson. Wordsworth believed it. How do we learn from Nature?'

'By listening for impulses, sir. But he doesn't tell you how to do it.'

'What about "Come forth and bring with you a heart/That watches and receives"? You've just read it.'

'How can a heart watch, sir?'

'Can anybody help Richardson here?'

Slim, spotless, doctor's flaxen daughter, Brenda's hand shot up as if it were reaching for the alarm cord.

'He doesn't just mean the heart itself, sir. He means more like a good heart, being willing to be influenced, more an open heart. Heart's a metaphor, sir.'

The master nodded. Brenda gave Joe a conquering and pitying glance. Her marks were better than his – in all three subjects, English, History and Latin. But such triumphant glances were helpful, he thought jealously, a goad.

Joe's gaze drifted to the window. Would she say yes? At least he was in the team. Linda would surely have told him if Richard had already asked her out on Saturday. How could he have waited so long?

Being in the team would help. He could follow what was going on in the lesson and still drift. They were going through their set books for the third time.

'We have to keep in mind that this poem is an answer to "Expostulation and Reply",' said Mr. Tillotson, 'hence the title "The Tables Turned". In one sense he's pitting the power of books against the power of Nature.'

'He gives a lot more time to Nature,' Joe said, 'so it's an unfair argument. But you learn from books.'

'It depends what sort of learning we're talking about.'

'Wordsworth thinks that moral learning and truth and wisdom can be learned from Nature,' said Brenda, 'better than from books. Just by listening to a wood.'

Yes, thought Joe, somehow you do learn. But he could not talk about it openly.

How did it happen? When first they had read Wordsworth, Mr. Tillotson had explained the poet's 'neuroticism' and 'disturbances', and Joe had been attracted by that. It encouraged what he was already daring himself to do in solitude, sit on a hedge bank or a hillside and just simply be there. Until the sense of it became unbearable. This now seemed a greater thing because of the experience and poetry of Wordsworth. And at times he had felt a sense of replenishment, a dream of calm, a proportioning in his mind, marked by a physical experience of lightness, inward smiles at recognitions untraceable. He did feel his thoughts, sensations, whatever they could be called, acted on just by being there, open to impulses as in the poem. But how did it happen?

Yet the boy's liking for argument crashed through the fragile evidence he had gained for himself.

'Listening to a wood won't get you through A levels,' he said.

118

Mr. Tillotson smiled with the others, but the teacher knew that Joe wanted more.

'Wordsworth wasn't interested in getting you through A levels, Richardson,' he said.

'God made Nature,' said Arthur loudly. His family was strict Unitarian in one of the remote, Norse fell villages. 'So it makes sense. Real country people have a lot of wisdom. Our preacher says that.'

'But we know about God through the bible,' said Joe. 'That's a book.'

'No it isn't,' said Arthur. 'It's God's word.'

Joe backed off. Reason had, gently – fearfully – begun to question faith. But he was not remotely ready to joust with the axehead certainties of Arthur's upland nonconformism.

'There's something going on here behind the lines, you see,' said Mr. Tillotson. 'I'll give you notes on this next week. It might come up as a question. A poem is always both of its time and it has a history. Now with Wordsworth we have to remember the French Revolution – which he saw as a student – and he welcomed it – "Bliss was it in that dawn to be alive" – remember? We talked about that – and then what happened after the Revolution? – The Reign of Terror, which he put down to the fanatical application of Reason. "We murder to dissect." Reason, you see, had led to tyranny. Reason was suspect. And in this century also so-called Reason has led to tyranny time and again.'

'It needn't,' Joe said, although he could just glimpse that it might.

'One moment. Add on to this another revolution, the Industrial Revolution which Wordsworth thought destroyed the balance between man and Nature. Now that Revolution as well was based on Reason, and he thought it had gone wrong in much the same way. So you can see why he looked for something else to hang onto. Being brought up in the Lake District helped – Nature all around him, you see, overwhelming him, and he thought that Nature and instinct – our own internal deepest nature – would answer the questions that Reason and both Revolutions had failed to answer satisfactorily. Nature and – this is a key point – a new understanding of childhood – "the child is father of the man" – we discussed that last term, this is crucial, we've discussed that before – which brings us to the Immortality Ode. Veronica, you can start us off.'

Joe did not really understand. How could Nature be against industry when his father used to tell him about looking for trout on the way to the factory and the mining lads from Aspatria all kept dogs, went rabbiting, knew more about trees than he did? And wouldn't you be the poet you were going to be whether or not there was a revolution? You just wrote a poem, didn't you? Because you had to. That's what poets did. As Veronica's monotone and dogged delivery nevertheless brought lines of soaring magnificence into what Mr. Tillotson called the domesticated and Jane Austen part of the school, Joe wanted to ask the teacher to spell it out more. But not yet. If he looked out of the rear window he could catch a sight of the new block where she was at that very moment, sitting and listening, like him.

Should he write a note? He could use poetry. 'She walks in beauty like the night.' Change it to 'You walk in beauty like the night.' Too soft? Too early and too soft. How could he put on paper how much he fancied her when 'fancied her' was not good enough? She couldn't possibly be impressed that he was blind side loose forward. Or just made up to a prefect. Richard was deputy head boy. If his gang had got the skiffle group organised and were playing somewhere, that would have helped, but they were still struggling just to make the right sound and finish at the same time. What could he give her?

Great waves of words rolled quietly through the small warm

schoolroom. 'Turn whereso'er I may, By night or day, The things which I have seen I now can see no more.' 'Our birth is but a sleep and a forgetting: The Soul that rises with us, our life's Star, Hath had elsewhere its setting, And cometh from afar.' 'Earth fills her lap with pleasures of her own; Yearnings she hath in her own natural kind.' The diffident voices of the Wigton schoolchildren, shy before these cliffs, scaled the heights with difficulty. These were new ways of seeing worlds external and internal, surprise views, sudden clearances, and their hesitant voices expressed the uncertainty of being in unmapped territory.

It was Mr. Tillotson himself who read the passage Joe most wanted to hear. He was a good reader, Joe thought, never rushed, made sense of it as well as finding the poetry in it. 'Not for these I raise, The song of thanks and praise; But for these obstinate questionings/Of sense and outward things, Fallings from us, vanishings; Blank misgivings of a creature/Moving about in worlds not realised.' How did Wordsworth know that? How did he know exactly that and to be able to say it like that? First time round he had plucked up courage to ask Mr. Tillotson what it meant, which was when 'neuroticism' had turned up, and also 'disturbances'. The teacher had then told him that in a letter Wordsworth as a boy had written how he had to grab hold of a rock to make sure he was still in touch with the external world. That was when Joe's loyalty to the poet had been forever clinched. The final words rolled into the air and dissolved into silence. The teacher let the enclosed silence linger. Then the lesson was at an end.

'Don't be late again, Richardson,' the teacher said as the boy made for the door. 'It can become a bad habit.'

At their table in the girls' canteen there was conflicting advice.

Linda said, 'Richard's better but he fancies himself a bit too much for my liking.'

Jennie said, 'Joe's hopped about from one to the other. You'd be safer with Richard.'

'I don't have to go with either of them, you know,' Rachel whispered, but fiercely: though they had attempted to isolate themselves at one end of the table, ears were pricked up all around the compass.

'You don't have to but you will,' said Linda as, heroically, she pushed aside her apple crumble and custard because the other two hated school puddings.

'Richard is . . . Well.' Jennie struggled. What superlative could be found for him, especially in a company which distrusted superlatives?

Linda said, 'I don't think Joe'll give up.'

Rachel bent her head slightly and smiled. His clumsy bungled advances that summer in the lane in front of her farm had been comical. Standing holding up his bike as if frightened to let go of it. But still.

'Richard,' Jennie was firm, 'is, well, anybody would go with Richard. And not only in this school either.'

Again Rachel smiled. Was his reach so wide? But 'not only in this school' was somehow comical as well.

'Richard was with Marion for nearly a year,' said Jennie. 'So he's a sticker.'

'I like Marion.' Rachel nibbled her lower lip, as if in vexation.

'She was too slow for him,' Jennie said.

'Who told you that?'

'It's what they said.'

'I heard it was the other way round.'

'That makes more sense to me,' said Linda, grimly longing for the clearing up signal so that she could banish those puddings from her sight. 'Marion's in a rush.'

With dishes cleared and 'For what we have received may the Lord make us truly thankful, Amen' mumbled by the host of green-clad girls, they went to look for a quiet spot and settled behind the tennis courts where anyone approaching would be clearly exposed and so deterred.

They took off their blazers, rolled up the sleeves of their white shirts, kept the buttons shut to the neck, sat on the grass secure on their thick green skirts and looked over to the elegant school, young men and women most of whose mothers and fathers had been out at work at their age, tentative and rather restless in the new privilege of staying on, raw implants, their role unclear, ambitions confined, unused to this academic air.

'He's coming over.'

Linda heaved herself up and went out to face him. The passage between the tennis courts and the wall which shut off the grounds from the rest of the crofts was rather narrow and effortlessly she barred him. Rachel looked away.

Linda walked back as expressionless as she could manage. Joe stood his ground.

'He wants to talk.'

'He said more than that.'

'He said he would book two tickets anyway.'

'What if I don't go?'

'He said he could always get rid of one.'

'What else did he say?'

'He asked if you were already going out tomorrow night with somebody else.'

'What did you say?'

Linda paused. She was concerned lest she had done the wrong thing. She had, however, told the crucial truth.

'I said there was nothing promised. It was left vague.'

Rachel nodded, rather solemnly. Richard's friend had said that he would be at the coffee bar in the neighbouring mining town in which he lived, half an hour before the first house. His gang always gathered there. Unlike Wigton, Aspatria had a coffee bar with a jukebox next to the picture house. This made it an adolescent social market, a place of trade with no necessary previous commitments. For Richard, invitation enough.

Joe stood there, knowing he was a target. Rachel got up.

'I can't just leave the poor lad standing spare like that.'

As she walked across to him, the air seemed to part in a special way to let her through, the boy thought, the sun behind her darkened her skin to a mystery, the nervous smile on his face opened from the heart and Rachel saw that and was suddenly, unexpectedly, abashed, gave a crooked smile in return, wished she were not wearing short, hooped green socks.

Joe had an intimation, at the outermost limit of his mind, that with Rachel the siege would be lifted, not only the fallings away but other fears, that she would heal in yet unknown ways what work and will had only staunched and subdued. With Rachel all would one day be well and yet if his feelings and thoughts could have been summed up in a single word as she came to a stop a mere pace in front of him that day, it would have been 'Help!'

She saw how much he wanted to go with her and was impressed. She had never felt herself to be the object of desire. And though he had stood his ground and taken on Richard, she sensed, in what flowed between them under the hot September sun on the land of the old Saxon crofts, that he was uncertain. Rachel felt safe with that.

'Where'll we meet?' she said, surprising herself.

For a moment he was winded. Then he grinned, a gormless grin.

—✺—

At the end of the school day he circled the bus queues on his bike to make sure that Richard did not approach her. Rachel took the bus which went down to the little farming villages on the Solway, past the ruins of a mediaeval Cistercian Abbey, past fortified churches, across fathomless ice-age peat bogs. Her father's farm was about three miles north of the town. Richard would bowl west towards coal, iron ore, the slag-heaped industrial eruption which rimmed the western fells and lakes. Joe circled the chattering bus queues intent as a kingfisher, ready to dive in.

Nothing happened.

Nothing happened for the rest of the evening either, nothing to compare. He did the three hours homework he had set himself for Fridays in the regime for this A level year. Nothing there but the pleasant slog, the notings and underlinings, the first draft of the final essay, the full-stop entry in the accounts book registering subjects done, time taken. No mention there of the faint fuse of excitement which nudged him to pause, a quiet pleasure in anticipation along his nerves which seemed to percolate into all the intervals in concentration. Restless after the essay he went down into the noisy pub but nothing took his fancy and he was not needed. The street was warm from the day and still some light but he did not want to go to see his Uncle Leonard or Mr. Kneale even though noisy Friday nights in the pub had become the time he went across for an argument or even for peace to get on with his homework. The phone box on Market Hill was a temptation but he knew it would not do to phone her – and she would have a phone, farms had phones: best to do nothing.

In bed he read *For Whom the Bell Tolls* but his attention was not quite as raptly secured as usual in the grip of the fiction. The customers left. Those who had served them would be in the kitchen now, the round-up, the unravelling of the day. He preferred to be on his own, cultivating the thought of her, the look of her which came to him like a scent, through the Spanish Civil War, through the essay on the Dissolution of the Monasteries, the apprehension of Richard, the fearful prospect of being blind side loose forward in the first game of the season the next morning, through all the usual rumble and rubble of impressions, memories, impulses swirling, clogging, infesting, irradiating inside the skull, like a scent it came, the look and thought of her.

He found the Beethoven concert he had circled in the *Radio Times*, paused a while but a few minutes would have to do, he could not be drawn away from his purpose, not even by siren sounds in which he could utterly submerge himself.

These concerts were a secret vice. Neither his parents nor any of his friends knew. It was not that he was too embarrassed about it, though there was some of that. Nor was he altogether ashamed, although there was a little of that too. Classical music was for posh voices, different accents, expensive clothes and outings, references chiefly designed to exclude, or so it could seem to Joe. But there was none of that when the music itself came from that common little maroon plastic box and played over him, played him, as the best singing in the choir had done, as the occasional happy few bars in the steeplechase of his own piano grinding lessons had delivered, there was none of that when the music carried him out to seas of

126

unknowing that he would never understand and never want to leave. But tonight he needed simpler excess, someone he could be like, someone who could inhabit him, not an ocean but an island, a rock, hard, immediate, even savage. He had an appointment out there in the universe of music and he could not break it.

He said his prayers quickly, including A levels now, but put tactfully. Then he knocked off the light. He reached down in the dark, left Beethoven and sought out the station which would weld him to that new music, that new voice, that sorcery, the promise of disturbance. He had to be patient: Frankie Laine, Doris Day, 'Whatever Will Be' which made him smile and sing along and then the needle hit bull on the nerve, Elvis Presley. White boy, black soul. The man. 'Houn' Dog'. The song. Rock 'n' Roll. That beat, that sex. The revolution. It shot into him.

Would she be there?

CHAPTER TWELVE

Joe rushed in, made it to the stairs but Sam had been watching out for him and stepped out of the bar.

'You did well.'

The boy had to turn and face him though he felt glued to the ground with embarrassment. His dad had turned up at the game: so had other dads, a brother or two, a few girl friends, a scattering of the town's sporting punters who now followed the school side playing so well but none of that mattered, it was his dad who mattered and Joe had not been prepared for it, left at nine-fifteen in good time for the ten o'clock kick-off, changed, the sweet skin-satiating feeling of pride when the dark green jersey was handed out and pulled on and then without warning there was his father, chatting away to Mr. Braddock, his History teacher, which doubled the embarrassment if doubling were possible of such a large quantity. At least he did not shout encouragement like one of the dads or instructions like another.

Now he wanted to talk about it! Joe faced him up and then his head dropped, as if expecting and deserving criticism. He had missed an easy tackle. Plain to be seen and certain to be judged and condemned by all.

'You were too strong for them all round.'

The pub was quiet. Past dinner time. Joe had taken his dinner in the canteen with the opposing team. Ellen was visiting her father's grave. Mr. Hawesley had said he would get her back by six. Sam was a bit lonely.

'Richard dictated the play . . .' said Joe.

'He's a natural.'

Joe nodded over-emphatically. Richard had carved them apart, dummied, side-stepped, slung out passes unerringly, tackled with force, scored, twice. In the dressing room before and after the game he had had the grace to say nothing. Joe had had the sense to do likewise.

'But you played well,' Sam insisted, fishing out a cigarette. 'Good covering.'

'I missed that tackle.'

'Everybody misses a tackle now and then. And he was a very nippy little lad, their best player, that scrum half. Everybody misses the odd tackle.'

But not because they're suddenly frozen in fear, Joe thought. Will I ever be picked again?

'For a first game I would say very promising.'

Sam smiled, wishing he could do more. The boy turned to go, hesitated for a fraction of time wanting to say thanks or talk further about the game or just give back for what had been given but 'I've got to go' was all he could muster and both of them knew he was running away.

'Can I have *For Whom the Bell Tolls* when you've finished it?' Sam asked the question of the boy's back. Joe turned his head.

'I like it better than that other one,' he offered. 'There's more to it.'

'After I've read it we can talk about it. Maybe. If you want.' But the boy was gone.

Joe took the stairs two at a time, dumped his strip into the bathroom and shut himself into his bedroom to sweat out that missed tackle. Would Rachel get to hear of it?

Sam stood at the foot of the stairs for a moment or two. He had to let the boy go his own way. He had to accept that Ellen was changing. He lit up, breathed in deeply, went back into the bar. After closing time he would go to the British Legion, put on a bet, play a few frames of snooker with the lads. That should shake it off.

— ∽ —

Joe did not do homework on Saturdays but this day it was a near thing. At least it might have distracted him. He went to help Alan in the shop but trade was so slow and Alan was put out that Joe was not coming to the dance with him that night. He liked to take Joe on the back of his new second-hand motorbike. It was not the same going on your own, he said. He would find somebody else, he said, and Joe, jealous, slid away as soon as he saw an excuse.

Malcolm was playing some of the records in his neatly catalogued jazz collection. He had come to it through the English jazz players – Humphrey Lyttleton, Ken Collier, Chris Barber.

Malcolm embraced the new world of jazz. There were clubs he read about – there was even a club in the attic of a Victorian building in the middle of Carlisle. Wild and dangerous men went there in berets and older women hung around temptingly. One day he would be old enough. Meanwhile there was Louis Armstrong, of course, and Miles Davis and all the great as yet unseen Americans; but most of all, for Malcolm, there were the two gods – Dizzy Gillespie and Charlie Parker. When he listened to their music, however much he liked the other more popular American music, he felt sophisticated, superior and always charged to wind up Joe.

Malcolm started picking on Rock 'n' Roll – 'music for peasants' his father called it, Elvis Presley was 'white trash', Bill Haley was 'jungle music'. Joe's defence was heated. Malcolm teased him. Joe gave up – not wanting to spend his passion on such a wasted effort. He left and circled around the streets for a while, willing his bike to nose out interest, rifling through the narrowest alleyways, but all that happened was that he ended up at his Aunt Grace's house for tea, as usually happened on a Saturday afternoon, and he listened to the football results in suspenseful silence while his Uncle Leonard marked his pools and for a few moments seventy-five thousand pounds was a real possibility. 'Win the pools and never have to work again,' Leonard would say, 'the English working man's highest ambition in life.' But again, fortune had just eluded Leonard's careful clerkly skills.

'Another week,' he said as he had said on so many Saturdays before. And immediately new hope began to trickle in, no respecter of experience.

Joe helped his Aunt Grace with the tea. She was slower on her feet these days. Sometimes there was a dribble from the corner of her mouth.

Afterwards, Leonard went up street to net any latest gossip and be ready for the pink sports edition which would be through from Carlisle. Joe decided not to help Alan out with the paper deliveries. He had been stung.

He was relieved when his uncle left the house. Usually he enjoyed discussions with Leonard and Mr. Kneale. Today he was too restless. And it would have been the Suez crisis and Joe's opinions were volatile. As we had won the Second World War and just lately had the Greatest Empire the World Had Ever Known and always fought on the side of Right, how could anybody object to the decision to keep the Canal firmly under our control? This even more emphatically stated was Leonard's position, to which Joe was viscerally sympathetic. Yet Mr. Kneale's respect for the United Nations and Mr. Hawesley's uncharacteristically fierce advocacy of the anti-government position of the Labour Party also had its influence on the boy – it was another world of fairness, another view of the Empire, a difficult new order to consider, a budding feeling that invasion could be morally inferior to restraint. Mr. Braddock had set up a debate on it and told Joe he would be speaking Against the invasion. But he was glad to avoid this argument. His Uncle Leonard's anger would have taken too much energy. Uncle Leonard wanted to blow Colonel Nasser to Kingdom Come and he wanted Churchill back pronto to make sure the Americans didn't stop us. It was our show.

Joe could only concentrate on meeting Rachel. He wanted time to flick past. He wanted a guarantee that she really would be there. He fingered the tickets in his inside pocket so often that they began sweatily to stick together. No friend or activity he could think of could do what he most wanted – eliminate ninety minutes. He had circled a concert in the *Radio Times* but simply listening would not be enough. He ran with restlessness. The pub kitchen would make him restless. Alone in his bedroom would make him restless. He forced himself to bike around the far boundaries of the town – that could put in fifty minutes and more if he doubled back on himself. He could have been on an abandoned planet for all the traffic he met and while he rode, he dreamt of her, saw her, rehearsed what he might say, worked out a list of topics, worried that the grey skies might be full of rain which would put her off the bike ride into the town, thought to go out and meet her, decided that would spoil it, the clouds were too high, weren't they? For rain?

And then she was in front of him.

It was a different her.

CHAPTER THIRTEEN

Rachel had taken trouble. This would be the first time she had gone on a date to the pictures. Before that, village boys, an evening stroll, escorted back from a village dance, what now seemed merely girlish days. The second house of Wigton pictures on a Saturday night was serious. Whatever came of it, word would get around.

Her father was the problem. It was essential that he did not pick up the scent. They were two peas in a pod, he said, in looks, in character, it was a pity she was not a boy. The two boys were like their mother, fair, willowy, placid, unforthcoming. Rachel was his. That was the chief reason for the circumspection of the village boys. 'You're turning into a honeypot,' he would say to her: it was a criticism of sins uncommitted, it was jeering as if she were getting above herself, it was a warning, no doubt of that, and there was something else which she could barely fathom, it was hurt at the approaching betrayal, a staving off of loss. As a child she had trailed around the farmyard behind him as if attached by a piece of string, the short shadow to the light of his furious mission to transform the weedy, bog-ridden, over-small tenant farm, wanted by no one else and only landed in the lap of the former labourer because of the few hundred pounds down payment provided by his wife, whom he

133

tormented for that benison. The war had given him his chance – the war had made him.

Rachel had been his 'luck', he said, the youngest, the only child born on the farm. The boys were hammered into shape but he never let his physical temper loose on Rachel, and for years she was outside the rule which willed the wretched farm to improvement, to lease more acres, to start a pedigree milking herd, and through fine husbandry force it into a property which made Isaac Wardlow a man admired in the district although no amount of admiration would ever satiate his ambition. Rachel was his pet. He made no affectionate gestures, no kissing after she was a baby, no hugging, no expressions of love in word either, but she was outside the force of his passion to show them all, protected. Until she grew up.

Now she feared him. She saw him lead in the bull, holding the pole, steering but utterly alert and she felt like that. His temper would fire at any time now, just as with the others, but Rachel was not used to it and she fought back, which he liked because it meant she was him, but he could never let her win and steadily he was crushing her. Twice she had threatened to run away and once he had all but hit her.

The Friday night was easy because she went up to the village hall to the Youth Club but on Saturday she would have to take care. She stayed in the house throughout the day. She felt as if he were shaming her; he would give her no air. In the heavy-beamed, old-oak-furnished Victorian kitchen, which her mother hated and longed to replace – but there was never money for inside – she literally kept her distance, helping to serve the food when the three men came in for dinner, clearing away, washing up, not even risking a walk up the village but filling any free time in her bedroom, vainly trying to read. The date with Joe had become important.

It was quite usual for a few of them to cycle into Wigton for the pictures on a Saturday night and no surprise that it was the later, the second house, because the young men and older boys would never be finished work in time to get to the six o'clock. So she did not need an excuse. But her father could pick things up about her, as she could about him, so Rachel said less than usual and gave her mother as an explanation and an excuse that it could be the time of month in case her father asked any questions.

As the time for supper approached and her brothers rushed to clean up and be off on their motorbikes down to the nearby coastal resort where Saturday night was big, Rachel had to fight herself not to catch his eye. The constantly twilit room was more than usually oppressive, the fire, burning peat and logs got for nothing, too hot, the whole enterprise taking too much effort even before it began. How much calmer to sit in and listen to the radio or go around to Linda's house where they could play records and dance together in Linda's bedroom. Her father seemed to take such a long time at the table, one cup of tea after another, dark-faced in the dark room, powerfully barrelled body, thick leather belt which he had often taken to the boys, collarless shirt, open waistcoat concealing braces, smelly stockinged feet, boots at the door to be cleaned for him for the morning. He drank his tea in the old way from the saucer and dipped digestive biscuits in it, as if he were down to gums.

Rachel was made even more anxious by the nervousness of her slender, fair mother, who was in on it. There was an excitement in her gestures, the swift smiling knowing looks, which, Rachel was sure, would put him on the scent. More than once she had to get out of the room to lower the tension and whenever she came back she expected the man to fix her and say, 'Now what's all this?'

He looked at her carefully before she left. There was a moment. This time she stared him out. The green school raincoat. Flat shoes.

No make-up. Assurances that 'a few' of them were going which was true although she dared not catch the glittering glances of her mother.

She was free. The bike seemed a thing infected by her escape to freedom, rushing her away, spinning wheels colluded, the greetings of the others like cheers. They pedalled through the still-light lanes close-ranked as a flock of chittering starlings, migrating through the dim countryside for an evening's pleasure.

Unusually, Rachel did not park her bike down Meeting House Lane next to the Salvation Army but turned into Church Street and found the little yard where an old unmarried aunt of her mother's lived – Aunt Claire. It was there that Rachel put on her make-up, changed into the high heels she had borrowed from her mother and smuggled into her saddle-bag. She put aside the school raincoat. The old lady smiled. 'You're on the gad, eh?' she said, her sweet country face innocently complicit, gleeful. 'Well, good luck to you. I hope he deserves you.' Rachel blushed.

There was still a feeling of blush about her as she made her way a mite unsteadily down the crooked street and across to the mouth of Meeting House Lane where Joe stood looking up and down the road. The first thing she thought was that she was glad he was not wearing his specs. Mostly he did not outdoors but she had feared that for the pictures . . . But not. And even better he was not wearing the school blazer. A charcoal grey suit, white shirt, tie, like a man out. His hair was as she liked it and so was his obvious uncertainty, which flipped to startled when he saw her.

She had turned into a woman. Was that it? She had changed utterly and yet she was the same. The same framing black hair, jet eyes questioning him – do I look all right? Why are you staring here on the street? – blue dress dipped, as Joe would describe it, at the front so that the rise of breasts could clearly be noted, a whipped-in waist, a gentle fall of soft textured pleats. He wanted to touch her. It was very difficult not to, but King Street was alive and both of them were certain that they were under intense observation.

You look beautiful, he wanted to say, but was an age from saying it. It makes me very embarrassed to see you looking at me like that, Rachel wanted to say, but please don't stop. How could I have waited so long, Joe would have said, in another world, maybe in a film: wasting a whole summer. There is something about him, Rachel thought, that suit sets him off well, I like his mouth.

The split seconds embraced not only formulated thoughts but a draught of sensual impressions, past comparisons, building of future possibilities, fears of recognition from others, delight of recognition in each other, a sudden nucleus of unspoken affinities which only months would unravel. Yet even such split seconds had to come to an end and descend into conversation. Joe had not a clue what to say – despite repeated rehearsals in front of the mirror as he had vainly attempted to Presley his hair – and so he nodded. The best you could manage, she would say, later, much later, was a nod!

'Did you get seats on the back row?' she asked.

The hot seats, the bold seats, the seats for young lovers.

'No.' Already defeated. Booked too late. Not even next to the back row.

'Good!' She smiled. It would have seemed too fast, too soon.

Joe did not understand her obvious relief but there was no time for that as they were tugged in by the flow which indicated that the doors had opened for the second house.

First they sat straight in their seats, three rows from the back, attentive to the bits and pieces that came on before the main film, staring intently ahead as if afraid to miss a frame. In the interval Joe bought two ice-cream tubs. Rachel did not like to refuse although she wanted to shove it under the seat. Conversation through the wooden spoons over the damp little tubs was not easy but Joe found a useful vein in the caricaturing of teachers. When *On the Waterfront* began they snuggled closer, as if that was what they ought to do, and behind them there was a ripple of snuggling up and the beginnings of such gropings and suppressed groanings as would be tolerated in a small cinema peopled exclusively with locals, part of whose entertainment was to watch and report on the real-life love stories in the back rows. Joe's eventual looping of an arm around Rachel's shoulders was a small masterpiece of nonchalance, he thought, only partly spoiled by his hand bumping into the knee of the large lady directly behind Rachel. Her cough was a test. Both of them giggled. Rachel eased closer.

Joe did keep a check on the screen but his time was now devoted to answering the question which would not go away: what to do next? He fished the hand down in the direction of a breast but a mere shrug ruled out that route. He looked at her, hoping that she would look as intently at him but she was eyes front, unyielding. He turned a little sideways so that his other hand could touch her waist, her arm, anything so long as more parts of her could be in contact with more parts of him. This was not satisfactory at all: she seemed frozen to him, alive only to the screen.

Finally she did turn and by this time a turbulent Joe thought he had earned a kiss.

'Isn't he sexy?' she said.

Joe looked at Marlon Brando as for the first time. He was affronted. What was sexy about him? Old jacket. Mumbling. Squashed face. Not a trace of a smile. And in the fighting bits they always used doubles. Girls weren't supposed to find men sexy, were they? It was girls who were sexy. But her use of the word excited him. When he turned back to Rachel, once more she seemed enraptured by the massive stumbling creature on the screen. Joe studied Brando.

He eased off. To be beaten by somebody in a film! But as soon as he eased off, Rachel's body softened to him and she seemed to melt a little, prepared to be part of him. He made no further move.

And then he flew. Welded to her by the lightest of touches, he saw them take off together. That he had so nearly not secured her! That was now the urgent goal, securing what had become in that short time, and however hard to articulate, someone absolutely necessary to his life.

In bed, later, wide awake in the silence of the countryside, Rachel knew that it would go on. His mixture of urgency, anxiety and undisguised affection – could she risk anything stronger? – had flung itself at her with an unsettling, a flattering, force. In the tingling silence of her bedroom, with the memories of that shyly looped arm, the sexiness of Marlon Brando, the full long kiss pressed against her which Joe had claimed after fetching his bike and riding home along the unlit by-roads with her, the wiping off the lipstick at the door, even though her father was long asleep, that good suit of his, good mouth, she felt that she had made the right choice.

She knew her father would somehow have sensed it all and anyway there would be the gossip over the next day or two.

CHAPTER FOURTEEN

Sometimes Ellen thought she scarcely knew him. Even now when as usual he was reading, cigarette dangling, cup of tea long cold, customers long gone, town a tomb, and she as usual had pulled up the low stool to the embering fire, her *Woman's Illustrated* to hand, drowsily grazing on the spent coals, even now, even there she could think she scarcely knew him.

There had been the strict innocence of knowing him as a girl, then the knowing as a woman, the strange mix of longing and memory and inevitable numbness of knowing when he was at war and in danger of no return and perhaps that had strained it for good, or maybe time was responsible. William had talked about time and pain finally snuffing out any flicker from the original fire until only a memory was left. The rest was habit, William said, shored up by will.

It was not so bleak or so clear cut with her although William's arguments always beguiled Ellen, who was not used to analysis and reflection of this kind. She would declare, stoutly to herself, that she still loved Sam and could show it and did and always would. But she could look at him as on this night and see the man, the outward form, the familiar slouch over the book, the cigarette, and feel that what had really been him had gone, replaced by efforts and memories on both their parts. The length of the absence in war and her unrelenting current of fear had taken part of his life away from her. He could as it were vanish from her in such a strange way. She knew him and she did not know him, and what she did not know could sometimes seem everything.

'We called in the Traveller's Rest,' she said. 'You were right about it being a lovely place.'

Sam smiled.

'Did the Queen have a half with you?'

'She told us she was already spoken for.'

'And?' He put down the book.

'It's . . .' She struggled: praise did not come easily but the Traveller's Rest was a very fine pub, a cut above all the pubs she knew in Wigton, a pub with a rose garden, a ladies' bar, ample amenities. 'I can see what you saw in it,' she said.

'We did what we did.'

'I can see what you could have done with it.'

'There would've been no point.' The words were philosophical but the regret could not be disguised, the anger was not fully gone, and he picked up the book.

'I was willing,' Ellen said, and he nodded without looking up.

But Joe was not. When the brewery had offered Sam what the director called 'one of the jewels in our crown', a pub in the rich steel town of Workington down on the West Cumbrian coast, Joe had instantly announced that he would stay the week in Wigton at his Auntie Grace's and only come through at weekends. Nothing would shift him. And Sam had seen the eyes, seen the uncontrollable force of the fear of leaving the town, the school, the Known, and sensed a little of the boy's deeper unconfessed terror.

'I wouldn't know anybody,' the boy had said.

'What's the point of having him if we never see him?' That had been Sam's sole and stoic statement. 'We'll stay where we are till he's through.'

'We saw her three times,' Ellen volunteered and this time Sam checked the place in his book and put it down for the night. He had laid on a coach for those interested in seeing the Queen on her visit to open the new Nuclear Power Station on the West Coast.

'You were like a pack of kids when you set off,' he said.

'Gerald knows the back roads.'

'She must have thought you were on her tail. Three times! The Wigton Mob.'

'She's lovely.'

'Did she give that wave?' Sam did a fair impersonation of the royal half-salute.

'She's lovely.'

'For King and Country,' Sam murmured. 'That was what we were told.'

'William wants to get up a bus to go to Carlisle to hear Mr. Gaitskell speak on Suez.'

'He told me.' Sam lit a last cigarette. 'I said I'd lay it on.' That had taken some of the sting out of it. 'Do you two talk about politics when you're in that car?'

Ellen's throat dried. They did. Or rather she listened. William saw her as a clean slate on which he could write the story of his mind and on their trips she had been drawn in by his talk. Sam read books, as many she would guess as William Hawesley, but Sam did not talk to her about them. To Joe, yes, when they caught each other. But Sam's books were closed to her, they were somewhere in which he lost himself.

'He reads a lot,' she said. The wrong thing.

'He's an educated man,' Sam responded, doggedly fair. 'I'm surprised he still wants to help us out here.'

'But he really likes it here!' Ellen's face shone, Sam noticed. 'It's the people and the gossip of it, he says. He feels he's in the middle of real life. He wouldn't be without it now, he says.'

'So you talk about politics? You must. You going to hear a speech can't be an accident.'

'Why shouldn't I?'

'No reason.' Sam smiled. Except that I feel left out.

'Do you think what we're doing in Suez is right?'

Ellen's earnest question made her seem strange to him. It was as if she had been asked to say it on behalf of someone else. As if it were not her. But it was. The question was rather diffidently asked but put sincerely. Perhaps it came too from the new hinterland she had been forced to find for herself in the war, one which William now gave her the energy to explore further. As strange to Ellen herself as to Sam.

'I can see why Nasser got confused,' he said, 'the Americans promising a loan and then backing off. But everybody has to be on the same side when you send in our own lads.'

'But don't you think,' Ellen tried to remember William's words, stumbled in her mind, used her own, 'it's a bad thing to do?'

'It depends what you mean by bad.' Sam spoke the sentence for the quotation it was, but Ellen had not listened to Dr. Joad on the Brains Trust. It was Joe who joined him now that it had moved onto television on a Sunday afternoon, sat together in the empty pub kitchen, silently intent on the giants of conversation – Dr. Bronowski, Julian Huxley, Isaiah Berlin, Alan Bullock, Professor A.J. Ayer – who spoke to them and so fluently of what most mattered. They would know what was meant by bad.

'Bad's . . .' Ellen did not like debate on ideas. She had no faith in herself. William made it easy by somehow putting the answer inside his question. 'You know what bad is.'

'Sometimes you don't know,' Sam said. 'There's some think the Atom Bomb was bad. We were glad of it. More would've been killed without it. Maybe it'll stop big wars in the future. Then it'll be seen as good.'

'The United Nations,' Ellen said, determined, 'they should decide on wars – otherwise nothing will ever change.'

'I wouldn't disagree. But sometimes life can't wait for the United Nations.'

'Why don't you come and listen to Mr. Gaitskell?'

'One of us has to look after the pub.'

'I'm not out much.'

'I'm not saying that. You go. Take Joe.'

'I seem to see less and less of him these days.'

'He does lock himself away,' Sam nodded. 'He's going his own road now.'

There was a pause of shared sadness, a few minutes which almost formally marked a passing, a change, the end of a time, the boy beginning to leave them, their son on the solitary way to becoming the man he wanted to be, having to loosen bonds, even to shake them off. Both had registered that in small signs, oblique remarks, changed glances, outbursts, sudden oppositions, and in that pause they did know each other. Out of this unexpected wholeness, Ellen said,

'It's good of you to let Colin travel on the dog men's bus.'

'He would have found it hard to get to the trails without.'

'But it's still good.'

Sam wanted none of this subject but there was in Ellen's voice a yearning to which he had to respond. She longed to be proud of something in Colin.

'He's got himself a good dog,' he said and it was true. Colin had sold off his budgerigars and bought two well-bred young hound dogs, one of which was now emerging as a champion. He needed what was known as the 'dog men's bus', laid on by Sam every day of the hound trailing season, making the Blackamoor the dog men's pub in the town. Ellen had made the request for him. Sam made a final effort.

'It's smartened him up,' he said. 'It's made something of him.' He stood up. 'Sometimes all that's needed is a bit of success.' He yawned, widely. 'Bed,' he announced. 'I know. You'll have a last cup.'

'No,' Ellen decided, out of nowhere. 'You're not always right. I'm coming to bed now.'

CHAPTER FIFTEEN

It rained. It pelted down. It sluiced. The river by the station flooded onto the road and for three days the school buses could not come in from Rachel's area. There were floods elsewhere in parts of the sodden town, streams in the gutters, waterfall spouts from overcharged or broken drainpipes, low-lying land pooled in shallow lakelets as they had been on and off for months now. On the farms on the Solway Plain the harvest was delayed yet again. Men went round the unprotected fields with sacks over their shoulders, boots squelching ankle deep in mire, the smell of damp indoors as thick as the rain haze outside. Like an unpitying invasion the clouds came in from the Atlantic, over Ireland, over the sea, squadron after heavy-laden squadron, dropping their tons of cargo on the water-brimmed land below and Isaac Wardlow was a man to be avoided. The flattened saturated corn in his fields looked on him as a failure.

Cut off from school Rachel helped her mother dry things out in front of the kitchen fire, pulley overloaded, clothes horse sending up steam as if it had nostrils, her brothers unwilling, unmanly to change out of soaked clothes at midday, her father like the wrath of God, her mother said, just you watch out for him, like the wrath of God.

Between times, Rachel pulled on her wellingtons, buttoned the tough school gabardine to the neck, found a use for the hated school beret and went to see Linda where she enjoyed her friend's sly enquiries about Saturday night, told her in detail about the attractions of Marlon Brando and skated around the topic of Jennie, who had happened to turn up at the Aspatria coffee bar, and was rumoured to have found herself on a back row double seat with Richard. 'It doesn't mean she isn't one of my best friends still,' said Rachel, although it was a disconcerting development.

'Why should it?' Linda agreed, but later she would float a remark, 'Jennie always had her eye on the main chance,' or rather cuttingly, and in a strictly neutral tone, 'Mind you, nobody can deny her vital statistics,' or, more forgivingly, 'Jennie's always fancied him,' or, most telling of all, 'If he's that fickle you're better off with Joe.' Rachel agreed. On the Monday Joe had been like a dog with two tails. At break time she had scarcely been able to move without him there, smiling, beckoning, chatting, just preening himself on being with her, until she had to send him away, but he understood. Now three days without contact although they had agreed on the second house once more. But still not the back row. He said he understood. She laughed at his expression when he said that.

Linda's passion was records and the money she earned working in her parents' village shop went to vinyl. Mel Torme's 'Mountain Greenery' and The Platters' 'The Great Pretender' were her latest purchases and she played them until she was word perfect and then she played them again. She had also worked out the basic steps for Rock 'n' Roll but her father had forbidden those records and so she just sang it. The attic bedroom was a little small for the size of Linda in full flow and the awkwardness of Rachel. They ate only slightly stale fancy cakes from yesterday.

As she walked home along the flooded lane Rachel laughed aloud at the ducks proudly claiming the human right of way. Looking very pleased with themselves, Rachel thought. Their world winning. And Linda's support for Joe, given in her own indirect way but given, had been a help. Linda was shrewd as well as being a friend. She would be extra friendly to Jennie if they got into school on the Friday. The rain had eased a little: the forecast was not as alarming: it was surprising how quickly it drained away. She wanted to be back at school, out of the house, seeing Joe.

'There was a young man phoned while you were gallivanting about the village.'

Her father had waited to say this until Rachel had put on the large black kettle at his order for tea. Her back was to him. She did feel, and literally, a chill about her. The tone was menacing and when she turned she saw her mother was frightened. The boys, as her two older brothers were always called, were out taking the herd back to the fields after the milking.

'Name of Joe. He said he would telephone later. I told him not to bother. What do you think, Mother?'

She shook her head, but giving what signal it was impossible to judge.

'It was Mother persuaded me to have that telephone. The rich, you see!'

His smile showed his strong straight white teeth and it could have fooled a stranger. Rachel knew she was in for it.

'Is this the fella you were seen with on the back row of Wigton pictures last Saturday making a fool of yourself with?'

'I wasn't on the back row.'

'That's not what they told me.'

'Well, they were liars!'

'And who are you calling liars, young lady?'

148

'Whoever told you.'

'She's getting her dander up, Mother, eh? So what about this kissing and canoodling in public?'

'I didn't. That's another lie.'

'Don't you set yourself against me.'

'I'm not.' But she was.

'So who is this fella?'

'I'm not saying.'

'Oh. Are we ashamed of him then?'

'No.'

'Or are we mixed up with the sort of fella we shouldn't be?'

'He's at my school if that's what you're worried about.'

'Don't tell me what I'm worried about. I'm worried about my daughter making a public exhibition of herself at Wigton pictures and some good for nothing thinking he can just make a telephone call whenever it pleases him and have you at his beck and call. That's the start of what I'm worried about.'

His words stirred his rage. The game play he had been drawn into by her gutsy daughterliness dissolved as his fury sped to the surface. He gripped the arms of the wooden chair as if to manacle himself to it.

'I've only been out with him once!'

'And I suppose you think you'll be going out with him again?'

'Yes!' A recklessness now began to possess Rachel. She wanted to throw off this, this man, this dark place, this fear all about her.

'Well, you won't.'

'Who says?' She ought not to have done that. Isaac gave the two words space as if waiting for them to reach the final boundary of their echo.

'Who says?' Softly spoken now. 'Did you hear that, Mother? Did you think it would come to that?' The voice began to rise and so, with a terrible slowness, did Isaac himself. 'Who says? I'll tell you, young lady. I says! That's who says. I says!' He was now on his feet.

'You shouldn't have said that.' Her mother's intervention – addressed to Rachel – was a plea to both of them. 'You should pay your father more respect.'

Isaac was baulked: a wild look of frustration was directed with venom at his wife who yet had come in on his side. But a break in the rhythm had been made.

'I'm sorry,' Rachel said.

'I can't see it in your face.'

'I can't help how I look.'

'Well,' he sat down slowly, stiffly, 'thank your mother for letting you off.'

The kettle began to sing. Rachel turned to lift it and pour it into the pot and discovered she was shaking. She checked it. She used both hands to steady the large black vessel. With her back to him, he said quietly,

'You'll not go to Wigton pictures again until I say.'

This time she sensed that saying nothing would be the most effective response. After a breath she turned to face him once more: and just looked.

'Not until I say.'

'I'll pour the tea.' Rachel stood aside to let her mother pour and took in the full meaning of her stare – stop now, no more.

'I have no time for tea,' Isaac said.

He went across to the door without looking at either of them. In the porch he pulled on his old coat and jammed on his cap. Without turning he said,

'Some of us work.'

The rain had begun again. A soft drizzle this time, but penetrating. Rachel now shook violently.

150

'I won't stay here if he does that,' she said to her mother. 'And you can tell him if you want. I'll live with Auntie Claire in Wigton and I'll get a job in a shop. I'll be sixteen in three weeks. Then he can't stop me doing what I want.'

—⁓—

Rachel did get to school the next day and told Joe that her father had gone mad. She would not be able to come to the pictures. It was not an excuse. It would be better if he did not phone. In fact she would much rather he didn't. She would phone him from the village. No phone? Well, they would have to wait until Monday. Better not to write either and not come through. It would blow over. She let him kiss her in the doorway of the school hall where they had loitered after the dinner break, lolling around conspicuously until all the others had drained back to their classrooms. He wanted to tell her he had been picked for the team again but it did not seem appropriate.

Joe had been listing the girls he had fallen for. Time and again he had fallen. Lizzie out on her own. Girls on Market Hill and Water Street before that. At school, Kathleen, Marjorie, Jennie, Christine, Betty, Jean, hopeless loiterings, embarrassed encounters. A few times it had been more than letters passed across the classroom, S.W.A.L.K. capital-lettered on the back of the envelope, sometimes a date to meet at a social, at the pictures, a walk, high blocked spiked excitement, and once it had lasted a month until she had packed it in. Only twice had he done the packing in. The Glasgow girl at Butlin's in Ayr who had been perfect until she had put on a fancy dress for the barn dance and somehow become so different that Joe had run away; and the girl on a holiday from Maryport who had been a mistake from the beginning.

There had been the Catholic girls met at the socials set up by

Sister Philomena and Sister Francis at St. Cuthbert's. Margaret, Cecilia, Theresa; and Eileen from Carlisle, met in that city of dance halls' most junior academy, meeting again on Burton's Corner at the end of Sunday afternoons to go to the pictures, and that had seemed good for a while, letters through the week, poems, a feeling of arrival with a girl from Carlisle and slightly older. But she too had gone, though it was his own fault, he knew; the reckless kissing of another girl from the same school on an A.Y.P.A. outing.

He knew he was always on the lookout. Nothing yet had happened for which he could be accused of being fast, although the moist and grassy fumblings and tugging of clothes, hands on, hands off, and extreme clinging with the second girl from Carlisle had seemed close, until she suddenly just sat up, tidied herself and said she had to go home. There was a perpetual longing and lust about him, buried deeply and subjected to many religious forebodings and social strictures, but unmistakably there, waiting, wanting to be released. It was as if he were the only sufferer, though he had to assume that every other boy had it. Certainly Alan talked enough about it. Joe did not like to spell out any details: there were very few.

There could be flashes of wildness which caught him unawares. A photograph of naked breasts in the *National Geographic Magazine*. A pouting seductress in *TitBits* studied in shame at the barber's. The lift of a skirt on the screen when a Hollywood Goddess spun in a dance or Ava Gardner and Rita Hayworth just gave their look. There were days when he thought he fancied every girl he saw and believed that he would have made a go of it with any of them, however they looked, whatever their reputation, as long as they said yes. He wondered everyone could not see it steaming from his ears. But except for those confused gropings in the grass it had not really taken off. Lena Barton had been reported as saying, 'I just don't fancy him.' It was Lena Barton simple: they just didn't fancy him.

But Rachel did. He could tell. Rachel did and that certainty offered the promised land. Rachel did.

—◊—

Rachel made a point of going out at 'pictures' time when she would have joined the others anyway. Linda, who only went to the pictures when she got a lift, met her outside the shop and they went to the Donaldsons, where they played cards in the big light farm kitchen and Mrs. Donaldson made them sandwiches and tea. She got back while they were still up. She was civil but went to bed immediately.

Isaac burned.

CHAPTER SIXTEEN

Mr. Braddock had told them they need not wear school uniform which put Joe in a dilemma. There was his best suit – too good to waste on a school outing which would involve scrambling about in the open, most likely in the rain. There was his old suit but that was only for knocking about in. And there was an old sports jacket, too battered, he thought, for the occasion. There was the uniform, which he settled for but without the school cap or tie.

Most of the other boys wore sports jackets as did Mr. Braddock, whose prized ancient garment was leather-patched at cuffs and elbows. Malcolm's sports jacket was almost new but it too was leather-patched, which Joe thought daft and somehow showing off.

The trip to the Housesteads Camp, fifty miles away on the Roman Wall, was open to all Sixth Forms, Upper, Lower, Science and Arts, basically in order to fill the bus, although the Headmaster had put on the circular to parents that the visit could be useful for the General Affairs paper they all had to take alongside their more specialised exams. The early autumn morning was fine: Joe did not take his mac. It began to rain after half an hour or so. He tried to get a sing-song going – 'Ten Green Bottles', 'One Man Went to Mow', 'I've Got a Luvverly Bunch of Coconuts', the usual starters –

but there were few and timid takers, as if there were an unwritten rule against such singing in such a bus. A vague disapproval. Brenda looked snooty. It soon petered out. Joe felt embarrassed. You always sang in buses on trips. He was sitting next to Malcolm and put up with Malcolm's inept impersonation of Al Read until he recovered his composure.

The bus moved north, through the Wastelands over which the Scots and English had battled themselves to a standstill nationally, tribally and family to family for more than three hundred years. The teacher brooded on the small villages which had only recently felt confident enough to build in stone. This had been nomad land. The few cities were fortified, Carlisle itself, Newcastle to the east, Lancaster and York to the south, Edinburgh to the north and between them, smaller forts, peel towers, fortified farmhouses, fortified churches, a land of ravage and plunder, boys of eleven and twelve in the saddle, cattle raids by night, blood feuds unending even when ringleaders were shipped west across the sea or fled further across the ocean. Even though he had been a navigator in the war, Mr. Braddock's imagination and his sympathies had always been excited by the army, armies, men in combat, battles which could still, just, trace their source to Homer. Epic battles had been waged here, tragedy and glory, and now they were headed for the magnificent outermost wall of one of the greatest military peoples and Mr. Braddock chewed over how he could pass on what he knew.

They were good, the children. He took out his pipe and stuffed it tight with cheap tobacco which stank. They enjoyed that. That was Mr. Braddock. Haddock was his nickname, but not many bothered with it. His sentimental determination to give them the best he could earned him their respect. Son of a missionary, educated far from his parents who were devoted to Central Africa, marooned with reluctant

155

relatives on too many school vacations, finding both solace and companionship in war, in the air, in danger, he had landed in this far northern town as a staging post but was increasingly drawn in to it. The Lakes are so near, he would tell friends; property's so reasonable; a great spot to bring up kids – he had two, both under five.

But it was the schoolchildren, the variety and character in them, that held him. He liked to imagine them as the crucible of a new England. Some came from the mining town of Aspatria, others from the port of Silloth, others from the hill villages still speaking the dialect of their conquerors eleven hundred years ago, others from the rich Solway Plain, others from the market town of Wigton. The enduring land, the industry which had made England so great, the trade which had made her so wealthy and the history which seeped from the place, intoxicated the keen young teacher. And in the children themselves he thought he could discern those differences and yet also see those qualities held in common which made the English, as he thought, such an exceptional mongrel breed.

The schoolteacher saw some of them as the first of their kind to be off the land after centuries in thrall to it, first out of the mines, out of the factories, and he saw himself bringing them to a new and better life through the salvation of scholarship. At times he could feel deeply moved by the journey they were about to embark on and connected it to the emotion he had felt when in his study of History he had first encountered the life stories of ordinary people.

One in particular he had cut out and kept and though now it was buried in some overstuffed drawer, he knew it was there. It was the testament of a ploughman of the eleventh century speaking to the Lord of the Manor: 'I work very hard, dear Lord. I go out at daybreak driving the oxen to the field and yoke them to the plough; for fear of my lord, there is no winter so severe that I dare hide at home; but the

156

oxen having been yoked and the share and coulter fastened to the plough, I must plough a full acre or more every day. I have a lad driving the oxen with a goad, who is now also hoarse because of the cold and shouting. I have to fill the oxen's bins with hay and water them and carry their muck outside. It's hard work, sir, because I am not free.' Learning would free them, and he would bring them that.

As the bus climbed north to that waist of Britain, between the Solway and the Tyne, where the Romans had thrown down their final word in stone to the barbarians, Joe looked out of the window and wished Rachel were sitting next to him. She had not been able to come out on Saturdays for a fortnight now and while Joe told her he understood, he did not, really. Seeing her at school had become more important, finding the moments in the day, the places. Linda and occasionally Jennie too, on guard.

He used to get sick on buses and the trace of it remained and so he breathed deeply and made himself think of something other than the queasiness imminent in his stomach. Brenda suddenly looked attractive in those non-school clothes, he thought, yet whenever he caught her eye she seemed to look mockingly at him, some sort of taunt which was both provocative and provoking. Veronica had turned up with a ponytail, quite unselfconscious, and again transformed as all the girls were in their non-uniforms. Joe had attempted a wolf-whistle and then bit his tongue because it could get back to Rachel and there was nothing in it at all. The only one with whom he felt wholly comfortable was Arthur, who had arrived in full school uniform, not a single concession. Joe did not know why Arthur's fidelity pleased him so much. Like Mr. Braddock's stinking pipe and tramp's jacket.

It was odd about Malcolm. He riled Joe and yet Joe thought of him as a friend, one of his old gang with Alan and John – now at the factory – and Paul who had drifted away. There was something in

Malcolm which made Joe feel inferior and while he resented it he was also attracted to it. Malcolm's posh detached house, Malcolm's posh things, Malcolm's father's posh car. But it was not all that. Mr. Braddock had branded into them that money was of no real importance. One of the many lessons in living he gave to children whose superfluous income was negligible, most of whose houses were rented, whose holidays were 'a day at a time' or at home, whose material possessions were few, was that money did not matter. He drove this into them. Character mattered. Duty mattered. Loyalty, honour, humour, humility, grit – yes – but money – no. Money was no more than a means to an end and the ends sought in this life had to be modest. A gentleman was modest, though he rarely used the word 'gentleman', for he wanted the girls to be advised of this first social commandment too. And modesty had nothing to do with the making of money, the mere accumulation of cash and possessions, the waste of life in a trade for profit. Modesty had to do with helping others, cultivating decent values, playing the game in the right spirit. On that scale money was unfortunately necessary but its pursuit was not for the finest. Joe was a devoted disciple of Mr. Braddock and so it could not merely be Malcolm's advantage in money.

He felt Malcolm thought he was better than him.

'I can't see the point of doing History,' Malcolm said. 'I mean, it's O.K. seeing things – castles, cathedrals, stately homes – but that's buildings – engineering like this Wall – my dad says the Romans were the greatest engineers before the Germans – but History! As a subject. It isn't even hard. I did hardly any swotting for O levels and got just as good marks as Joe.'

To whom he turned. Joe was stumped. The others around the back seat in the old coach were impressed. Joe usually came back with something.

'Science is what's important.' Malcolm was Maths, Physics and Chemistry. 'And Science is hard. You can't flannel in Science.'

'You can't flannel in History,' said Joe. 'How can you flannel about dates? How can you flannel about causes of wars? How can you flannel about religious persecution?'

'I flannelled in my O levels,' Malcolm said, coldly, 'and I got the same as you.'

'It's different in the Sixth.' But Joe knew it was a weak argument.

'This is the age of the Sputnik,' said Malcolm. Veronica was kneeling on the seat in front of him, the ponytail bobbing as she nodded. Veronica's always easy to impress, Joe thought. 'What does History matter when we're off to other planets?'

'You'll always want to know where you came from,' said Joe. 'You'll always want to know how you got to be the way you are now.'

'You don't have to do it in the Sixth to find that out.'

'Surely it's simple enough,' said Brenda, who had come to the now-crowded back of the bus to sort things out; and besides, she and Malcolm were friends, their parents were friends, they played bridge together, people expected the two of them to click one day. 'History tells us what our past was, Science tells us what our future might be. You need both.'

Malcolm smiled at her. She did look good out of uniform.

'Science tells us about the past as well,' he said. 'Look at the history of the universe. Only Science can tell us about that. Or evolution, that's Science. D.N.A., that's Science. Geology, that's Science. Medicine, Science. How you got here's just the easy part.'

Brenda returned Malcolm's smile. It was as if they were a Freemasonry of two. But she did not like to be argued down, not even by Malcolm.

'Many of those subjects are part of History anyway,' she said.

'And if you think it's easy, it's not. Maths was easy. I got the same marks as you.'

'History,' said Joe, taking care, 'tells you the most important things of all. It tells you how people lived, it tells you how religion mattered to them and how they fought for liberty and that; you learn about conditions not just of the rich but the poor and how they can be changed and how thinking improved, that's History as well, it's to do with what we're all made of. That's why it's worth it.'

'I'll sign up for that,' said Mr. Braddock. He gave the briefest of nods to Joe, a Morse blink, a darted compliment to the boy who would nurse it. 'Prepare to land,' he said. 'Housesteads awaits.'

Joe was not the only one initially disappointed. He had expected a mighty wall, something on the scale of the photographs he had seen of the Great Wall of China. He had been promised an excavated camp and anticipated amphitheatres, a forum, temples, avenues – instead of which there was a network of ruins never more than two or three feet high, with stumps of columns, mown grass and small detailed signs, the whole looking forlorn under the damp sky. And no Wall in sight. Mr. Braddock gathered the two dozen volunteers about him and knew their sense of anticlimax.

'You have to use your imaginations,' he said. 'That's something we simple historians try to develop,' he beamed at Malcolm. 'And so think of this place, on a wet day like this, nearly two thousand years ago, great thick walls, here; splendid columns, sixteen of them, over there; hundreds of horses and chariots, footsoldiers slogging up to the Wall and back on guard duty, many of them hundreds of miles from home in warmer climes, the womenfolk in the kitchens and some of the senior wives with their music and their own little courts, locals conscripted into the army itself and all sorts of camp followers. Imagine this place on this hillside looking down to the road there that goes seventy-odd miles from Wallsend in the east to the Cumbrian coast on the west, and beyond that road there is another ditch and beyond that another mound, deep defences constantly under repair, the whole place seething! And think of it when they might have been under attack from the Picts to the north, with the orders flying out, the brilliantly organised Romans falling into battle order, the wild screaming of the barbarians from over there . . .' Mr. Braddock pumped away and Joe for one was helped to the enchanted chimera of the past, encouraged to believe that he could indeed feel what it was like to be alive then, experience the sounds, the fear of the enemy, the resolution to face them. From the small academically reconstructed piles of underfunded ruins grew a settlement fit for warriors.

'And we see here the final line drawn around a great Empire.'

'Ours was miles bigger,' Joe said. 'And miles better.'

'That's another question. Let's go and look at the Wall itself.'

The schoolteacher smiled to himself as he led his little army up towards the clump of firs beyond which was one of the most spectacular runs of the Wall, cresting what seemed a frozen cliff wave of rock, clinging to its steep contours. Joe's patriotism pleased him. Mr. Braddock had emerged from the war with one credo intact – his belief in the superiority of the English, especially the decent Englishman. He had seen much to disturb child-taught beliefs about the nobility of his countrymen. But the History teacher was a relativist and from his own experience he still believed that the Englishman, by whom in some absolutely clear but inexplicable way he meant most of those who lived in Britain as well as Australians and New Zealanders and Canadians and some sections of other colonies – who were admittedly different but all also really 'us' – Englishmen had indeed created an Empire 'miles bigger' and, yes, 'miles better' than any other. They had taken all the Roman virtues and humanised them.

They had held onto that amazing Celtic mad courage which had so impressed Caesar. And they had taken on the torch of liberty and democracy from Greece. That was the basis of it – conquests, colonisation, were a bonus.

As he led the young troops over fields which must have prepared for so many wars, he rehearsed what he would tell them in the talk scheduled for the end of the morning. He would say that war not only tested individuals – their bravery, their selflessness, revealing unexpected cowardice, unanticipated heroism – but also nations. Look at Europe as the prospect of a Second World War had grown more certain. Germany completely gone, lost its head, lost its soul; Italy following on, tinpot; Greece, Spain and Portugal almost as bad; France shaming its great history; Russia a new authoritarianism; Sweden and Switzerland pretending to be neutral but arms open to the fascists; Ireland on the side of England's enemies as usual; Eastern Europe in Stalin's shadow; only Britain and the core of that, England, with the combination of moral courage, will and force to stand up to brutal tyranny, to fight for decency and liberty. Despite all faults, all failings, it had stood alone and in the greatest danger until Hitler had fatally turned on Russia and then America had piled in. He would tell them all that. They must know the best of their country. And America, the teacher would say, despite its many immigrants from all over Europe, had still built itself on the ground cleared by the Pilgrim Fathers with the language of the King James Bible and in fruitful opposition to the English Crown. He wanted them to be proud of what England had done, especially as this Suez shilly-shallying made him uneasy over its future.

'You've been divided into six teams of four,' he said, after they had recovered their breath and, he hoped, taken in the awesome nature of this dramatic fortification. 'I've drawn up a list of questions. I want you outside the Museum at twelve-thirty prompt.'

162

Later, after they had eaten their sandwiches and been driven down to Hexham for a brisk tour of the Abbey, they were given a free hour to walk around the quaint streets of the ancient Christian market town. Joe peeled back to the Abbey. He did not quite know why but he wanted to be alone there. The way the worn steps swept down into the church had stirred his imagination.

He sat in a pew in the middle and let the place seep into him. It was as if he had trained himself by that testing of himself when he had stopped in those walks and faced the order outside and the disorder inside his head. Soon in the cool near-empty Abbey he felt wrapped around with the sense he sought for, of a world of devotion, of monks rising in the middle of the night and padding down those broad shallow stone steps from their dormitories into the choir to celebrate and commemorate their faith. Just as on the Wall gazing north he had seen himself as a centurion alert to the next attack, his forces well deployed, his own sword arm ready, so here he let the present dim down and in a fragmentary but felt way, he lowered himself into the past, finding in it a dreamlike satisfaction, a simpler, other, achieved life.

The tap on his shoulder made him turn sharply.

'Time to go,' said Mr. Braddock.

Joe stood up rather slowly as if he were tired. He was silent as they walked towards the bus.

'That essay of yours on the Dissolution of the Monasteries,' the teacher said.

Joe waited.

'Best you've done, I think. Straight alpha.' Joe's first.

The boy looked at him. The man looked away.

On the bus in the dark after very few minutes the cocktail of good fortune which had come Joe's way on that day and over the previous few weeks would not be denied. He began another sing-song, this time with a fair imitation of 'Walking in the Rain'. Brenda, who had a good bluesy voice, sang 'Swing Low Sweet Chariot' and 'Motherless Child'. Malcolm did 'The Ying-Tong Song'. Mr. Braddock set them off with 'Pack Up Your Troubles in Your Old Kit Bag' and 'It's a Long Way to Tipperary'. Joe attempted 'Houn' Dog' but that was hard solo and Malcolm sniggered. Some cheered. They were in the mood now as the unlit coach sang on along the Roman road and Mr. Braddock remembered there might be a bottle of light ale somewhere in the pantry.

CHAPTER SEVENTEEN

Diddler came to collect Joe just after seven. Sam had let him off his Saturday morning work and there was no rugby match. Joe was not too old to dismiss a ride on the flat cart and they trotted briskly through the near-deserted streets of the old town and out beyond the river.

'They put barbed wire across the end of that road in the war,' Diddler said. 'To stop the Germans getting to the park.' He shook his head and then spat, the usual controlled jet. He flicked the reins to gee-up the piebald which galloped up the steady incline towards Pot Metal Bridge. 'Look at him, Joe.' He grinned widely at the rump of the horse. 'Where's his like? Not in this town.' The gallop jostled the bundle of old blanket. Joe saw the gun which gave him a jolt of pleasure.

He slowed the horse down to a walk when they turned into the lane, a rutted mediaeval way leading eventually to a neglected farm, run down over decades by the ageing brother and sister who had inherited it. Along the way was a huddle of poor rented cottages, one of which housed John, one of Joe's old gang, now an apprentice at the factory. It was at his house that the hunt met.

Joe had never been on one of these sweeps through the countryside. He had not realised there would be so many there. Six men including Matt who kept a tame fox and John's father in his most valued possession – a poacher's jacket handed on just after the war. All the men had guns, .22s. Sandy Fletcher, a dog man, had an old twelve-bore. There were three lurchers, four terriers and, as Joe would see later, six ferrets currently deep-pocketed. The men stood among boys, about ten of them, sons, friends of sons, one or two, like Speed's younger brother, magnetically attracted by the lure of the scavenge. There were sacks to be carried, bread for the day. John's father counting heads, the small crowd impatient to be gone. Diddler put his horse out to grass in a lush field. Diddler had advised him to wear his wellingtons and wrap up warm. Most were scarved and booted save for Speed's brother and his friend.

John handed Joe a stick, almost straight, about three feet long.

'This is your skimmer,' he said. He smiled in appreciation of Joe's ignorance. John thought Joe was making a bad mistake. There he was, still stuck in school – what was the point? No money. No apprentice-ship which would lead to a steady engineering job and security. If you wanted school, well, he was on day release once a week to Carlisle Tech. And paid for it! And he worked with men who could tell you useful things, not just teachers forever spouting what was no use to you.

'It's to break rabbits' legs,' he said. He made a space, swung and skimmed his own stick grass-top high. 'When the ferrets have flushed them out and they make a bolt for it. Then you can just go and break its neck.' Joe had never done that. 'We got nearly three hundred last time. Last year. We got nearly half a ton of stuff.'

They swept through the country in a line using the long nets at the warrens, taking vegetables, eggs, thirty pigeons the year before, and two roe deer, everything edible, anything sellable, farms swift to check their poultry after the line had moved through, sacks squawking.

'Stick by me,' said Diddler. He pointed to Speed's brother. 'I want you as well.'

The boy came over. He was bigger than both his brothers. Worked for the council, digging ditches.

'Speed still in Malaya?' Joe asked, to say something, to make a connection with the final fierce member of that family.

'Still shooting folk, Joe,' the boy said, smiling rather dreamily. 'I get my papers in a fortnight. I hope there's some left for me.'

They moved off. The long-haired ginger lurchers, lean, loose-limbed, something of the wild about them, something unbiddable, loped ahead like scouts. They spread out as they went past the neglected farm where the pickings were easy.

As the autumn lift of wind whipped his face and Joe gathered a sense of the coherent intention of what had seemed a rag tag and bobtail gaggle, a feeling of exhilaration began to grow. He was near the middle of a line widely spaced now, mowing purposefully through the fields, something of an army about it, the boy thought, and something piratical or like the Border Reivers Mr. Braddock had told them about after that trip to Housesteads. Sweeping through the country, living off the land, 'back to the roots of war', he had said.

As the boy settled into the line, safe between Diddler and Speed's brother, he took more detailed stock of those about him.

There were men and boys who, since his days with Speed and his time in Water Street, he saw only at the edge of his daily Wigton round. Once the boys had been encountered nightly in games in the streets, gang battles, the robbery of orchards, building of bonfires, damming of the river, but now the increasing possession of the grammar school emphasised a distance, his difference, still at school

167

way past working age. The men were generally from the poorer end of the town, not always steadily employed, some of them drinking away too much of what they earned. They were always with dogs, always with each other, perhaps the last of a deeply persistent tribe that had scavenged over centuries, now set to disappear from the landscape, local poachers, small-time dealers, near to the tinkers, whose camps at Black Tippo they would visit to trade, bake hedgehogs, pass the time with that old improvident, self-ruling nomadic group. They somehow panhandled a living from the shallow stream they stood in and yet, as they hunted and cleared the land, Joe felt grateful to be there, to be alongside men and boys who were so certain in the land itself, so dominating the land which would feed and please and profit them.

They put the long nets around a big warren. Joe was told to hold one end. They sent in the ferrets. 'A rabbit can come out of one of three holes,' John had told him, pleased to teach someone who had stayed on at school for nothing but teaching. 'You have to cover the lot. The net is across the main holes. This,' his skimmer was brandished, 'is for the others.'

It was not a glorious posting, to stand just holding the net, but maybe he would graduate, Joe thought, maybe have a chance to use his skimmer. He looked across the plain towards the fells which rimmed the north of the Lake District and felt something grand in the reach and climb of the prospect before him, began to dream a little, Rachel that evening and at a dance, to be close to her, would they dim the lights for the last waltz? The line of Skiddaw cut clear in the cloudless autumn brightness, no thought of the fury in the earth as the ferrets attacked, the panic of the rabbits until the net went tight, and again, as out they came trapped, too terrified to turn back, blocked from going on, men and older boys walking along the net to break their necks with a swift stick lash. Joe felt his mind tremble between thrill and horror, that life could be so swiftly ended, that this was hunting, that he was allowed there at all.

At the end of the field they came across a rabbit, couched in the grass, shivering, eyes desperate, fixing him personally, Joe thought. Speed's brother knelt down beside it and laid aside his stick. He rolled the rabbit over so that he could break its neck. He stiffened his hand, palm open, held the rabbit's ears.

'This is a real rabbit punch.' He grinned up at Joe who had the uncanny feeling that it was Speed now before him, Speed who had been his friend and been watched over by Sam standing in for his own father who had cracked up and gone on the tramp after the war, Speed who had lain between the railway tracks and let the train go over him, Speed who had been destined like his older brother Alistair for Borstal had not Sam helped him into the boys' army. 'Speed was great at this,' he said, as if reading Joe's thoughts.

He chopped his hand down. The rabbit shuddered but did not die. The boy cursed. Licked his hand. Held it higher, the executioner's weapon of choice, and then slammed it down, accurately, fatally. Life went from the animal and Joe felt a little sickness of excitement. He had missed Speed.

———ᴍ———

A week or so later in what Captain Fitzjohn described in a letter home as a God-forsaken hole, filthy, stewed in heat, totally off the map somewhere in Malaya in a bitter war nobody at home was the slightest bit interested in, Speed was in terminal trouble.

They were in a tent, the two of them, the officer from Wellington College via Sandhurst, the private from Wigton via the Boys' Army School in Harrogate. The officer was unusually agitated, the younger private stiff-backed and on full alert on the chair he had been unexpectedly offered.

'Why did you do it?'

Speed said nothing. The officer took out yet another cigarette.

'C'mon, man. There must have been some reason. Nobody does that without a reason. Why did you do it?'

Speed looked straight at the man. He knew him so slightly save in one action which he knew more searingly than anything else in his life. The officer was floundering and Speed wanted to help him but it was impossible.

'For God's sake. If I'm going to help you I need to know. There must have been a provocation.' He grimaced. 'Even for you, you bloody savage. What was it?'

Speed shook his head. It was a lock of shyness, avoiding a form of showing off. He would tell no-one. That was that. Yet inside him was in turmoil. Perhaps this was real fear? Fear in battle egged you on if you were Speed. Fear was a spur. Fear was exciting. It made you more brave. Fear was good. But he had a new fear now and he could not use it. How could he fight his way out of this?

'Look.' The officer on a generous and unplanned whim passed over the pack of Senior Service: Speed took one greedily. He reached for his own matches but the officer beat him to it with his lighter. 'Look,' he repeated after both of them had sucked the harsh tobacco deep into their lungs, 'maybe I can help you.' He gazed around the empty tent, cautiously. 'You know I want to help you. After all.'

After all, the sword-lean, strained-faced private soldier in front of him had saved his life. The ambush had been brilliantly executed. He himself had been totally exposed when Speed had come out of nowhere and drilled the man through the skull. He had then hurled himself on Speed to knock him out of the way of a man bayonet

170

charging. Speed had got that one too. And on at least two other occasions Speed's galvanising ferocity had been what, the officer thought, a British soldier was about.

'What did the man say to you?' he asked.

Speed paused, took a drag and then, only just noticeably, shook his head.

'For God's sake! I know something was said! But I need you to tell me. This will be a court martial unless I have something to work with. This will be you out. Out in any case. But maybe we can beat the court martial. It's not the first time you've done it and it is just not tolerable. You daft bugger.' He flicked the ash away far too emphatically. 'For the last time – give me something to go on.'

Speed managed a half-smile. The officer went silent, suspended between understanding and frustration. 'Last call.'

Although there was half of the cigarette left, Speed stubbed it in the ashtray.

'I can't.'

'Then you're out. Do you understand? I might get off the court martial because of your record, but you'll be out.'

Speed's face tensed up.

'You mean out of the army?'

'Yes.'

'Altogether?'

'Yes.'

'But what will I do?'

The question was so forlorn.

'You can tell me what the hell happened.'

Speed shook his head.

'Then there's no hope. You'll be out.'

'But what will I do?'

The young officer was moved which, he knew, was the wrong thing to be. But he was, and he let silence grow perhaps to heal it.

He lit up another cigarette from the stump he had and waited.

'Let me stay in,' Speed said, his eyes cast to the floor, his voice very quiet, his demeanour humbled, even begging. 'I'll do anything,' Speed mumbled. 'You can put me on jankers as long as you like.'

'Last call.'

Speed looked at him, helplessly. He could not.

'Let me stay in.'

Speed had never pleaded for anything. The effort of it caught the young officer by the throat.

'It matters to you, doesn't it, being in the army, even in a malaria-infested shithole like this?'

Speed merely nodded but in the enduring pause he managed to say,

'There's nothing else I want to do, you see, sir.'

'So for Christ's sake – tell me why you did it?'

The men looked at each other, intently. Across a chasm of class, education and privilege. They knew that in those perilous moments under fire they had been welded together. The look held: and then Speed once more shook his head.

Later, in the Officers' Mess, the visiting V.I.P. Lieutenant-General Oliphant asked him what sort of day he had.

'Lousy,' he said, and explained.

'We can't have the wild men,' the General said, sadly. 'But I've never really known why. Look at Mad Jack Sassoon – out after snipers night after night. Mad as a bat. Great man. Great soldier.'

'This lad,' the officer nodded, 'he's wild. The others looked to him. He was not just brave – they're all brave – he was – I don't know – fearless – a bit of an inspiration.'

'He has to go?'

'He has to go.'

'God knows why we lose our best like this,' said Oliphant and turned away.

Speed was blind drunk in the guardhouse. They'd bought him beer. Now they left him alone.

The man from the other regiment had picked on Speed's officer and said he knew him from time back and he was a bit of a nancy boy. Speed had warned him. Then he had said worse. It took three or four of them to drag him off the man who was still in a critical condition. They said that had they not stopped Speed in time he would have murdered him.

—⁂—

Joe walked back to Wigton through the fields. He had promised to be with Alan after dinner but it was with no deep reluctance that he left the hunt. He had felt rather left out. He was not as good at it as the others, not even the young boys, not as eager at snouting out the prey, and after two or three hours this grew uncomfortable. It was as if he were failing all the time. And there was something else, something he could not name, but it troubled him, a sense that this mattered to them, really mattered in many ways, whereas he was just a strolling player. Diddler waved him away with no reproach. He passed one of the younger boys who had been told to guard sacks which they would pick up on their way back. The boy was puzzled that Joe wanted to go home and asked him to guard the sacks so that he could rejoin the others. Joe's refusal elicited a spit, to the ground, but no doubting its target.

It was too good a morning for the boy-man to resist. The leaves

173

were still heavy, hedges thick, the thrill of the chase, now that it was behind him, stirred feelings of valour, the exercise had blown away the usual cobwebbed organisation and constraints of duties, fears, plans, controls, projections, insurances, and he was intoxicated by the rhythmic pace of his walk, the sense of Nature all about him which seemed to flow into him and reach the heart and soul of him. He was young, he was doing what he wanted, he was in love, the fields were fair, beyond him like a beacon was the Italianate tower, pride of Wigton, the day would end with Rachel; all this was his.

As he strode at full stretch, he found himself humming. He was alone in the fields, looked around to check, began to sing. It became just a noise, a crush of sounds from chants and hymns, songs and the music heard in secret – all just one sound which matched his mood, which floated as he himself seemed to float through the autumn fields. It was a song of himself. Everything seemed to be in harmony. Everything seemed good. The world was a blessed place, all things committed and flowing through him and through everyone. He saw that everything moved to a single purpose, everything was earthed in the grass beneath his feet, and it was as if he simply ceased to be but was part of all around him, the sky within his reach, air, earth, stones, trees, he was part of their song and they of his.

<hr />

It was fish and chips in the back room. There were two wooden tables bare but for salt and vinegar. No chairs, four benches. He had cod and sixpennyworth of chips, a heap of scrams and a pot of tea with bread and butter. They were supposed to charge you threepence more for having it off a plate in the back room but mostly they forgot. He was alone for which he was thankful. Sometimes eating out could be

174

embarrassing, a show off, especially at the café above McGuffie's, even in the Spotted Cow. The fish and chip shop was the easiest. It had been his mother's decision a year or so ago. Saturdays were just too busy for her to get three different dinners cooked for three different times.

But alone, he could make the chips into sandwiches and put on lashings of salt. Alone he could keep up the singing in his head and conduct with his knife and fork. Alone there was no one to whom he felt he ought to explain and apologise. Manuel the owner came back for a cigarette and talked sport. Joe told him about the hunt. He found he was exaggerating and boasting about the hunt to impress and entertain the fish and chip shop owner. He knew he was doing it but it careered out of control and he ended up edging into some fibs, small fibs but fibs, and he left the place rather cast down, knowing he was bound to be found out. He had to stop doing that. He was always doing that. Especially when he was happy he was always exaggerating, fibbing. Even if God forgave him, there were others who wouldn't if it got back to them.

—⚏—

Alan had decided to wear a helmet. No proof could have been stronger to indicate the significance of the enterprise. He saved it for the aerodrome and he and Joe – on the pillion – drove there faces naked to the wind, bare heads tingling as the air rushed past them.

They had cycled there often enough with the gang when younger. A few old Spitfires, Lancasters and Wellington bombers had once stood in neglected corners of the place to which in the war they had hedge-hopped for urgent repair. Irresistible to the boys. Inside the cockpits. Battle of Britain. Messerschmitts at five o'clock. German ack-ack below, steady through the anti-aircraft fire, bombs away, noise from film sound tracks – eeeeee-ow – pum, pum, pum – or da-dat-a-da-dat-a-da-dat-a-da as the Spitfire scimitared into the sky then swooped on the outwitted German to blow him to smithereens. Now the weed-infested former emergency ward for fighting planes was being repossessed by the land.

The aerodrome was where the motorbike boys went to try for a ton-up. Hitting that hundred had been Alan's ambition for months. He had souped up the engine with the help of one of John's friends from the factory and now he reckoned he was ready. Joe envied him. His own attempt to save for a motorbike had failed. The money he got or, as his father said, earned in the pub somehow trickled away, dances, bus fares, the occasional packet of cigarettes, a couple of halves out of town, on a Saturday night, sweets. Alan got a big extra from Christmas tips and his mother liked to spoil him.

Colin was there – without Paul. Colin was one of the oldest of the crowd who had now made a club of these Saturday afternoon tests on the abandoned Solway aerodrome. Joe cringed a little but also felt, as usual, that Colin had been hard done by and in this confusion went across to him. Alan had immediately started tinkering with the bike.

'So you'll come and speak to your uncle?'

Why not? When had he avoided him? What did this mean? Colin was dressed in a leather jacket, leather trousers, dead smart, Joe thought, all the gear, heavy boots, goggles slung around his neck, the winning dog had given him funds.

'Hello,' Joe said.

'Is that the best you can manage?'

Colin quiffed his hair. Joe was instantly aware of his own wind-flattened hair and shoved a hand through it.

'No good, pal,' Colin said. 'Sandy hair's too thin for the job.'

176

He leaned easily on the gleaming saddle of the propped-up bike, took out a cigarette.

'I'll not offer you one. Your mother'd kill me.'

No she wouldn't, Joe thought. She needn't even know.

'Where's Paul?'

'Paul's not here.' Colin was abrupt.

I know that. But you're always with him. So where is he? He persisted.

'I used to see Paul a lot,' Joe said.

'He's into U.F.O.s now. He's just a crazy mixed-up kid!' Colin smiled – the smile was for Paul, Joe knew that.

'Do you believe in U.F.O.s?'

'Paul does. I'm thinking of getting a sidecar. For the dogs, mainly.'

Joe waited, sensing another volley.

'Your dad doesn't really want me on that dog men's bus. I can put them in a sidecar. It'll give me my independence. Take them anywhere.'

'Dad says the dogs are running well.'

'No thanks to him.'

Joe's stomach clenched.

'I'll help Alan.'

'That's right. Run away.'

Colin held his nephew's gaze for a few moments, saw what he wanted, turned, let him go.

Alan was one of two going for the ton that afternoon. He did a few warm-up runs. The men and boys gathered around his bike as if it had been involved in a terrible crash, as if by gazing alone they could improve it. Joe was outside the technical talk. Again he did not know enough. As the motorbike men closed in on their day's object, he looked across the flat lands towards the sea and Scotland beyond. This was supposed to have been outside the range of the German bombers which was why so many planes were nursed over the counties of England to come here to be repaired. Yet how had the Germans managed to reach Glasgow? And Liverpool was not so very far south. Maybe it was a difficult target, no city, no river to guide them, only the Solway Firth and that at a clever distance. Sometimes he looked forward to his coming two years' National Service and today he thought the best option would be to try for a pilot. You could always get a good job after that. But they needed perfect eyesight, didn't they? He was sure he could remember in some photographs of R.A.F. pilots that there were men wearing specs. He looked in vain for the old planes they used to play in so blissfully.

Colin had brought a stopwatch though no one knew what use it would be. He said a stopwatch was second nature now, with the dogs. He said he had measured out the perfect mile and put in two sticks. If he stood far enough away he could get a reading to within a fraction. Alan said his speedometer was reliable enough. Colin said that in this sort of affair you needed a second opinion. He walked away to take up his position. Alan gave Joe a look which said, 'You are responsible for that Colin.'

Finally and reluctantly all the elaborations important to the event were completed. Alan put on his helmet and went slowly down the disused runway. He was a very small figure in the distance and Joe, who had not brought his specs, had to squint hard. He revved up and higher and then the dot began to move towards them, straight at them, it seemed, as if launched on a course to blast directly into them. They began to cheer and Joe waved as Alan bombed past, decelerated, turned, came back.

Colin came across, stopwatch in front of him.

'It's got to be thirty-six seconds at least,' Joe said. They knew that. He need not have said that. They had been here before.

Alan took off his helmet as Colin arrived.

'Well?' Colin demanded.

'I think I did it,' Alan said. 'I think I did.'

Colin's nod was grave. He took the stopwatch to Alan and showed it to him, close up. Alan gave no reaction.

'Thirty-five seconds!' Colin announced, as triumphant as if he'd done it himself. 'Better even than a ton.'

Joe let the others beat him to clap Alan, though awkwardly, on the back. He was almost too pleased to move. He wanted to savour it a little longer. Better even than a ton!

———— m ————

He helped Alan with the sports editions and they swooped around the town on their bikes pretending to be on motorbikes. Alan was going to the dance with him: he would be on the pillion again. They would go to the Bird in Hand for one or two halves and then on to the Institute. He had promised Rachel he would be there at eight-thirty. She said she wanted to be there at eight on her own for a bit.

As he and Alan came down Southend at the end of their round, they caught up with Diddler. Speed's brother was standing upright in the cart, steadying himself between the full sacks. Alan swerved past. Joe slowed down.

'We had a good day, Joe,' Diddler said. 'Tell Sam I'll bring him a fresh rabbit or two and some spuds. We found a lot of spuds.'

'Thanks.' Joe wanted to linger but Alan was opening the gap and so he pushed on the pedals, but turned after a few yards, to wave, and admire Speed's brother, a charioteer, standing high on the flat cart, riding into Wigton with the plunder of the day.

CHAPTER EIGHTEEN

Rachel decided to put on her lipstick in the house. She even left the bathroom door open. She had put on her own low heels – her mother's shoes would be hopeless to dance in – and she decided to carry her coat downstairs rather than wear it, which had been her original intention. She wore the dress she had worn on their first date, her second best but the dance in the village hall was not for best. Instead of wearing her cardigan she draped it over her shoulders, which meant that her bare arms were clearly visible. And as she dabbed Yardley's eau-de-cologne between her breasts she tugged down the dress. The breasts still had some way to go. She hoped.

Isaac was drawn up to the fire though it was not cold. Although her entrance was deliberately unquiet he did not turn to look at her nor did her lingering provoke him in any way to alter his hunched concentration on the fire, simply tapping the grate with the poker. Her mother also looked away. Rachel was flustered and the walk to the village hall was a fortunate opportunity to calm down. Her anger at him had yet again flooded violently into her mind.

It would soon be over. Tomorrow was her sixteenth birthday. He could not legally hold her after that and her preparations were under way.

Her mother had noticed the steady departure of clothes and possessions, on the way to Claire's at Wigton. Should she tell him? If Rachel did go, and now she feared it to be a real possibility, then Isaac would ask her if she had known about it or suspected it and she would have to confess she did but had not told him and then God help her. If she told him now – she dared not think, truly she dared not imagine what he would do.

'Cup of tea?'

'I was thinking should we go up to that dance,' he said, without turning. 'There'll be plenty there.' He meant adults, farmers, their kind. 'You used to like putting your glad rags on.' He turned and smiled. She could not interpret it. 'You were very light on your feet,' he said.

'You weren't as bad as I'd expected either,' she dared.

'Better at the slow ones. Things with a bit of class to them. The valeta.'

'That did surprise me.' That courtly dance, hands on hips, fingertips touching, something like the dances in historical films. 'I've half a mind . . .'

And for a moment peace flared, years were wiped off, he was the bold strong country labourer come to court her, defying her disapproving parents, that irresistible smile of his and while they were out that warning to others that to touch her they would have to step across his dead body. Even now she could remember that basking in being so protected and cherished. How had mere time changed all that, eroded so much until now there was scarcely a grain of her which could escape the demands of his ambition, the rays of his driving rages. Moments such as this were as rare and as potent with brief pleasure as the sight of will of the wisp down on the moss.

'I'll get you that tea,' she said, for she knew he would not go.

181

She went to the sink.

'What've you got her for tomorrow?'

Her back stiffened.

'We went to Redmayne's on Tuesday. She needed a new coat.'

'New coat! Money talks, Mother, eh?'

She filled the kettle too full and poured some down the sink.

'I'll give her a fiver,' he said.

'She'll appreciate that.'

'A fiver.'

Isaac's tone was neutral but it spoke in tongues. The fiver meant amazement – how could he give to his sixteen-year-old daughter a sum of money he would never have dreamt of as a weekly wage until well into his late twenties and even then it would mostly be spoken for: it meant arrival, he had got there, he was one of the rich, a fiver was no sacrifice, no hardship; it implied contempt, that it was so easy now, that it was just a bit of money, that after all it meant no more than it did; it was an act of bitterness, that he could feel no gladness in it, no feeling of this expressing love between father and daughter, mere payment in recognition of a date; sadness, that a few paper notes were all that he could give; it meant anger – this would show her, this was a cold transaction and more than she deserved. It was a bribe, it was a peace offering, it was the best the man could manage.

She brought him the tea and he poured it into the saucer. She would have enjoyed the dance. So would he, once he got there.

Isaac's generation were there in force and at this early stage dominating the dance floor together with the very young, mostly girls, party dresses, velvet bows in their hair, being tutored by elders, the hall brightly lit, three-piece band – drums, accordion, trumpet – refreshments laid out at the back, sandwiches, cakes, soft drinks, ready for the interval. Of those to whom the dance was vital, the adolescent, the courting age, those on the gad, on the prowl, on the chase – the males fortified themselves at the Bird in Hand, some in pubs further afield, the females arrived in good time but located themselves in the refreshment end or danced with each other as Linda did with Rachel.

When Joe came in he searched her out with such ardour! Rachel felt both calmed and clarified by the direct and open unspoken declaration. He walked across to her looking neither to right nor left, the room might have been empty and deserted but for her and she felt her heart unclench, could feel it, she would swear much, much later to Linda 'just kind of melt – I know it sounds daft'.

Alan trailed behind him determined not to get stuck with Linda. He needed to click. These village dances were usually lucky, especially for somebody from the town with a bit of money and a motorbike.

A slow foxtrot was just what Joe wanted, but Rachel held him firmly at arm's length. There was torment in this. She was dancing with somebody obviously her boyfriend in front of everybody she knew, everybody she had been at school with, everybody of her parents' generation, younger brothers and sisters, guaranteed to say something embarrassing, at least two former boyfriends, all of whom, she thought, were studying him, weighing him up, scrutinising her, was it the real thing? Smooching in any shape or form was definitely out and Joe felt a little deflated. They had stormed up from the pub, he had come in like a hurricane and now in his arms he held a tense, stiff dancing partner who seemed unwilling even to look him full in the face. He walked her back to the chairs which stood in neat order along the walls and as they came off the floor, Rachel whispered, out of the corner of her mouth, 'Dance with Linda!'

A quickstep was announced. Joe said, 'May I have this dance, please?' Linda put her handbag on the chair. The bag was dark green. It matched the voluminous green satin of her unafraid and stupendous dress, wave after wave of heavy material enfolding and caressing wave upon wave of Linda. She came quite close. The three-piece band tried to imitate the Glen Miller Orchestra.

It was like dancing on air. Delicate hands, trim ankles, smooth unfat face, all these commanded Linda and the bulk of the body that afflicted her dropped away as the music sped on and Joe discovered the dancing partner of his dreams. Rachel was fine of course but awkward; other girls had been good; Sadie was marvellous but she was a touch too inclined to lead even though she pretended he did. Linda was gossamer. The slightest pressure on the hand that held his and she would spin into a perfectly achieved diagonal of scissor steps scything the floor. A tad of pressure from the right palm which was placed on her back and she would go into reverse spins. A mere indication and they would stop for dramatic effect and then begin again. They could have been dancing together for years. It was extraordinary, Joe thought. It was almost not dancing but gliding, skating, moving effortlessly like hawks on the wind. He led her back, intoxicated.

'You're a great dancer.'

Linda smiled and nodded slyly.

'You two should be in a competition,' Rachel said, very pleased that her best friend had scored such a hit. And Joe got one of those rare quick fully exposed smiles that floored him.

Next was the Dashing White Sergeant and so he could dance with both of them. Alan, he saw, had been collared by the Thompson sisters: Alan would like Sarah Thompson. The old country dance, in a circle, steps to the left, steps to the right, set against your partners, hold hands, duck under the neighbouring trio, join up the circle, start again – filled the hall and brought in six to sixties, those who could really and those who could scarcely dance, mixed the crowd, raised a sweat, called for Scottish-sound whoops as the bit of Highland Fling made its appearance and joined hands with the reels and two-steps, the Palais Glide, the Three Drops of Brandy, the Gay Gordons and the Hooligans and old waltzes which linked back to court and village green, to lute, drum, tabor and also to massed violins in ballrooms centuries and half a continent away. The new dances were spliced in. There were excuse-mes and ladies' choice, statue waltzes and, the only failure, an over-ambitious, overselfconscious and mediocre attempt at Rock 'n' Roll. Linda walked off the floor and said it was pathetic.

For the last hour the much older lads and the bolder young men came in rather tanked up from the pub and Joe curtailed his wide choice of dancing partners – which had been encouraged by Rachel, and was implanted in Joe's own education. But he did not want these men around her: one who must have been well over twenty-one years old did ask her up and Joe, dancing with Sarah Thompson, stalked them around the floor troubled by jealousy quick as lightning about him. The sensation was disturbing and Sarah's attempts at conversation foundered. He handed her over to Alan a little too eagerly and went to stand beside Rachel, who was being talked at by this burly latecomer.

'Donald Pennington,' Rachel said as they walked to the chairs, 'they have a big farm near Abbeytown. Really big. And a big house with it.'

Joe wanted to consign all farmers, especially big farmers, to a sexless limbo, to show in fireworks of wit how far superior staying on at school was, to wring from her now a declaration both absolute and binding.

'That was his brother who got into Durham last year, wasn't it?' he said.

'It's a shame with a farm that size.'

They put out half the lights for the last waltz and she let him hold her tight which meant a slow and deep plunge into the feel and smell of her hair, the press of her body, the slight taste of salt when he risked a light brushed kiss on her cheek, the music drawing her into him, the movement pulling him closer to her, his hand moist on the thin cotton of her dress, even their thighs close at times when he paused for a split moment and just clung to her in a state of bliss that should never have ended.

'God Save the Queen' then Alan came up, Sarah Thompson hovering behind him.

'Meet outside her gate in half an hour?'

'Who's "her" supposed to be?' said Rachel, but she smiled.

They set Linda back home. Joe had danced with her three more times and her talent gave Rachel and himself something to talk about as they walked towards the farm.

'This gate,' Rachel said.

It was the upper gate, leading to the barns.

'Watch your feet.'

She led. They went into the open barn and the sweet ripe scent flooded into his lungs and its sickening sweetness set off a fuse along his veins.

'Bit of a stench,' Rachel said.

'I like it.'

'Takes all sorts.' But she only said that out of nervousness, Joe knew.

There was a little light from one of the far street lights in the village. Scudding clouds kept obscuring the moon. The constant barking of a few dogs, a car or two, a motorbike or two distantly heard, the wide silence of the great plain, the big sound of themselves together unseen, unhindered. She put her arms around his neck and they kissed hard and lingeringly, again and again, repositioning their lips as if for a better expression of all that was being said and done in this partial and chaste meeting of flesh, came up for air, even managed a few sentences now and then, but soon dived back to the kiss, the slender focus of all their lust, all sensuality confined to two slivers of flesh far away from the forbidden sexual zones, lips, the unspeaking voice of their desire, those kisses invested with such a charge by poetry and song, tender and powerful silent mouthings, longings, the seductive blend of internal and external skin, the tentative touchings of the tip of the tongue, extraordinary and numerous expressions and satisfactions in the only permitted lasciviousness of a budding uncertain love. After some time Joe put his hand on her breast. She did not take it off, indeed she seemed to lean into it and Joe left it at that: truly grateful.

While resting her head on his shoulder she looked at her watch. 'I'll have to go.'

She broke the clinch immediately. Joe felt he had bobbed up after too long under water. Outside the farm gate he said:

'I'm coming through tomorrow.'

'You can't.'

'It's your birthday.' It sounded like a complaint and in a way it was. He had spent hours thinking about her present.

'What time?'

'Four o'clock?'

He had worked it out. Church. Eat. Three hours' work. Get there. Back for evensong but not essential. As long as back by eight for another hour or two's reading or the concert he had circled.

'Two.' Rachel had made her calculations. 'Outside the Hall. I'll see you there.'

She went into the dark farmyard. He heard the door open and close, quietly both times. There was no option. He would have to miss sung eucharist in the morning and then he could guarantee getting the three hours in after he had helped his dad. She had said two o'clock but who could tell how long it would go on for – the longer the better for him – best to get the history done in the morning. He had only ever missed the eucharist before when he had been on holiday.

'What was she like?' Alan had taken about an hour. Joe was shivering.

'Good,' said Joe, as flatly as he could. 'Sarah?'

'Bit slow.' Joe climbed onto the pillion. 'But I've fixed something up for next week.'

'I'm set.'

Alan cruised out of the village and only hit the accelerator when he was well clear. He was still basking in the ton which Joe had helpfully introduced into the general conversation and with Sarah present.

Joe held on. He saw the stare-eyed rabbit, he saw Speed's brother high on the cart, he saw Rachel across the dance floor waiting, and in the palm of his right hand he carried the softness and comfort of her breast.

CHAPTER NINETEEN

In the morning Rachel helped her mother with the baking and cleaning. Advantage had been taken of her birthday. There would be a Sunday tea for favoured relations. High tea. Cold meats, a token salad, farm butter, rum butter, brandy butter, jam, pickled onions – all home made – home-baked bread and too many plate cakes, trifle with cream, and continuous tea. The house had to be burnished clean as on no other day. The men would be uncomfortable. Strapped in suits and stiff collars grown too small – they would sweat before the reckless fire. The conversation of the men would be stock prices, subsidies, land; of the women genealogy and intense local gossip. Suez would be lucky to get a mention. Rachel enjoyed these occasions and even today there was an excitement in the anticipation, fanned, as always, by her amusement at the seriousness with which her mother took the whole thing.

'You would think you were going to be inspected by the Queen.'

'The Queen would be a walkover compared with this lot.'

'They're family, Mam!'

'There's nobody worse for finding fault. You'll see.'

'It's like a showroom.'

Rachel opened her arms to the plain, solid but glassily polished table, chairs and sideboard in the sitting room already laid for the tea even though it was only late morning.

'They'll find something. You know my sisters.'

'Why don't you put a vase of flowers in the middle of the table?'

'Somebody would knock them over. And imagine what your dad would say! Anyway, who has flowers on the middle of a laid table?'

'You could open up new frontiers.'

'C'mon, we have to get the men their dinners.'

But the prospect of sitting down with her father and her brothers dampened Rachel's spirits. Perhaps her excitement had been whistling in the dark. She was going to carry out her threat, which meant that in a day or so she would be in full confrontation with him. Her mother had not spoken to her about it for the past two weeks, believing that to ignore it would be to solve it. And Rachel's good mood that morning had reassured her.

'Was he at the dance?' she asked, skittishly.

'He was.'

'It's Ellen Richardson's boy, isn't it? We were both at school with Ellen.'

'Does Dad know?'

'We don't talk about it.'

Rachel wanted to tell her mother that she planned to leave the next morning. To stay with Aunt Claire. To leave school at Christmas, which she was entitled to do, to get a job. She ought to tell her. Her mother would get part of the blame. It was unfair not to. It was such a big thing to do on her own. Perhaps she would not have the strength to do it. Perhaps her mother would help.

'Potatoes,' her mother said. 'Peeled. Now.' And she was gone.

After dinner the brothers went out to tidy up – even more scrupulously on this day because once tea was over the men would expect a tour of the farm buildings and sightings of the home fields. Isaac waited until the washing-up had been done and then took out his five pounds. 'Here,' he said. Rachel knew the command was to her. She turned from the sink. He held up the notes and flapped them a little, boastfully, so that the full five could be seen. Yet there was also a diffidence in Isaac; he had waited until his sons had gone. He wanted it over with. He was aware of the wall between them now and uncertain whether the gift was a show of weakness.

'No thanks,' Rachel said.

'Take it.'

'I'm happy with the coat. That cost enough.'

'I want you to take it.' He was winded. He was hurt.

'Take it!' Her mother was angry. 'Your father's giving it to you.'

'I'd rather not. Thanks all the same.'

'Well, Mother. She doesn't want my money.'

He folded the notes carefully and put them in his waistcoat pocket.

Rachel untied her apron and made for the door leading to the stairs. There had for a moment been a crushed expression on her father's face which had made her want to cry.

As she passed by him, he lunged out and grabbed her wrist, held it very hard.

'You're very close,' he said.

'It hurts.'

'You're still my daughter.'

'It hurts!'

He let go. There was a red mark around her wrist. She reckoned that to go upstairs, get her make-up and cardigan, come down, cross this kitchen once again with Isaac even angrier would be dangerous. She made for the door which led to the farmyard. Her school coat was on the peg in the storm porch. That would have to do.

'I'll be back in time to help with the tea,' Rachel said.

Isaac waited for the door to close.

'Well, Mother. She must think she's rich if she can turn down a fiver.'

'She shouldn't have done.' The tone was sincere. 'It was bad manners.'

'Bad manners. Is that what you call it?'

She looked out of the window, miserable. In the gaiety of the morning's preparations, in the normality of the family dinner, in the dramatic prospect of tea, she had felt that all could be well. Now she was certain that Rachel was hell bent on it.

'Is there something I should know?'

What was in the quiet voice? Menace? Pleading?

'I don't know what'll happen between you two.' She waited for more from him. None came. 'I'd better get a move on.'

—⁓—

It always ended up with scent and soap. Joe had tried very hard but scent and soap it was. Even in the chemist's, where Ellen had once worked part-time, where they were indulgent to his indecisions, and suggested many combinations for the money available, it still ended up in scent and soap. 'The very best there is,' Lawrence assured him, 'what the rich people go for.' As she waited for him in the porch outside the village hall, looking at the drizzle as if she might read signs in it, Rachel knew it would be scent and soap.

He was also wearing his school mac, plastered from his ride through the rain, his hair soaked flat, but his face, washed bright, lit up the moment he saw her. She would tell him.

They went to the bus shelter opposite the school. There was nowhere else. She could not risk the barn. The chapel was open but that was unthinkable. Farm buildings on other land were too risky. Too wet to walk. The bus shelter it was.

There was a narrow bench. They sat side by side very properly in case someone she knew went past. One rapid squeeze, one swift kiss, then he handed over the present. She looked surprised, told him it was the best you could get, gave him another squeeze, another swift kiss, took a deep breath and told him that she was leaving home the next day.

'Where will you go?' Joe's voice was solemn. He was awe-struck. She told him.

'What will you do?'

'I'll finish at Christmas and get a job.'

'What about your exams?'

'They wouldn't have mattered anyway. I'd have had to leave. You must tell nobody.'

Joe looked at her, searching for a new person. She looked the same, save for a seriousness about her, a grown-up seriousness, sad and calm.

'What'll he do?'

Rachel shrugged, wearily. She had asked herself that question so many times.

'What can he do?'

'I'll . . .' Look after you? Help you? It was all too sudden for Joe. But there was excitement.

'I know,' she said and took his hand. 'I'm glad I told you.' And this time it was a real kiss, not caring who saw them.

But after that there was not much else to do or say. He walked her back to the farm. She did not ask him to bike ahead and let her arrive alone. They parted chastely at the gate, both by this time utterly drenched.

—ɯ—

After an hour's homework in her Aunt Claire's front room – the kitchen was tiny, it was just a glorified one up, one down – she went to see Jennie who lived in an Edwardian sandstone house on West Street. They watched television and then went to Jennie's bedroom to talk. Jennie and Linda were the only others in on it. Jennie talked to Rachel like a doctor to a patient.

And as she walked back through the town, Rachel felt that sense of being someone less and other than yourself, that displacement which accompanies illness. The evening town seemed a foreign and a hemmed-in place. The people on the street she did not know. She felt she was being looked at and talked about. She was glad to find one of the alleys that took her into Church Street and down to the yard.

Her father's car was there.

There was a flight of sandstone steps which led up to Peter Donolly, Photographer, in a studio which overlooked the pig auction. She sat on these. In the twenty minutes which seemed hours, three men passed her – all nodded – and a gang of boys began to cluster significantly near and creep relentlessly nearer. She left the steps and stared through the gate at the empty auction pens. She liked pigs. They made her laugh. Her father butchered his own and she had watched him do it ever since she could remember. What a big grinning beast a pig had seemed to the small girl and how wonderful her father who could suspend it so easily, cut its windpipe to stop the squealing, scrape off its bristle and then, when all was set, open its throat, wasting scarcely a drop of blood. He would watch her to see if she flinched, but not once. She would find it harder to face now – school had softened her, her father often said that.

She had to face him. The boys who had gathered around her in a loose semi-circle parted easily with only one or two little hoots. From her look they could see she was way beyond them.

He let her come in and sit down. He was uncomfortable. He was always uncomfortable in any house but his own and wanted to get out as quickly as possible. Her Aunt Claire sat on a hard chair by the table. Her father was in the big armchair. Rachel took the smaller one opposite him. The light had not been put on and the small room was only relieved of its thrifty gloom by the modest coal fire.

'I'll just finish this tea and then we'll be off,' he said in a pleasant tone. 'It won't take you long to pack your things.'

Rachel had not been prepared for this. Not this calm. Not this gentleness. Her Aunt Claire looked at her: what did the look say? What could she say?

'Cat got your tongue?' He smiled, and in the smile she saw the anger in him and knew how deep it was.

'I want to stay here.'

'Upstairs.' He slung back his tea from the unaccustomed cup. 'I haven't all night.'

Rachel looked at her Aunt Claire, who sat stiff-backed, knees pinned together, full apron flowing to her ankles, anxious as a schoolgirl under examination. The glow of the fire made her sil-ver-grey hair gleam. Her hands were on her knees, palms down.

'He is your father,' she said, 'after all,' knowing she was expected to say something, having to feed the silence, wanting to be fair all round.

'Upstairs.' He looked at his watch.

Rachel could not move. There was a burden on her, as solid-seeming as a weight. Her father commanded the room outside her and the space in her head. All she could be was still.

'Would you have done this, Claire? Defied your father?'

The little countrywoman concentrated on Rachel and in a measured tone she said,

'I'm not having you hit the girl, Isaac Wardlow, not in my house.'

'I've never struck her.'

'I know you, Isaac. And I'm not frightened of you.' Again said very carefully, very fearfully, but said.

'Maybe it would be better if I had.'

His look to Rachel had in it an anguish which made her turn from his gaze. But she took strength from it.

'I'm not coming home,' she muttered and waited for the blow.

Isaac stood up and the force of the man spread to the walls. The two women were frozen, neither daring to catch his glance. He looked from one to the other.

'Do I have to carry you off?' he asked hoarsely.

Rachel had said all that she could manage. He turned to the older woman. Claire was gazing directly into the fire, her skin's rosy sheen at odds with the tightness of her expression.

'I could take you,' he said, holding up his right arm, 'in this one hand.' He opened the palm of it and then, slowly, he closed it. 'Like that.'

But all he got was silence.

Finally.

'If I'd defied my father like this, or if any of my sisters had done this, and the same goes for you, Claire, however hard you look away, by God we would have known about it!' He walked to the door slowly, like a man wading waist-high through sea.

'He is your father,' Claire repeated.

'She doesn't want me for a father,' Isaac said, opened the door, and left.

In the yard where he had parked the car, he stood still for a few moments, feeling rather dizzy as happened to him now and then. The boy came round the corner, hands in trouser pockets, expression clear as a bell, whistling. He made for Claire's cottage.

'You!'

Joe had no doubt who was being called out. He turned and smiled at the stranger in whose face he then recognised Rachel. He took his hands out of his pockets.

'What name do you go by?'

'Joe Richardson.'

Isaac paused. The dizziness had not cleared.

'Off Sam?'

'He's my dad.'

The older man looked him over as the boy just stood there.

'You're more like your mother,' he said, eventually.

He watched the boy knock and be admitted. Then, cautiously, he got into the car and drove off slowly.

'He didn't hit you,' Claire had said, as soon as Isaac had left. 'He didn't even offer to.'

'He would have done if you hadn't been there.'

'But he didn't. I think he wanted you back.'

'He wants his own way, that's all.' Rachel spoke in tones older than the older woman. She was tired.

'We'll have some tea now,' Claire said. 'And I made scones this afternoon.' She put on the light. The central bulb under the transparent shade blinked the small room bright and yet Rachel had preferred the dark. When the knock came to the door, her stomach clenched once again.

197

'It's open,' Claire said.

He came in.

'It's just Joe.' Claire's relief made Rachel smile. 'I was just making a cup of tea, Joe.'

She went into the minute back kitchen, leaving them alone.

'I saw your dad.'

Rachel waited.

'He seemed all right.'

'I thought you did homework straight through.'

'I wanted to see you.'

She crooked a finger, flashed a look at the back kitchen and lifted up her face for a swift kiss. Joe felt bold.

'These scones have to be eaten now,' said Claire, 'they'll be stale tomorrow.'

They ate dutifully. Joe and Claire had no trouble talking the news of the town which for the older woman was more engrossing than fiction. Joe's access through the pub made him a valuable source and Claire took advantage.

Rachel followed him out, dark now, and they found a doorway in one of the narrow alleyways which slit back into High Street. She told him why her father had come but could not and did not want to try to articulate the confused deeper feelings she had, how moved she had been by her father, how – could this be true? – sorry for him, yet the anger was still there, unsoftened despite the softer feelings. Joe kissed her consolingly without suspecting the quiet revolutions she was undergoing.

He stayed up an extra hour to fulfil his stint. Rachel slept badly: she missed the night noises of the countryside.

—⚭—

Her mother was waiting for her after school three days later and this time Claire left the two of them alone.

Rachel saw her mother's distress and caught it. Yet for a while the two of them just fussed over the tea Claire had laid for them and her mother answered questions about the dogs and dug up some gossip from the village and told her how much the aunts and uncles had liked the birthday tea, admired the house, admired the farm. There was, though, a bus she had to catch back to the village. She took out a cigarette and, after a brief hesitation, offered one to Rachel.

'Dirty habit,' she said as she waved away the smoke from her face. She was not a skilful smoker. Rachel had already learned to breathe out the smoke steadily through her nose.

'Now then.' She flicked a tiny amount of ash into the fire. 'I'll tell you the truth, Rachel. I feel shamed.'

Again she tapped the cigarette at the fire. Rachel had not expected this.

'It's getting around. I was here on market day and there were one or two questions and looks. Just enough. We've never known anything like this in my family, Rachel. I call them everything when they deserve it, but we've never had anybody running away from home like this and in public.'

Rachel did not want her mother to start crying.

'What's he like?'

'He says nothing. But I know he wants you back. He's moping, that's the best way to put it, he's moping. The house is very empty without you.'

The girl was moved.

'It's more than him, though. To tell you the truth if this gets out much more I'll not want to show myself.'

Rachel looked closely at her mother's face, at eyes which would not look directly at hers. She saw it lined too early, too thin, once fine now worn, the good fair hair too cheaply attended to. She knew the work, early morning until bedtime, a toil inside and outside the house to serve the ambitions of the man who had captured her and held her. She wished she had enjoyed a kinder life.

'So it's for my sake, you see,' she whispered, afraid she might be tearful. 'He didn't put me up to it. If you do come back I want you to say nothing about this. I don't want him to think it was me.'

Rachel waited until the weekend and returned at an inconspicuous hour on Sunday afternoon. She strapped the bag on her back carrier seat; Joe put the case on his handlebars. He did not go beyond the gate.

Isaac took it carefully and so did she. A new degree of politeness entered in, not elaborate, not so dramatically different from before, but less shouting, more respect, a tension but no anger and, for a time, a sadness that had not been there.

CHAPTER TWENTY

Sometimes his father brought his cup of tea upstairs, half way through the evening, a break from the pub. Joe now worked in the otherwise unused parlour of the flat, more space. It was difficult for him not to feel impatient when his father came in, a resentment that his self-allocated routine was being breached, his time raided, the job he had set himself casually interrupted, but the impatience was also fuelled by guilt, that he could not meet the modest expectation of attention his father wanted. Sam was aware of that but arrived with his cup of tea nonetheless. He stood beside the fire, Joe at the table.

'Handy in a way,' he said, 'me and your mother downstairs all night gives you this place to yourself.'

'Yes.' Joe had often thought that but in the grip of this almost panicky resentment he resisted any agreement which might lead to conversation. 'I'm doing Latin,' he added, hoping that this would act as a deterrent. But how could his father know how much he hated Latin and therefore how much harder Latin was than any other subject and therefore how much edgier he was about interruption? Yet it was complicated, as everything seemed to be getting more complicated these days, reasons, explanations, excuses, qualifications, subtleties, glosses, all taking over from black and white, wrong and right, good or not. Because he could have liked Latin had it not been for his teacher, Miss Castle, who disliked him so much. He would have liked to like Latin, it would have made him better at it and when he read the translation of *The Aeneid*, part of which was their set book, he was wrapped up in it, but then the Latin got in the way. When he read Cicero's speeches in English he thought they were such great ways to make arguments. It was some language for speeches! But the language lay there on the page resentful, offering him no help. It was Miss Castle who sat on that page like a thumb on his neck and he could never get her pressure off him.

'I'll just be a minute or two,' Sam said. The boy's surliness was transparent. Sam admired the way he stuck at it. He had made a point of never pushing him about his homework, never asking about it. It'll do him good to know he's done it on his own, he told Ellen when she pointed out his lack of encouragement.

'I read the play,' he said, 'most of it.' Sam smiled broadly and even sunk into himself as he was, Joe responded to the fun and fullness in that smile. 'I liked it. I'm not saying I understand all of it by any means. Still, I tackled it. And I liked it.' And he wanted an argument about it with a son who no doubt understood every word and liked an argument. He knew he had to begin it.

'King Lear goes all wrong from the start,' Sam said. He took out a cigarette. Despite all, Joe had to repress an inward groan. It would be at least a full cigarette's worth of time.

'He should never have given away his kingdom.'

'They were his daughters.'

'I don't care who they were. He signed his own death warrant then and there.'

'He's old. He's over eighty, it says. He's not well. It's very hard

work being a king. Especially then when you were in the middle of it.'
Joe rose to the bait.

'He could have given them titles. He could have given them money. But why he wanted to give them his kingdom I'll never know.'

'Maybe he needed to be looked after for a change.' With a rather rude obviousness, noted but ignored by his father, Joe put down his pen and leaned back in the chair. 'I know it turned out to be a mistake but he couldn't have thought that at the time. He must have thought it would work out O.K. Look at what they said.'

'Flarch. Just sucking up. He must have been in negotiations. Kings did their own then, didn't they? He must have learned diplomacy. How could he be taken in by that pair of fishwives?'

'Cordelia doesn't flarch.'

'She's worse. I can't understand Cordelia. Why does she make such a fuss? I thought she was just showing off, how much better she was than her sisters.'

'Well, she is.'

'I'll grant you that.' Sam nodded, took a puff, smiled broadly again. 'That Fool's got more sense than anybody else, even though he is only a Fool.'

That was what Mr. Tillotson had said. Joe nodded it through. But the main challenge had to be resisted.

'Maybe he thought they'd all end up fighting among themselves when he died and so he wanted to sort it out before then,' Joe said.

'Who told you that?'

'I thought it up.' Mr. Tillotson had said he had a point.

'Well, he miscalculated that one, then, didn't he? They're at his throat in ten minutes and then at each other's throats.'

'Did he need a hundred knights?' Joe asked. 'That was the problem.'

'You sound like her in the play. One of the daughters.'

'But how would you like it if somebody said they'd let you rule and then turned up all the time with a hundred knights who caused havoc and did whatever they wanted?'

'Whose word do we take for that? The two ugly sisters?'

'You make it sound like a pantomime.'

'P.G. Wodehouse would have made a great comedy out of it.'

'Mr. Tillotson says it's Shakespeare's finest tragedy.'

'You listen to Mr. Tillotson.' Sam meant it. Enough.

He dropped the stub of the cigarette into the fire. Joe was relaxing now. He could always add on ten minutes at the end to keep up his hours.

'That's not what I came to talk to you about.' Sam took out another cigarette. 'I think you can let go some of your jobs downstairs,' he said. 'You've enough to do up here. So,' rather hurriedly, 'if you help me to carry up on Friday and Saturday mornings and chop the week's kindling – we'll manage the rest. Same pay.'

'And sweeping the front?'

'You hate that, don't you?' Sam's smile was sympathetic. 'Especially when your friends come on those school buses and catch you at it. Sadie says she'll share it. You're coming up for the final furlong – so. You do hate sweeping that front, don't you?'

Joe nodded, not knowing whether to grimace or smile. He felt trapped when his father knew him so well and yet he also felt pleased, even flattered, to be so thoroughly known.

'There's this.' He fumbled in his school bag and pulled out *A Selection of Essays* by William Hazlitt. 'There's a really smashing piece on boxing.'

'I've not read many good books about boxing.' Sam took it. 'Thanks.'

'It's just an essay,' Joe said. 'But it's still good.'

'I'll let you know.' He went to the door. 'I suppose there wouldn't have been a play at all if he hadn't given his kingdom away at the start.'

Joe laughed. He would tell Mr. Tillotson that one. The Latin Unseen ought to be easier now: more relaxed, as, unexpectedly, he was. 'Omne appetitum appetitu sub specii boni.' The familiar alarm bells rang – 'appetitum appetitu'? He reached out for the dictionary.

———※———

There were good days, Sam thought, and that was one. As he read in the kitchen after closing time he found his mind drifting back magnetically to that earlier exchange in the parlour. He wished he'd said more: there was so much more to say but it had been enough.

'What are you looking so pleased about?' she said.

'Never you mind.'

'Bad manners to keep secrets from your wife.'

'Bad manners it is then.'

'It'll come out when you least want it to,' she warned.

'Let me get on with my book, woman,' he said and there was concord with Ellen, and that, too, was enough.

———※———

He knew that 'Houn' Dog' and 'Don't Be Cruel' would be a risk but surely the skiffle numbers should have worked – 'Rock Island Line', 'Cumberland Gap', 'Bring a Little Water Silvie' should work, while there was at least a bit of belt in 'Cool Water', 'Jezebel', 'Walking My Baby Back Home' and 'Rock Around the Clock'. But the reaction was hardly a reaction at all. No sympathy vote for this being their debut.

True, the two ukeleles were not in tune and Malcolm tried to be too complicated on the drum and washboard; Joe's own thumping of the home-made broom, twine and tea-chest double bass was very patchy, largely owing to his attempt to put in the actions while he sang, and Alan's saxophone was spectacularly under-rehearsed. But still, he thought, it was the new sound. It felt good to be inside it. Now and then it really rocked. Why didn't they just stand still and listen instead of walking around eating sandwiches? It had seemed such a safe bet for a debut – the Scouts Annual Autumn Fund Raising Dance, music wholly from records save for them, the Memphis Five, in the interval. But they just fizzled out. Nobody even seemed to notice when they finished. Some of the younger Scouts had begun sledging across the floor and most of the girls who mattered had gathered in a huddle in the furthest corner, including Rachel and her pals. All of the band had themselves been in the Scouts and felt aggrieved that their act of generosity had been greeted with such indifference, even, in some numbers, with hostility.

Joe had not imagined this. None of them had. Triumph or near-triumph had been the only possibilities. They came down from the platform shiftily and split immediately.

'To tell you the truth,' said Rachel, as they tried a modern waltz, 'I had to laugh. You looked so serious.'

It was serious. They had practised for hours on the Saturday in the singing room. They had thought they were nearly great. Just a bit of polish from a live performance – and who knows?

'Linda liked your Lonnie Donegan,' Rachel conceded. 'She's got good taste in music, hasn't she?'

'What about you?'

'I thought you all looked a bit clueless.'

Joe danced on. He kept his nerve but his confidence flew out of the hall like a trapped sparrow through an open window.

206

'I was interested,' said Mr. Braddock, 'in that "Rock Island Line" business – quite a story there. I didn't realise they were folk ballads. Do we really need the American accent?'

That was little comfort either.

'Perhaps if you had the right instruments,' said the Music teacher, 'and learned how to play them.'

'We weren't ready,' Malcolm said, when they regrouped, moodily, sharing an illicit fag in the cloakroom. 'I told you that.' He had. He had been the only one. He had been overruled. He had only agreed to join because Joe had sweet-talked him about how it would impress the girls.

'That saxophone,' Alan said. 'It's a matter of getting your mouth round it and your fingers going at the same time. It's not easy.'

'No ukulele,' said Edward, 'however hard you twang it, can compare with an acoustic guitar.'

'If you have one foot on a tea chest and you're supposed to be making a broomstick and a bit of thick string sound like a double bass while you're singing, you can't always guarantee a result,' said Joe.

'Maybe if we cut out your singing next time,' said Malcolm, 'then we could concentrate on the real thing.'

'Who'll have us next time?' Joe asked Rachel.

'There's always somebody,' she said helpfully, 'who'll be looking for something to fill in while they get the refreshments.' Then she burst into giggles, the only consolation being that she leaned her head on his shoulder and so he could feel her breasts. 'Sorry, Joe.'

Later, as the buses drew up outside the school hall, Linda said, 'You need a microphone. And an echo chamber. And get rid of the tea chest. You should wiggle a bit more. People like that.'

The Scouts had laid on buses which would take home those who came from outside the town. Joe went back in to help clear up. The buses had been laid on far too early, he thought. Maybe the group should have come on later, when everybody was warmed up. When they did not have to contend with the full lighting in the school hall and all the junior Scouts in their short-trousered uniforms rushing around. They should have stood in the centre of the stage not at the side, even though it would have meant moving the headmaster's assembly desk. They should have had another rehearsal before the performance.

Alan really had to learn the saxophone. Who would tell him? And Joe had been so nervous. Before, during and after. Why did he do a thing that made him so nervous?

The floor was swept. The chairs were put back in their rows for Monday morning.

—m—

Brenda was good at table tennis which she called ping-pong and there was a rather battered table – for use of the Upper Sixth only – in what had once been a large kitchen. Joe had learned his game at Butlin's, free of charge (if you discounted the down payment), just as everything in that heaven for the boy – the roller-skating, the swimming pool, the dancing, all the games, the meals, everything – was gloriously free and if you could hog a table you could play all day for all anyone cared. Brenda had been coached. The only way he could beat her was by smashes and his smashes were erratic.

She had suggested a quick game after school and here they were on game five, two all, Brenda coolly in the lead in the decider. Joe had become uncertain of his smashes. Her spin was hard to deal with: it even seemed a bit unfair, Joe thought, but kept the thought to himself. She won. He congratulated her.

'Another?' She held up her bat.

'No thanks.'

'Frightened to be beaten again?'

'No.' But not too keen.

'Homework calls?'

'No.' Nobody liked to admit that.

'I don't believe you. People say you're just a swot.'

'What about you?'

'I don't have to swot much. People say you do.'

'What people?'

'Everybody.'

'Everybody who?'

'Everybody who doesn't like you.' Brenda was putting on her coat. She glanced at him quite calmly. 'Most people don't like you.'

Joe forced out the smile. He had sensed and suspected it but this bluntly? From the source of all truthfulness?

'One or two do,' he said, very weakly.

'Lower forms,' said Brenda. 'Not us.'

He let her go ahead, pretending some business with his satchel. He walked back slowly through the northern streets already dark now that the clocks had changed, now that winter was coming in. He took a detour around Vinegar Hill but Diddler wasn't there.

It was not until he telephoned Rachel at their agreed nine o'clock, after he had done his homework, that he felt easier. When she asked what was wrong with him he said he was having trouble with the Latin.

They were going to a dance in Carlisle the next day, the Saturday, with a gang of them, down on the six-twenty, back on the last train. This was the first time Joe and Rachel had joined this gang – Malcolm went, Veronica, Brenda sometimes and others who, Joe now saw,

209

meshed together in several ways. He had been looking forward to showing all this off, the gang, the County Ballroom in Carlisle with the full orchestra, the last train home, but now the thought of it after Brenda's assault made him rather miserable. Yet at the same time the prospect of being with Rachel was nothing but happy. How could he be both at once? He wandered across towards the pub from the telephone box with no stability in him: the noise of the pub pushed into his face. He veered up the hill to see his Aunt Grace.

—◦◦◦—

'What we're seeing,' said William, 'is a real change in the way people think, especially the young.'

They listened respectfully. They usually did. Even now there was still a frisson of pleasure that William worked alongside them in the pub, just doing the washing-up and for nothing. Alfrieda, unmarried, was attempting to attract warmer attention from the desirable widower but so far he seemed content as he was. Everyone accepted he had a soft spot for Ellen which did not go over the mark. But Alfrieda had now set her sights on him. First step to get in on those car trips with Ellen. Jack Ack and Tommy sipped at their free drink, tired after a heavy Saturday night, Ellen on her usual low stool in front of the fire, Sam in the corner where he could most easily get to the bar. For William, it was something of a court.

'Look at the way the young protested about Suez. And look at how gallant the young have been in Hungary against the Russians. Two sides of the same coin. They won't stand for the old ways much longer.'

'So what will they do instead?' Sam asked. There was the slightest hardness in his tone. Ellen chose to ignore it.

210

'They want a new world order,' said the secretary of the Wigton Labour Party with certainty. 'Out with the old, in with the new.'

'What is it that's new?'

The other men scarcely listened. They had chewed through the good stuff, the gossip of the night. Alfrieda though sensed a conflict and squirmed forward on her chair. Ellen ceased to glance at the magazine which had been mopping up her tiredness.

'It all comes back, doesn't it, to socialism?' Mr. Hawesley sounded both deeply confident and resigned.

He stuck the pipe in his mouth without lighting it, something Sam always considered rather comical. But it did give him a more studious air – that and the brightness there was about him, the bird-like brightness which came from a week's undemanding work and one night only behind the bar, but more than that, the brightness of the zealot, bright morning, bright day.

'Why should it?' Sam asked. 'Why should it all come back to socialism? America isn't coming back to socialism, as far as anybody can see. Russia's just another tyranny, nothing socialist there. Socialism here in Wigton's only just recently got any sort of a grip.'

'But surely, surely,' the pipe was taken out and tapped and cleared preparatory to the last charging of the evening, 'bringing America and Russia and Wigton together misses the point.'

'What point?' His look was direct and William held it only for an instant.

Ellen looked at Sam more intently. He would not give up. But William was the intellectual in the company.

'Both here and in Eastern Europe,' said William, speaking thoughtfully out into space and charging his pipe with St. Bruno '– and I'm sure in America and Russia, but it doesn't make the news – young people are saying, "We've had enough of your ignorance that

211

led to fascism and Stalinism and we want a more equal society but one where you have enough goods for all as well as freedom for all." In other words I see it as an altogether different mood. The authoritarian idea is on the way out – it will take time – but it is on the way out. In whatever form it has assumed. So is the worship of mere self-interest. Maybe it's the legacy of two world wars and all that terrible suffering, maybe it's just a historical shift,' he tapped the top of the tobacco with his index finger, 'but to my mind the young today are, in essence, Sam, in essence, saying no to war, no to oppression, no to force.'

'Fat lot of good it did them in Hungary.' Sam jabbed out his cigarette.

'This will take time. The Uprising itself was what was significant. The suppression was not unexpected.'

'It found out a lot of your communist friends.'

Sam's tone was harsh. Alfrieda looked to William. Ellen thought of how to bring down the temperature. William snapped on his lighter and the flame leapt out. He sucked it through the pipe. The action hollowed his cheeks ghoulishly. Alfrieda thought it made him look distinguished.

'It's a very common mistake, very easily made, to lump communists and socialists together, but you know better than most, Sam, that it's a mistake and a bad mistake. The British form of socialism owes more to Methodism than to Marxism, it has a long tradition of its own in this country through the trades unions and the Philanthropic Societies. Marxism, Stalinism, that's just fascism by another name.'

'I can't see how you'll ever be able to give up war.' Sam had caught Ellen's eye and he was calmer. 'Lads today are just like we were, and when the call comes, they'll fall in. I'd bet on it.'

'Human nature can change, Sam. We don't have gladiatorial combats any more. We don't have bear-baiting.'

212

'We drop bombs from thousands of feet up instead.'

'I'm for bed,' said Ellen, and everyone knew it was time to go.

'I enjoyed that,' William emphasised as he stood on the doorstep for his usual last word with Sam. 'Nothing like a vigorous difference of opinion between friends.'

'You're an optimist, William. It's nice to see.'

He watched him go across the road for his car. Waited until he climbed into it. Waved. Turned back in.

—⚏—

News had filtered through about Speed. Some said cashiered. Some said dishonourable discharge. Found work in Liverpool on the docks.

Sam smoked a couple of cigarettes alone, watching the fire die out. He was sad about Speed. His father, who had not been seen for years now, used to come into the district now and then, not for years now. Dead most likely. Unidentifiable. Poor Jackie. The Japs got him in the end. There had been such good reports about Speed before this.

—⚏—

Joe came in wearily, pushing his bike up the outside steps, stood it in the hall where he would park it for the night.

'Good night?' Sam's voice from the kitchen.

'Yes,' the boy said. But still that lump of misery. Even despite the time alone together in the empty train on Carlisle Station when they had crept away early from the dance. Cycling back from the village, the misery had returned and with it, or prompting it, the unbalance in his head, the dislocation, the bursting into nothing. He thought that had gone for good. He thought he had seen the last of that.

'Fancy a cup of tea?' Sam would have enjoyed a few minutes' chat.

'No thanks. Night, Dad.' Still from the hall. Going up the stairs.

'You're a good lad, Joe,' Sam called out. 'Everybody says that.' The boy stopped, checked himself for a moment and then took the stairs two at a time, lifted up by the words so casually but authoritatively thrown at him.

Stripped, fast prayers, too late for music, Rachel, now in the dark alone, think over every move they made. This had to last.

PART THREE
TESTS, 1957

CHAPTER TWENTY-ONE

He was in. There was no precedent for it. Not in that house. There was no need for it. Benefits would have been hard to quantify. Yet, when the relationship had achieved a certain weight, you met the parents. It was not an announcement but it was a recognition: that this was not a childish matter.

'It seems daft him hanging about outside the gate all the time in the cold and dark just waiting,' her mother said. 'Why doesn't he come in?'

He came in on a night early in the New Year, after a Christmas holiday of walks and dances and three parties in the houses of friends which had defined for both of them the glamour of their new social life as a couple. Four months, Joe would say to himself, still going together and not sick of each other yet. So he came in on the last day of the holidays and Mrs. Wardlow told him to sit down, though not at the table. She had just made some tea, Rachel was upstairs getting ready, they were going down to the Donaldsons' to play cards.

The brothers were clipped but civil, absorbed in pulling off their boots, splashing their faces with water, hauling up chairs to the table, arming themselves with knives and forks for the rapid demolition of the third big meal of the day. Insofar as it is possible to be genially ignored, Joe was genially ignored, which gave him time to settle. He liked the gleam of the old wood, the beams in the ceiling, the bulky highly polished furniture, corner cupboard, sideboard, the smell of fresh food, the routine of it all, the family being together, words to each other, he guessed, varying little from one night to another, Mrs. Wardlow feeding them. He liked the brothers. Their hunger satisfied, they cocked back their chairs which seemed an essential prerequisite to taking out a cigarette, offered him one, refused, he did not really smoke and it seemed too intimate a thing, too presumptuous, as he waited, they all waited, for Isaac.

Isaac had been warned that this might happen. He had seen the boy's bike propped against the wall as he conducted his last tour of the barns and sheds in the dark evening. He carried a storm lantern and liked the private light it gave. It was the time and the weather that suited him most. All the animals early accounted for. Provisioned well for winter. Clear but not frosty. A feeling of snug, of territory bounded and claimed, a time to recharge. Fewer things could go wrong. He counted his stock like Silas Marner counting his golden coins.

He padded straight to the table in his stockinged feet and a hush came on the kitchen. He ate carefully. Compared with his wolfing sons, he ate delicately. Such talk as there was was murmured between the three men at the table, farm talk, detailed talk, checking the accounts of the day. Joe enjoyed listening in. He liked the whole mood of the place, the everybody being there solidity of it, the sense of being enclosed and self-sufficient, fortressed.

'So,' Isaac said, turning directly to him. 'Sam Richardson's lad.'

Joe smiled. It was almost funny how closely Rachel resembled her father.

'What does Sam think about you not working?'

He poured the tea into his saucer.

'He doesn't seem to mind,' Joe sought to excuse his uselessness. 'I help a bit around the pub.'

'Sam was a clever lad at school.'

Joe felt complimented.

'So what'll come out of this school business?'

'I don't know.' He didn't. But he needed to be obliging. 'I could go on to be a teacher.'

'Hear that, Mother? We have a teacher in the house!'

'A clean job anyway,' she said.

'Not a lot of money in it,' Isaac said.

'Money doesn't matter,' Joe began but got no further.

'Money doesn't matter! Hear that, Mother? Hear that, boys? Money doesn't matter!'

Isaac leaned back in his chair and laughed. He laughed a big deep belly laugh, a laugh he may not have enjoyed for years, a laugh so sincere that it was infectious and first the brothers, then his wife, then Joe himself joined in and Rachel, who entered at that moment, was immobilised in astonishment.

'Well!' Isaac's great laughter gradually ebbed away. 'That beats the band. That beats the band!'

'What was all that about?' They were walking to Donaldson's farm. Joe explained.

'I can see why that would set him off,' she said, and smiled, more to herself than to him. 'Well, you got off to a good start. A sight better than I thought, to tell you the truth. He must like you. He doesn't like many people.'

'You've got your feet under the table now,' said Alan, when he told him. There was pity in his voice. 'She'll want to meet your lot next.'

'Do we think he should have abandoned her?' Miss Castle asked of Upper Sixth Arts' small corps of Latinists. 'Not left her "an abandoned woman" as Richardson translated it.' The error still amused the schoolteacher and there was almost affection in her teasing. 'But deserted her after promising to marry her.'

The radiators were on full and creaked with effort. The northeast February wind cut through the neglected frames of the old windows. Double Latin at the end of Monday afternoon was never a pleasure. They were in the last lap before the Mock exams.

There was, as usual, a tactical silence after Miss Castle's declaration. You never knew with Miss Castle, or Two Ton Castle as she was hurtfully known, even though she was nicknamed after the equally plump but much loved ukelele player Two Ton Tessie O'Shea. 'Aeneas has been saved by Queen Dido, on his way from Troy to Italy. She has fallen passionately in love with him,' here the vigilantly sensitive schoolteacher stared down her small crew to quell any titter at her, especially her use of 'passionately in love': but they knew better. 'And then the gods tell him he must resume his destiny and leave her. As we know, she kills herself, falling on a sword. Should he have left her? Brenda?'

Brenda had prepared this one.

'I think there are two points,' she said, alert as a hare, shining as a full moon. 'Firstly, it was his destiny and that's what he'd been saved for after the burning of Troy. Virgil says it in the poem.' Filling Miss Castle's ears with music and streaming her back to the comparably small Latin Sixth of her own youth and the young Oxford man who had led her through the poetry of Virgil, Brenda quoted, in Latin and not a stress out of order. Brenda was capable of pulling off the school's first distinction in Latin for years.

'And secondly?' she prompted.

'Secondly,' Brenda mirrored her teacher's proud smile, 'Mercury comes from Jupiter to tell him that he must leave, which (a) terrifies Aeneas and (b) gives him no choice because he has to obey the gods. To illustrate how fearful he is –'

But Brenda would never complete the sentence because Arthur said, 'They're not real gods,' with such force that she was halted and all the intensity of Miss Castle's scowl could not prevent Arthur pursuing the point. 'It's a mistake to call them gods,' he said. 'There should be another word. The Greeks and Romans just made them up to suit themselves. They've no idea how to be a real God. They just muck about.'

As he spoke and continued what had become a predictable diatribe, Miss Castle had to decide whether or not to take him on. He was a lost cause. She had never budged him, not once, not an inch. But how could she defend the principal comfort of her intellectual life, the glamour of her scholarship, those liberated, licentious, arbitrary, untamed pagan metamorphosing gods, whom this nonconformist clod from the hills simply dismissed.

'We have had this discussion before,' she said.

'We have,' said Arthur. 'It needs discussing.'

Could she sacrifice the rest of the lesson? There were the Mock exams to prepare. 'Does anyone disagree with Brenda?' said Miss Castle and Arthur knew he had won.

'I think he shouldn't have left her like that,' Joe said. 'Especially when she's gone mad. He shouldn't have left her like that.'

'I'm impressed, Richardson.' The dart not loosed at Arthur had to find some target. 'I thought you'd be the last to comprehend Dido's emotional distress.' Joe's face tightened – then, as happened very rarely, Miss Castle softened, for a few moments, to the boy she almost compulsively enjoyed tormenting. 'I agree,' she said. 'I think Aeneas should have defied his fate.' Miss Castle shared a deep fellow feeling with Dido. 'She loved him, she was prepared to give up everything for him, she made a public spectacle of herself, lost her reputation, shamed herself for him.' Miss Castle's delivery became increasingly urgent: the children were spellbound, not and possibly never knowing why. 'And then he just left her. He just walked away.'

She stopped. Out of the silence, Arthur said,

'Sailed.'

Miss Castle looked at Arthur as if he were insane.

'Sailed?'

'He sailed away,' Arthur corrected her. 'You said walked.'

'He should have taken her with him,' Joe said, somehow under-standing that somebody had to say something. 'She would have brought her navy and army with her as well. But he never even offered.'

'No,' said Miss Castle, abruptly awake. 'He never even offered.' A breath. 'A difficult case to argue, Richardson, but if the question comes up you might get good marks for trying, although,' and she was back on open ground, 'you will also have to make the points made so well by Brenda, especially, as she pointed out, as Virgil gives us so much evidence. Examiners like quotations.'

'Mind you,' said Joe, and hesitated.

'Yes?'

'She says some terrible things to him.'

'Perhaps he deserved them.' Even a smile now, the tone alto-gether lighter. 'A broken heart, Richardson, you should know about that from those awful songs you sing. It can do terrible things to a woman. Men will never understand that.'

Joe nodded because he thought he ought to. Miss Castle left him alone for a week or two.

—◇◇◇—

A fag, a cup of tea, work done with half an hour to go before the eleven-thirty opening time, Sam drifting up street, Joe away playing rugby, Ellen willing just to sit and talk in the kitchen: for Sadie this was bliss. She would not, she said, have swapped places with the Queen of Sheba.

She stirred both her tea and the conversation very gently: there was something she wanted to winkle out of Ellen. In the winter morning dark grey, the kitchen, which backed onto a small yard and a high wall, would have been gloomy without the fire. It drew the gaze of both of them.

'Penny for them.'

'I was thinking about Joe.'

'I miss Joe, pottering about.'

'So do I.' Ellen spoke softly as if this were an immoderate confession. Yet she continued. 'He'll be gone soon. Just like that.'

'How come?' From Sadie's nose came perfect double tracks of smoke.

'Mr. Kneale told Sam he thought he just might be university material. He'll have to leave Wigton for that.'

'Not for long, Ellen. Not Joe. Not Wigton.'

Ellen turned to Sadie and smiled.

'There is life beyond Wigton, you know, Sadie.'

'Not Joe.'

'He'll have to get out if he wants to get on.' Sam had said that. Ellen would murmur the sentence to herself.

'What does he want to get on for? It's been good enough for you and Sam.'

'Things change.'

Sadie did not persist, sensing that her disapproval of Joe's hypothetical abandonment of the town would upset Ellen who had

223

drifted into a world of her own in which once again she tried to begin the process of focusing on what life would be like without Joe, Joe whom she had protected throughout the war, even in the first years taking him to her bed, Joe whom she had steered unobtrusively but relentlessly, cutting down any tendency to excess, watching over him, Joe who was in and out of her daily life like her thoughts, always there, within reach, available. How would it be with him gone? She shook off the mood: maybe it would never happen and anyway, cross the bridge, as William always said, when you get to it.

'There's talk,' said Sadie, trying, hopelessly, to be cunning, 'that William's got you thinking of standing for the council.'

'Who told you that?'

'Tom-toms,' Sadie said and bared her small tobacco-stained teeth. 'Them old tom-toms.'

'What do you think?'

'You'd be bonkers.' Sadie looked at the wall-clock, the one with the rearing horse cresting it, and took another Woodbine. 'They only get moaned at, councillors. Women's worse.'

Ellen had already made up her mind against doing it, but William's suggestion was so well argued and so flattering that she wanted to give it an airing – especially with such a confidante.

'It's a chance to do something useful,' she said, toning down William's head-turning speech on public service and the public good, the dependence of the health of the community on the willingness of its stronger members to help the weaker and how this was essential to the continuing march and eventual triumph of socialism. That was too much for Ellen. But it was an appealing idea, of being someone who could be useful to people in Wigton – as she had been when teaching the girls who danced at the Carnival, especially when William told her that her experience of dealing with a range of people in the pub and the knowledge it gave her of the workings of the town meant that she had an ideal grounding. Which came out as, 'William says being in the pub's quite helpful.'

'They'll never be off your back.'

'Who?'

'We know who.' Sadie's tone was severe. 'We all know who, Ellen.'

'It would be doing something, though, wouldn't it?'

'You work hard enough as it is. You'll do more good behind the bar. Anyway, it turns their heads, being councillors. Look at that Mrs. Browne with a E on it. Tells one off on Greenacres for having too high a polish on her floor, she says, tells another off for having too much furniture, poor old Jane for making wedding cakes and selling them on council premises, not allowed. Who's she?'

'She was criticised for it,' Ellen said, 'by the council itself.'

'She still thought she could say it in the first place! It goes to their heads.'

'I hope they don't let Greenacres go back,' said Ellen. 'When we went there, right at the start, it seemed it was going to be paradise.' She laughed. 'I used to stand in the bathroom pulling the lavatory chain just to see the water go whoosh!'

'There's lavatories blocked up now,' Sadie said with a touch of it serving the tenants right for agreeing to move out of the centre of Wigton, betraying the old town for these new and fancy estates. 'There's windows warped and lino put on wet concrete.'

'I know.' Ellen was dismayed by this. It was as if she shared the blame for paradise going to seed so quickly.

'That's why people go on the council,' she said, 'to sort it out.'

'They never will,' said Sadie. She threw the stump in the fire. 'Five minutes,' she said. 'Sam should be back.'

'He said he might be a bit late. I'll open up.'

Sam was less than a hundred yards away, in another kitchen, with Mr. Kneale, checking through the questions for the Sunday Quiz. Leonard had taken Grace to the Cumberland Infirmary for a check-up. They were alone, which was perfect for Sam's purpose, one which rather embarrassed him because it seemed weak. All it amounted to was that he wanted Mr. Kneale to repeat the sentence he had uttered in such a casual way, so easy and natural about it, as if it were so ordinary, but when he had said that Joe 'might turn out to be university material', Sam had been elated: and yet. 'There's a long way to go,' Mr. Kneale had warned, 'and he's fallen away before, you remember, two or three years back. If these things happen once, they can happen again. But: there is a distinct possibility.'

Just why the idea of Joe at university moved Sam so deeply he could not, ever, fully explain. What he had to do now was to damp it down, damp it right down for fear evidence of his eagerness might raise the stakes, tilt towards imbalance, interfere. But, and this was the weakness, he just wanted to hear Mr. Kneale say it again so that he could have it confirmed before burying it. Which was why he had chosen his time with care, knowing of Grace's appointment. Yet face to face with the ageing schoolteacher, he found he had no strategy at hand to gain his end.

'This block of wood,' Mr. Kneale said, holding up a block of dark oak about the size of a building brick, 'is part of a humanly fashioned piece of timber which they found in Wedham Flow when they were digging down. At least seven thousand years old, Sam. At least. Seven thousand years ago there were men like us just a few miles away getting on with their lives, just as intelligent, not with our science but with their own knowledge. They would live where we would starve – there's no end to the past, Sam.'

He handed it over. Sam did his best with it and then handed it back.

'For somebody not born around here you take a big interest.'

'A man must cultivate his own garden, as the French philosopher said.'

'The lads on the allotments would say the same.'

'Now then, Sam. You know I respect the lads on the allotments too. But you can have both. You need both. Just as in the study of history you need your Great Minds – Toynbee, Spengler, Macaulay – but you need the local detail too and we haven't had enough of that.'

'We will by the time you finish.'

'If I ever do.'

'It must be coming on by now.'

'It isn't started, Sam. Not as a book. I've got notes. I've got outlines. I've got chapter headings. I've developed a talent for chapter headings.' He laughed at himself, affectionately. 'I've got a skeleton. I've got all those things but as a book *Wigton Men at War* has yet to get under way. It's rather depressing.' He looked keenly at Sam. 'Now where did that come from? Eh, Sam? I don't feel gloomy about it, not at all, not usually. Maybe it's this ancient piece of wood. Will anything I do last as long as this block of wood?'

Sam laughed. Mr. Kneale queried it in his glance.

'A queer sort of contest,' Sam said. 'You against an old block of wood.'

'Words,' said Mr. Kneale, 'last to come, first to go.' He put the wooden block on the kitchen table between them, reverently. Still looking at it, he said,

'Some of the lads let me see letters they had kept, letters they had received from their wives and sweethearts and families and two of the wives have shown me one or two of their husbands' letters. Very moving, Sam. And they were moved when I looked through them – I wouldn't take them out of their house, of course. They let me make a few notes – all above board. But I also thought, how soon have those words been robbed of much of their meaning, and in a few years they'll be no more than reminders – historical evidence, yes, but in a personal sense almost quaint.'

'Letters are a mixed blessing,' said Sam. 'We used to wait for them like kids. But when they came, it was always a bad day. This fellow's wife was pregnant – not by him. Another one had run off. There was a Colonel Oliphant with us used to say the war had turned out a regiment of amateur prostitutes. And there were those who got no letters. Poor sods.'

And Sam was again in Burma, in the place he most feared to be which was why a private encounter with the beavering Mr. Kneale was always a risk. Back there, far away from this house which had been his precise destination on arrival, the place which had housed his wife and son, the place he had seen behind the letters. The memories were too numerous, like a cloud made up of swarming insects. Now, as always when he feared questioning on Burma, he wanted to leave and soon found an opportunity. On the pavement outside he took out a cigarette. How stupid to go for that reassurance. How timid, having gone, not to get it. How relieved, though, that he had not exposed his need.

He wandered across to the Blackamoor. Jack Dickinson was coming up the hill, the black stetson jauntily set on the back of his head. Jack liked to think of himself as the reincarnation of the cowboy Tom Mix, spoke the American drawl, told stories of gunfights, worked for the council, born a hundred yards down from the pub, still lived with his mother.

'Howdy pardner,' he always said, 'the usual poison. Draw.'
And Sam would draw him a pint of mild.

—⚏—

'Speed!' There was utter delight in Joe's voice. Speed, who was heading for the Lion and Lamb at a smart lick, stopped, a touch reluctantly even though he too smiled. But he glanced around like someone who, merely by standing still in public, made himself too easy a target.

'Been playing football?' He glanced at Joe's bag, rather swaggeringly unzipped so that the boots and jersey and shorts could be seen.

'Rugby.'

'Still no job then?'

'On leave?'

'Out, Joe.' He looked about him. 'Booted out.'

'How was it before they booted you out?'

'Great. When do you go?'

'After my exams.'

'Go for the army, Joe.' He paused. 'Tell your dad I might not be able to get in to see him this time. I'm just up to see my mother for a day or two.'

'What do you do now?'

'As little as I can, Joe.' He grinned. 'I'm down at the docks. Some good lads.'

He was impatient to be gone. Joe knew that he did not have the resources to engage him further. What Speed did was beyond him.

'Still got those boxing gloves?'

Joe shook his head.

'See you, Joe.' And Speed was gone.

He was jarred by the encounter and instead of rushing upstairs, he went behind the bar to join Sam who told him he could take a packet of crisps. The only two customers were absorbed in the racing pages.

'How'd you come on?'

'Drew.'

'St. Andrew's has always had a good team.'

'Their ref. cheated. He was a priest, in a cassock.' Joe paused, but better it came from him than it got back. He spoke quietly. 'I nearly got sent off.' Sam waited. 'Well, this priest. He was just biased. Whenever we had a scrum near their line he said we didn't put the ball in straight. He picked us up for passing forward when we didn't. Then Richard scored a great solo try and he pulled him right back down the pitch saying there'd been a knock on and there hadn't been any such thing. Everybody knew that.'

'So?'

'I told him he was wrong. I told him he was being unfair. He stopped play and warned me. Then I said something about a priest not supposed to behave like that and that's when he nearly sent me off.'

'Did he make you apologise?'

'Yes.' Joe's answer was wrenched from him. Why should he apologise for telling the truth? He felt that, again, he had been cowardly.

'That was the best way,' said Sam. 'Sometimes it's the only way out. Even if you're in the right. You had to stay on with the team.'

Joe looked closely at him, for the briefest moment, to make sure he meant it.

'I saw Speed,' he said. 'He's just here for a day or two. He wanted me to tell you he might not get in.'

'Oh. I'd like to have seen Speed. So he might not get in.' Sam drew his conclusions, sadly.

230

'I had my dinner at St. Andrew's.'

'Your mother's off with William. And Alfrieda. Maybe we'll go along with her some day.'

'They're coming at four o'clock.' The band. For a rehearsal in the singing room in preparation for their interval appearance at the Rugby Club dance in the Drill Hall.

'I'll make sure to be out.'

'We're getting better!'

'It was the only way to go.'

'We're going to make a tape.'

'Bing Crosby, Mario Lanza,' said Sam, firmly, 'Kathleen Ferrier. They can sing.'

Joe went upstairs. He just had time to go to the Baths. The pool was never very full on a Saturday afternoon and he lolled through some lengths, lazily changing strokes, crawl, backstroke, breaststroke, the occasional flurry of butterfly, luxuriating in the buoyancy given him by this mass of clear liquid, sometimes just lying on his back, scarcely paddling his hands, just drifting, but safe, supported. He biked home the back way, over the hill which had once so terrified him, and even now, in the still-light afternoon of the northern winter, bright grey light, he felt a tremor of fear, remembered, a reminder or still there? He did not know but faced it before swooping down past the gasometer along to the old gaol, back home.

The rehearsal went well. They would meet up at the Drill Hall at eight-thirty. They would wear white shirts, dark trousers and black shoes. Malcolm's dad's microphone worked.

—ɯ—

Joe was strict about not working on Saturdays but Mr. Tillotson had told them that reading great English literature could improve their style and so *Our Mutual Friend* did not count. He was enthralled by it, hauled in, teased, angered, made to laugh aloud, indignant, almost dizzy with the concentration it brought out of him. He could see them all so clearly. They were like people he knew. He seemed to breathe in and breathe out with every character. The book took him over.

—❦—

The following Saturday, Rachel, blushing vividly, came into the pub kitchen before they went off to the dance in Carlisle. Joe's excuse, which almost wholly overlapped with truth, was that he wanted her to see the *Six-Five Special* on which they had been promised an appearance by Johnnie Ray singing 'Walking in the Rain'. Ellen asked Rachel about her mother. Sam bought her a glass of orange juice. Joe looked at the television as if he were attempting to hypnotise it.

'She's a lot like Isaac,' Ellen said. They were in bed. Joe was not yet back. 'Isaac was trouble in his time.'

'She does take after Isaac,' Sam said. 'But she's a bit like you.'

'Me?'

'Just a bit.'

Ellen smiled, in the dark.

'He can't get away from his mother,' Sam said, 'that's what it is,' and he turned to her, found her mouth and kissed her, moved closer to her.

CHAPTER TWENTY-TWO

His results in the Mock examinations were not good. No matter the received and painkilling wisdom that teachers always marked you more harshly in the February Mocks to whip you on to greater efforts for the real thing in June. No matter that all the others, save for Brenda in Latin, had not done much better. No matter that he still had four months to sort himself out. The results were not good. They would not get him the distinctions he secretly aspired to and even once or twice prayed for. They would not take him to university. Most of all they seemed such a mediocre reward for the hours he had put in. If this was all he could manage after all his timetabling and application then what did he amount to? Rachel's Mock O level results, by any comparison, were excellent.

'You should stay on at school,' he said.

'Can you imagine what he would say if I asked him that!' Rachel smiled, rather proud of the anvil certainty of her father's reaction.

'I could talk to him,' Joe said.

'I bet you would, as well.' Rachel nodded. Joe's ease with her father impressed her. As did his ease in the big kitchen, with her mother whom he was soon helping lay the table, take away the dishes, his ease with her brothers who teased him only ritually now and preferred him to 'spout on' about what he was doing at school, his ease with anyone who came and went into the farm or farmyard. She was aware too that his presence cushioned her from her father and yet unlike Joe she was made aware from time to time that Isaac was watching the boy, sizing him up, ready for him.

'Which is your strong arm?' he said. Joe would proffer his right. 'This is my weak 'un.' He put out his left. They would grip. 'Push now,' he'd say. 'Push.' And Joe would push, play the game, push as if his life depended on it and Isaac would laugh, he budged not a quiver, sometimes he would even fish out a cigarette, ask for a light, glance at Rachel who would not return his look, until one swift twist and Joe's aching arm would be levelled. But the boy just rubbed it and said, 'That's my writing arm, Mr. Wardlow. I'll give it a couple of weeks' rest before I try again. Must eat some spinach.' And Rachel would see Isaac's bare glee cloud into respectful puzzlement.

But much as he deflected his disappointment in celebrating Rachel's success, it was with his own results that he was massively more preoccupied. He had not dared make concrete the hopes raised, though obliquely, by Mr. Braddock and Mr. Kneale and even with almost inscrutable gruffness by Mr. Tillotson – but he had begun to let them buoy him up. The possibility of going on, before his National Service, to a university had become his sneaking expectation.

After these results it was: eighteen, out of school, into the army and a job. It smacked him in the face. That would be it. Two years wasted in the Sixth Form and letting everybody down. That would be the story.

All their results came in by Wednesday afternoon. On Thursday they analysed the papers in the public court of the classroom. Joe got nothing from this but a reinforcement of the inadequacy represented by the marks.

234

'It was quite a nice touch,' said Mr. Tillotson, in that bass monotone which could sound like a growl, 'to say that the main reason King Lear gave away his kingdom to his daughters was because without it there wouldn't have been a play in the first place. Quite a promising opening. But you said nothing at all to develop the point. You'd boxed yourself into a corner in paragraph one. Not to mention Holinshed's account which you can't have forgotten – Shakespeare thought he was writing a real history here – and we have to assume that, unless we can prove otherwise. And saying Cordelia was just showing off won't get you very far with the examiners. Examiners like Cordelia. If you want to be the iconoclast, Richardson, you'll have to try harder than that.'

'How did *you* think you'd done in the Unseen?' Miss Castle was inscrutable.

'O.K.' Joe was very guarded. His Latin had just scraped a pass. The confusing fact was that he had thought the Unseen a walkover. He had translated it in about five minutes and spent the next fifteen smartening up the prose.

'It was almost a hundred per cent wrong,' she said, flatly, not needing to call on any of her tools for making him squirm.

How could that be? Joe thought. It had seemed so clear. So he said nothing and tried to reveal nothing in his expression as the Latin teacher undid the test piece of Latin prose, proving without question that he had headed down the wrong path completely.

'It is a collector's item, Richardson,' she said.

Joe hoped for better from Mr. Braddock. He had achieved his highest mark – though nowhere near a distinction – and he had always felt the friendliness of Mr. Braddock to be personal as well as schoolmasterly.

'Your answers are too mechanical, Richardson. I know you've

had your laughs that I say there are always three or four reasons for this and three or four reasons for that, but that is merely a way to clarify matters. You banged them off as if they were the sole reasons, it was like watching a post being banged into the ground, one, two, three bangs, maybe a fourth, and move on. It wasn't bad. But it was too much like reading multiplication tables. Do you understand what I'm getting at?'

Not really. It was at this point on the Thursday that he felt his stomach shrink with something like the old fears which had once possessed him. Not really. He had given back to Mr. Braddock what Mr. Braddock had given to him. What else did you do? It did not matter that most of the others, as with Mr. Tillotson and Miss Castle, had also been similarly analysed. Joe could not get out of himself. He alone seemed to be hanging there, the target for these arrows of criticism. He felt it was unjust, he knew it was just, he felt he was being picked on, he knew the others were in the same boat, he felt he had failed totally, he knew he had failed only relatively, he wanted to do all the papers again, he never wanted to see an examination paper again, he should not have put A levels in his prayers, he should not have touched Rachel's bare breast, it was entirely hopeless.

'It's by no means hopeless,' said Mr. Braddock, to all of them. 'We'll get out some old examination papers. We'll start revising in earnest. The thing is to realise your full potential and none of you did that: but you can.'

Joe did not feel convinced.

Friday was a ghost day. Nobody seemed inclined to make a fresh beginning – nobody wanted another requiem for the Mocks.

'Were we a little too hard on them?' Mr. Braddock asked after lunch in the Staff Room.

'It usually works.' Mr. Tillotson spoke from behind the *Manchester Guardian*. 'It brings out their character.'

'I was harsh,' said Miss Castle, 'but fair,' and went back to her marking of the Lower Sixth.

Mr. Braddock wondered: it was difficult to get the balance right, especially, he thought, with some of them who were in uncharted waters, already adrift from their parents and their past, as he saw it, more than usually reliant on those who had encouraged them to slip their moorings. He packed his pipe with abstracted emphasis. Miss Castle moved to another part of the room and opened the window. Richardson had been extremely nervous. He would go further and say that the boy had got himself into a funk. It was as if the whole of his life depended on this, was at risk from this. There was an almost comical aspect. He had declared he would wear a different-coloured pullover for every exam, even though he had to borrow from his father and, so Mr. Braddock understood, one of the men who helped in the pub. He had seen that sort of funk with junior air crew. Mr. Braddock thought he might ask Richardson to baby-sit.

Joe did not reveal his results to Sam and Ellen. They knew he had been taking exams although, become increasingly dependent on fetishes and superstition, Joe had asked them not to mention them, certainly not to wish him good luck: that worst of all.

He felt ashamed. There was a game on Saturday and the Sports teacher told him he had played quite well, which was odd because his mind was not on it; odd, too, that he was not as pleased as he would have expected. Nor did a swim change his mood. Even the usual Saturday evening zoom around the town with Alan and the pink football results edition did not lift spirits which had been cowed by this disheartening appraisal by the outside world. What he had thought he was and more importantly might become, those waves of possibilities cultivated in the dreams of solitary study, hit the rocks.

Rachel was genuinely surprised that she had done so well and slyly pleased that some others, especially teachers, were just as surprised. 'It must be you,' she said to Joe, on their way to the dance. 'It must have been your notes, and what you said. My notes were terrible.' She snuggled against him, in the train on the way to Carlisle, in front of the others in the gang, unusually.

And as the evening developed, it was Rachel who took the initiative, suggesting – invariably his restless call – that they go early, leave the multi-coloured County Ballroom and the fifteen-piece orchestra, walk into the sandstone Victorian magnificence of Carlisle Central Station, sit on their local train already in its local dock, dark, open, find a corner seat, the orange lights from the station platform the only warmth on this winter night. They kept on their coats which provided cover anyway, and being Saturday he could put his hand inside her brassiere and nurse the soft bare breast. She even let him go to the top of her leg, across the top of her stockings, and stroke her there tentatively, hushed, until she moaned, he did not know why, but it excited him immeasurably.

It was a brilliantly clear night as he cycled back from her village and he did not go flat out. If the old fears were going to come, they would, he thought, however fast he pedalled. A rush of stars across the sky. He had been supposed to learn about stars in the Scouts but never got round to it. His mother, one night when they had been coming back from a social, had pointed out the stars and told him that in the war she used to look for the Warrior. He thought about Rachel and what they had done and felt brim full of a feeling something like happiness, but stronger.

The old town was all but dark. Three thrifty street lights were all the illumination and they would switch off at 1 a.m. He dawdled past the Fountain, past the arches leading down old lanes, past gap-toothed alleyways and yards even now inhabited. His bike and his breath seemed the only sound.

He would get up early for first communion, he decided. That would be his routine. He would never again pray to do well in exams. He would draw up a new schedule and spend more time 'reading around' as Mr. Braddock had advised him. He would add an extra hour to weekdays and two to Sundays. Saturdays had still to be kept free: long ago Mr. Kneale had drilled into him that one day a week was needed for recreation, whether it was the Lord's Day or not, Genesis knew what it was talking about, he said. He would underline everything important in red once, very important twice, to learn by heart three times. As he was likely to be very bad on his Latin Unseen, to compensate he would set out to memorise the translation of key passages from Cicero and *The Aeneid*. That bit on Rumour for instance he bet would come up: 'Fama Malum qua non aliud velocius ullum.' He would always use the Parker pen his parents had bought him for his sixteenth birthday and not alternate with the flashier article which had come earlier from Colin. He would not listen to music while writing English essays.

The black boy, the Blackamoor, on the stained glass in the internal door used to frighten him. He butted the door open with his bike and glanced at him without even a whisper of fear. He had got through that.

As he walked up the stairs he was possessed by sensations and thoughts of Rachel and himself alone on the empty train, the smell and sound, the touch of her and her face, eyes tight closed, pale, strained, lit so faintly by the orange station lamps, and that moaning sigh, the surge of it. Joe was consumed by a fierce feeling of the two of them.

CHAPTER TWENTY-THREE

On the last Saturday of the Easter holidays they biked to Bassenthwaite Lake. There was a boating station on the west side, Joe remembered it from a choir trip. He remembered a very small bay, high slate rocks giving it shape, old trees, beeches, oaks, densely clustered, lending it a seductive feel of secrecy. They had sandwiches for the day which was kind enough, cloudy but high, warm as they pedalled their heavy bikes the dozen or so miles up into the fells. Once or twice it was too steep and they had to give in and push the bikes. Cumberland Gap, Joe sang, fifteen miles to the Cumberland Gap. The group had just added it to their repertoire, along with 'All Shook Up' and 'The Girl Can't Help It'.

They felt they had the narrow roads to themselves, a few cyclists, fewer cars, the one major hold-up when a herd of milkers walked with majestic udder-swinging slowness in front of them back to their farm. There was a growing quietness about the place they were about to enter, Joe noticed, and grandeur, the hills rising up before them as finally they pushed themselves up into the mountains, waters and forests of the Lake District.

At half term Mr. Tillotson had taken Upper Sixth English to Newcastle to see extracts from Shakespeare's plays. On the way they had gone to Durham Cathedral. It was late afternoon when they climbed the steep twisting street whose quaintness and sense of past wholly enveloped Joe. Yet when they breasted the hill and came on the Cathedral across College Green, his feelings, his imagination soared in an attempt to match, to meet the mighty, dour magnificence of the Cathedral, so massed and solid, a building to withstand time. But there was more. Inside that mass was a space vastly captured by a weight of stone, columned, steep arched, tapered, squared, such an unlikely earth-locked material for the creation of this lofty ethereal effect that the boy's spirits were humbled, deference came on him, an amazed piety. This was a proper space for God, he thought.

Their bicycled entrance into the Lake District was like that: the sense of a hallowed place, a feeling of omnipotence, of a soul set free, coupled with an equally strong feeling of insignificance, yet an insignificance somehow glorified because you had become part of the world at its most inspired, and that was good.

They freewheeled down from Castle Inn, Bassenthwaite Lake on their left, the clouds breaking up, some blue, the wind sweeping back Rachel's hair, pressing the blouse and skirt against her body, all but immobile on the marvellous machines which took them as fast as a galloping horse.

He wanted to get a boat, go out onto the lake. He wanted to go into that dense wood and lie down with Rachel. He wanted at least to kiss her and press himself against her, best with her leaning against a tree. He wanted to unbutton the blouse and in a place of utter privacy and disturbing silence. He wanted to forget everything he had planned to do. His thoughts rioted in sexual fantasy. The spiritual exaltation of the Cathedral arrival was metamorphosed into young lust, glory into the itch of desire.

Joe believed that what he felt was wholly new. Surely this feeling

241

had never been experienced before. There had never been anyone possessed as he was. He had read about it. He had seen it on the screen. He had, a few times, thought that he had been caught up in it. But nothing like this. Nobody had told him about this – urgency, this saturation of desire. Or if they had told him he had not been listening. Perhaps you could only listen when you already knew about it, and the only way to know about it was to drown in it. It was a feeling which was as deep inside him as the circulation of his blood.

He looked, jealously, as the brawny young boatman helped Rachel board the long Edwardian rowing boat with unnecessary fuss and felt superior – clearly the boatman did not know anything about this, this elevated life composed of flesh and feeling and something rarer, something inexplicable, more than flesh, more than feeling. Nor did anyone else on the lake, he was sure, as over-effortfully he pulled the heavy oars in their rather insecure rowlocks, lifting himself out of his seat as he rowed, guiding the boat away from the eye-stroking young boatman.

Rachel lowered her left hand into the water.

'Freezing,' she said.

The word threatened Joe's strained and heightened mood. He wanted to sustain the mood. He wanted to articulate it. He wanted to be a match for it. Poetry, he thought, would do it. He jumped in, rather breathlessly, his rowing unpractised and far too violent.

'Shall I compare thee to a summer's day?

Thou art more lovely and more temperate:

Rough winds do shake the darling buds of May,

And summer's lease hath all too short a date . . .'

But he faltered. Rachel had first looked startled, then attempted to assume her forced-to-listen-in-school face, then she laughed, not cruelly, not loudly, it may have been a laugh of affectionate under-

242

standing, an embarrassed, flattered laugh, but Joe, high on his euphoric mountain, was too distant to make such distinctions and the laugh sounded like an almost polite way of saying, 'Oh do shut up!' He did.

'What did you stop for?'

'It sounded soft,' he said, though he thought it sounded wonderful.

'It sounded great!' Rachel said. 'You're good at Wordsworth . . .'

Joe knew he should let that pass.

'It's Shakespeare,' he said.

'And you want me to stay on at school?' She laughed.

'Wordsworth most likely walked around here,' said Joe, gamely, using talk as an excuse to rest on his oars. 'He walked everywhere. He used to make up his poetry while he walked. He used to recite it out loud.'

'He was lucky not to be locked up.'

'He thought you could learn most about life just by letting yourself listen, well, not quite listen, listening's the wrong word, he thought you could learn about life just by walking – around here, especially in isolated places.'

'Learn what?'

'All about moral evil and good, for instance.'

Rachel nodded rather earnestly but Joe could tell her heart was not in it. Yet he wanted her to understand because, at this moment, he knew that Wordsworth was right. The difficulty was to find a way to tell Rachel.

'I don't understand all that.' Rachel smiled, leaned back and closed her eyes and Joe urgently remembered the holy, tense look on her face in the orange light in the train when he had stroked her. 'You're getting quite good at Little Richard,' she murmured.

243

He picked up the oars. He had seen his destination. There was a copse fringing the lake and beyond it, alone in a wide field, was a small white church. He kept glancing over his shoulder, taking his course from that. He was on fire with longing for Rachel.

She wanted to paddle in the lake and he skimmed stones while she stood, water up to her knees, skirt tucked up, arms folded, face aimed at the sun, unscreened at last. Joe had taken off his shoes and socks to pull in the boat. He rolled up his trousers and joined her. She glanced at him.

'Why don't you take your trousers off?' she said. 'Nobody'll see.'

Nobody would. The few rowing boats on the lake seemed miles away. They had landed on a spot which felt as remote as Robinson Crusoe's island.

'I didn't bring any swimming trunks,' he said.

'Neither did I.' Rachel waded back to the shore, slipped off her skirt, revealing stout white knickers, and her blouse revealing an equally stout white bra. Then she waded back in, her smile a challenge. Joe kept his trousers on.

'It's no different from a bathing costume,' she said, 'save for being three times bigger than a bikini.'

But a bikini was a bathing costume. Her underwear, that hidden first covering, was altogether and disturbingly different. A bikini was meant to be like that and for outdoors. What Rachel was wearing was not meant to be seen by anyone but her: and perhaps him. And it was for their new world, not for standing in the shallows of a lake for everyone to see. Her slim white body, whitely clad, looked across the steel white-flecked lake up to the white-grey clouds. The way she looked, Joe thought, was what started off love poetry. He stood a step or two behind her. The poetry went away. What he wanted, more than anything, was to walk into the dark copse and find a place to lie down together.

'I'm famished,' she said. 'I hope that flask works.'

They opened up their picnic. Between them they had sandwiches – egg, tomato, ham, corned beef; sweet biscuits; a chunk of cheddar cheese; cold sausages; pickled onions; boiled eggs; fruit cake, gingerbread; apples; a bar of milk chocolate; crisps; lemonade; tea in a flask.

'We should have brought the Five Thousand,' Rachel said, but they ate a surprising amount of it. After they had tidied everything up, Rachel produced a pack of ten Players. There were seven left, Joe noted. She smoked much more expertly and pleasurably than he. Joe liked the idea of a cigarette, of holding it, lighting it, echoing poses and gestures of his screen heroes. He was not keen on the taste. He would just have to smoke a bit more, Rachel said, then he would get used to it.

Joe simply could not harness together the two drives within him. So much of him was ecstatically entrapped in this sound of joy, to which he was unable to give words, it was like the best music in his head, it was what he felt for Rachel, it was singing, all the good things in his life crammed into this sound, a harmony of everything, as if everything he ever needed to know of why he was there was being played inside him now in this spot on this day.

Yet, and at the same time, alongside this, all he wanted to do was make love to Rachel. Surely the one feeling, the higher feeling, should drive out the lower, he thought. But no. His fantasies were torrid, and soaked in guilt and shame, which just spurred them on. He had to look away because he knew he looked at her so hungrily direct. The long black hair framing the face, he wanted to push it back, to kiss the face, to stroke the soft cheeks, the strong nose, see the crooked smile. Her white skin made his fingers tingle to touch. He was growing more certain that he could tell what she felt but could she not tell what he felt now? How could she eat a boiled egg so calmly when they had the perfect conditions to embark on the first real love affair in history? Again he thought – surely nobody ever before had felt like this. He shivered a little although it was not cold and tried to call up the greater harmonies as she took her time over the gingerbread.

Joe remembered being told that they once made sacrifices in Bassenthwaite Lake. It used to be a place for druids and magic before the Romans came. He decided to keep this to himself. He could not predict how Rachel would take it.

It was not easy to find a place which was comfortable. The copse was cluttered with undergrowth, fallen branches, roots rearing out of the ground, rock barely under the turf. Rachel went back for her skirt, Joe offered his shirt and the two inadequate garments served as a groundsheet.

Rachel was very loving. On Saturdays he could touch her breasts, but today she also let him touch elsewhere as she had in the train, even though neither bra nor knickers were removed. They said nothing. She held and stroked him passionately until he was spun once again into that high, intoxicated state of acute joy, a state which consumed everything into nothing and yet filled and fulfilled him.

They heard the dog bark but broke free of each other only when it was on them. It shivered beside them, a big, golden, labrador puppy, long pink tongue slung out of a corner of its mouth, legs square planted, lunging and retreating, half wanting to play, half ready to run.

Rachel reached out to it, instantly re-directed.

'Hello! Hello! What's your name, then, eh? Aren't you lovely, aren't you?'

The dog barked happily. Joe resentfully sat and watched. Rachel was very taken with it, stroking it, nuzzling her face against its face, then pulling back as the tongue flopped over her cheeks.

246

The owner was there almost before they knew it. He was wearing wellingtons, corduroy trousers, an old sports jacket and a checked cap. He carried a gun. He was exceptionally tall. Rachel felt naked but did not know what to do: she had nothing to cover up and to do so would have been silly, but he looked down on her with a seigneurial flirty expression which she did not like at all. She drew up her knees to her chin and clamped her arms around them.

'Sorry about that. Here! Brute!' The accent was above that of Mr. Braddock, Joe reckoned, even above that of the vicar. He wished he would go away. He still felt rather dizzy. Rachel was alert.

'Private land,' he said. 'Not to worry. Don't want you mistaken for a pair of rabbits, that's all.' He glanced at his gun. 'Enjoy yourselves. Carry on. Brute! Heel!'

They crashed away.

Rachel put on her skirt.

As he rowed back across the lake they were rather subdued. Joe had wanted to go and look at the small church – it would somehow absolve him – but Rachel had said no, it was on private land, it probably belonged to that man and she did not want to see him again. They were still subdued as they pedalled back alongside the lake, but when they came to Bothel, with the Solway Plain beneath them, and seven or eight miles of downhill swooping ahead of them, their natural mood broke through and they raced in top gear even pedalling down the hills, laughing at the speed of it, already crystallising the good that had come from the day and knowing there would be more, more days, more together, more love, though the word was too big for either of them to have spoken it yet.

—⁓—

He reserved Sundays for the scholarship papers. Despite their mediocre marks, Brenda and Joe had been entered for scholarship exams in English and History, which were 'more advanced than A levels' as Mr. Tillotson put it, drily. The work involved an enhancement of their regular syllabus. 'Take more risks,' said Mr. Braddock. 'Just enjoy yourselves,' said Mr. Tillotson, 'it's a bonus.' Brenda had also been entered for Latin S level.

Sunday was eight o'clock communion. Then breakfast. About half an hour to get through the few jobs now required of him. Back in the empty parlour before ten to start at ten on the dot and work in fifty-minute stretches until one o'clock. The fifty minutes were strictly kept – he had read that the British Army marched for fifty minutes and rested for ten, which enabled them to march all day. Even if he were 'reading around', he would stop, mooch around, go down to the kitchen to get a cup of tea or deal with the business of the band.

The arrangements always landed on him. They had been offered an interval spot at Abbeytown, a village six miles away. But it was on a Friday, a work night. Yet they needed to do it. Joe found it hard enough to keep the band together – they had only been asked to play in public twice in the last three months – and if they did not go they would lose heart. But Friday was English. When it got noisy downstairs on Fridays he went across to his Aunt Grace's house for the last two or three hours: English was the most portable subject, he had found. He knew that if you broke a rule once, it was fatal. But Abbeytown dances drew the crowds. Could he break his Saturday rule and work three hours on the Saturday afternoon to compensate?

He deferred the decision as the ten minutes were up and went back to reading *The Prince*. It could be useful three times over, Mr. Braddock had said: once for the Scholarship Paper – power was a regular question and Machiavelli was a primary source. Again for the

History A level – for the influence of the philosopher on crucial ideas of sovereignty and the most successful way to govern. Lastly, and least, for the General Paper all of them were required to take alongside their specialised subjects. This second time round, Machiavelli was beginning to make sense to Joe, who had struggled his first way through, stumbling over what sometimes seemed too elaborate, sometimes too obvious. It needed to be re-read, often more than once.

He kept finding sentences with which he disagreed. 'It is better to be feared than loved,' for instance. Well, was it? Jesus Christ was not feared and he had far more influence than any Prince. But best, he sensed, to keep that to himself. Best to settle for it for the exams.

He thought he saw how Henry VIII might have used it. He could write an essay on Henry VIII which would include Machiavelli's ideas on the way to organise a state. He had already written a test S level essay for Mr. Braddock comparing Machiavellian princely rule with the Welfare State: the teacher had said he was getting the hang of it. One of several bets Joe had on with himself was that Henry VIII and the state would be a question: evens were the odds. Elizabeth's foreign policy was two to one, Coke and Common Law three to one.

He had dinner at one, the simpler the better, fish fingers, chips and peas, and then half a tin of fruit drowned in condensed milk.

Two to five was English, which Mr. Tillotson suggested was best used by reading.

'Just reading?'

'Just reading, Richardson, as widely as you can, poetry most of all, try to learn some of it, examiners like quotations.' It seemed too easy to count as work and Joe felt guilty. You did your own reading in bed, at free times, between other things, whenever there was a chance. Just to sit and read whatever took your fancy and call it work made him uneasy. Mr. Tillotson had yielded and offered up a few general lines of study. Joe was on the history of the sonnet from Da Lentino and Petrarch to Milton, the Romantics and finally Wilfred Owen.

He liked sonnets. It was a partiality which, like that for classical music, was kept strictly private. He had to study sonnets in Wordsworth who was one of the set books but he liked sonnets anyway. He liked their neatness. He liked the way they rhymed so easily. He liked the punch lines. He wrote love sonnets which he knew he ought to tear up but he kept in the old cash box which used to hold a collection of foreign coins. He wrote patriotic sonnets, local sonnets and cod sonnets. It was odd that although cod sonnets were the best fun to do they were never any good at all, whereas one or two of the others were plausible fakes. 'Juvenilia,' Mr. Tillotson called them when he submitted them for the school magazine. 'But imitation is a tried and tested way to kick off. Save free verse for later, Richardson.' Over his flat northern voice came a small gravelly chuckle.

They had tea in the kitchen at five, the main meal of the day. Joe took time off until eight. Usually he went to see Rachel, even though the sabbatical possibilities for a young courting couple were very limited unless you were Chapel. Linda was Chapel, the soloist in a devoted choir. Rachel rarely went and then only to put in an hour or so. Her parents liked her to be in quite early on Sunday even though they were not religious and Rachel went along with that as did everyone else and what else was there to do except on the long light summer nights when strolling down to the Moss was the fashion. There was another fact about Sundays. On Sundays their rule was you touched nothing. Sometimes and always when it was raining, Joe would just go to the telephone box opposite the pub and talk for as long as the money held out.

At eight o'clock his options were open. He could go across to see *The Sunday Play* with Mr. Kneale and his Uncle Leonard and Aunt

Grace. Ibsen, Chekhov, Shaw, Tennessee Williams – 'All good stuff,' Mr. Tillotson said, and useful too. Or he could read whatever he had on the go: currently it was Aldous Huxley, pressed on him by William. Later he would search the air for music.

He set the alarm for seven-thirty every morning to put in half an hour's dogged memorising of Virgil and Cicero.

As long as he was working and keeping to a plan he could keep at bay the strong anxiety which threatened him. An anxiety which he feared. It was a force on its own, he thought, like Rumour in *The Aeneid*. It was close to fear. Perhaps it was fear. That he would fail. And then? There was nothing on the other side. If he failed, he fused.

The other day Mr. Tillotson had reminisced about his university days and told them of the trials of learning Anglo-Saxon. But the story of Beowulf had gripped him and he re-told it sufficiently well to his small Wigton flock for Beowulf the warrior man and Grendel the dragon monster to dig themselves into Joe's imagination. To help himself he thought that Grendel was like his fear, loping in at night looking for blood, looking for lives to end, bodies to gobble up. But Beowulf destroyed Grendel in the end. He would be Beowulf.

Yet the fear was deeper still. He had seen *The Hunchback of Notre Dame* when he was a child. Quasimodo played by Charles Laughton had so thoroughly terrified him that for weeks he could not cross the line into his bedroom without his mother as escort and she had to stay there while, using all his courage, he looked under the bed. And still further down there were those times, far less frequent now but not wholly departed, when what he was had left his body: that was waiting out there. Fear was in the roots of him.

It was Rachel, after he had said his final prayers and turned off the light, it was thoughts of Rachel which saw him through the night and might see him through the days until he faced the monster of those exams. She was his way through.

He saw Rachel standing in the lake, beyond her the shimmer of water smudged with a few boats, beyond that the steep rise of fell and then the sky to the west. Standing, white body white clad, black hair a waterfall down her back, gazing over the magical water to the abrupt rise of dark wooded hills.

CHAPTER TWENTY-FOUR

'So why would he want to do a thing like that, Mr. Hawesley?'

William did not want to be drawn. Sadie's energy always felt like an assault. He had hoped for a few minutes alone with Ellen which is why he had plumped for a Saturday afternoon when he knew Sam was away at the hound trails. Sadie, though, had been called in to help over the last hour while Ellen fitted in a hair appointment. She had stayed to clear up and enjoy being alone, the chatelaine of the pub. William's visit had spoiled that and besides she had never been easy with him, always glancing at Ellen.

'I really don't know, Sadie.' William looked at his watch. He would give it ten more minutes.

'He comes in,' she lit a cigarette from the live butt of the other, the sole charge of the pub led her to extravagant gestures, 'on one of them Sunday trips from Scotland because the pubs is closed over there and he plays the piano. Nothing wrong with that. Then he starts to tip folks who sing! One pound, two pounds, five pounds to one woman! Everybody crowds in. He tips everybody. Off they go back to Scotland full of drink. Then we get the police and they say he'd pinched all that money, but why does he give it away, Mr. Hawesley? It's all psychology, I know that – Ellen says you're very clever at talking in the car.

And I've heard you myself once or twice after closing time. So where's the psychology in that?'

Her sparely fleshed face, brown already though midsummer had not yet brought much sun, her bony nose – something of the sparrowhawk about her, William thought, black eyes fixed on the prey.

'Perhaps,' he struggled to oblige: it was his habit, it was, he thought, his duty, 'he felt so guilty at stealing it that he gave it away to get rid of the guilt.'

'So what did he pinch it for in the first place?'

'There are hundreds of explanations for that, Sadie: poverty, overwhelming desire, an illness . . .'

'There isn't hundreds of reasons, Mr. Hawesley. He was a thief. Why does he give it away, though?'

'Well, as I said, his guilt may have got the better of his greed.'

'You'll have to say that again, Mr. Hawesley.'

He did, and explained more fully. Sadie thought on it.

'I can see that,' she said, eventually. 'Guilt's the worst thing. Catholics knows all about guilt.'

She was impressed.

There was a clatter outside the kitchen door as Joe hustled downstairs on his way to the Baths.

'See you later, Alligator!' Sadie shouted.

'In a while, Crocodile!' Then the outside door slammed.

Sadie nodded, rather proudly.

'Me and Joe.' She crossed the index and middle finger of her left hand, illustrating intimacy.

'Ellen tells me he's working very hard for these exams.'

'Too hard.' Sadie tossed her stub into the empty grate. 'He's like a ghost.' She stared at William, who shifted uneasily. 'What was it . . . ?

254

His guilt got the better of his greed? That's a good one, Mr. Hawesley. I'll remember that one.'

He left after twenty minutes. Sadie lit up again to celebrate her sole sovereignty of the Blackamoor.

—ᵕᵕ—

In the small café of the Spotted Cow, Ellen waited for Annie to relax. Ellen had sought her out in the Victoria Arms where she worked as a cleaner and general 'swiller-out' – in her own phrase. With some difficulty she had persuaded her to come to the Spotted Cow for a cup of tea. Though this was as casual and homely as could be, a stopover for those catching a bus or taking a break in shopping, it was, for Annie, an ordeal. Annie had never eaten out. Other people did that. Nothing she was wearing was good enough. Nothing looked right. Everybody else looked right whatever they had on. But Annie did not want to invite Ellen to her damp and meagre basement in Water Street and Ellen was too good to refuse.

So it was the Spotted Cow. A small room beside the ice-cream counter and milk shop. Half a dozen wooden tables and wooden chairs. Squared lino. Just a cup of tea. No sandwich and certainly no cake. One cup of tea. Ellen had secured a table in the corner. Without being seen to look, Annie tried to take it all in.

'Some of them come here every day,' she whispered. 'How can they afford it?'

Ellen took a sip of tea as if to encourage Annie to do likewise. Annie had always looked ill, the heavy white face, bad skin, cheaply cut hair clipped back, always a coat winter and summer, a covering. Sam had kept in touch with her after her husband's breakdown and disappearance on the tramp, and Ellen was trusted by Annie because of that. They had never sat down to talk. Ellen felt that she was putting Annie at a disadvantage by bringing her to the café but as the customers for ice-cream trickled through despite the gloomy summer day, as more people crowded in then drained away according to the timetable of the buses, and a few nodded and said hello as if being there were just a normal matter, Annie began to relax, conceded another cup of tea, took out her cigarettes, offered one to Ellen, was pleased to learn that Ellen did not smoke. 'Well,' she said, 'I never knew that.' She leaned forward, to whisper, 'Speed told me you didn't drink. I think that's good in a landlady.' She puffed out a messy huff of smoke. 'There are those. It's too easy, isn't it? No names.'

'I think you should reconsider this offer of a bungalow, Annie.' Ellen, too, spoke quietly.

'What do I want with a bungalow?'

'It'll be dry, Annie, and there's a toilet inside.'

'I like where I'm at.' Her tone was grim.

'There's plenty of people you know up at Brindlefield. Those bungalows look right over towards Skiddaw. There's a bit of garden – plenty will help you with that.'

'It's too far out of the town. I've got to be in the Vic at half past seven. I'm swilling out in the pig market on Tuesdays and Thursdays. I'm just next door where I'm at now.'

Annie's point was well made. It would be a good fifteen minutes' walk to the town centre from the new bungalows and uphill all the way back.

'And you'd get soaked most days,' said Annie, seeing a chance to press home the advantage.

'I still think it would be worth it. The boys would come and give you a hand.'

'They send me something, now and then,' said Annie. 'I'm grateful for that. I wouldn't want them worrying about a bungalow.'

'They could be knocking Water Street down some time, Annie. It might be best to get a good bungalow now.'

'How could they knock Water Street down?' She was totally disbelieving. 'It's the middle of Wigton.'

'A lot of the houses have been condemned for a long time.'

'That hasn't stopped folk living in them. You used to live in that yard just off, worse than Water Street, you never took no harm.' Ellen said nothing. 'Well then.' She took a full mouthful of tea. 'It's good tea,' she said.

Ellen could not do the next things: she could not cajole, she could not utter dulcet threats. It was clear that Annie's mind was closed. So she had failed. Annie saw that Ellen had given up.

'If they put bungalows in the middle of Wigton,' she said, 'then I might surprise myself.'

'Good idea,' said Ellen. 'That's a good idea.'

'But they won't,' said Annie, and finished the tea.

Back on the street she said,

'I enjoyed that, Ellen. I thought I wouldn't but I did. Smart spot. I enjoyed it. Tell Sam hello.'

—⁂—

Sam always tried to avoid Colin. But it was inevitable that their paths crossed at hound trails where Colin had recently become one of the princes of the field, the rare article, the owner and trainer of an outstanding trail hound. On the trail field, with the ring of bookies, which boundaried the day for serious punters, it was hard to avoid the man. Colin enjoyed meeting Sam in such a public place. And when

Sam turned away from Henry Allen's board, there he was, a country suit, dog on thick glistening leash, greedily accepting nods and words of approval from the passing cognoscenti.

'Bet on mine?'

'I did.' Sam nodded at the dog. 'On the nose.'

'Poor price.'

'That's favourites for you. I took Speetghyll each way.'

'Waste of money.'

'Won't be the first time, Colin.' Sam spoke that as a closing remark, moving on.

'I've been keeping an eye on Joe.'

Sam stopped.

'They say he's swotting too hard.'

Colin flicked out the word 'swotting' as if he were flicking back his hair.

'Who's this?'

'Lads I know from the school. They tell me things. They say he'll blow up.'

Sam looked at the scowling grey summer sky for a moment. He did not want to say a word: he just wanted to step out of reach of this creature so indissolubly linked to him. Lads? 'Blow up'. 'Swotting'. Colin did not deserve an answer.

'You don't need to swot hard if the talent's there. That's what I say. You keep your cool in those situations when the heat's on. That's what I tell the dog.' He glanced down at the docile prizewinner.

'Well,' said Sam, 'I said I'd look out for Tom Johnston. Seen him?'

'Joe won't listen to me these days.'

'He's busy.'

'You should never be too busy for family, Sam, that's what I say. Isn't that right?'

'I think I've just spotted him.'

Sam side-stepped the dog and walked across the bookies' ring, out onto the open field, took out a cigarette, looked across the plain towards the sea.

Colin would be round his neck for ever.

—ɯ—

On the way back from the Baths, Joe called into his Uncle Leonard's.

'He's taken your Auntie Grace to the hospital,' Mr. Kneale said. 'Just a little scare, I think, but you can't be too careful.'

Grace's plight registered only lightly with Joe. He had known her since the dawn of knowing, her home had been his and still felt his first place. His mother fretted and was sometimes pessimistic about her. Leonard had changed. He had taken charge and at the same time become much more openly concerned about Grace. Yet the deterioration, though Joe could see it, though it moved him, did not really register for what it was. He was too full of his own life, too ripe in his own growing and getting.

'She'll survive,' Mr. Kneale said, sturdily, as he thought to cheer up the boy, 'she's an old warrior, your Auntie Grace.'

Joe made to go but now that Mr. Kneale had got him so unexpectedly alone, he wanted to say what was on his mind. It was a delicate and difficult matter, and very personal, and yet he had known Joe all the boy's life, stood in, as he liked to think, for the boy's father during the war years, and sometimes it fell to those in authority to say things which were delicate and difficult, however personal. Yet in the kitchen, the boy now taller than he was, some-thing of the animal about him, with that hair soaked from the swimming, the tremble of effort around him, the alertness, the older man felt diffident.

259

'How's the revision coming on?'

'Not so bad.'

'Mr. Braddock tells me you've improved by leaps and bounds since the Mocks.'

Joe let the compliment sink in. He would hold onto that.

'Is it all beginning to come together?'

'In a way.'

That was exactly what was happening. Patterns were emerging. The facts, revised again and again, ceased to be the object and the obstacle – they had settled in, quickly and easily available, ready to fall into one of several formations depending on the question. More than that, there was a sense of relaxation on the page; somehow he had time now to set up the essays, in English as well as History, even to play around. Latin was still a grind. Mr. Kneale had put his finger on it. It was coming together. The old Pickwickian figure, as he could now describe him, had often made the telling comment.

'It's a time of concentration, Joe,' Mr. Kneale went on. 'I've always thought that it was rather unfair of the Creator to put the young through this when they are so very confused and preoccupied by the uncomfortable changes in their biology but there it is. He does. And we have to put up with it. But,' and now there was no retreat, 'we must never let the Lower Self distract us from the higher aim.'

He had spotted Joe and Rachel in a particularly passionate embrace in a classroom doorway in the dark corridor which connected the hall to the library. Its groping intensity had alarmed him. As soon as he said 'the Lower Self', Joe blushed at that memory.

'There will be time for the Lower Self,' said the long-time widower, battling on, 'but that time is not when you are taking your A levels.'

Joe looked so sheepish that the schoolmaster stopped. 'Has Mr.

Braddock advised you to spend the first few minutes reading through the questions, all the questions?'

'He did.' Joe had not been too impressed. He thought that the sooner you found a question you could answer, the more time you would have to get on with it.

'It is crucial,' said Mr. Kneale, severely. 'I've known many who failed to do their best because they did not consider the paper As A Whole.'

That stuck. He could not wait to tell Rachel about the Lower Self. He would tell her in the train after the dance. He would make her laugh by exaggerating it. Mr. Kneale was her History teacher which would make it all the better. She liked him poking fun at the teachers, even though he felt guilty about it.

—∞—

'What did William have to say?' Sam asked after they had all gone.

'He came back about me trying for the council.' On her low stool, still drawn up to the grate though there was no fire, she yawned. 'Joe gets himself back very late on a Saturday.'

'He has to set her home. So what did you say?'

'I told him I'd think about it.'

'I thought you'd already turned it down.'

'I had. But it's hard to go against his arguments.'

'Why don't you do it, then?'

Ellen shook her head. Sam waited.

'How could I stand up there and ask people to vote for me?'

'So why don't you tell him that?'

'I will. I think he knows. I said I'd make my mind up over the weekend.'

261

'But you've already made it up.'

'Don't be difficult, Sam. It's bad enough.'

'I can't see what's bad about it.'

'Sam. Please.'

He nodded and returned to *Nineteen Eighty-Four*, a book William had brought for Joe to read. But its grip had gone.

'I was thinking today, at the trails, maybe we should get a car.'

Ellen stood up, yawned again, fully stretching. Sam smiled at the naïve baring of herself.

'What would we do with a car?'

'We needn't be so dependent, on buses, on lifts.'

'I'm off to bed.'

'You could learn to drive.'

'Me?'

'Why not?'

'I'll fall asleep on the floor if I don't get to bed.' She went to the door, paused, sought out his eyes, and said, 'I think Alfrieda's starting to get her claws into him.'

'I'll just finish this chapter.'

'You're waiting up for Joe,' she said.

'You're dead on your feet.'

He closed the book. Joe would have nothing to say.

'Just looking at you's made me tired,' he said. 'Go on up. I'll join you.'

'Will you now?'

CHAPTER TWENTY-FIVE

He was awake before the alarm clock rang but he waited until the pointer crawled up to seven, then killed it instantly. It was *The Old Curiosity Shop* now and he was uneasily addicted to the evil Quilp. He drew the curtains and looked hard across Market Hill to the Baths, to Highmoor Tower and beyond as if his look alone put them in their place. He scarcely noted the sun, the bright June sky, only a few light white clouds, promise of heat. The large illustrated edition settled comfortably against the reading stand formed by his thighs as he pillowed up against the bedhead, knees bent. Just before seven-thirty he flicked ahead to see where he could sensibly finish. By letting his mind go into the novel he could ward off other thoughts.

Then the bathroom routine. Again unvarying. And while he dressed in his bedroom, his mother prepared the unvarying breakfast. Cornflakes, poached egg on toast, tea. He would have preferred not to talk at all but he felt he could not ask for that: insisting that neither of them wished him good luck, ask how it had gone or made any reference at all to the examinations was enough. The poached egg was overdone, which he liked – you could paste the yolk onto the toast. Ellen tried not to fuss but poured him his tea which she had not done for some time.

He had filled the Parker fountain pen his parents had given him. The spare was the pen from the pen and pencil set bought him by Leonard and Grace when he had passed his eleven plus. Colin's pen would bring bad luck. The only lucky charm he took was an old tie pin given him by Sam: he put it in his inside pocket. He left the house at eight-fifteen, just got up and left, a gruff 'cheerio'. Sam came downstairs after the front door had banged.

Joe had decided that he would walk and walk a long way round. He had timed and tested the route on the Saturday but this was the first time he had ever gone to school this way. That felt good. To do something altogether new marked out the occasion. It made it special. It evaded the lulling slide of that several thousand times journey long become automatic. It had to be different. And more: this route meant he had to cross a scarred frontier.

He walked past the old gaol, local sandstone slabs built down into the darkest stretch of the river, misery coming from it even now, decades after it had been abandoned and simply refused to rot away. Along by the river between the cottages of the tenters and the sweet smell from the town gasometer and up the hill which led to the Baths, escorted each side by the sandstone walls. He stopped at the top of the hill. He had timed it so that he could spend an easy five minutes there and he stopped deliberately. Until the previous Saturday when he had done a trial run, he had never in his life dared stop on top of this small hill. Either he had been on his way to the Baths, seen the building across the field and biked down towards it as hotly as someone urgently seeking sanctuary or, coming back, he had seen the light outside the gashouse and made for it as a target of safety. To pause at all on this crest – day or night – would undoubtedly have resulted in an attack of unsustainable terror.

Now he leaned on the wall, looked across Willie Johnston's field and made himself feel calm. Below him the sandstone swimming baths: ahead of him the auction fields and auction market flanked by the sandstone grammar school and the sandstone church. He rubbed his palm on the sandstone wall. Across to his right was the tall pencil chimney of the factory and beyond that the trim Victorian station, again in that warm local stone. As he walked towards Lowmoor Road he found himself looking out for it. Out of nowhere it had become essential reassurance. He looked across Crozier's field up towards the exotic Highmoor Bell Tower, but it was the sandstone bulk of the once lordly Georgian mansion which took his eye. It was as if he needed to find and feed on this stone. It was such a subtle colour – so many shades and rusts of brown. He had not really noticed it before. As he came to the corner of Lowmoor Road he felt a lift of his spirits when he saw the sandstone run of weavers' cottages and the double-fronted sandstone mass of Flosh House, which stood by the town's third river. What power of distraction or displacement was at work he did not begin to understand but his pace slowed as he passed the sandstone cottages, known to him since his first years at his infant school, cairns which guided him back home.

And when he passed between the National School and the old Nelson School, inevitably constructed in the brown stone which had come from the quarries a few miles away, he felt as if he was being given safe conduct on the final furlong to the school, to the place of examination.

They had been excused morning assembly and as the first exam did not start until nine-thirty, Joe arrived at a school already buried in its closed classrooms. He walked in quietly and went straight to the lavatory, into a cubicle, put the seat down and sat on it. The stone had got him this far.

The truth and the certainty as the boy saw it was that if he failed in these exams the world would fall apart and he was a cast-iron certainty for failure. His life would be ruined. He would be humiliated and have to bear it like the mark of Cain. He could not remember a single fact or date. When he opened his eyes to his mind it was like opening a hive and discovering anarchy among the bees. He had to put his hands on his knees to steady himself and felt the taste of poached egg threaten the back of his throat. It was not just failure. It was the sure knowledge that when he sat down he would not be able to answer one question or write one coherent sentence. He would black out, start to shout aloud, swear, be sent out, somehow explode, collapse . . . The spring in himself had now been wound so unbearably tightly that instead of releasing it would break him. He closed his eyes the more formally to mutter an apologetic rush of last prayers, but he knew that was no way to use prayers and took deep breaths instead.

It was nine-twenty-three! They had been ordered to be there at nine-twenty. He was out, a fumbled unnecessary pee, merest dab of fingers under tap, down the corridor, nine-twenty-five! They were going in. Brenda caught his eye and smiled a quick tense smile and he smiled back, a rictus. Veronica's head was bowed, she muttered dates to herself. Arthur looked so calm it resembled a trance. The other three were already over-anxiously early at the desks. Joe put on his specs and unscrewed his pen.

The invigilator handed out neat pads and told them there were extra sheets on his desk should they be needed. The wall clock stood at nine-twenty-eight. He walked between the desks and laid down the examination papers, closed. No one was to touch them until nine-thirty. This was the first of nine papers. English History.

Joe was now in an inward scream of panic. He doubted he was even in the room. He must not let that happen.

Nine-thirty.

'You can begin,' said the invigilator.

Joe's fingers did not seem to work properly as he turned the paper over. The questions were in very small print. His eyes immediately gobbled them down and his mind registered nothing. He looked outside for a moment, across to the tennis courts and the old crofts. Then he looked at the questions again. Henry VIII and Thomas More . . . Elizabeth's foreign policy . . . Coke . . . Laud . . . the names were like a summons, the names called up what he had been taught, what he had learned. Like tribal chiefs they called up their clans. The connections began to gather and organise for action. He breathed out very heavily. It was almost a sigh.

He could tackle this.

—⁓—

'So how was he?' Sam asked, eventually.

'Very nervous,' Ellen said. 'I hardly dared say a word. He looked so white. I wish he wouldn't clash himself so much.'

Sam sipped at his second cup of tea, then drew on the cigarette.

'He's going into battle,' he said quietly. 'That's what it is.'

—⁓—

Rachel's results came through and they were good.

'Four As. Two Bs. Just one C.'

'Chemistry.' She laughed. 'I hated Chemistry.'

'History, Geography, French, English Language – As. You could easily stay on.'

She was pleased. They were walking down to the old quarries

which had been worked out some years before and had gradually built up into a tarn, with clumps of islands and marshland around the periphery, ideal for home-lashed rafts and hideaways. Called the Moss, it was nearer than the Flow but with similar advantages. Her results had arrived that Saturday morning. They had agreed that Joe would phone after dinner so that she would have time to sort herself out.

Excitement and restlessness shimmered on her. Although Joe was determined to congratulate her properly and attempt to change her mind about staying on, her unusual heightened state interfered with his purpose as he guided them towards a favoured secluded glade. She was wholly aware of this and made no resistance.

'They must be among the best results of your year.'

'I don't know about that.' Rachel tried to sound severe. It would not do to boast but she was very pleased.

'I bet the teachers will say you should stay on.'

Rachel gave her quick, shy nod. But that was enough for the moment. She looked around carefully. It was a bright day, a light grey covering of thin cloud, warm, muggy, some of the farmers were still haymaking after a rainy summer. They were next to Donaldson's land. The four brothers and their father were building up a larger holding even more successfully than Isaac although, as once or twice he pointed out, they had started from a much bigger base. They monitored and picked over their fields and they were mischievous beggars, Rachel knew that, very keen to flush her out, her and this Wigton dancer always sloping off to a quiet corner.

It was the wrong time of day for it but she was as keen as Joe now. They found their place – cool, thicketed, almost a cave, on one of the tiny islands. They did not break the Saturday rules, not even on this day, but they came close. Joe spun helplessly into a sort of ecstatic trance which took possession of every part of him, mind, body, spirit, and Rachel, he felt, fully met him there.

As they smoked their cigarette, Rachel smiled at the revving of a nearby tractor.

'We just timed it right,' she said.

'What do your dad and mam think?'

'I think they're pleased.' She drew on the cigarette delightedly. 'I think he's dumbstruck. He never thought I had any brains. Girls don't, you know, on farms.'

'That shows him then.'

'I doubt it.'

'I'll tell him how good these results are.'

'You can do that until you're blue in the face,' Rachel said, smiling still.

'You could get a better job if you stayed on. You could make more money – would that help?'

'Joe.' She stubbed out the cigarette on the turf. 'I wouldn't stay on at school for all the tea in China. We'd better move. Those lads are capable of anything.'

She stood up, buttoned up her blouse, adjusted her skirt, slipped on her shoes, clipped back her hair, and led him, head bent low, out of the cave into the bright grey light and by way of a narrow causeway back to land, back to the lane. She waved ironically at the young Donaldson reared high on his tractor who roared up behind them and grinned knowingly down on them as he stood to drive the throbbing machine as hard as he could, clattering past them, forcing them to stand aside.

'They're cheeky buggers,' Rachel said. 'It'll be all round the village by tea-time.'

Although the village did not begin for a hundred yards or so along the lane, Joe did not put his arm around her. They even walked a yard or so apart.

She led him to the bus shelter where they could sit for everyone to see, happy to be seen by everyone, thus causing no comment.

'Now look,' she said, 'it's very nice of you to go on about me staying on at school but I'm not going to.'

'Why not?'

Where did she begin? Joe was still only a boyfriend. Family was always family and the worse the more private.

'You see the best of it,' she said.

It was almost said as a complaint. Joe's ease in their kitchen company, his interest in what they did, his taking for granted they were interested in what he did, meant that they were now much kinder to Rachel and not only when he was there. Isaac looked at him as a tolerated curiosity. The boys enjoyed trying to catch him out. Her mother welcomed the Wigton gossip with which the pub so plentifully supplied him. But that, Rachel wanted to tell him, was not what it was really like. Yet how could she do that without betraying them all and revealing far more than at this stage she wanted to or could?

'Let's just say that I want to be independent. I can maybe get a job in a bank in Wigton – they came and told us there were vacancies – and I'll have my own money and so.'

'Sounds to me as if you're forcing yourself.'

'I'm not! Joe! You like school. I don't much. You like the work and that. I like the bits when we're not doing any work. You really liked doing revision, I could tell that. I hated it. If Linda hadn't been there so that we did it together I wouldn't have done it at all. Or hardly any. I'm well out of it and that's the end of it. I'm not arguing about it.'

Joe was silent for a time.

'What did Linda get?'

'She did fine. She's going on to do Domestic Science at Carlisle Tech.' Rachel laughed. 'You know what she said? She said, "When you're like me" – meaning, you know, "When you're like me you need that bit extra in the assets department!" Isn't that great? "In the assets department!" She has her eye on Michael Donaldson and she'll get him, she will, will Linda. She likes farming.' Rachel looked around at the rich alluvial landscape occupied solely by farms and their cottages. 'I don't care if I never see another farm as long as I live.'

'But you're not leaving home?'

'Not yet. We'll see how it goes. And it'll be cheap. Now I'm free they'll have to take into account some of what I do and dock it off my keep. Now if you had a word with Dad about that!'

She saw him go and waved until he disappeared. She would see him again in a few hours. She felt a great relief and peace in herself. They were going to the dance at the County in Carlisle. She felt a regular there, now, knew some of the Carlisle girls, had become friends with those in the Wigton gang too old to know properly before. Even with Brenda, though she was wary of Brenda. She did not always like the way Brenda looked at Joe.

Her mother was the only one in the kitchen. On the middle of the table there were two five-pound notes.

'One from your father,' she said, 'the other from me.'

Rachel went across and picked up both notes. The relief showed plain in her mother's face.

'I didn't expect this,' Rachel said. She looked at them. 'Thank you very much,' she said, formally.

'Your dad as well.'

'I'll thank him when he comes in,' she said. 'I'll make a point of it.'

—m—

271

'The S level was quite impressive,' said Mr. Braddock. 'It can be quite a tricky paper.'

'You'll enjoy English more than History, you know,' Mr. Tillotson said. 'Same marks. The way universities teach History is dry as dust. Spend your three years reading great literature, Richardson.'

But there was his loyalty to Mr. Braddock.

'Oh well, at least you'll be spared Anglo-Saxon.'

'I was pleasantly surprised,' Miss Castle looked on him intently, as if he had somehow pulled a fast one, 'to be frank, Richardson, I was rather taken aback.'

'On these results he'll be entitled to scholarships,' Mr. Braddock said to Sam. 'The cost to yourself will be minimal. He'll have to brush up on his French. They need Latin and one other language.'

'He said "will be",' Sam reported to Mr. Kneale. 'He seems to think it's home and dry.'

'Good odds, anyway, Sam,' said the old schoolteacher. 'But Braddock's aiming rather high.'

'My dad'll just not believe it! Staying on for even more schooling,' Rachel rolled her eyes. 'I have to be there to see his face when you tell him.'

'So he will be going away.' Ellen looked into the fireless grate as if it had delivered an ancient prophecy. 'We'll have to start to get used to living without him.'

CHAPTER TWENTY-SIX

They flew, that summer, the two of them, they just flew.

She was more free than ever she could have imagined possible.

From the moment Rachel got out of bed in the morning she could at last steer her own course. The swift acceptance of her application for a position in Martin's Bank in Wigton, the so solid-seeming terms and conditions from day one until the happy pension, with holidays all laid out as inviolable as law, had dissolved the anger which had threatened Isaac at the prospect that she might leave his dominion. It was, too, a very fair wage, he thought, for just standing there and adding up, doing nothing very much, finished by late afternoon. She agreed, which quite pleased him. She would start in mid-September and until then she would rehearse her imminent independence. It was, she told Linda, like having a bubble bath all day and every day. And there was her father's slightly altered state. He had heard that they had asked her to stay on at school. He saw she had refused. Both impressed him. He yelled at her less often and rarely with fury.

Buddenbrooks thudded in, *Death in Venice*, *Tonio Kröger*, *The Gambler*, *Resurrection*, *Women in Love*, as much of Scott Fitzgerald as he could lay hands on – Joe slab-read daily. Gorgings of literature were wolfed down ill-digested, undiscussed, half comprehended; for a time it was a need. In the permitted gentle anarchy of the last weeks of term, exams over, lessons pointless, results not in, he plunged into the empty space like a sky diver. Suddenly there was all the time in the world to listen to the circled concerts in the *Radio Times*. He discovered the Proms. He discovered Stravinsky and felt a wild sense of agitation, which he could neither explain nor share. The band found time for three lengthy rehearsals and agreed that Autumn was make or break. They adopted 'Putting on the Style' as their theme tune.

Together, though, was where the real life lay. They had never had so much time together and these last idle weeks at school were a lesson in the daily business of being in a public courtship. But after term ended, they emerged into a toxic freedom of their own. And when the results came, liberating Rachel from some anxiety and Joe from fear, all their careful young regulated love was lit to a bonfire.

They found reasons to be away together as often as they could. Day trips, spinning bicycle wheels to small coastal villages undisturbed, it seemed, for centuries, duck ponds bordering the narrow tracks, hens strutting outside farm gates, still working horses here and there, old-fashioned breeds of fat cows munching through their seven stomachs, a buttercup and daisy time of small family holdings on lush fields by empty shores which looked over the Solway Firth to its mirror image. In the dunes they found privacy easily and spent long afternoons following the tide, finding animal- and human-looking pieces of driftwood, picking sand out of sandwiches, Joe feeling obliged to swim despite the cold water, Rachel taking one quick dip and that was quite enough, the days long, the sky filling the empty landscape, and coming closer to each other as their love began to move away from school uniform.

They talked for hours but would have been hard put to recount much of it a few days on. Rachel let Joe loose on fantasies of aspirations. She could not credit that he could talk like that and she admired him for it, though some of the time she listened under sufferance and some of the time she punctuated his sentences with 'Don't be soft!' or 'I don't know what you mean,' to which, at his best, he would respond, 'Neither do I,' or 'I just wanted to say it to see what it sounded like.' These were times when Joe's talk was nougated with gobbetted bits from books and the bible and what he'd heard in debates on the radio, seen in plays on television. This cluster, unique to him in their circle, moved her and she liked him more for it because he was like nobody else. And he could make her laugh. He imitated people. He'd got her father off to a T.

'Mother! He says school's work!'

'Mother! He wants her to stop on and end up just like him!'

'That bloody bottom field. I'll tame it or I'll burn it!'

Or Mr. Tillotson, Rachel's favourite teacher.

'Watch me saying poetry without moving my lips.' The Yorkshire drawl, the gravelly cough-laugh. 'If you move your lips, sounds too soft. It sounds like prooooose.'

In this summer she began to weave their own history. Remember how they had outfoxed the Donaldsons one day and strolled up behind two of the brothers – one of them with an old pair of German binoculars! How one of her brothers had said, 'You only die once!' and Joe had replied 'But you were dead before you were born,' which had been the subject that evening, for maybe an hour, of the only non-family, non-farming wrangle Rachel had ever heard in their kitchen. And when they had finished the haymaking, just recently, and when she was supposed to be saying goodbye at the gate, they slipped away and climbed up to the top of the stack, just under the roof of the barn, practically eating the great sweet stink of it, sweating as the cut hay sweated, half undressed, so much, wanting so much more, when Rachel had heard the sure tread of Isaac. He had come either to seek them out – for no sexual feelings, gestures or references of any kind were tolerated at any time in front of Isaac – or just to look on his store, this barn of hay, this land hoard which would secure another good winter. They had breathed so softly Joe wondered whether he was breathing at all. Isaac had stayed for an eternity and then there was the bark of a short laugh. Rachel was always convinced that he knew they were there.

They talked about Linda the courier in the early days, about their madly risky embraces in school corridors, about what they had 'really' felt for each other that first time in Wigton watching *On the Waterfront*, about when they 'really' knew.

Joe became more and more entranced with Rachel, there were hours, sometimes it seemed days, when he could not take his eyes off her. He could not look at the way her shining jet hair curved across her forehead – a 'failed fringe' she called it – without a feeling of tenderness. The mane of black hair made his hand itch to hold it, plunge into it, stroke it. The eyebrows were straight and black and blackened further sometimes by a well-licked stub of pencil, perfectly, he thought, he tried to write, framing her eyes just slightly almond-shaped, big, long-lashed, deep brown in the day, darker as night came on. Her nose, which she ridiculed – 'What a blessed hooter!' – he thought was bold and to mind came the phrase in Hazlitt speaking of Coleridge's nose – 'the index of the will'. It was not a nose to peck, not the pretty small snub of the P.G. Wodehouse perfect English rose: it was strong. Thinnish lips and that crooked smile as if smiling hurt a bit or was not quite allowed in its fullest expression which is why he loved it when she laughed, when her mouth opened and the teeth showed and she laughed so loudly. Finally the skin, country-clear skin, white and peachy until the sun struck and then brown as Sadie's gypsy face. It was the touch of her though. Underneath the breasts, inside the thighs, sometimes self-consciously trailing a finger over her cheek, skin so soft it beggared silk, he thought, made satin coarse, all but melted under his tentative breath-held fingertips.

It was the summer of long bicycle rides when sometimes Rachel wore the blue shorts which she hated because they showed 'my stumpy little legs!' Stare as he did, Joe did not see stumpy little legs. True they were not exciting. That was because they were uncovered. But they were her legs. When the legs were under that new pink dress which flowed out almost like a crinoline, tented by the starched petticoat, when they were sheathed in stockings, supported on high heels, suspended, chaste, forbidden only to him, then they were exciting. Or perhaps the hidden clothing was exciting: as sex had not yet been consummated the hidden was the sex: the underwear was the sex.

It was the summer of permitted adventures together. They went youth hostelling into the Lake District for three nights and trudged from Patterdale over Kirkstone Pass with a group of students from Durham University, in whose party they were somehow included that day, Joe in his element, Rachel confirmed at the end of the day in her decision not to stay on at school even though, she protested, some of the students were 'very nice people'. The whole of the Lake District's narrow latticing of sparsely vehicled roads was on the move with rucksacks, greetings, tales of perilous ascents of Scafell and the Langdale Pikes, comparisons between the different lakes. The more learned spoke of 'high thinking and plain living', looked out for famous dons who holidayed in the Lakes, saw a landscape layered in literature and art.

277

The hostels themselves delighted Rachel, their neatness, everybody equally joining in to cook, clean, wash up, a constant feeling of freedom and privilege, she thought. Tightly bandaged emotions began to loosen among these rather diffident joking flocks of island youth plodding in the paths of genius, raking the scenery for sensation, often taking their first sore footsteps away from adolescence. She was reserved when they invoked Nature, heartily, jovially, ironically. She had been brought up with it and its meanings were different for her, its presence no great infusion into her life. But she held her tongue.

She liked the dormitories. Girls in one room, boys in another. The sense of being in an all-female team. She had never been encouraged to play hockey, although she was good at it, because the matches were on a Saturday, always, Isaac decreed, the busiest day for her mother who needed all the help she could get. Rachel enjoyed watching the way the other girls disposed of their clothes, this one over-fussy, that particularly fine-looking young woman with a cut glass accent as slatternly as a tinker, two girls talking non-stop and a bomb could have dropped, she thought, and the talk would have gone on, and she overheard some of it, they talked about nothing but what they had done in the day. It was her first holiday not spent in the house of a relative and everything captivated her – laundry room, drying room, even the neat lists of rules. They had to be in by ten and up at seven and they were and everybody joined in, so easy a company. She one of the youngest but not made to feel it and then away to walk to the next hostel, all leaving at the same time, mostly going in different directions, goodbye, good luck, good to see you.

Rachel had never known such polite cordiality.

It was the summer of the Roman Wall and Holy Island. They hitchhiked to what became Rachel's favourite youth hostel at Once

Brewed where they stayed two nights. From here Joe led her up to the Wall where he remembered enough of Mr. Braddock's speech to convince Rachel. The journey to Holy Island was a haul. They left the hostel as early as they could and hitchhiked north. They had to walk across the causeway: another rule which made Rachel smile was that you could only arrive at a hostel on foot or on a bicycle. 'Even if it's pouring down?' she said. 'Even if you've twisted an ankle?' She enjoyed Joe's stiff defence of the system.

The causeway was under water but they waited and picnicked and finally walked across to the half-time island of Lindisfarne, Holy Island – a place, Joe vaguely knew, of learning and spirituality. He was disappointed. He had been to the Island of Iona with the Scouts and there the dramatic setting, the atmosphere, which wrapped around him the moment he landed, the Christian presence and scholarship of the place had swallowed him whole. He had hoped for the same here. He wanted Rachel to feel what he had felt on Iona. Instead, his disappointment fed her low enthusiasm and he could tell that she was not interested. Even when he tried to do a Mr. Braddock on the site of the ruined mediaeval church, mistakenly believing it was the site of the Celtic saints, her reaction was merely good mannered, her attention wandering as if it were a lesson. But her attention was not caught wherever it wandered: a little castle at the far end of the island which she bet Joe would suggest they walked over to; a few boats beached below the church; a higgledy-piggledy little village with no shops of interest. After that, marram grass.

Yet it was she who insisted on how much she enjoyed it once they were safely back on the road, thumbs cocked for a sympathetic driver. She would not have got to any of those places without Joe, she knew that. She would be stuck within a stroll of the farm. And Joe tried so hard. He made her laugh sometimes he tried so hard. But he tried for her. To please her. To show off to her. To entertain her. She could not think of any of the others who would do that. Most of her girl friends reported that their boyfriends said nothing most of the time. Jennie claimed that Richard could be more or less silent for hours.

It was the summer when they finally made love. Not in the woods leading to the spectacular cliff drop of Lodore Falls, as Joe had wished and manoeuvred for; not in that remote milecastle beyond House-steads which he had aimed for so resolutely; not in the marram grass on Holy Island which was so tempting but would have been doubly a sin, somehow; not even in the ancient traditional invitation of the barn.

They had been to the dance at Carlisle and clung to each other in all the slow dances, often merely swaying. The train had been a torment. Aunt Claire, at whose house Rachel left her bike, was as usual in bed. 'Sound as a top,' she said, but they were always welcome to make a cup of tea before they set off for Rachel's house.

They lay on the floor. There was just enough space between the two armchairs and the table. It was all very quick. Both were afraid to speak, afraid almost to breathe in case the sound alerted Claire. Rachel took off her knickers, put them in her handbag and snapped the clasp. Joe unbuttoned but did not take off his trousers. Be careful. Yes. Rachel tugged a cushion off the nearest armchair and put it under her head.

He went into her. His excitement was challenged by intense nervousness. Careful. He had to push. She put her fist in her mouth but only for a moment and even then she nodded. He was there. Yes. There was such a sweet sting about it. It was so strange being inside her body, one, deep inside her now as he thought, her flesh tight around him. It was fantastic! He began to move and she opened her eyes and whispered again, careful. He moved harder. Yes! Her lips parted, he too felt his mouth strain to open. Suddenly she heaved him off. Startled, he spilled over her and flopped on top of her quite unable at first to separate in any way the whirling of colours, sensations, a maelstrom of sensations only slowly cooling to thoughts.

So at last, Rachel thought. That was it at last. It hurt but it was done, she thought, and it would be better now that it had happened.

Rachel leaned forward, put an arm around his neck and kissed him lingeringly on the cheek. 'I do love you,' she whispered. Awkwardly he returned the embrace. Such thoughts as he could muster were hard to shape: the blinding fact and bewildered joy of it: the distant rumble of punishment for sin, the anxious consequences of sex.

'Time to go,' she said, gave him a final peck, and was on her feet.

CHAPTER TWENTY-SEVEN

It was as if, sword still in hand, he had slain the dragon and turned the corner only to find himself confronted by a cliff, sheer, unscalable, no holds to be seen: Oxford University.

Oxford University was so foreign, so remote a place. Like all boys who played rugby union, from the richest English public schools to the most modest grammar schools, the Varsity Game, where Oxford took on Cambridge, was as essential as an International, though from a better haughtier Corinthian age. And though the twin citadels of scholarship were seen across a chasm of class as wide as a continent, and set on a moated peak of widely unbegrudged privilege, the British public still followed intently their simple annual rowing race on the Thames. Oxford was the academic cousin of Camelot, it was in the constellation of courts, protector and purveyor of rulers in the Government and the Empire. When informed it was Oxford he was being entered for, Joe could merely repeat the word itself: 'Oxford?'

After close consideration it had been decided not to enter Brenda. Her Latin A level mark had been excellent but the others not quite as good as they could have hoped for. No sooner was the hint given than Brenda turned it to advantage by announcing that as her father and his father had gone to Edinburgh University it was on

Edinburgh she would set her sights, tradition being paramount in these matters. Joe felt put down.

But not too much. Oxford was a fight worth taking on. He did not have long. The exams would be on him in October. Five weeks. After discussion with Mr. Braddock he had the plan. Latin was to be kept up. French was to be crammed. History of the S level variety was to be further groomed. He set about it.

Mr. Braddock was an Oxford man and it was to his old college, Wadham, that Joe was to apply. Mr. Braddock told him much that was enticing and daunting about Wadham and about Oxford and Oxford Men. He loaned him his lovingly thumbed copies of Evelyn Waugh's *Decline and Fall* and *Brideshead Revisited*. Mr. Tillotson advised him to read *Jude the Obscure*. Miss Castle at last worked without sarcasm to take the curse off Latin Unseens.

Joe told his father and mother he had no chance and did not want to talk about it.

He left early on the Monday morning. Rachel came to the station to see him off. She was to start at the bank the following week.

On Mr. Braddock's recommendation he had been reading *The Times* and the *Spectator* to help put him in shape for The Interview. For however well he might do in the written work it was, Mr. Braddock assured him, only in the alchemy of The Interview with The Dons themselves that the true Oxford Man could be discovered. He was also reading *On the Road* – that would be the life! – and his head pulsed excitedly with its transatlantic, free, druggie, rolling life, free-flowing prose. What a sound! But he must not sound like that in the exams and especially not in The Interview. He took *Barchester Towers* for that. Mr. Tillotson said it was about right for Oxford.

—⁓—

On Saturdays they would carry up the beer before breakfast. Joe now brought up two crates at a time. He wiped the bottles and put them in the usual military formation on the shelves while Sam cleaned out the pumps, replenished the cigarettes, tidied up the glasses. The bar was extremely narrow but they did not get in each other's way. Ellen called them when breakfast was on the table, always boiled eggs and toast on Saturdays for some reason or for no reason at all, but it was always boiled eggs.

The letter was next to Joe's plate. In the top left-hand corner, it read 'Wadham College, Oxford'. His breath seemed to evaporate inside him. He forced himself to pour a cup of tea, put in the milk, put in the sugar. Sam was staring at the sports pages. There was no telling whether he was reading. Ellen had gone out to join Sadie in a two-handed assault on the singing room.

Joe slit open the letter. It was two short paragraphs. He read it two or three times and a smile grew from way inside him, finally breaking onto his face. He handed the letter over to Sam. Sam read it as Joe had read it, intently, several times. Then he looked up, a touch bemused. The boy's face was now a beacon of grin. Sam gave that quiet smile, shook his head and half rose so that his hand extended across the table.

'Well done,' he said. It occurred to Joe, some time later, that this was probably the first time he had shaken his father's hand. 'Well done.' Sam looked at the letter again, then handed it back.

'Will you tell your mother?'

'Rather you did,' said Joe. To tell her in the mood which had seized him would be showing off. He was bursting to show off. But she would not have that. 'You do it.'

The boy put the letter back in its envelope. He would go up to the bank and find a way to slip it to Rachel.

There was such an unaccustomed shyness in Sam's tone. 'Can I have another glance?'

The letter was passed back.

'Off up street?' Sam asked. Joe gave the most fractional nod he was capable of.

'Say something as you go out,' said Sam. 'Something like "Dad's got a bit of news for you." That'll do. She'll feel left out if not. She'll know anyway, as soon as you say it.' He looked up at the boy, mad to go, scarcely able to bear the spot he was standing on.

Ellen came in as soon as Joe had banged the front door behind him. She was excited, apprehensive, proud, fearful of seeming too proud, not quite knowing what to do about this alien news.

Sadie said, 'I'd've put money on it.'

Sam went about his work rather more quickly and quietly than usual. He wanted to talk to somebody. Just chew it over, for himself more than anything else, just sit and talk, let it sink in. There was a man he'd known well in Burma, Alex, a schoolteacher with whom he had set off for Australia. Alex would have fitted the bill. Leonard, Grace, Mr. Kneale, Tom Johnston, Jack Ack, Mr. Hawesley, his own father: there were others. They would all have to be told.

It was not the telling. He wanted to seek somebody out. He called out to Ellen that he might be a few minutes late which she expected now on a Saturday morning. Unusually she called back, 'Sam?' and he waited at the door. She looked around the pub empty save for Sadie now battling with the Ladies' in the backyard, and kissed him.

As he turned into Water Street he saw himself, how many? Eleven years ago, on the corner looking on empty streets, determined, absolutely as he had thought, to emigrate the next day. He passed the yard of their first house, now boarded up for demolition, along the little world of Water Street, until he was almost on the Congregational

Church where he turned to his left and went down to the near derelict grass-moated pile of Vinegar Hill.

Diddler was unloading the cart.

'Just the man!' he said. 'This mangle, Sam. A fella helped me shift it on.'

They got it off with some effort. Diddler looked at his assortment of morning plunder with satisfaction. 'A woman down New Street,' he said. 'Wanted her wash house cleared. I was doing her a favour, she said.' His voice was full of pity that there lived in Wigton those who valued so much so little.

'I thought we might have a drink.' Sam pulled out a quarter bottle of whisky.

'Now that's a thought.'

The tinker led the way into one of the four small dwellings which all but collapsed into each other. Nothing prepared you for the kitchen in Diddler's house. The ground outside was a place of scrap, of the caravan at the ready on its blocks against the wall, the two horses, the piebald and the old nag, hobbled, eating the feed he'd forked out earlier and trying to get some purchase on the grass. Vinegar Hill was a place most people passed by quickly, some with a shudder.

The kitchen glowed. There was good china well displayed in a glass fronted mahogany cabinet. The walls were studded with fine plates. There was a ruby coloured rug on the floor, two broad and deep leather armchairs which gleamed from the polish that seemed to have been applied just that minute, nowhere more lavishly than on a long elegant walnut sideboard on which there were what looked very like silver candlesticks. His wife stood beside the blazing fire, which threw into relief the autumn darkness of the room, morning though it was.

'Hello, Sam. We don't see you so often now.'

When he had first met her, Sam had immediately been attracted by her sly lulling voice. He had always liked the shawled dark-skinned mocking look of her. And still it was there, in her full middle age. And disturbing.

'When you're in the pub trade,' she said, 'it's people paying you a visit all the time, I suppose, so there's not so much need to visit in return. Life comes in through your own door.'

'That's right.'

'Will we take some water with it?'

Diddler was holding two squat crystal tumblers.

'Half and half,' Sam said.

Almost stealthily, the shawled woman brought them a jug of water.

'I'll leave you,' she said. 'Come again, Sam.'

'Back to the old place, then, Sam.'

Diddler held out the glasses. Sam's measures were generous.

'Back to the old place.'

'You were a game little beggar.'

'You were a hero to me when I lived here.'

'A hero is it?' Diddler's mouth split wide across his face, the bare gums making it all the merrier. 'That's something, Sam. Here's to you and yours.'

'Here's to you.'

They sat in the deep armchairs across the fire and supped the whisky in silence for a while.

'It tastes good in the morning, whisky,' Diddler said. 'It tastes good any time of day, mind you, Sam, but in the morning while the stomach is still fresh, it tastes very good.'

'I thought you'd've sold the piebald long ago,' Sam said.

287

'I was made many an offer.'

'I heard.'

'You can get very fond of a horse, Sam.'

'I can understand that. A top up?'

Diddler held out his glass.

'What are we drinking to, Sam?'

'The boy. Joe.'

'I'll drink to Joe.'

He reached out and the men tapped their glasses against each other.

'He's won himself a scholarship into Oxford University.'

'Well now.'

'That's what he's done.'

'Oxford University,' Diddler said, spoken as one who was encountering these two words for the first time.

'I never imagined he'd go that far.' Sam poured himself a second and final glass and again topped up Diddler's tumbler. 'To be honest, there was a time when I thought he'd been thrown.'

'But he got back on her.'

'He got back on her.'

'To Joe.' Sam raised his glass once again.

'What about the army?'

'He doesn't have to go. They've just stopped the call up for his age group.'

'A clear field then,' said Diddler.

'I wish he'd had to go. He needs toughening up.'

'But he won the university, Sam.'

'The scholarship.'

'Wasn't that tough enough?'

Sam wanted to reach out and take the man's hand. This, he now knew, was what he had been looking for. He took his time. 'Yes,' he said, 'that was tough enough.'

He sank the whisky and it was good.

CHAPTER TWENTY-EIGHT

'Don't let it go to your head.'

'I won't.'

'Now don't! I've seen it ruin the best.'

'Yes.'

'I mean the very best.'

'Yes.'

Joe would agree with anything to get out. Colin had ambushed him in the kitchen and embarrassed him up to the room he had now made a den. Rosettes were hung on the walls in neat order. Cups and bowls and other prizes were displayed on what had originally been designed as a bookcase. Photographs of the prize-winning dog with proud owner were inescapable. Colin had urged a cigarette on Joe – a Sobranie, black paper, tipped with gold. Joe was enjoying the sight of this exotic stick between his fingers. Would Rachel smoke Sobranies? Colin wore a green three-piece tweed suit bought 'at the top of the range' from 'Redmayne's, the celebrated Wigton Tailor'. 'Take me. If I'd let it go to my head I would forget what it was that made me in the first place.' Colin coughed, hard: it was getting worse; he banged his chest with his fist. It was, Joe thought, a bit like that gorilla beating its chest on TV.

'Yes.'

'Don't just say yes! Listen. This is experience talking. The day I take training that dog for granted is the day it will start losing.'

'These are good.' Joe watched his hand wave the black cigarette. 'They're decadent.'

'They're cool, Joe. That's the expression. You should know that.'

'Like Elvis.'

'Rock 'n' Roll's crap.'

'I said crap at school the other week and Miss Castle made me apologise. She says it's a swear word.'

'I'm talking about your prospects, Joe! This is where I come into my own. I'll get you the best briefcase money can buy and I'll get you one of those rolled up umbrellas they all have.'

'Thank you.'

'Don't thank me, that's just the start. Somebody's got to take you in hand.'

How could he get out of this room?

When, eventually, Colin released him, it was into the waiting hospitality of Mr. Kneale, who ushered him up the final flight of stairs to his suite under the roof.

'It's a few minutes before six, Joe, but I think I can offer you a sherry. Sit you down. Sit you down.'

It was not easy to find a space. Mr. Kneale's notes had long ago filled up the shelf space and the broad surfaces of the good furniture he had brought with him: now they occupied most of the table and three of the chairs, leaving only one wholly free: obviously Mr. Kneale's.

'I can stand,' Joe said.

'I'll clear a chair.'

He poured out two small glasses of sherry from the great

291

decanter so admired by Grace. Then with some pottering he lifted a heap of notes from a chair, looked around in vague despair and put them on the floor. Joe sat in the vacated space.

'A formal congratulations, Joe,' Mr. Kneale said.

'Thank you.'

He sipped the sherry and tried not to wince.

'You'll get to know sherry,' Mr. Kneale said. 'That's all part of it.'

Joe took another sip. No real improvement.

'Your father's very proud of you, you know.' Joe was puzzled by this. He had seen that Sam was pleased. 'Proud' indicated a new range of reaction, altogether more resonant, more important. He would never have thought it. Now that it had been presented to him it took his thoughts clean away from the decorous and encouraging remarks of slippered and eternally present Mr. Kneale: 'proud' of him. He was proud of himself that Sam was proud of him. He could still be afraid of his father. There were still times when a look in blue eyes so much harder than his own softer blue, just as his sandy hair was a dilution of Sam's copper crop, could alarm him, just as a sudden movement of his arm could make him flinch. Something of Sam's war had trickled back through two or three men who had been in the pub now and then or met at hound trails, men who had been in Burma with him, and Joe's hazy sketch of his father's character included the certainty that his father had been tougher and braver than he could ever possibly be. Yet this man was 'proud' of him. He did not know what to make of it.

He caught up with the conversation when Mr. Kneale produced a small almost black wooden box.

'This is for you.'

Joe got up and went across for it. Mr. Kneale was too deeply wedged in his seat to rise easily.

'Thank you very much.'

It was difficult to respond with real enthusiasm to a small almost black wooden box. He returned to his seat. It was inscribed: 'J. Richardson. Wigton.'

'You can open it.'

'Oh, Thank you, Mr. Kneale!'

A slim pair of cuff-links rested on a pillow of cotton wool.

'They were given me by my father,' Mr. Kneale said. 'You should have them now.'

All Joe's shirts had buttoned sleeves.

'Thank you.'

'It's more the box,' Mr. Kneale said. 'You can use it for cuff-links and collar studs and such, but it's the box I want you to notice, Joe, as a historian. I got Mr. Wilkinson onto it.' The old man's tone grew holy. 'That box, Joe, is fashioned out of a piece of worked timber – it could be from a house – which was found preserved in the peat, in Wedham Flow, and, Joe, it is at the very least seven thousand, maybe nine thousand years old, the box that you are holding in your hands now.'

Joe stared down at it wondering how to react, waiting for the spell of its great age to be released through his willing hands.

The final call in the tall home on Market Hill was on his Aunt Grace and Uncle Leonard. It was not a good day for Grace but she had waited for him to come and see her. Joe was used now to listening to her slow hesitant talk and responding with sentences which did not demand long answers. Leonard patted him on the shoulder and shook his hand and a little tightly folded wad of paper was transferred from palm to palm. Outside, opened up, two five-pound notes. He bought drinks for Alan and the others.

There had been a photograph and a short write-up in the

Cumberland News, people in the street knew, so many of them knew Ellen, knew Sam, were customers, well done, Joe. He ducked into side alleys. School had to be endured. The headmaster announced it in Assembly and Joe was relieved that Rachel was not there.

'Well done, Richardson,' said Miss Castle. 'I still think it was a mistake not to put Brenda in but it is literally seven times more difficult for a girl. I have reason to know. I was in the same predicament.' Joe was too self-consumed to pick up the sadness in her voice.

'As long as you don't take it at its face value,' said Mr. Tillotson. 'No doubt there'll be some very interesting people there. Did you read *Jude the Obscure*?' Joe shook his head. 'Do!' The English teacher gave a rare opening of his lips, a smile. 'While there is yet time!'

He stayed behind after school to talk to Mr. Braddock. They sat across the big table in the library.

'They sent me your marks.'

He pushed them across. Joe scanned them rapidly.

'It means you wear a long gown,' said the teacher, steadying his enthusiasm. 'Commoners – I was a Commoner, most are – wear short gowns. Bum-freezers. And you might room in college for two years. And of course as a scholar you'll have to do grace with the Warden, before dinner. In Latin. Longest in Oxford.'

Two things were happening to Joe simultaneously. He was taking it all in. And it was going right over his head. It was in plain English. And it was in Sanskrit.

He rejoined the conversation when Mr. Braddock talked practical sense.

'Have you thought of what to do? Between now and next October.'

Joe shook his head.

'Tricky one. National Service was such a natural bridge. Most of the men you'll meet will have done it. Watch out for that.'

'Why, sir?'

'They won't take prisoners.'

Once again baffled: but he let it go.

'Let me make a suggestion. Give yourself another term here. Finish the rugger season. You can concentrate on that now. I know Mr. Tillotson has a play he wants to do with a whacking great part of some sort in it and only you'd have the time. Then I think you should push off, somewhere, anywhere, abroad, we'll find something, just get a perspective.'

'That sounds a decent plan, sir.'

'Meanwhile there's the Cumberland and Westmorland Old Oxonian Association's annual dinner coming up in December. I take Marigold and I would like to invite you to join us. It'll be at some hotel somewhere and I can promise you a very enjoyable evening.'

'Thank you, sir.'

Mr. Hawesley gave him R.H. Tawney's *Religion and the Rise of Capitalism* with the inscription: 'By their fruits ye shall know them. Wishing you every success at Oxford, William Hawesley, November 1957. Wigton.'

'You'll need to be togged out when you go,' Sam said. 'Your mam and me'll do that.'

Ellen had said very little. She was uncomfortable with the photograph in the newspaper. She did not want everybody to know their business. After the first day or so she became politely ruthless in shifting the conversation on swiftly should anyone bring up Joe. She looked at him very closely. It would not do if he lost himself.

CHAPTER TWENTY-NINE

'You're going up in the world,' said Isaac.

Rachel did not immediately return her father's smile. Was it an accusation, was it a compliment, was it mockery?

'She looks the part, Mother!'

Mrs. Wardlow was on her knees, pins in her mouth, marking the adjustment to the hemline of the new dress they had bought Rachel for Christmas.

'Who is it again?'

Rachel obediently muttered the name of those who would be going to Brenda's Boxing Day Party and Dance in the Kildare Hotel – once the Conservative Club, now both a residential hotel and a place where the cut above drank: it was never called a pub. Its main room was the natural reception room for cut above receptions and private parties such as this being thrown by the doctor and his wife for their daughter's annual party. Almost all the names she called out were punctuated by Isaac.

'Solicitor's son! He sends his boy away to school.'

'Auctioneer's lass!'

'Red Hall! Another that gets sent away.'

'Bank Manager! The pick of the crop, Mother. Top Johnnies.'

Her mother glanced up at Rachel and they laughed, a warm compliant laugh. For all his volume he was in a good mood.

'The high life! Which knife and fork to use, eh?'

And life had changed since Joe had got the scholarship. This party was the clearest evidence. Joe had never been invited to Brenda's parties before. But that did not stand alone. Joe had used the money given him to take her to Carlisle to see Lonnie Donegan and his skiffle group at the Lonsdale: good seats. They had been to Carlisle Pictures a few times on Fridays, Joe's excuse that you saw the best films weeks before they came to Wigton and so much was in the papers about *The Wayward Bus, Gunfight at the O.K. Corral* and *Lucky Jim*, but it was a statement, Rachel knew that, a probing of a broader life, perilously near showing off but not quite. Joe's enthusiasm for it all was catching.

Small flickerings, acknowledgements along the way. A difference. Mr. Braddock had a chat with her when he came into the bank on a Saturday morning, a dignity-enhancing adult to adult chat which she was sure would not have happened had she not been Joe's recognised girlfriend. Linda said it was a shame he was going to university because students were too poor to get married and it put the whole thing back for years.

The dress was packed very carefully into a suitcase, with the new shoes, the good handbag. She would be staying overnight at Claire's. Her mother was driving her into the town or rather letting Rachel drive: she had asked for, and to her amazement been given, driving lessons for her seventeenth birthday.

'You've never been in St. Mary's, have you?'

They were ahead of time. The Anglican church stood directly opposite the Kildare Hotel. Joe went in, found the lights and switched some of them on. Rachel felt awkward and solemn but mostly awkward. Joe's religiosity was his own business. A change came over him, she noticed. It would have been impossible not to notice. A stiffness in his walk. A dreaminess as he looked about and pointed out one or two of the features. He went into himself, where she could not nor did she want to follow. They walked side by side down the nave to the chancel steps where they stopped. Joe bowed, unobtrusively, to the cross on the altar: Rachel felt no part of this. It seemed he was saying a prayer, to himself, but still a prayer. She looked above the altar. The vicar had painted the ceiling deep blue. There were golden stars, the biggest of all hovering over the cross. Rachel tried to force back her reflection that it was a bit obvious. When they turned and walked back towards the west door, Joe put his arm around her.

'Smack on time,' Joe said as they went up the steps through the big door, up a thickly carpeted staircase which curved gracefully and into the party.

Rachel saw Jennie immediately and was reassured. She needed someone she knew well. Richard waved to them both. There was Malcolm, who was at least a familiar face, Brenda of course, and Veronica, but few others from school. Everybody save Jennie had been two years ahead of her, but it was not as bad as she had feared. There were those she did not know, a few who went to the private Quaker school on the edge of the town, three or four boys, as Isaac had forewarned, who were at local public schools. Joe seemed to know most of them. He was easy enough with everybody, even a bit cocky, she thought, but better perhaps than overawed, as she was. And part of her liked his strut.

The doctor and his wife and a few of their friends kept their distance, skilfully allowing the party to seem entirely in the hands of Brenda and her friends. Brenda's mother was eccentric, Joe thought. He would see her and another woman early every Sunday morning from Easter to September waiting for the first bus to Keswick. They were dressed in trousers and boots, big socks, old jackets, bulging haversacks. They would lean against the black railings just along from Grace and Leonard's house, smoking, off to climb mountains. There was something about them that said they didn't give a damn. Joe picked up a faint resonance and liked it and was pleased to see her.

Malcolm organised the records and apart from a little too much jazz, the music was good to dance to. Everybody joined in every dance. By the time they panted to a halt at just after ten for the buffet supper, the country dances, the excuse-mes, the ladies' choice and gentlemen's choice had thoroughly mixed them up and people whose initial expressions had put Rachel off proved perfectly friendly. She relaxed and forgot she was the youngest, the 'country cousin' as she had dubbed herself to her Aunt Claire, just there 'because of you', she had told Joe.

'I'm enjoying this,' she whispered to Jennie.

'I didn't think I would either. It's just because Richard played for England, you know.'

Rachel did know. Jennie made sure of that. Richard's triumph six months ago – not only playing for but being Captain of England Schoolboys – had roared through the county. Joe's achievement was not in the same league. Rachel knew that Jennie, once again, was making this clear, but she rather liked her for it.

They were sipping lime squash through a straw. There were bottles of light ale available for the boys but supplies were limited and demand was monitored.

It was all so posh but it was also good! Rachel brought these two observations together as she freshened up in the Ladies'. Posh was usually to be avoided. Posh made you uneasy to be there. Posh was the other side of what you were. Well, this was posh. A grand and glamorous room, big chandelier, deep armchairs with those English rose patterns all over them, a decorated ceiling, massive wine-coloured velvet curtains, down to the floor, a big buffet, everybody dressed up to the nines, accents you never heard.

'Good, isn't it?' They were dancing a slow foxtrot which allowed them to come quite close to each other though nowhere near as close as at the County Ballroom where you could really cling. She gave him that quick happy nod.

Later, 'Let's have a look at that eye.' Brenda's father put a thumb on the tiny scar. He turned to the other two men. 'This young fella was within an ace of losing that eye. Three stitches, was it? Four? Not a whimper. How old? Eight? Nine?'

Joe felt like an exhibit.

'You've done well, Joe. We're all very proud of you.'

He stood dumb.

'I always think it's a pity the best brains have to leave the county,' said the solicitor. 'Carlisle should have been given a university years ago.'

'What do you think about the future of Nuclear Power, Joe?'

Joe had no thoughts at all but he was being included and he had to.

'It's better than coal-mining,' he said.

'For the individual, undoubtedly, but what about the Nation as a whole?'

He tried to think of an answer.

'It's the future,' said the solicitor. 'It is the only way we can keep up with the Americans.'

Brenda's mother, who was on gin, made her customary intervention. Everybody who could had to do an act. Brenda kicked it off with her comic recitation. One of the public schoolboys did a funny mime of someone trying to get a piece of sticky tape off their fingers.

Two of the Quaker girls sang a medley from *The Pirates of Penzance*. Joe itched to join in. Rachel tugged at his jacket to try to keep him in the safety of the deep three seater sofa.

Malcolm, whose initial reluctance to be part of the Memphis Four (Edward had quit) had been outweighed by the pleasure he took in public performance, was taking lessons in jazz piano. He and Joe had tried to run something up once or twice, while rehearsing in the pub. There was a piano in the corner of the Kildare reception room. Malcolm needed little urging. They were cheered as they walked across.

'Bye Bye Love' was a good opener. You could just do it on chords and Malcolm managed. The song was popular. They did it as a duet. Everybody hummed along.

The applause was emboldening. 'Rock Island Line' was virtually a single chord and the applause included whoops of appreciation. Rachel beckoned him back.

They attempted 'Jailhouse Rock'. Joe got carried away with his impersonation which at first went down well – cheers, even. Joe was Elvis. He could feel everything Elvis felt. He could get right into his skin. He'd seen the film twice. He did Elvis to a T, he thought. But quite suddenly, the piano seemed to go in an entirely different direction. Malcolm panicked, hesitated, attempted a covering chord, missed, made a final effort, desperate, then stopped, leaving Joe strung out in the middle of the floor half way through the song, gyrating helplessly. He turned to Malcolm who just raised up his hands. He withered to a halt.

'I should have gone on,' he said, later, in the course of the tenth or twelfth analysis with Rachel. 'I could have gone on without him. I should have gone on without him.'

'Nobody minded. It didn't stop Brenda eyeing you.'

'Oh God!'

'Everybody'll have forgotten about it.'

'All he had to do was bang out a chord!'

'You were great till then. Everybody clapped anyway.'

'That made it worse. Oh God!'

'Brenda's mother seemed to get a good laugh out of it.'

'She did.'

'What did she say to you?'

'Nothing much.'

Brenda's mother had said, 'Quite extraordinary. And going to Oxford? You know, while you were doing all that, I had the distinct impression you weren't really English. You'd be far better off being an American.'

They had played charades for a while and then the final dances when a couple of lights were turned off and light smooching was permitted, but not by Rachel.

But on the floor in Claire's house in Church Street there was less restraint. Joe knew that the whole world was in them, a new world, never known before, as they made love in silence in front of the last glow of the fire. Outside the clouded midwinter night wrapped them round in deep erotic secrecy.

PART FOUR
OPEN COUNTRY,
1958

CHAPTER THIRTY

Joe met her after work. They biked towards her home slowly, almost wordlessly, and stopped at the convenient wood. They took the bikes into the wood itself. It was damp and Joe's usual fidgety attempts to find 'a good place' were, Rachel thought, a waste of time. Finally she said, 'This'll do,' and sat on an uncomfortable but dryish heap of stones from a long-forsaken drystone wall.

They smoked.

They had not even kissed but, Joe thought, it was too late now. 'There's nothing we can do.'

We could talk, Joe thought, talking helped, talking could unwind the fear for a few minutes, why won't she talk?

'I put it on too late,' he said.

'It's done now.'

Sometimes he was too carried away and too fumble-fingered to deal with it. And there was a phrase of Rachel's — 'It's like fiddling about with an inner tube' — which had stuck in his mind. Pausing to put the thing on interfered with what they were really doing. It was more than just reluctance: though he could not articulate it, the intervention spoiled what was essential; instinct had to be shackled.

'It's both our faults,' said Rachel, offering a small smile. 'We get carried away.'

'When do you think the stuff comes out? The real stuff, the stuff that counts?'

'I don't know.' Rachel was cornered. There was no one she could ask. There was no book she knew of which could help her. Even Linda was out of the question because even Linda could not be expected to keep this sort of information to herself.

'That first stuff's rather watery,' said Joe, hopefully.

'I've thought of that.'

'Maybe it's only, you know, when . . .'

'I know.'

'I generally get it on before then.'

'Or you don't.'

'But then I pull out.'

'But it goes everywhere,' Rachel said. 'And all over your fingers.'

'Doesn't it die off in the open air?'

'Does it?'

Although she did not want to talk about it, Rachel yielded to Joe's persistence and her resentment began to fade.

'How do you feel?' Joe's eyes narrowed as he examined her face for clues. She turned away.

'Normal.'

Which was true enough, save that Joe's questioning threatened to depress her. This was the second time. On the previous occasion she had been distressed by the fury of his anxiety, a state of uncontrol which in some way chimed with the worst furies of Isaac and set up a similar resistance in her. It was crazy that it might have happened again so soon.

'What would we do?' he said, as he had said to her on several occasions.

Rachel lit another cigarette and breathed in deeply.

'There's ways of getting rid of it. That's something I have heard about.'

Joe's throat caved dry.

'That'd be wrong.'

Rachel gave that bare flicked nod.

'Let's wait and see; it's only one day overdue.'

Maybe, Joe had thought, it would be just as well. They could get married. He would find a job in Wigton. So he need not leave Wigton. His Uncle Leonard had just the other day said, teasingly but still said, that there was always the junior clerk's job waiting. It was not, in truth, an unattractive prospect. Yet there was within this coiled frenzy of anxiety, fear, that if It happened, his world would end. Those moments of relief when in his imagination they were married and homed in Wigton and doing much as they were doing now were always bombed: it would be the end. It was unimaginable, he could not deal with this fear: it would wipe him out.

When Rachel got home she went straight to her bedroom. Her mother had guessed what was going on but said nothing, waiting to be called on. She took up a soft boiled egg and toast.

'That's kind,' Rachel said. The women looked steadily at each other.

'Anything else you want – just give a shout.'

Rachel went back to her book. She wished Joe were calmer.

—m—

'There's no need for an American accent, Richardson.'

'It's an American play, Mr. Tillotson.'

'Standard English can cope.'

'I've been practising, Mr. Tillotson.' Joe could tease the teacher now.

'Unfortunately, it shows.'

'But it won't make sense. I know it's called *Our Town* but it isn't. It's an American town.'

'It's an archetypal small town, Richardson. It's just as much English as American. It could even be Australian. As a matter of fact, I have a hunch Thornton Wilder pinched the graveyard scene from Thomas Hardy. Ideas move around, Richardson, so can places, and the same notion can address superficially different circumstances. This is a small town in America which is much like a small town in England which is one of the reasons I chose it.'

'And because it's got a big cast.'

'And because it has a big cast. May we proceed? You have a lot to learn.'

Joe hurled himself into this first rehearsal, gabbling, over-emphasising, over-dramatising, acting like mad.

'It's a quiet piece,' said Mr. Tillotson, amused, the chuckle in the gravel voice. 'It's a modest piece about a modest town, Richardson. We decided not to do *Macbeth*.'

But Joe would not be bound, not on this afternoon. He had been into the town and met Rachel in her break and they had walked up Church Street where she said,

'Good news.'

—⁓—

'Make or break?' Malcolm said.

'Make or break.' Joe nodded. Alan, miming with his saxophone, also nodded. John had gone to the lavatory.

They were the eighth on. The skiffle group competition was in Workington, a West Coast coal and steel town, about twenty miles from Wigton. Twenty-five pounds for the winners, but much more importantly a guaranteed place in the last three for BBC Television's national county versus county entertainment programme.

'There would be no stopping us then,' said Malcolm.

'Cool,' said Alan, sweating steadily. 'Cool.'

'That lot sound good,' Joe said. Only a thin wall separated the hall from the back room, the tea room, now dressing room crammed with fourteen skiffle groups.

John came back.

'I think I want to go,' said Alan.

'There's a queue. And somebody's been sick.'

'All the way from Wigton, Ladies and Gentlemen, a big hand, four young lads, the Memphis Four.'

The rule was that the first song be classic skiffle. Then they were allowed a non-skiffle but pop piece and they went for 'Houn' Dog'. Malcolm's father had put in relevant oooh-aaahs and this was far and away Alan's best shot on the saxophone. That went down well. The judges compared score cards.

'They want to see you again, lads,' the M.C. said, looking at the note. 'So don't go back to Wigton yet. Another round of applause please, Ladies and Gentlemen.'

They went outside. Across the road, towards the sea, the sky was lit up from the steel works. Joe remembered that his grandfather used to work here, in the pits, under the sea. He must have been brave, Joe thought.

Fags were lit up.

'It'll be sudden death,' Malcolm said.

'One number.'

'One number.'

'Will they want skiffle?' Alan always felt just a touch redundant in skiffle with the saxophone.

'It says skiffle competition.' Malcolm was firm.

'It didn't seem to matter when we did "Houn' Dog".'

'We could do it again,' Alan said, 'that way they could hardly complain.'

It was cold, a light drizzle coming in from the sea, across from Ireland, across from America. They knew they had to suppress any excitement: it would be bad luck to be excited.

'Lack of originality,' Joe said. 'They could get us on that.'

'"Wake Up Little Susie",' Malcolm said. 'We can make that sound skiffly.'

'That means two singers,' said Joe, the singer.

'We've done it before,' Malcolm sounded just a touch heated. 'My dad says that at least the Everly Brothers have a bit of musicality in their songs.'

But they don't have the thump, Joe thought, they just don't hit the spot like Elvis Presley. He was warmed up now. The crowd had really liked 'Houn' Dog'.

'Maybe we should just do "Houn' Dog" again,' said Joe, 'like Alan suggested. Tried and tested.'

'You were the one who went on about originality,' Malcolm said.

'I can do "Wake Up Little Susie" now,' Alan said. 'I've sorted it out since then.'

'Good,' said Malcolm. 'And it's an easy one.'

Malcolm always wanted to sing. He was all right but they all knew he was no real good. He looked too worried. They all knew but no one wanted to say.

'"Jailhouse Rock"?' said Joe, hopelessly.

'"Wake Up Little Susie"'s easier.' Malcolm felt he was on winning ground. It would be impossible for Joe to push himself forward as the soloist on such an occasion.

'We should go behind the lavatories and have a rehearsal,' Joe said.

If Malcolm thinks 'Wake Up Little Susie' is an easy one, he knows nothing.

'I can't make head or tail of it,' said Malcolm's father as he drove the silent four back in the van he had borrowed for the evening. 'That last song – beautifully rendered, I thought – nothing raucous about it at all, Malcolm and Joe blending in almost perfectly, that little stutter by Alan somehow adding to it, all round a fine performance. You came fourth. No disgrace at all. You were a credit to yourselves.'

'Wigton can never win in Workington,' Alan said bitterly. 'They'll never let us. If we had won they'd have beaten us up.'

———∽———

Rachel agreed to go youth hostelling in the Lakes at Easter with Brenda and Malcolm, but she was not keen. But Joe seemed so keen, as if he were now the host to those two better off figures, taking them into his domain. Rachel was often caught up in his enthusiasm and if she regretted it later she was fair enough to admit it was her own fault.

It was nothing like as good as when they had been on their own. Brenda had somehow to be looked after or expected to be looked after or was just a bit incompetent, Rachel could not work out which. Malcolm sort of droned on, Rachel thought, saying interesting things but somehow from him they soon lost all interest for her. Joe, on his own, could talk rubbish and she would enjoy listening. Now he seemed determined to meld in with Brenda and Malcolm. Rachel tried to squash the fear that he was trying to impress them. Why should he bother?

And it kept being complicated. There were times in the evening when she wanted to be on her own with Joe. She thought that should be obvious. Malcolm and Brenda, though, who were not going out with each other, made it clear that it would be unfriendly to leave them, even bad manners. Rachel was amazed that Joe seemed to find it so hard to walk away. They would drink two or at the most three halves in the nearest pub and either Joe would expand or Malcolm would talk about jazz or Brenda would say anything that came into her head as if that was interesting enough to impress everyone, especially Joe, she thought. Rachel was bored, an unusual state for her to be in when with Joe, and annoyed that Joe did not notice it.

Moreover, trudging from hostel to hostel in patchy weather, which had seemed such an adventure the first time with Joe, now seemed a bit senseless. They could have caught a bus and just sat about at the other end. She looked longingly at the cars – her driving test was due in a few weeks. Although she was the youngest by a couple of years, she had a faint feeling there was something childish about all this. She had only lasted a fortnight in the Girl Guides. To her surprise, one of the features of the walks which most fascinated her was not the famous mountains nor the famous lakes but the sheep, hundreds and hundreds of them, almost hanging off some of the crags, a wonder they did not fall off, she thought, and all so carefully segregated flock from flock by the net of drystone walling – the best thing, in her opinion, about the whole of the Lake District. It was not an opinion she wanted to air. She reassured Joe that everything was fine.

Two of the girls in the bank had gone to Spain for their holidays. Rachel could have gone with them and it took an effort not to regret that she had turned it down.

They met the two men at the Patterdale Youth Hostel. Ben and Victor had been to the same public school, they had just finished their National Service in the army, they too were off to university in October and this was their first time in the Lake District, their first time in the North, and the six of them ended up in the snug bar of the pleasantly old-fashioned country pub at the edge of the village.

Ben, Rachel thought, was exceptionally handsome. Tall, broad, nearly blond hair, swept back but not with Brylcreem like Joe's, the right kind of casual shirt on and the best blue jeans on a man she had ever seen. Rather surprising to see somebody with that accent wearing jeans and all the spicier for it. She knew that he liked the look of her. She noted that Brenda, even as they walked to the pub, was glancing appreciatively all over him. Malcolm, Joe and Victor were ahead, discussing politics: Victor, Ben had already told them, intended to go into politics. This announcement, she saw, had rather stunned Joe.

'So let me get this straight,' said Ben, as they sat crammed around a small oak table under heavy oak beams holding up a low ceiling just repainted white for the new season. Ben and Victor had pints. 'You, Malcolm, are going up to Durham to do Natural Sciences. You' – Brenda – 'are off to Edinburgh for Classics – sooner you than me!' The quip was taken by Brenda to be a compliment and Rachel rather squirmed at the way Brenda squirmed – Ben had that effect. 'You' – Joe – 'are up to Oxford, bravo! And you' – Rachel caught the pause, caught the softening look, maybe this whole little game had been for this moment – 'refuse to reveal your hand.'

'Nobody asked,' said Rachel, tapping her cigarette ash into the ashtray. 'I am going up to Martin's Bank in Wigton as from next Monday morning and by the look of it for the rest of my life.'

'Good on you!' said Victor, and he raised his glass.

'The only one of us,' Ben said, 'earning an honest living.'

Joe saw the way he looked at Rachel and he observed the way she took and returned the look and jealousy flash-flooded through him. The pain of it was sudden and unbearable.

'Victor's brilliant, of course,' Ben said, and the rather sallow-faced, slight-framed, five-o'clock shadowed Victor crossed his arms and shook his head vigorously. 'Oh yes you are,' Ben chided him. 'He's always been too modest,' he explained. 'But this idea of going into politics is bonkers.'

'Why's that?' Joe's question was harsh, Rachel noticed. So – she saw – did Ben.

'They're all power mad, aren't they?' said Ben. 'Bound to be. That's why they do it.'

Rachel laughed. She felt like saying, 'I agree,' but she held her tongue.

'I agree,' said Brenda, who couldn't mean it, Rachel thought. Brenda would be bound to think that politicians were to be looked up to like bank managers and doctors.

'Why are they power mad?' Joe asked.

'Because they seek power. And when they get it, they want to tell you and me what to do with our lives.'

'No they don't.' Joe's attempt to soften his tone failed. 'They pass laws which they're entitled to pass because we elect them.'

'I think Ben might be referring more to the psychology than the actuality,' Victor said.

'It's the same thing,' said Joe.

'Hardly,' Ben said.

'How isn't it, then?'

Rachel was beginning to cringe. Even Brenda looked a touch bemused at the turn of the conversation.

'I suppose we're distinguishing between the inner man and the outer man.' Ben's voice became something of a drawl. 'Internal, external: private, public: intimate and public. That sort of thing.'

'It still doesn't explain it.'

'I think,' said Victor, 'what Ben means . . .'

'I think I know what he means,' said Joe, who was very far from sure, 'but what I'm saying is what you think and what you do are bound to be connected so if somebody wants to be a politician to do good, how can that make him somebody who does it just to seek power or tell you what to do?'

'There's a point there,' Victor said to Ben.

Joe really should have left it there, he knew that, but only in that overwhelmed minority in his mind, which fought hopelessly to stave off the jealousy.

'And somebody has to have power, haven't they? Have you read Machiavelli?' Ben hesitated and then, almost truculently, shook his head. 'Well, read him if you want to know about power. Except I disagree with him because he's too general.'

'You. Disagree. With Machiavelli?'

'Yes. Because he didn't take real democracy – our democracy – into account. He couldn't. It hadn't been invented. But power in a democracy is an entirely different thing. All power tends to corrupt and absolute power tends to corrupt absolutely, I'll grant you some of that. But Lord Acton wasn't the greatest believer in democracy either.' His voice had risen: the pub was embarrassed.

Rachel blushed when Ben said, in a sarcastic tone, 'So it's Lord Acton now?'

'Yes. Because in a democracy we can kick them out. We can kick them out whenever we want. And in our democracy which is the best there is, they have to report back to their constituencies and at a pinch they can kick them out as well. So if they are seeking power – at all –

and I would dispute that – then it's a very limited sort of power, isn't it? Not the sort of power that does people real harm, not fascism.'

'Nor communism,' said Victor, seeing perhaps a way to divert this.

'Do you think they're on a par?' Joe, surprised, changed his tone.

'It's an interesting one,' Victor said. 'I happen to disagree with my friends on the Left on this one.'

'There can't be worse than fascism,' Joe said. 'How can there?'

'Tyranny takes many forms,' Victor said.

'Victor knows A LOT about politics,' said Ben, rising to his feet, 'we have an Angry Young Man here. Another round everyone?'

'I'll have a pint this time,' said Joe.

'I'll help you.' Brenda picked up the glasses Ben could not carry and went across to the bar with him, where their whispered huddle convinced Rachel that they were talking about Joe, who had suddenly lost energy and merely listened as Victor talked about Stalin. Why was Joe so jealous?

Joe kept close by Rachel as they walked back in the dark to the hostel. Brenda lingered behind with Ben. Victor and Malcolm had discovered true happiness in a shared infatuation with Charlie Parker.

'Let's go down here.' A path alongside the hostel, leading to woods.

'It's time to go in.'

'We've got seven minutes,' said Joe, and took her by the arm.

Scarcely past the gable end of the old hostel when he said, in a voice of torment,

'You fancied him.'

There was no reply. Only the dimmest light from the end of the path. The moon was not up. But he saw well enough that Rachel's

316

expression was sullen. The jealousy, though suppressed, seemed to infect his blood and press into his head, invading it.

'You did. You fancied him!'

'He's very good looking, that's all.' She was defiant.

'But I could tell.' Joe's throat tightened. 'I could see by the way you looked. And he looked.'

'Oh for goodness sake! I can look at somebody, can't I?'

No. No. No.

'I'm not your blooming slave, you know!' Rachel would not be meek. 'I'm allowed a mind of my own. Maybe I did fancy him! Maybe I did! So what?'

Joe's feelings fused. How could what was them be so easily betrayed? How could 'fancying' somebody else ever come into it? What did that mean? He felt breathless. No! A right hand leapt towards her face and stopped the merest space before the skin of her cheek. She pulled away and even in the low light he caught the fierceness of her expression, the fury, maybe hatred. The tightness in his mind broke into a confusion. Then shame. Then, seeing her face unchanged, fear. And silence.

'We'd better go back,' said Rachel, eventually, in as level a voice as she could manage.

She walked past him, rather as if sleep walking.

'I'm sorry,' he said. Ignored, he repeated, 'I'm really sorry.'

She went in ahead of him. Joe walked into the hostel as if he were a condemned man set to begin a life sentence.

—m—

'I'm not so sure it's a good idea for Richardson to stay on into the summer term, even if it is only for a month.' Miss Castle had picked her time and company carefully. Both Mr. Braddock and Mr. Tillotson liked to hog the place on Fridays.

'He's getting way above himself. He simply barged into my class yesterday as if he had all the right in the world. Of course I sent him out but that's not the point.'

'He's reading enough,' said Mr. Tillotson. 'That can't be wholly bad,' he offered the Latin teacher one of his sly smiles, 'even if it is in English. But you're probably right. You usually are.'

Miss Castle was flattered. Mr. Tillotson was not a flatterer.

'I admit he's gone off the rails once or twice.' Mr. Braddock had already charged his pipe but in his agitation made no attempt to light it. 'I admit that. But he has to have his fling, don't you think? Find his feet? Make his mistakes?'

'He's never been bad at that,' said Mr. Tillotson, and Miss Castle laughed.

'They called it Sowing Wild Oats when the young bucks did it,' said Mr. Braddock.

'Is he still with that girl?' Miss Castle put as much disapproval into 'girl' as she could possibly muster.

'Rachel Wardlow? I believe so. I thought she was rather good for him.'

'Clever girl,' said Mr. Tillotson. 'Farmers!'

'Perhaps it would have been better if he'd pushed off sooner. Still, he's going to work for the Abbé Pierre in Paris. That should help sort him out.'

'As long as his French is up to it.'

'Rather pious,' said Mr. Tillotson.

'It was his own decision,' said Mr. Braddock. He lit his pipe. Joe had behaved erratically, especially since Easter. It was a disappointment. He blew out a lungful of smoke. Miss Castle moved to the window. Eventually Mr. Braddock announced his conclusion. 'He hasn't learned how to handle free time. That's the problem.'

—◊◊◊—

It had been nearly a fortnight now. They still saw each other. They went to dances, walked, though not as much, did not now seek out their cave on the Moss. He had asked her to forgive him more than once, beginning the morning after, and she had begun by saying, 'Let's forget about it,' but so sharply that it was obvious she had not forgotten about it. Joe believed he would never forget about it as long as he lived. How could you threaten the person you loved most? Even when all the excuses were laid out – you shouldn't be able to do that. Not to Rachel. He kept asking her, not nagging, he thought, just asking, sometimes no more than two or three times a day. 'Let's forget about it' softened into 'I'll have to think about it', which, in time, became 'I think we should both forget about it'. She could not bring herself to say, 'I forgive you.'

Joe was used to being forgiven by God Himself after the general confession. Not to be forgiven by Rachel was terrible. He deserved it but it was terrible. But she would not budge in those weeks and finally she said, 'I know what you want me to say, Joe, but I'm not saying it and that's that.' Hers was a harder ancestry than the forgiving Anglicanism of Joe.

He knew he had ruined it. There was a barrier between them now – something as thin as cigarette paper but it was there. It was there when they said hello, it was there when he put his arm around her, it was there when he danced, however much he joked, however tightly he held her, it was there in the train even – she was not as keen on the train now – it was there in Claire's house and even when they made love on the floor it was there and Joe knew he had ruined it.

319

As the time came for his departure for Paris the panic began to grow. He had not been altogether keen in the first place. It was Mr. Braddock who had pushed him to a decision and the work of the Abbé Pierre with the clochards, the down-and-outs in Paris, struck both a religious and a romantic response in Joe. This would be paying back debts due to a fading God; gratitude for former feelings of religious intensity. And the Abbé Pierre was a Great Man. But who was the Abbé Pierre compared with Rachel? How could he get out of it? How could she be changed back?

On his last night she was suddenly again as warm as she had ever been. They went for a walk. The evening was soft and light and the Moss was too full of others and so they turned back and sneaked into the barn. She was loving with him again and the difference and the pain of imminent absence combined to fill him with immense love for her. It was inconceivable she would not always be in his life. His head was in her hair. He breathed her in. They were still half dressed.

'I am really sorry,' he murmured.

'I know.' She stroked his shoulder almost maternally. 'It's all right now. You didn't hit.'

'I do love you.'

'I know.'

'Always.'

'Always?'

'Yes.'

She pushed him away to look at him rather solemnly. Always. Then she kissed him as deeply as ever she had done and they stayed there as late as they dared.

CHAPTER THIRTY-ONE

Joe hitchhiked to London and took the train to Dover where he caught the ferry. By the time he got to France he felt cocooned in unaccustomed solitude. It took him some time to find his way out of Calais. He had enough money to take the train to Paris but the hitching in England had been successful enough and it did not occur to him it would be much different here. It was strange, this sense of solitariness, when there was so much around that caught his interest. But that was the balance. Now one now the other swung into the ascendancy. He decided he needed to eat and went to a small café but all he could get was bread, a long roll of bread, which was unaccustomedly delicious, and a bowl of milky coffee which again amazed him by its foreign luscious taste. He was truly abroad.

He had been abroad once before, a school trip to Holland when he was fourteen. They had been allowed to pretend to bid for tulips in the tulip market, they had seen *The Night Watch*, they had been to Haarlem and taken a trip around the canals. Water pistols had become a rage among the boys. The girls had been astonished that people left their curtains open at night so that you could see into the houses. He had spent a good deal of time buying presents and then worrying because the teacher said they had to list them all and if they came to over five pounds they would have to pay tax or have them confiscated at Customs. Some of the food had not been cooked properly.

In Holland he had been shepherded, every step. Here on the road which arrowed to Paris, he stood in the morning sun with his father's old kitbag at his feet and the haversack from the boy scouts slung over his shoulder, shyly thumbing out at the right-lane traffic. He had just read *The Outsider* and he felt every inch the isolated self-absorbed anti-hero of Camus as he thumbed without success for more than an hour. It was as if isolation were a cloak which came out of the air and wrapped itself around him.

A small van stopped and he was picked up by a merry man whose French was pickled in an accent as unintelligible as Joe's boyhood accent would have been to a French student. But the lack of communication amused the Frenchman and they passed the time wholly content in pointing out 'hedge', 'road', 'farm', 'cow', 'field' and laughing for no reason at all. Joe felt lapped in a warm bath and both of them were a touch sad when their journey ended. On the roadside he tried to smoke the yellow cigarette the man had given him and all but choked. But he had broken his duck and he waited for his next lift with some confidence, even though *The Outsider* still threatened him.

—⟋⟍—

They had said it would be 'truly international'. So it was. About two score idealistic young men from all over Western Europe had rallied to the call to help the Abbé Pierre in his mission to feed and care for the poor of Paris, those who slept unromantically under the bridges, those who dressed in rags, drank cheap, vile alcohol, were the beggars at the gate.

The young men lived in a compound, small rooms, four bunks in each. The compound was grassless and saved only by a ping-pong table. There was a shop which turned over the goods either given or politely scavenged from the richer districts by those who went out in the small trucks early in the morning. There were regular prayers in French, Roman Catholic, although other denominations were invited to join in. The intensity of the others re-ignited some of Joe's former religious passion.

It was the clochards, the down-and-outs, who destabilised him. He could not cope with his inability to cope and his distress grew by the day. The young Christian men went under the bridges of Paris to feed the clochards and Joe could get through that. Then there were those who came to the compound. They had their prayers together and that was fine. He tried to talk to a couple of them, in the shade, sat on the porches to the bunk rooms. That was worthwhile though the smell was very ripe and the language was not easy.

It was the eating that finished him. They sat down to eat together, just as Christ had brought everyone of all degrees to the table, it was said. Joe could not eat. Not so much because the food often seemed raw. The bread was always good. It was the look of the clochards. In his prayers he castigated himself and tried again in the morning but it got no better. It was the ravaged, muck-streaked, often pocked, scarred faces, the matted hair, the multiple layers of tattered clothing; everything that a true Christian ought to embrace repelled him. The more he thought about them the more fiercely his re-inflamed Christianity burned. But what sort of a Christian was he if he could not fulfil the basic duty of embracing them?

Joe did not, perhaps could not, call into the account the disturbance still felt over Rachel in the last few weeks; or the deepening strangeness of the compound secluded in an inner suburb of Paris, isolated and bare in bounty. Or his further embarrassment at the curious flight of whatever French he had known. His conversations were brief, simple and meagre. He made no friend. Even when he took his turn at the ping-pong table he felt listless, unable to absorb himself in the game, a willing loser to get it over with. He wrote a very long letter home saturated in self-pity, asking for food and ending with the sentence, 'You must not tell anybody this. I don't want anybody to know about this.' He held back from posting it, gave himself the next weekend; but it was a close run thing. He felt stranded, hoist on a religion which did not support him when he needed it. Yet it was his own fault.

He liked being with the men in the trucks in the early mornings. They went to a small café, stood at the bar, ordered a coffee and a cognac and smoked the fat, loosely filled, yellow-papered cigarettes which Joe was getting used to. He liked seeing Paris out of the window of the truck. Some of the objects they were given – chairs, ornaments, books, jewellery – seemed very fine to Joe. In those mornings he felt the beginnings of interest, inklings of an infatuation with the city. The foreignness became beguiling, the tables on the pavements, the bookstalls alongside the river, the high elegance of those who directed the handing over of their rubbish, even the funny lavatories. But his stomach would clench as they drove back for the midday meal and by the time he got into the eating room he was faced with what had become repellent.

It could not be forgiven. And he was such a disappointment to himself. Is this what years of singing and praying in St. Mary's Wigton had turned him into? Was this the best he could do? Praying did not help. The more he concentrated on himself, the more acutely he thought about Rachel. He could not trust himself to post the daily letters – too big a wad to fit into a single envelope – scribbled in lengthy desperation. And what a thing to be desperate about! 'Desperate' should be reserved for much worse than this.

—m—

On the first free Sunday he walked into the middle of Paris and discovered the Jeu de Paumes. At first it was the coolness of the gallery which most struck him. The day was hot, the streets heavy with a heat he had not previously encountered, his route had been tentative, apprehensive, in such new, even alien, territory. The feeling of *The Outsider* had descended on him like a shroud. Who was this 'he' drifting along burning pavements among different-tongued people not one of whom he could say 'hello' to, not one of whom he knew, not one of whom knew him? If he vanished outside this *pharmacie*, who would notice? Who would care? Would he himself care?

The gallery was a refuge. Not very crowded, people drifting around in that underwater mode he had noticed when he had been to the Tate Gallery and the British Museum on the London Trip. The slightest burr of low appreciative sound; a sense of congregation, piety, even worship.

When he had returned to school after getting into Oxford, Joe had put himself through a crash course in Modern Art with a much amused Art teacher, whose own work, sculptures in the manner of Henry Moore, were gaining her a reputation in the county. She had been highly entertained – though she had kept it to herself – by the boy's blunt bafflements, especially with Picasso, Braque and Matisse. The Surrealists were stared at without comment and she could almost see the boy trying to fit together things which to his mind did not fit together. He laid out the reproductions on a large trestle table as if they were pieces in a jigsaw.

But these paintings, here in this stylish, cool French gallery in the middle of Paris, these were real, the real thing, the paintings themselves. He planted himself in front of the Van Goghs for so long he could have put down roots. They seized his mind. He not only saw the paintings, he had the novel and thrilling sensation of believing that he saw what the paintings were about. He had been told what paintings represented: a battle, a monarch, a landscape, a scene in the bible. But this was an insight of a wholly different nature and his own. He saw the pain of it: he understood the distortion: he thought he understood the strain in those thick raw daubs and strokes of colour, the over-emphasis of everything, everything being both what it was and also what it hinted at. Fallings away. The meaning of it, to Joe, was as clear is if he were reading it. He was mesmerised.

He drifted past Manet, Monet, Renoir, Degas, Cézanne. The Impressionists once so derided were now the study of so many whose recent forebears had scorned them. There was that, too, he knew, and it gave him a sense, unearned but pleasing, that this generation, his generation, understood more than previous generations, had more insight, more art, more knowledge.

At first, Joe looked as intently at the names and the titles as he did at the paintings themselves. It was like a little dance: in towards the wall, rather myopically staring at the name and the description, a few steps back to see if the painting fitted, forward once more to the wall to check he had got it right, back again to look, a final and, he hoped, profound, penetrating look. He looked at dozens of paintings but it was Van Gogh who rooted him.

Towards the end he tried to go round without looking at the labels, attempting to remember who was who just by the paintings. He stayed until they said it was time to go.

At the entrance he found a free leaflet which described all the principal museums and galleries of Paris. He felt he had picked up a string of pearls. He stopped in a café on the way back and ordered steak and chips which he gobbled down and, hoping no one would notice, ordered the same again. He drank light beer which was cheap and refreshing. Mostly he studied the leaflet. He had to get to all of these. He just had to.

He saw the entrance prices. Sunday was free. He could not wait another week. Nor was it just the prices. Although there was not a contract with the Abbé Pierre's organisation (he was never to see the Abbé Pierre himself) he knew that it was understood he worked six days a week, most afternoons. That gave him Sundays and only rare afternoons.

When he got back, worn out but with some stability inside him for the first time, he tore up all his previous letters to Rachel and told her about Van Gogh. He decided against sending the unhappy letter to his mother: in its place he wrote a cheerful note on a postcard – of Van Gogh's *Sunflowers* – which he had bought in the Jeu de Paumes. He would go to the Jeu de Paumes every Sunday he was in Paris.

—ɯ—

He told them he needed to go to the British Embassy and they let him off the following afternoon.

It was very grand. It was even grander than the halls Joe had seen when he was at Oxford. And it was hushed, hushed in such a way, Joe thought, that you felt you had to hold up your hand if you wanted to speak. Those in charge seemed uninterruptibly busy, though only among themselves, mostly smart men very smartly turned out, his mother would have said. Joe regretted his sports jacket but he had thought that to bring a suit to work for the Abbé Pierre would be a waste of space.

Another rather lanky, long-haired English boy sat on the bench beside him, reading *To Have and Have Not*. Joe wanted to ask him what he thought about it, but he observed the pervasive reticence. He had brought *Seize the Day*.

After a while, when no one official had paid any attention to them, Joe was offered a cigarette.

'I haven't tried one of these.' It was a Disque Bleu.

'The tip keeps some of the filthy French tobacco at bay.'

He snapped on a lighter. Joe had begun to acquire a taste for the filthy French tobacco but he kept mum. It was not a place to rush things.

'What brings you here?'

'I want to see if they've got a free pass for museums and galleries,' Joe said. 'I've read that they've got them for French students so I wondered if we had them as well.'

'I shouldn't think so. Not our lot.'

'I'll ask anyway. These are good.' He waved the cigarette. 'What brings you here?'

'I'm just hanging about for a friend who works in the place. Do you work in Paris?'

'I'm with the Abbé Pierre,' Joe said, feeling a cheat.

'Very worthy.'

'It is.'

'Bloody hard work, I imagine.'

'Not really.' Joe defended the Abbé Pierre with some spirit. 'And as you say it's worthwhile, that helps.' So why the sudden pit in his stomach?

'I had a nerdy number making hundreds of beds in one of those immense French schools they turn over for thousands of holiday students. It was quite larky. We made the beds in the morning. Got all our meals free and some sort of stipend. Day's yours after lunch.'

328

Joe wanted that job. The want of it went through him like a stake. That job would save him. The possibility X-rayed his misery. He stubbed out the cigarette: it took several attempts.

'Can anybody just go and sign on?'

'Welcome you with open arms. Especially English. University?'

'Going to Oxford.'

'Open Sesame. Which college?'

'Wadham.'

'I don't think,' he put back his head and obviously thought, 'no, I don't know anyone at Wadham.'

Joe took the address of the school. He got a plausible student card without any of the anticipated fuss. He caught the metro to the nearest station to Abbé Pierre, packed, said he had to go, and set off in the early evening for the school, which was in the Bois de Vincennes. He had to get in. He could not go back to the Abbé Pierre.

—◦—

After a fraught hour of waiting, suddenly, without formalities, the school took him on. He felt free – wanted to weep, weak as he was, wanted to sing but dare not try his luck, carefully followed directions in the balmy, late Parisian twilight. He went into a long dormitory, gratefully flopped on his bed, unpacked, then slept, fighting off the truth that threatened to overpower him: that he was a coward and had run away from what was difficult, and failed a test of faith. But he had done it. And he felt safe. His father would have stuck it out, his grandfather too.

—◦—

'English!'

He woke up immediately. Above him a very large boy, a giant teddy bear figure, black wavy hair, bright smile. There was a buzz of foreign voices.

'English! It is time to arise for *le petit déjeuner.*'

He dressed quickly and tagged along with the dozen or so other boys. They were all German.

'My name is Reiner,' said the beaming teddy bear over coffee and bread, this time with honey. 'You and I, we are working mates.'

'Work mates.'

'You will teach me English. The other boys said me that so I will be a work mate.'

'I'm Joe,' he said and put out his hand.

Reiner stood up and made a small bow.

'Joe is?' he said, lowering himself onto the bench with care.

'Joseph.'

'I will call you Joseph. Or English. Both. Joe is American.'

They were in a corner of a vast refectory. There were half a dozen girls at a nearby table. At yet another table was the residue of the regular school staff. Joe was to discover an enormous school, taking more than sixteen hundred pupils, on the very edge of the Bois de Vincennes itself. Classrooms had been stripped of partitions and turned into mass dormitories for visiting schools and Joe's job was not just to make the beds but to sweep out, generally clean the place and help with the preparation of the *déjeuner.*

'We have our rooms,' said Reiner, 'and we do it so. First we take all the clothes from the bed. We carry them away. Now we take the new clothes for the bed. I will demonstrate you. Is this English correct?'

Joe struggled. It would be better and certainly easier to say nothing. Was it duty or vanity or a desire to please?

'We call them sheets,' he said, 'not clothes.'

'Sheets?'

'Sheets.'

'Clothes are this?' Reiner pointed to his shirt, his shorts.

'Yes. And we don't say "I will demonstrate to you." We say "I will show you."'

'I will show you.'

'And we don't say "We do it so", we say "We do it like this."'

'We do it like this. This is very good for me. *Danke. Sprechen sie Deutsch*?'

'*Nein*. And that's it except for *Danke sein*.'

'*Danke* will be correct also alone. *Parlez-vous français*?'

'*Un peu.*'

'That is good also. But we will speak in English.'

Joe enjoyed it. The relief after the clochards made him feel giddy. Soon he was running down the narrow lanes between the drilled rows of single beds ripping off the single blanket and the two sheets with a sense of looting. The sleeve for the pillow was fussier but even that had the exhilarating feeling of off with the old on with the new.

Reiner talked relentlessly. He talked about the Opera House in Munich where he worked as a 'ticket collector' as often as possible so that he could see the performances. He talked about the youth orchestra in which he played percussion, which he illustrated. He talked about his plan to be the music director of a theatre, of the magnificent scenery around Munich, of the wonders of Paris, especially the Opera House. Later, when they had finished stirring the potato purée in the vats and laid the long tables for several hundred,

331

they went into the Bois de Vincennes itself and he talked on. Joe was disappointed at the meagre number of trees.

'At English schools I am told you are talking against the Professor.'

'The teacher. Talking back. Yes. Asking questions usually but arguing sometimes.'

'That is very good. At German schools we do not talking back at all. You are more democratic.'

'Oh.' Joe was pleased. 'I suppose we are. I suppose your method is authoritarian.' Should he have said that?

'It is not good for democracy. But it will change,' said Reiner. 'The French are the most democratic.'

'Are they?' Joe was stung, but his ignorance made him unable to do anything about it. 'How do you know that?'

'The French are all an individual,' said Reiner. '*Liberté, égalité, fraternité* – that is the French.'

'We have all that.'

'Not as the French.'

'Like the French. To be honest, Reiner, I think we do but we just don't boast about it as much.'

They came back to the dormitory less animated.

Reiner introduced him to the others as 'Joseph, the Englishman', and every one of them shook his hand, gave a little bow and said 'welcome' or 'very pleased' or 'good day'. Hardly any of them looked like Germans, Joe thought.

There was one, two beds away, chunky, blond, freckled, thick-lipped, guttural, just like in the films. The others were all shades and shapes and sizes. Maybe, Joe thought, they were rejects.

Germans were supposed to shout, hoarsely. The blond did, but only him. They were supposed to stomp around. These did not.

Germans were supposed to be arrogant and haughty. These were friendly although, thankfully, not too friendly and one or two were downright gentle. You were supposed to be able to see the evil they had done in the expression on their faces. Joe saw none of this. They were orderly but quiet about it and he liked that. They asked what he had done on his trips into Paris and when he told them they were interested. At least two of them, Joe thought, were exceptionally nice. One, Hans, a slim, slight, dark-eyed, long-haired physicist was keen on ancient civilisations, especially the Assyrian and the Egyptian, and explained to Joe where the best exhibitions could be found. The other, Manfred, was shy and, unusually, rather lazy, languorous even, much enamoured of lying on his bed reading poetry. 'Hesse,' he confessed when Joe asked him, 'very predictable. What you read is much more exciting.'

So where were the Germans his third and index fingers had shot down in their scores when he was a boy? Only the Japanese were greater enemies. And where were the Germans who had bombed London, blitzkrieged Belgium, stormed through Poland, and exterminated the Jews? Where were those Germans?

It was wrong, he thought, to look for those Germans in these boys. They would have been children when the war ended. Believing himself to be an original, a pathfinder in the perception of this matter, Joe concluded that the war, thanks mainly to the British, had 'cured the poisoned wound of Germany' as he wrote to Mr. Braddock, and victory had 'cauterised' it. These were new people and could not be judged as if they were their fathers. Joe worked that through carefully over the four weeks he was there. They had to be given a clean slate, a new start.

It was not always simple. One of the boys talked about his father's heroics as a U-Boat Commander and Joe's fascination was increasingly eaten away by the pressing realisation that it was British sailors who had been killed and he left the circle to go outside. Reiner came to join him and said nothing as Joe gazed rather bemusedly out of the window.

And one evening out of nowhere Friedrich, the very blond one, took exception to what Joe was saying about different armies. It began with a polite enquiry into Joe's father's part in the war and turned into a vigorous discussion of the Burma Campaign about which Friedrich was clearly and insistently more knowledgeable than Joe. Joe was irritated by this and claimed knowledge he did not have, only to be remorselessly unmasked. They turned to the strength and skill of the armies of different nations in the war. The Americans, Friedrich declared, were the worst next to the Italians. The Russians, he said, were the bravest, the French the weakest, the Australian Army was excellent and so were the New Zealanders and the Canadians. The British were gallant but poorly led. They were third. The Japanese were the cruellest but also the second best. The Germans were the best army. They nearly beat the rest of the world put together.

Joe disagreed. At first, as he thought, reasonably. Friedrich's dismissive smile became increasingly annoying. Joe had a problem with facts. Friedrich's came out of an incontestable certainty of superior study. Joe just knew, just absolutely knew that the British were best because in the end they always had been, look at Agincourt, look at the Spanish Armada, always outnumbered, but in the end . . . look at the Battle of Britain, outnumbered again, and at Kohima – they won when it mattered. Winning was only important when it mattered. It may have been Joe's vehemence. It may have been an unfortunate reference to Germany's fascination with Hitler, but fists were raised and then the two of them were leathering each other with interest.

It was Hans who led the raid to pull them apart. It was Hans who designated Reiner to stay with Joe and help bathe his lip while with the others he marched Friedrich to the far end of the room. All Joe heard was an intense growl of anger, one or two interruptions from Friedrich, even more intense anger.

They returned as a corps, Hans and Friedrich in the lead. Friedrich stuck out his hand.

'I apologise, Joseph. Please accept like an English gentleman.' He bowed.

Joe's anger melted away instantly.

'Oh, it's O.K.,' he said and took the offered hand. 'Thanks.'

—m—

Occasionally he went into Paris with Hans or Reiner but he preferred to go alone. He did not want to share what was happening to him. He did not want it explained to him, however skilfully by Hans, however sympathetically by Reiner. At times he did not want it explained at all. Just to look, and by looking try to draw out the meaning, by gazing at these paintings, these sculptures, these monuments, this stained glass, that statue, just by gazing and being there, he thought, he would understand. Like one impulse from a vernal wood. Like that.

At first there was so much that he did not know where to begin, nervous that there was little time and he knew so little he could be making wrong choices. The Louvre was always safe and he would walk around in a daze of masterpieces, gallery after gallery, fighting against museum fatigue, gorging beyond saturation, emerging stupefied. Notre Dame too never let you down. He could lose himself looking at those mighty doors, walking round the outside of the building to see the flying buttresses like the exposed roots of a vast mythical tree, sitting across from the Cathedral with a cognac, a glass of water, a

335

coffee and a packet of Disque Bleu, drifting into that deeply coloured candle-lit Catholic bustle of suppurating whispers, gazing up at the rose windows, hopelessly trying to absorb it all, drugged by it.

In Notre Dame he almost wished he were a Roman Catholic. He observed people going into the confessional and wished he could have done the same. It was all very well talking to God in a group at St. Mary's, but admitting your sins to one person alone in Notre Dame seemed more likely to succeed. Maybe in one of those boxes someone could help him about the sin of sex with Rachel, especially as he had no intention of giving it up.

That was one of the factors gradually driving him away from St. Mary's because there was no answer there except to give it up. Why was it a sin in the first place? If she got pregnant he would marry her. At some level in his mind this was a preferred option: for by marrying he would keep her and be with her always and if he considered his life truthfully, as he did when he felt particularly blue, that was what he wanted more than anything else. He would even trade in days in Notre Dame and the Louvre for a single afternoon on the Moss with Rachel, although his more pious strain might attempt to deny that. The longing for her was never far away and imagining her daily routine was not only a comfort but a pleasure to be saved up, to be savoured.

So pregnancy was not a problem. Surely sex could not be objected to because it was so good? That just left sin: the edict that it was wrong because it was wrong, but the Ten Commandments talked about what not to do after marriage, not before. Yet it was a sin. Everybody knew that. Even people in Wigton who never went to church at all. If you did it before you were married you were dirty and asking for it and there would be a terrible come-uppance. And if you went to church it weighed on you, as it did on Joe. It was something he had to bear, shrug and wrestle with alone as best he could. But here, in

336

Notre Dame, people queued up and talked through the grille (he had glanced in an empty box) and came away forgiven, absolved, free, after a few prayers, a candle perhaps, and a promise to sin no more; but they could because they could come back to the same box again next week.

Feeling that the eyes of all in Notre Dame were on him, Joe lit a candle, pressed it on a spike, knelt and prayed that Rachel and he would be O.K. together, and paid his franc faithfully. Surely non-Catholics were allowed.

Would he dare to go into a confessional box?

—m—

Rachel came out into hard sunlight and tilted her head down until her eyes adjusted after the twilight of the bank. She had imagined that the branch in Carlisle, where she had just been interviewed for a six-week attachment, would be full of light as it was so grand, but there was the same gloom as Wigton; banks were a bit like those village churches Joe had occasionally tempted her to visit, she thought, places built to deny the sun.

They had given her the Saturday morning working time off for the interview, which had been scheduled at the end of business. She had been nervous but the anxiety had evaporated as soon as she saw the man; it was clear that all he wanted to do was to get it over with as soon as possible and go home. He ran out of steam after three questions, spent some time sifting through the paper mound on his desk to find her C.V., gave up, asked if there were any questions from her, was openly relieved when she said no and, with the only flourish of the encounter, told her that she would be 'informed in due course'. And she had dressed up for that!

Linda was coming to join her for an afternoon's potter around the shops, but her bus would not arrive for almost an hour. Rachel stood on the hot pavement uncertainly. She did not want to spoil their afternoon by looking around the shops on her own; all she knew of Carlisle was the County Ballroom and the railway station, both at night; Joe, she smiled to herself, would have gone to the Cathedral or something – more gloom.

'You look lost.'

He sprawled at the wheel of the small red open-topped M.G. two-seater sports car, imitating someone in a film, she thought, and she laughed at the obviousness of his pose, the show-off little car whose like she had never seen before, the transparent way in which he fancied his chances. He was very good looking, she thought, in a film star way, and he knew it.

'Garry Powell,' he said, 'I kept looking at you while you were waiting to meet the boss.' Rachel nodded. 'You blushed,' he said, 'but you didn't look back.'

'Why should I?'

'Can I give you a lift anywhere?'

'I'm waiting for a girl friend.' Why had she said 'girl'?

It was an exciting car, she thought; she had never before considered a car to be exciting but she looked down on this red projectile in open admiration.

'Fancy a spin?'

She did. But what would that say about her?

'How long have you got?'

'About an hour.' Rachel looked at her watch. 'Fifty minutes.'

No one in Carlisle knew her.

'You can do a lot in fifty minutes.'

He offered up a smile which Rachel thought was both charming and fake, but again it made her want to laugh. It was entirely new for her, this encounter; there was something easy, fleeting, unencumbered about it: and a faint thrill of risk.

'How fast can it go?'

'Not much more than ninety on these roads.'

'Show off!'

He smiled as if delighted to be awarded an insult from such an attractive young woman.

'Yes or no?' He leaned across and pushed open the door.

Rachel looked around. What could possibly be the harm in it? Joe was in another country gobbling up art galleries. It was the middle of the day. Garry worked in the bank. People were allowed to be friendly. She had a right to some sort of life of her own. What was Joe up to?

So near the ground, the hot wind in her face, streaming back her hair, the heart-soaring sense of speed, of being free, twisting dangerously through the rich, docile pasturelands of the Eden valley, new country to Rachel, as new and as glamorous as the car, the man, the speed.

He snapped to a stop in front of what to Rachel seemed a very grand house, free-standing, one of several around a postcard village green, a pond with ducks, a church Joe would have hauled her into, a lane right next to the house leading, she could see, to a broad stretch of the River Eden, a sandstone cliff face on the further bank, an immense house placed on the top and very edge of it. Everything so unlike the working plainness of her own village; it could have been another country. And what was not on view was just as striking, Rachel thought later: a confident and entrenched feeling of assured wealth.

'I'll just take a minute to change into my tennis things.' He hesitated and then, in what he hoped was just the right negative tone, said,

'Want to come in and meet the folks?'

'No fear.'

She looked at her watch. He was so obvious that she was embarrassed for him.

'Five minutes max. Scout's Honour.' He gave the three-fingered Boy Scouts salute and Rachel let him off.

She felt exposed. Sat there in the flash sports car, alone and clearly waiting. The only person she saw was an elderly woman shepherding two Jack Russells down the lane. Two cars and one bicycle passed by. No one, she reasoned, was the slightest bit interested in her and yet she felt raw. As if she were seen by all to be betraying Joe. As if she had stepped unprotected into a new world it would be better for her not to know. She wanted Joe to be back; to go to the train with him in the evening; to go to the dance; to make love at Aunt Claire's. She looked at her watch.

'Did I do it?'

Rachel was puzzled.

'In five minutes? Frantic!' He displayed himself. Dazzling, crisp white shorts. White sweater slung around his neck. White shirt. White socks and tennis shoes. Two tennis rackets.

His enthusiasm, if even, as she suspected, it was only about himself, burst in on her fears, chased out the gloom, made her smile even at the silliness of it, his honesty, it appeared, the freshness.

'Why do you want two rackets?'

'It looks good,' he said, and Rachel liked that reply.

—m—

He felt lucky to find a table on the Boulevard St. Germain itself. The early evening, especially on a Saturday, was the most crowded time, he had noted, especially at the Deux Magots where the tables aproned onto the broad pavements in front and to the side of the famous café in which, Joe had been told, Sartre and Camus could often be spotted, sitting with a drink half the day, writing masterpieces at those heavy little tables. He never failed to hope he would encounter them even though his only visual references of the two men were indistinct photographs some years out of date. But their potential presence made the Deux Magots even more of an event.

He had spent the afternoon in the Latin Quarter, adrift in the web of small and narrow streets which were already his favourite area of Paris, streets that reminded him of the alleys and wriggling back lanes of Wigton. He had been walking for hours in the heat, ferreting in St. Séverin, accidentally encountered, half hidden, its barnacled mass of grotesque gargoyles instantly become a new treasure, one of the many with which the city was cramming his mind. He had achieved a helpful and soothing level of exhaustion which dulled dependent longings for Rachel.

He had endured the experience of intense solitariness before he had known Rachel, and he could reach back for it and the memory eased him into the lonely Saturday evening; lonely despite the pavement crowds who looked as if they were on a stage, Joe thought, or in a film. He too felt like an actor, but uncertain that he had found a part.

It could be embarrassing to sit for a long time with a small order – one cognac, one coffee with accompanying glass of water, one croissant – but not if you wrote. He had seen others do it. In Paris you wrote in public and writing excused the measly order. He had bought paper and biro. 'Dear Rachel . . .'

Saturday night. It would not do to think too much about it. What would he have told her if she had been with him at the table? Say she

341

had just joined him from one of those little hotels, one or two of which were so cheap (he had investigated for future visits with Rachel) that he could just about afford them. Maybe about the man in the shop in the rue de Seine, a shop stacked with African sculptures, figures, masks, weapons, what looked like totem poles, distorted animals. Joe had been magnetised by the display in the window and stopped in his tracks, seeing what he had never seen before, unable to begin to analyse what it was that attracted him; the owner had waved him in.

Joe would have mocked his self-conscious French and made Rachel laugh by caricaturing the tiny, almost dwarf-sized sickly faced man whose black hair stood upright as if electrified by fright, whose hands and nose and ears and mouth were much too big for the spindly little body, who was kind to him, knew he knew nothing, tried to explain sometimes in slow French, sometimes in broken English. He would have made Rachel laugh but been unfair, Joe knew that, he often knew that, but making Rachel laugh could be more important than being fair.

One of the points the man had made was that modern artists stole from these African sculptors, he mentioned Modigliani most indignantly, just as they had previously stolen from Oceanic sculptors, Picasso came in for his lash here, and this theft not only dishonoured them, he said, and robbed of glory the originals, it also made for inauthentic art which was corrupt. Joe had been swept up in the argument, wholly on the owner's side, and saw these artefacts not only as mysteriously powerful in themselves but also the plainest evidence of the poor people being exploited by the rich. Communism, the man declared, was the only solution to the problems of the world. Joe was not sure of that and said so, but did not want any further discussion: the man's thesis had become too intimate.

This owner would have talked on for hours, Joe would have told Rachel, in fact he asked him to come back when the shop was closed so that they could go out together for 'un petit verre', but Joe had fudged it, suddenly claustrophobic in the overcrowded little shop, suddenly menaced by the impenetrable statues, the over-intense man, the weight of unknown meaning, glad to be back on the pavement even in the stinging stone heat.

After he thought it over he decided not to write to her about that.

'I went to the Musée Rodin yesterday,' he wrote and enjoyed the pose of writing, he, Joe Richardson, there, at the Deux Magots, just like Albert Camus, 'and it was fantastic.' He did not write about the erotic sculpture, the secret parts of women lasciviously displayed by a man who clearly enjoyed making them for others to enjoy looking at their frozen eroticism which were exciting even in bronze. He had not cared to be seen standing too long in front of some of them. 'In the garden there was this massive panel of Hell. You could see how the people were being tormented. It looked very convincing. I bet Hell's just like that.'

He wanted to tell her that Hans had taken him to a jazz club just off the Boulevard St. Michel and he had actually seen Memphis Slim at the piano. Hans had gone on to another club but Joe stayed for the next set. Memphis Slim! But he feared that would sound too much like a 'night out' and wrote instead about Ste. Chapelle.

Darkness began to mingle in with the street lights but instead of alerting people to go home, it seemed to increase their determination to stay on the streets and the parade went on, entertained now by a man with a tame white rat, a fire eater, a unicyclist, a circus for free, and Joe ordered another cognac, another coffee. He felt absorbed in what was around him. He was part of this life, this play, the flow of it, just sitting there.

He had eaten little since the midday meal in the school and he was by now light-headed and finally he relaxed. He was in Paris, in the Boulevard St. Germain, writing, even though it was a letter, writing in a French café, and now young roller skaters appeared, racing towards oncoming cars and at the very last minute swerving away like matadors and the angry cars honked and honked and honked.

—m—

That night he woke up to the rattle of small arms. The boys crowded to the windows of the dormitory. Hans told him that the Bois de Vincennes was noted for its concentration of Algerian terrorists. It went on for more than an hour. Hans said it was war, by other means but it was war. They were lucky, he said, to witness this new war. Friedrich called the Algerians 'Les Nègres' and said he thought all terrorists were cowards. Terrorism, he said, was a coward's way to make war. Joe thought he might agree with that. Yet, as they talked, he found himself saying, what else do you do if you have no army and a real cause? What else can you do?

In the morning it seemed far away. That was the only night it happened. It was as if it had been in another world.

—m—

With just a couple of days to go the energy went out of Paris. He wanted to be back with Rachel. He hunted for a present. He had saved for it.

He went to Montmartre where he had noted that the painters and jewellers in the square offered what he considered wonderful works of art within his pocket. For some time he hovered over a small painting of Sacré Coeur. It was an original, no doubt about it. The painter was doing another while Joe made up his mind. Fantastic, Joe thought, to get it so right and yet so small. There was another painting, equally attractive, of the view across Paris from the top of the steps of Sacré Coeur. But would Rachel really like it? In the end, after about two hours of close inspection and the weighing up of rival claims, he chose a bracelet, a thick broad band of what could have passed for solid gold, shaped very unusually, Joe thought, like nothing he had ever seen in a shop or anywhere else for that matter. The artist said it was a unique piece and Joe knew he had bought not only a bracelet but very possibly a true work of art.

He walked down to Pigalle bearing his gift. He had not been to this decorous boulevard of strip. He was drawn along by the saucy photographs, the big bold elegant illuminations, the seductiveness, not at all sleazy, even cheerful, practical, business as usual. Yet inside Joe there was a distinctly sleazy excitement. He walked self-consciously, trying to pretend he was just out for a balmy evening stroll. Doorways opened to sexy music and photographs of sultry beauties already far further undressed than anything he had ever seen in *TitBits*. It was without any question a betrayal of his relationship with Rachel to creep off to a strip show. It was another needless sin, just when he was beginning to sort out the sin of making love to Rachel. It was what old men did, in mackintoshes. He had read that the girls who did it had a terrible time and only did it under protest or because they had to bring up young children. He would probably get robbed. They all looked too expensive.

Yet being in Paris for nearly six weeks without seeing a single strip show was surely not really being in Paris. It was part of what Paris was. He would never see one again. Everything ought to be experienced. What harm could it possibly do? Who would ever know? Could he afford it?

Just about. A small doorway with the word APACHE lit up over its portal. He went in as if he were entering the lair of Jezebel.

It was very well lit, which was a disappointment. He had expected something darker, sensuous drapery, side lights, maybe some snakes behind glass and half-naked waitresses. The usual man in his long white apron asked him what he wanted and, fearing the price of everything, Joe ordered a *demi-pression*. The waiter took his time.

No one was on the tiny cleared patch of floor which must be the stage but already Joe was all but suffocating with anticipation.

The lights went out. A spotlight hit the stage. Curtains at the back, which Joe had not noticed, parted with enticing slowness and revealed a long bare leg, scarlet painted toenails, a head, a torso, and then the whole woman, in what Joe thought of as a sort of Hawaiian grass skirty thing and a broad red band, seemingly made of red towelling, covering her top. Tropical music played and she swayed and so did the skirt, which kept opening up vistas of strong thighs. After some time the skirt was slid off, breathtakingly disclosing knickers that matched the towelling top. After an age that came off too. Joe was rapt. She made them wobble. She made them sort of do circles. He did not know whether he ought to look. He could not take his eyes off them. She pretended she was going to take off her knickers. Her thumbs hooked inside them. Her light went out.

The lights went on. Joe looked around furtively, swallowed hard and drank too much of his *demi-pression* in one go.

There were four more, one of whom, dressed like a cow-girl in a very short fringed skirt, was described as doing the original Apache dance. Joe was impressed.

More than that, as he walked to the metro clutching Rachel's present, he was giddy. He had not eaten since lunch and the force of what he had witnessed had stirred him as it ought not to have done. It was a pity, he thought, as the train approached the Bois de Vincennes station, that his last visit in Paris should have been to Apache. How much better . . . but it was fruitless attempting to dismiss it in his own mind. He could tell the truth there, couldn't he? Well then: he was glad he'd gone and if he'd stayed another night he'd undoubtedly have gone again; funds permitting. Especially as nobody knew or need ever know.

———∭———

He got fed up with hitching near Crewe and went into the town hoping he could catch the last train, later than usual on the Friday night. If not he would sleep on a bench until the first morning connection. But he was lucky, he could just afford it, and the train crawled into Carlisle at eleven-thirty, too late for a Wigton connection and too late for a bus. He had to walk clear out of the city before he got a lift, a lorry on its way to the West Coast. He offered the driver a Disque Bleu and enjoyed his cursing and coughing.

Sam opened the door.

'What time is this?' He smiled at the bedraggled young man, kitbag slung over his shoulder, haversack dangling from the free hand.

'Sorry.'

'Glad to see you.' He stepped back. He had slipped a raincoat over his pyjamas. As Joe came through the door there was a fumbled handshake. Sam wanted to hug him: safe home. 'Your mother'll come down and make you some tea.'

'I don't need any, thanks. I got a cup on the train. I'm fine.'

'Good time?'

'Good time.'

347

'I'll leave you then. You don't want to talk now.' Just a hope. 'Thanks for the letters.'

'Talk in the morning?'

Why was he so keen to be alone? What did a few minutes with his father matter? Why did he already feel bad about himself in his own house?

'Rachel brought a letter just this afternoon,' Sam said. 'She wanted to make sure you got it as soon as you got back. It's on your bed.'

'Thanks.'

'Talk tomorrow.'

'Talk tomorrow.'

'Hello.' Ellen walked down the stairs in that white silky dressing gown, Joe thought, like somebody in a film. She smiled shyly and gave him a quick light peck on the cheek. Sam nipped into the bar for a packet of cigarettes.

'You'll have to have some tea,' she said and led them into the kitchen. She looked at him intently and Joe felt the burn of her gaze. 'You need a haircut,' she said. 'And,' she turned to Joe, another smile, an order, 'your dad will want to know about Paris.'

There was Rachel's letter. He could let it lie in his mind, he thought, enjoy it twice. Once thinking about it, a second time reading it.

'What's the best thing you saw?' Sam did not offer him a cigarette.

'Third degree now, Joe,' said Ellen from the kitchen, 'just give in.'

Joe smiled at the raincoated figure on the seat opposite.

'You look funny dressed like that,' he said.

'I'm thinking of turning it into an act.'

'Maybe Notre Dame,' Joe began, wanting to keep Van Gogh and

Rodin to himself until he had talked to Rachel about them, 'especially the front of it.'

Ellen sat and watched them both. Said little. It was good to have him back.

An hour or so later he unpacked sufficiently so that he need do nothing after reading the letter. It was nice and odd to be back in the old, narrow little bedroom, the books still neatly on their shelves.

'Dear Joe,

'I've thought about this a lot but I have to say it. I want you to get it now, as soon as you come back. A few days after you went away I was sent to Carlisle for an attachment. To cut a long story short, I don't know how to put this, but I have taken up with somebody. He's older than you and I've gone out with him once or twice in Carlisle. I need to think things over. I really am sorry. We've had really great times and I know I said things etc. But times change, maybe you being away gave me time to think about myself a bit more. I really am sorry, Joe. Love. Rachel.'

CHAPTER THIRTY-TWO

He found Rachel in the second bank. At the first he had been told that someone on an attachment would be in their main branch and he walked in just before 10 a.m., less than half an hour after it had opened. Without noticing he had caught some confidence in Paris, he was lighter on his feet, there was no hesitation about him. It was a warm morning and he wore a fresh white shirt and the dark trousers that went with the sports jacket. The present had looked too obviously like a present, it had taken the artist an age to wrap it and so Joe carried it in a brown paper bag.

'Can I speak to Rachel Wardlow, please?'

The heavily spectacled man in the dandruffed double-breasted pinstriped jacket was tempted to send him away but Joe's uncon- cealed determination and the sense which came from him that he had every right to see her made the man smile. Besides he was not too fond of Garry, the bank's spoiled Casanova, who had taken her up. She looked a decent girl, and this one looked the right part as her boyfriend.

'Rather irregular,' he whispered. 'I'll see what I can do.'

There was one transaction going on, and two clerks working behind the tellers. Usually even that small audience would have set off a jangle of self-consciousness and general awkwardness in Joe. Now he did not notice.

Rachel came through the half-glassed door, reluctant, head lowered, hair half covering her face, that blue dress which used to be best and, when she looked up, she took his breath away.

He just stood, silent, looking at her with hungry urgency.

'Did you have a good time?' she whispered.

'I wrote.'

'You seemed to be having a good time.'

Joe wanted to take her away. He wanted to reach across the counter between them and kiss her, hold her, have her back. He had never seen her looking so good: the word beautiful struggled to surface. He wanted to ask her about this man. He ought to confess about the strip club, that was probably why God had got his revenge, but he would never confess. He just wanted it not to have happened.

'Can't we talk?'

'Not here.' Her whispering had edge. 'Not now.'

'What time do you finish?'

She looked flustered.

'I'll wait outside.'

'Don't wait outside.'

'Where'll we meet, then?'

She looked at him directly for the first time and a smile threatened, perhaps a memory. Joe was standing his ground.

'Burton's Corner,' she said, 'half past twelve.'

'Right.' He looked at his watch. 'I've got a present.' He swung up the carrier bag and it clonked against the counter.

'Thanks.'

'You might not like it.'

'You have to go now, Joe.'

'What are you doing tonight?'

'You have to go.'

The dandruffed teller coughed to second her motion. He had played fair. He smiled at the young man, the smile of dismissal. Joe understood.

'Burton's Corner. Half past twelve.'

He went out quickly with his brown paper bag. Rachel said, 'Thank you, Mr. Webster.'

'He seems a very personable young man, Rachel.'

'He is,' she muttered and went back into the back office. Garry did not even look up.

Part of the new Joe considered that he ought to spend the two hours in Carlisle Cathedral which he had never explored properly, or in the museum section of Tullie House, or even at the Castle which his father had spoken of but he had never visited. That part was trampled down within seconds. Joe walked the streets. He traipsed all over Carlisle, over the Viaduct, into Denton Holme, back into the city, down Warwick Road to Brunton Park, back up by the alleys he used as a boy going to the football, down Scotch Street, back up by Fisher Street. He tried to pretend he was doing some sort of research in case anyone wondered why this person with a carrier bag was pounding around Carlisle so relentlessly on a sunny summer morning, and now and then he stopped and looked at street names as if thoughtfully.

What he really wanted was one of those Parisian pavement cafés where he could sit and have a coffee, a cognac and a glass of water and read a paper and watch the world go by, let others' agitation soothe his own. He bought the paper. The best he could do for a café was the tea rooms on the first floor of an old-established ladies' clothes shop. It was full of women having clatter-cupped tea and scones. The coffee was awful. He gulped it and went back on the tramp.

He tried to work out where they could go. They could not chance a pub. Rachel was still not eighteen and they would not be able to get away with it in Carlisle. Tea rooms were out. The only open ground he knew of was beyond the Castle, quite a walk, and he sensed that like himself Rachel wanted to engage immediately. Standing in the doorway of a closed shop would be practical but it was not attractive.

'We'll go to the railway station,' Rachel said. 'All we have to do is to buy a platform ticket and find a bench. People are used to people sitting and talking at a station.'

The bench she found was on Platform Four at the opposite end of the station from where the Wigton train docked.

'Here,' he said, the moment they sat down. He bundled the carrier bag into her lap. He saw now that she was wearing high heels as well.

'I don't think I should take it.'

'I'll just throw it away if you don't.'

She sought it in the large brown bag and then undid it carefully. When it was revealed, Joe was proud of it. It shone. It was big.

'It's . . . gorgeous!'

Rachel put it on. It swathed around her wrist, its curvaceous shape, exotic, bold, bringing out the same qualities in Rachel. She pushed out her arm and admired it.

'It's,' she struggled for a moment, 'one of a kind, isn't it?'

'An artist made it.'

'It's really French.'

'In Montmartre. Toulouse Lautrec used to do his painting in Montmartre.'

She darted a quick kiss on his cheek.

'Thank you.'

'So I don't have to throw it away?'

'No.' She smiled and admired it again. 'I bet nobody round here's got one like this.'

Joe felt grateful and he relaxed, spread out both arms along the back of the bench, one of them inevitably going around Rachel's shoulders. He breathed in deeply: he could wait no longer.

'Have you and him done anything?'

'No.'

'Nothing?'

'Joe!' She focused on it. 'Since you want to know, we kiss and he wants to go further but I won't let him.'

Kissing was bad enough but the rest was good news and people kissed people they were not going with in games at parties. There was a great deal to be relieved about. Now he would go very slowly and carefully, even nonchalantly.

'Where are you going tonight, then?' The words rattled out.

Rachel would not be interrogated.

'I suppose it's with him, is it?'

She looked at the bangle. Was it rather too flashy?

'Who is he anyway?'

Joe was growing more angry and could be ignored no longer.

'We're going to a social at Carlisle Tennis Club,' she said. 'He's very good at tennis.'

'Anybody can be good at tennis.'

Again Rachel bit her lip.

'We could go to the County,' he said. 'It's bound to be better than a social at a tennis club.'

'I've promised.'

'What about me?'

The question, forlorn, essential, raw, eternal, rang to the glass roof of the Victorian station, outcrying the clacking of train wheels, the shrill of the whistle – what about me?

'We've been going out for nearly two years, Joe.'

'What's wrong with that?'

'I've never been out with anybody else. The village boys, before you, that was just a few of us walking around the village together. I've never been with anybody else ever.'

'Nearly two years is good,' Joe said. 'We've stuck at it.'

'When you were away –'

'I'm back now.'

'I started to think about it. Then Garry –'

'Garry!'

'Asked me out for a drink. He's got this little sports car. We go to a pub in the village he lives in, nothing like our villages, it's,' she paused, 'a moneyed village.'

'I'll earn money some day.'

'That isn't what I meant. The village. It's so – it's where his mother lives. In the Eden valley. It's not like where we are, Joe. It's different.' It had all been different and she had felt free, relieved from Joe's never-ending jealousy and pressures – on her, on himself, on them, on everything.

'What does that matter?'

'It was something different, Joe.'

'It'll wear off.'

The more placating her tone, the more hurt and angrier Joe grew.

'The train now approaching Platform Four is the eleven-o-five from Glasgow Central. Calling at Penrith, Lancaster, Preston, Crewe, Watford Junction and London Euston. This is the eleven-o-five from Glasgow Central.'

'So will you come out with me tonight?'

'I've promised.'

She looked at him and looked away immediately.

'I'm sorry, Joe.'

'That's all right.' His words were tight, his movement as he stood up stiff. He forced back the feelings which threatened him. 'I'll go then.'

He turned and all but marched along the platform as the heavy engine hissed and puffed towards him, slowly drawing along its retinue of coaches.

Rachel watched him until he went through the ticket barrier and then, wearily, she took off and wrapped up the gleaming bangle and put it back in the brown carrier bag. Just before he had turned away, standing there, he had looked great, she thought.

—∽—

'Can a mother say you're making a mistake here?'

Brenda turned from the mirror and presented herself.

'Charming! You're utterly charming.'

'Thank you, kind mother.' Brenda giggled and curtsied.

Her mother took another sip of gin. Only the second of the day so a big sip was allowed. She eased herself into the fatly cushioned sofa and looked both at her daughter and at her elegant sitting room with no little satisfaction. With Brenda safely off to Edinburgh University in a few weeks and Henry now boarded at school at Sedbergh, all was well.

'I suppose you have to get it out of your system.'

'He's different since he came back from Paris.' Brenda frowned seriously. 'Paris matured him.'

'Did it now?'

'He went to every gallery there was and every church. He talks about it.'

'Does he ever? Fag?'

'No thanks. He broadened his horizons.'

'Brenda, darling, he's a pub boy and he always will be a pub boy. You can take the boy out of the pub but you can't take the pub out of the boy.' The bell rang. 'He's on time. Must be keen, darling.'

'This is the fifth time we've been out in just two weeks,' Brenda said, driving a little too fast along the Roman stretch of road to Carlisle. Joe had not been prepared for her father's car. 'That's if you discount Saturday two weeks ago.'

Joe had finally forced himself to go to the County Ballroom on that first Saturday night. Maybe just to be in the same city as Rachel at her 'Tennis Club Social': maybe she would abandon it and come to the County Ballroom. Maybe she would be waiting for him in the train. Maybe he would bump into her as a few of them walked through Church Street on the way back to Brenda's house to have a final cup of coffee. Brenda had been very helpful. Every time they danced she had shown her concern about Rachel and listened to his few tight-lipped confessions, nursing every drop. Her father had popped his head around the door of the handsome room of which the half-dozen of them had taken possession after coming back from the dance. After a general greeting he had said,

'And how was Paris, Joe? It was Paris, wasn't it?'

'It was great.'

'You must come to a Rotary lunch and tell us all about it, Joe. I'm sure we'd be riveted by what you had to say.'

Later, as Brenda stood outside on the step, in no hurry to see him go, she said,

'My father really respects you, Joe. He really respects you. I can tell.'

357

There was some comfort there. Brenda had been keen to help. Then they had met as it seemed by accident at a Former Members of the Anglican Young People's Association Get Together; again the following Saturday at the County and twice during the week for walks. On both these walks there had been strong kissing but Joe was worried about it and Brenda sensed that a little. But the kissing, she reflected, was nevertheless strong.

They were going over 80 m.p.h. Joe took out a cigarette.

'Light one for me?'

He did. Two in his mouth at the same time. Who had done that? Humphrey Bogart? Robert Mitchum? It felt very adult. He guided it over to her outstretched fingers. He was not too happy about her driving at this speed with one hand but he would never have said.

'I thought we'd go to the Crown and Mitre,' she said, 'away from the gang.'

Joe nodded. He had been there once with Rachel on his birthday. It was much grander than the County. It had a real hotel bar beside the ballroom – in the County you had to go across the road to the pub in the interval. In the Mitre there were tables and chairs, some of them easy chairs, around the ballroom perimeter. Dancing opinion held that the Mitre's floor was second to none. And the band was not only bigger but had broadcast twice on BBC Northern Radio. It was more expensive to get in and Joe had noticed a definite mark-up on the price of drinks. Away from the gang? Maybe just as well. The gang were so used to Rachel and himself being together. He was glad not to have to brazen it out.

'It means we'll be stuck with each other all night,' said Brenda as they went into the first quickstep, 'I hadn't thought of that.' She giggled and Joe smiled and looked at her. Mostly he had looked away from her. For dances, she let her hair down and it rested, blondly, silkily, on her shoulders, which were almost bare, the dress designed to reveal as much flesh as possible above the breasts without risking strapless. There was a dark purple ribbon in her hair which Joe liked and a necklace which she called 'costume jewellery'. She was good-looking, Joe thought, some would say very. Not as fine a dancer as Linda, but, he had to admit this, better than Rachel, less stiff and always happy to be close together whatever the dance. Since they were embarked on the unusual, unique adventure of dancing every dance together, they would simply stand at the side of the floor, between dances, their arms around each other's waists, ready for the off. Brenda was never short of something to say and Joe's hurt, which had made him much more reticent, welcomed the balm of her intelligent chatter. She was attractive, he thought, and nice, he concluded, she had changed, he thought, and once or twice when she pecked him on the cheek proprietorially, he pecked in return and hugged her closer.

That was how Rachel first saw them and her head rocked back as if she had been hit on the chin.

'Do you think,' Brenda asked, as they went through the motions of a foxtrot, 'that we are the two most intelligent people in this ballroom?'

Joe did not know how to answer that. But when he laughed, and Brenda laughed, she added, 'You pig! I'm serious.'

Was being called a pig, in fun, O.K.? He had to suppose so, she had said it so inoffensively.

'I think we should get to the bar before the interval and beat the crush,' he said.

'Intelligent!'

And she pulled him towards her, burying her head into his shoulder. Joe's face was up against one of her big earrings. He let it bounce against his mouth.

Rachel was in the queue for the Ladies', when he came out of the Gents'. His heart leapt up. She saw the look that transformed him and knew she was the cause of it and her face reached forward for a kiss but in an instant all that vanished and they tried to be cold to each other. She stepped out of the queue.

'You seem to be having a good night,' she said, careful to keep it neutral.

'Brenda. Yes. Have you been here very long? I didn't see you on the floor.'

That was because I steered well away from you.

'It's a big ballroom.'

But I should have seen you. Or known you were here. I knew things about you that never needed explanation. Why didn't I know you were here?

'Are you with –?'

'Garry. Yes. We're going soon. He's not the world's keenest dancer.'

And he is understandably fed up that for no reason he can fathom I have gone dead on him.

'So you're off.'

To make love somewhere? To go to that pub in that 'moneyed' village of his? In that sports car? To spend time alone with him? Without me?

'You and Brenda seemed to be chatting away ten to the dozen.'

'She said we were the two most intelligent people on the dance floor!'

'Big head! That's terrible! What did you say?'

'Nothing.'

'More fool you. Sorry. It's none of my business. Look, Joe, I really

360

do have to get back in this queue or there'll be a nasty accident. You'd better get back to Brenda.'

I don't want to.

I don't want you to.

'Away you go.'

His sole purpose in the dance that followed the interval was to get a close look at Garry. What he saw was not too upsetting. The man had very wavy blond hair, corrugated, Joe thought, or permed; he was not that much taller than Rachel; he was not much of a dancer; some people might just have found him good-looking; and although they danced close together, Rachel was miles away from clinging while this Garry's head never kept still, twitching around in every direction, picking people out, for one moment even picking out Brenda, passing on.

They were not there for the next dance. Nor the next.

'They've gone,' Brenda said, rather drily but with humour. 'It must be funny seeing her with another man. How long were you together?'

In the full dark of the return journey, Brenda drove the car no less recklessly but she did slow down at the zigzag death trap of Carlisle Bridge, a mile outside Wigton. She stopped, looked back, and reversed the car unsteadily down a tiny side road. Then she knocked off the lights.

'This was the best place I could think of,' she said. 'Let's get in the back.'

It ought not to have worked, his thoughts infected by the sight of Rachel, his spirits lifted by the sight of Garry, his hopes raised by the way Rachel had said what she had said outside the Ladies', but it did; that is they kissed without restraint and began to move on.

Brenda talked and made noises whereas he and Rachel tended to be intensely silent, but the noises were encouraging and the talk was even appreciative, sometimes an instruction – 'keep your hand there', 'keep doing that': the back seat of the car was peculiarly erotic. Making love was what you did not do in the back seat of a car, making love was the last thing it was designed for, making love was all but impossible in the back seat of a car, even the elementary, early and opening stages of making love, even sitting side by side and getting close was an acrobatic feat but all the difficulties added up to an enclosed, claustrophobic, tented excitement. The back seat provoked performance.

He slipped off one of her shoulder straps and slid his hand down and not only did she not object, she pushed her breast into his hand with words and sounds that matched the crude urgency of his own growing involvement. This was not really betraying Rachel, was it? After all, she had gone off with Garry in his sports car. That evened it out. What were they doing in the sports car? He stroked Brenda's breast more emphatically which seemed to give equal pleasure to both of them. And there for a while they stayed, in a state of mooncalf sex, confused but with intent, breasts now bared, jacket off, shirt undone, shoes long discarded, each wanting to see if there would be a next move, what it would be, most of all, who would make the next move.

But for a while they stayed as they were, young, inhibited, chained to their place and time, already looser than they'd anticipated this early on in their dating game but was there even more? They smoked a cigarette, between them: passed it across. That seemed the best way. Brenda opened the window and threw out the red-tipped stub. The fresh night air zipped into their sex cave and she shut the window tight and then turned to Joe and they draped themselves against each other, bared against each other, poised to consider the next stage.

362

The approaching car did not dip its headlights and almost blinded them. It drew up a few yards beyond them and the driver sounded his horn, several times, before making off. Brenda was jelly.

'It'll be someone who knows my father. Oh God!' she said. 'They'll know his number plate. They'll know it's me. Oh God!'

Finding shoes, buttoning the shirt, trying to clip on the bra, losing the tie, oh God! They drove into the town soberly. Brenda stopped in front of the house. The lights were still on.

'They'll expect you to come in,' she said.

'Should I?'

'It'll be obvious, won't it?'

'Yes. Will it? Yes. I won't then.'

'I'll say –'

'Tell them I have to get up to go to early communion.'

'Will you?'

'No.'

Brenda took a deep breath, opened the window wide and said, 'Calm down, Brenda.' She took several deep breaths. 'We can deny doing the worst of it,' she said, 'and there's nothing wrong with just kissing in the back of the car.'

'Nothing.'

Joe just wanted to go. By Church Street. To see if Rachel had left her bicycle there. Brenda was so sensible.

'It was good, wasn't it?'

'Yes,' he said, truthfully. But not the same: nothing like the same.

'Maybe just as well.' All the time Brenda had been talking she had been putting on make-up, patting her hair, fiddling with her dress. 'That they came. The headlights.' She giggled. 'Maybe it saved us!'

It had done, Joe thought, it had done.

'Are you sure you won't come in? It might arouse less suspicion.'

'Next time, I think. Next time.'

'Okey-dokey.' She turned a face now calm and cool towards him. 'Last kiss?'

A tame one.

'Ring tomorrow?'

'Yes.'

He got out of the car, waited until she had parked, got out and reached the front door, then waved and hurried towards Claire's in Church Street, too full of too many contradictory sensations to be able to think at all.

—m—

Sam waited until Ellen had gone upstairs to read in the parlour as she did on Sunday afternoons now that Joe was not immersed there in his work. The room had to be lived in, she said. Joe cleared the last of the tables and sat down with that unrelenting feeling of emptiness: usually at this time on a Sunday he would be off to see Rachel or out on Market Hill phoning her.

'I saw Rachel yesterday,' Sam said, 'on the street. She's back working in Wigton.'

Joe had tried his level best to avoid seeing her. It seemed only fair. But twice he had found himself opposite the bank at the time she came out and both times had been embarrassingly awkward.

'I've seen her once or twice.' Sam took his time. Joe's face was fastened on a page of P.G. Wodehouse. He had gone back to him over the past fortnight.

'I always liked Rachel,' said Sam. She had looked unhappy.

'I think she might not object to a call,' he said. 'She looks a bit down. Of course it's none of my business,' he said.

Sam took his time.

'If you love her, Joe, you should see this other fella off. At least try.'

Joe turned over the unread page.

He was on the phone to her for over an hour. He had to come back twice for more change. Before he set off to bike out there, he phoned Brenda, took a breath and told her he was going back with Rachel.

'So it's all over then, darling,' her mother said. 'Mother did tell you so.'

'It was just a fling.'

'Good for you.'

'We'll be at different ends of the country in a few weeks' time.'

'Good thinking. Edinburgh will be jam packed with eminently more suitable bachelors. Just forget him.'

'I will,' said Brenda, firmly.

'He's a type,' said her mother, finally. 'He's good of his type, but I'll never like the type. Nor will you. You'll see after you've met much better boys in Edinburgh. He just isn't worth you and there's an end to it.'

Rachel and Joe took a short pause for breath and then continued what might have seemed an attempt to crush each other's faces together through the act of kissing.

'Sorry.'

'Sorry.'

'Sorry.'

Never, they knew, they vowed, they said repeatedly, they would never ever split up again. Never.

CHAPTER THIRTY-THREE

Joe was there, on the street at the legendary time they came around the corner. He was forever grateful that he had been there. It was just a couple of weeks before he was due in Oxford, a drifting time, nothing to do but wait, nerves stretching by the day. It was mid-evening, still a clear September light. He was talking to Alan at the mouth of Meeting House Lane when they came around the corner into King Street, past Middleham's the butcher's, past the Fountain, and began what Joe saw as a fierce, almost savage and imperial progress. He would have sworn that everyone on the streets that night, the lads leant against the Fountain, strollers, window shoppers, those turning up early for the second house of the pictures, all of them were as frozen to attention as he was by the force of the two of them, transfixed by them. Speed, with Lizzie close, holding tight onto his arm.

There was murder in his eyes, unmistakable. Violence in every step he took, a terrible raging for vengeance about him. Tall, black-suited, wide-open-necked white shirt, blond hair long, heaped back from his brow, a face set in stone. And her, almost as tall on high heels, a matching stride, a black skirt, lavishly scalloped black blouse, extravagant black hair extravagantly styled, face white, barely concealing the fear, holding his arm tight, holding on, Joe understood, for dear life.

He would never forget those moments when Speed brought Lizzie into the heart of the town. He wanted to shout 'Hello!' but like everyone else was too much in awe.

Everything about Speed said: one word, one look, one gesture which even hints at what happened to her and you will be meat. She is mine and this is her town and we are just going for a drink like everybody else. Lizzie's silence was if possible even more direct: help me to do this, it said. Help me. They looked so magnificent, Joe thought, they were gods on that night.

Speed went first into the Victoria, one of the prime watering holes of the lads, and it was reported the next day that when they went in the silence slammed down so hard it was like a door slammed shut. Speed ordered their drinks, took them to a table in the corner and only when he leaned forward to take Lizzie's, observed trembling, hand did a looking-away-we're-ignoring-you conversation resume, but low, to listen in. Speed talked briefly to a couple of old pals, knocked back the pint and stood up to go. Lizzie had not finished her drink but said she didn't mind leaving it. Speed went across the street to the Vaults, the pigeon men's pub: it was later reported they had been in the Lion and Lamb and finally they headed for the Blackamoor. Each pub they left behind talked of nothing else for the rest of the night. There was an excitement, even something of a privilege, that they had come into the pubs, relief when they left, no mention made of the fear Speed spread all around him.

'Speed!'

Sam's smile was wide, his hand held out, a surge of affection went through him.

'And Lizzie! Lovely to see you!'

Speed looked at Lizzie to register that she was fully aware of the honour being done him, the high place he held in the affection of this man, Sam Richardson, the pride of it.

'Sam, you old bugger,' he said, and clasped the hand strongly.

'The kitchen's empty,' Sam said, 'if you want a bit of peace.'

Lizzie nodded immediately. Facing them out had been a strain.

'What is it you want?'

Speed ordered.

As Sam drew the pint of bitter the smile never left his lips. Speed! He had come back.

'They're on me,' Sam said. He looked directly at Lizzie. 'I'll tell Ellen you're in,' he said, 'she won't want to miss you.'

Again Speed turned triumphantly to Lizzie. There! the look said. See how nice people are. See how easy it is slotting back in with friends like these: my friends. Ellen came downstairs immediately. With an unaffected and unusual public display of feeling, she held out both hands the moment she came into the kitchen and said,

'Lizzie! I'm so glad to see you, Lizzie.'

'We're getting married,' said Speed: the sentence was a punch. 'Next week.' Another pause. The final one. 'In Wigton.'

Sam looked on him even more tenderly.

'Good on you,' he said, quietly.

'She's a Wigton girl,' Speed said.

'At St. Cuthbert's?'

'We're both Catholics,' Lizzie's face bore a defiant and hurt expression. 'Why shouldn't I get married in my own church?'

'Is your mother making the dress?' Ellen asked.

'She is.'

'I bet it's beautiful. She's a wonderful dressmaker, your mother.'

'Can I have a word, Sam?'

Speed saw that Lizzie was safe with Ellen and wanted to get on with his business.

'Just a minute.' Tom Johnston was in the darts room. Sam asked him to look after the bar for a few minutes. The two men went into the empty singing room.

'Have one with me, Sam?'

There was only a minimal pause. He had broken his rule only once before and this was surely comparable.

'Gladly. Another half for you?'

'A pint'll be better, Sam. Sure it's only a half? You can have a short, you know.'

'A half will do nicely, Speed.'

The drinks were brought. Sam raised his glass.

'Good luck to you and to Lizzie. Good luck to both of you.'

'Thanks.' Speed felt clumsy in the exchange and compensated by sinking half the pint. The draught resolved him.

'I want to tell you why I was kicked out, Sam. I've never told nobody except to my mother I said I'd done nothing bad, which is the truth. Now then.' He described the circumstances, briefly, with no self-pity, the facts.

'I thought it might be something like that,' Sam said. He took a sip of the clear bitter. 'I'm glad you've told me, Speed. I'm very glad. And you couldn't find a way to let the officer know what the fella had said?'

'Was I wrong, Sam?'

'Well.' He took his time. 'You did your own cause no good, Speed. But you were true to yourself. That matters a lot.'

'I want our reception here,' Speed said, 'in the Blackamoor. Lizzie's family seems to be dithering about. I said I want it here. I said you and Ellen's the best people in Wigton and that's where we should have it.'

369

'And we're nearest the church.'

'There's that, Sam.' He laughed. 'Cut down on cars! Sean said he'd come and talk. I'm just giving you an early warning.'

—⁓—

'How did you find Lizzie?' Sam had been waiting all evening to ask Ellen but only now, in their last nesting place of the day, did the opportunity offer itself.

'Terribly strained,' Ellen said. 'Poor Lizzie.'

'I've seen young horses look like that,' Sam said. 'Just so high strung you can't touch them without there's such a pulling away, their eyes never stop looking frightened, mad with it.'

'Will he be any good for her?'

Sam had thought about that since the young couple had left. He sipped his tea. He had made no attempt, this evening, to read.

'He won't let anybody touch her, that's one thing. That must help her. She can feel safe with him.'

'But how can she feel safe with anybody? And I know you think well of Speed but he can be a violent man.'

Sam had thought of that as well.

'He'll look after her,' he said. 'I'm sure of that.'

'Oh, I hope so. Poor Lizzie.'

'They want to have the reception here.'

'We've always turned everybody down. No exceptions.'

'I made an exception for you, once, about the Labour Party. No politics in the pub, remember, but you would have the Labour Party here for its committee meetings. I said yes. That was an exception.'

Sean came to see him the next day. They went into the kitchen.

Sean had accepted just a half of bitter and he sipped it carefully and looked around.

'Fine house you have here, Sam.'

'Cigarette?'

'I don't use them, thanks all the same. We go to the Half-Moon, you know, and the Crown, the other end of the town.' He grinned rather shyly. 'This place is a long walk home later on at night.'

'They're two good houses.'

'I like this bitter, Sam. Bitter has to be kept just so.'

They were silent for a while. They did not know each other well. Things were not to be rushed. Sam noticed that when Sean picked up the half-pint glass it all but disappeared inside his hand. Yet there was about him that almost daintiness of some big and powerful men.

'So what's the verdict, Sam?'

'We'll do it.'

'There's them told me you'd never do it.'

'Well,' said Sam, 'they were mistaken.'

'You've known Speed since a boy.'

'I have. He's done well.'

'That army matter now, there's a puzzle.'

'He did no wrong, Sean.' Sam paused for emphasis. 'I know that.'

The Irishman looked at him, scrutinised him, nodded.

'I'll take your word, Sam.'

Sean took another sip at the beer.

'They told me you didn't drink, Sam.' The notion amused him. 'Now that's something I've seen. A landlord that doesn't drink.'

'Not in this pub, that's all.'

'I'll have to get you up to the Half-Moon then. So. Kathleen will be down to talk to Ellen about the food arrangements. They'll bring it in in the morning, she was thinking. I was thinking of a free bar.'

'Maybe a free bar from half past two for an hour or so and then beer free and pay for your own spirits.'

'I don't see that working out, Sam. How long have we got?'

'As long as you want to stay here, Sean, but it'll be tricky to cope with a private party after about six.'

'We'll close the free bar down at six then. It'll fit in with you after six, that'll be the way.'

'Ellen and myself will wait on. And I'll get Alfrieda and Tom Johnston to help out. Jack Ack said he'd bring his accordion.'

'That's the way it should be done,' Sean said. 'I had that in mind to ask you. And a rough idea?'

'Let me take care of that. I'd like to.'

Kathleen came down on the following evening and they agreed that the whole of the pub would be available from two-thirty to six. The food would be laid out in the kitchen. There would be glasses of Asti Spumanti lined up on the bar for everybody who wanted one, as soon as they got back from the church. Kathleen asked if the darts could be put away.

Ellen took her to the door and Kathleen said,

'I want to thank you, Ellen. Lizzie's always looked up to you. Since the Water Street days. She's not in the family way. They'll be going back to Liverpool after.'

Joe's job was to collect the empty glasses and help Alfrieda wash them when the pile got too high. William, Alfrieda explained, would have been there but a Labour Party Conference in Whitehaven had to take priority. He was getting more involved now, she said, and was much called on.

Sam looked around the pub the few minutes before they arrived. The kitchen was transformed. More tables, whitely clothed, a banquet, Sam thought: my God, had Kathleen laid on the food. The singing

372

room, extra polished by Sadie, who insisted that she would come over and help with the main clearing up at about five. The dartless darts room made more cosy with some of the chairs from the upstairs parlour. The bar with the Asti Spumanti bottles ready to fire and the glasses ready to be charged. There was, Sam thought, a real anticipation about it. Ellen was at the wedding itself. Joe was upstairs already changed, ready, waiting for the call. Mr. Kneale, whom Sam had recommended to do the wedding photographs, wandered contentedly from room to room, a Wigton schoolmaster in a Wigton pub but on legitimate business.

The photographs outside on the steps of the pub. The confetti on the front, in the corridor, in the kitchen. The men, dark suited, white shirted, the tie essential, black shoed, mostly sporting white carnations, and the women vivid in coloured wedding outfits, bold in new wedding hats and gloves and shoes, bosoms pinned with a rose, make-up re-perfected almost hourly, the afternoon moving from diffidence and politeness as the families and friends found the common ground to a welding around the wedding feast, praise for the food, and the service, wonder at the flow of free drink. Joe slipped in and out spying for glasses, collared by Alistair, a talk with Lizzie's sister, sent by Ellen to talk to Annie who looked left out, Sam calm at the centre of it all, Sean and his brothers planted in the hallway, three guardian oaks, kids in white, trailing ribbons in their hair, playing their giggling games and a gradual movement towards the singing room where Jack Ack swung the accordion and little reluctance was expressed when it came to singing a song.

'Joe should sing!' said Alistair, ordered Alistair. 'Joe has a band.'

Others were willing but now they wanted the landlord's son to sing to them and it was no occasion for any show of false modesty. He had sung there before. Frankie Laine's 'Cool Water' to begin: Jack Ack was well on top of that and the boy's choir-trained voice, the group, the layer on layer of good humour, good will, in the place lifted him, and the ham, the show off in him so long and so successfully repressed, let loose and he belted it out – 'Water,' they echoed, 'cool, clear, water'. Then he did 'April Showers'. There was scarcely a man in the pub who did not think he could not imitate Al Jolson singing 'April Showers' and the roof was raised. One more!

And in that haze of wedding, the deep undertow of risk and relief of Speed and Lizzie, the heady feeling that the noise was encouragement for him, alone, Joe had a premonition that it was for the last time. He went flat out for 'Houn' Dog', played with it, inhabited it, made a glorious fool of himself – and they cheered the fool, they whooped him home, when he looked up even his dad was laughing, but most of all there were Lizzie and Speed, side by side just inside the door, she beyond words, Joe thought, tall and victorious in her white dress, and Speed, glass in hand, tie long loosed, an arm around her waist, laughing his head off. Joe saw Lizzie when they were in the same gang in Water Street and Speed flying into battle after he had been cut in the stone fight and lying between the rails while a train went over him and Lizzie breaking in the piebald. There was no one to touch them in that town or anywhere. On this day they stood apart in the world.

'Good old Water Street, eh, Joe?' Lizzie said when it was done, her face rearing nervously but smiling straight at him.

'You're a better singer than a boxer, Joe.' Speed clenched and shook a fist at him.

'Somebody else's turn now,' the boy said, 'I'm supposed to be clearing up the glasses.'

He pretended to look put upon but it was a charade. He was elated, flying, proud that he had looked Speed and Lizzie in the eye and they had admitted him.

CHAPTER THIRTY-FOUR

Oxford was closing in on him.

A week before the departure date he went to Carlisle on the bus with his mother, to visit Jespers, 'Gentlemen's Tailor. Outfitter to the County'. Joe thought this a wholly unnecessary outing. He already had a perfectly decent suit. His mother had taken him to Redmayne's in Wigton and had a sports jacket with leather buttons made up for him by people she had once worked with. 'I used to make the buttonholes, Joe. Buttonholes, buttonholes, day in day out, buttonholes.' And he hated shopping.

'Why are you wasting money on a new suit?'

'Your dad and I said we'd tog you out and that includes a new suit.'

'Why do we have to go to Carlisle?'

'Because we do.'

It was odd, Joe thought, sitting next to his mother upstairs on a bus. He had not done that since he was a kid. It was a boyfriend-girlfriend thing to do. Ellen thought how nice it was, when was the last time? Would this be the last time?

She went into Jespers visibly nervous, Joe saw that and it made him feel arrogant. Who was Jespers to unnerve his mother? But inside he understood a little of what it meant for her. It was hushed and leisurely and the clothes were clothes that important people, ambassadors, Joe thought, politicians, civil servants, wore in films, in newspaper photographs. Something about the style of them? What they were made of? He could read appreciation in his mother's glance but he had none of her interest or expertise and a blur to him was to Ellen detailed evidence of class. This is what she wanted.

'Madam?'

The man was lean, pink-complexioned, a fine three-piece county suit, a paisley-patterned silk tie and handkerchief, a face which shone, gold-framed depressed clerical spectacles over the rims of which he peeped as he thought engagingly. Joe took against him.

'We'd like a suit, please.'

'For the young man, of course?'

'For my son,' said Ellen firmly.

'Hard to believe!' The eyes twinkled. No reaction. 'And may I ask what is the destiny of this suit? Are we talking sports suit, outdoor, casual, indoor, even so, rough tweed, fine tweed, lounge suit, double breasted, single breasted, town wear –'

'He wants a suit for university. He's going to Oxford next Wednesday.'

'A suit for Oxford then! Well now. I dare say we will find that suit, madam.' Out of his pocket came a tape measure. 'Could you oblige by removing your jacket: thank you. Very good. And if you would stand with your legs apart. Very good. A fine specimen, madam. Come this way.'

He led as if he were leading a regiment on a triumphal entry. They were now in another, even quieter, cooler room, a room of suits and nothing but suits, suits of all sizes, suits for all occasions.

Joe wanted the first one he tried out, two piece, dark, 'complemented', the man said, by a lime green waistcoat in which Joe saw himself as the bee's knees. Dapper, natty, snappy, smart, none of those words could do justice to what Joe saw in the full-length mirror. It was a bit of Rock 'n' Roll in a posh suit.

Ellen insisted he try on others which he did, knowing it was a waste of time but keen to please especially now that lime green waistcoat was in his sights. He had seen young men in the papers in fancy waistcoats but it had never occurred to him he might join them. This was worth the trip! After suit four, Joe was done with dressing up, staring at himself and being stared at, but Ellen would not relent. The man too, Joe could tell, felt a little driven by Ellen's persistence.

He had to try two of them on again. It took an effort not to groan.

Ellen sat on a stool and looked at him intently.

'The suit we first put on him is the most dashing,' said the man. 'Can be worn with or without the waistcoat, of course, and so would be entirely flexible.'

'I'd like him to try that other one on again.'

'The clerical grey?'

'The clerical grey.'

Joe liked it well enough. It was stylish: a mid-tone grey jacket, trousers, matching waistcoat; sober, worn by men of a certain background from eighteen to eighty, a uniform of the serving and the ruling classes.

'We'll have that,' she said. 'It's very well made.'

'It is an Oxford Man's suit,' the Jespers said. 'He will not go wrong in Oxford with a suit like that, I assure you.'

The boy did not like watching his mother pay over all that money. One day, he would pay it back.

'The other one was better,' he said, back on the bus, clutching the big parcel.

'Yes. It looked better on you.' She paused. 'I liked the waistcoat.'

'So did I.' He could see himself dance in a suit like that.

'Clerical grey will be easier for you,' she said. 'You'll blend in better.'

She had not enjoyed it but the job was now done. She felt tired and looked out of the window as the familiar countryside wound past them, tugging them home.

$$—\text{m}—$$

Then it rushed him. Then it was there. The last night out with Rachel, her father let her borrow the car. They made for a small country pub where they sat alone in a saloon bar surprisingly elegantly furnished. The landlady was Spanish. 'They've just done it up,' Rachel whispered, 'a lot of professional people come here at weekends.' They served sandwiches and Rachel bought two rounds. Eating helped because they had already talked everything over more than once – how they would write on alternate days, how she would take a Friday off in a month's time and come to Oxford for a weekend, how they would manage to fill in time without each other. As they were leaving, the landlady asked if she could try on Rachel's bangle. Both of them glowed in her praise for it. 'He must love you very much to buy you this,' she said. In the car Joe imitated the way she had said it – not to mock, but to have the words repeated.

Now that the departure was imminent, Joe felt deadened. His one overwhelming feeling was that he wished he did not have to go. Where he was now was bound to be better than anywhere else because now was as good as life could get.

They made love in Aunt Claire's and she heard them as she often had, listened a while as she often did, and then turned over to sleep

378

again. He waved Rachel off in King Street. He would not see her in the morning. The town was empty as she drove away and that matched his mood.

He took his time, walking slowly down the night street. He was leaving all this. He stood at the end of Water Street and looked around him, trying to summon up a feeling of departure, a moment of drama, a sense of an ending. Nothing came, save that deadness and the faint recurring siren whisper that he wished he did not have to go.

'Let me look at you,' said Ellen, the next morning, and he stood still, dutifully, for her inspection. 'Pack everything?' He glanced at the bulging suitcase. 'Enough to eat?' He indicated the haversack, picnic packed, flasked and lined with books. She stood there for a few more moments, wanting to say more, wanting to say much more, not knowing what to say. 'You'll do,' she said and she gave him a rushed little kiss.

Sam walked him down to the station. When the door banged, Ellen came into the kitchen where Sadie was pretending to work.

'He's gone,' she said, and Sadie turned away. She knew that if she looked any longer at the expression on Ellen's face, she would cry.

'The bar top still has to be polished,' Sadie said, eventually.

'Yes.' Ellen took the duster out of her pocket and looked at it. 'I'll do that.' And she went out tentatively as if afraid she might trip or bump into something.

They were some minutes early at the station. The cold made clouds of their breath. Sam looked at the bridge and wanted to tell Joe a story but he decided against it.

'Cigarette?'

Joe was surprised.

'Thanks.' He took one. Sam lit a match and cupped it to Joe's cigarette and then to his own.

'I should have landed here,' he said, 'when I came back from the war.' He scratched the back of his head with the hand holding the cigarette. 'But the engine broke down a mile or two away and we had to walk.'

'I remember climbing across that bridge,' said Joe. 'Stupid.' The cloud of cigarette smoke was darker than the breath.

The train was ahead of time. Sam levered in the suitcase. Joe leaned out of the window, lost for words, wanting words, needing a sort of conclusion.

'Just be yourself,' Sam said, 'that's all. And be decent to people.'

The boy had no immediate response but when the train edged forward, gathered itself, began to pull away, he waved and he found the words.

'Thanks, Dad,' he said, and wanted to add more.

He hesitated. But Sam nodded. That was enough.

PART FIVE
UNIVERSITY
ENTRANCE, 1958/9

CHAPTER THIRTY-FIVE

'Dear Rachel,

'Why does it hurt so much? And what is it? The moment I wake up my stomach feels as tight as a drum but at the same time it's queasy and I want to be sick. I don't think it's because I'm frightened because I can't see what there is to be frightened of. I just don't want to be here. In its own way it's as bad as those things that used to happen in my head. There was a bit of this in Paris, but it's much worse here. I want to be in Wigton and I want to see you! This feeling never goes away for long and I find I can only damp it down if I really concentrate on something else but I can't concentrate on anything else because of this feeling! The day crawls along whatever I do. I look at the clock and only ten minutes have passed. To tell you the truth, I'm ashamed of it. It's as if I'm going to burst out crying all the time! It's such a sign of weakness. Isn't it? What a baby! He wants to go home! What a kid! But I do. Sometimes inside my head feels frantic. And I can't tell anybody because they would just laugh. The truth is I daren't tell anybody.'

Not even Rachel.

'Dear Rachel,' he wrote, and sent,

'Thanks for your letter. You collect letters in the morning from a pigeonhole in the Porters' (sort of receptionists) Lodge (reception). It

383

was great to get your letter. One so far, fourteen more by my calculation until you come down (I think the proper word is 'up') to Oxford. I live on a staircase (it is a real staircase but what it does is let off to eight different rooms or sets of rooms). I share with James Carr-Brown who went to an independent (you pay but you don't board) school in London. I like him and he's very kind. We dine (at night) in the Hall – the canteen! – about three hundred or more men (nobody's called a boy or even an undergraduate – and student is not a word used in Oxford: we're all men) and the cost of it goes on our Battels (end of term bill). You wear gowns for dinner and for lectures and tutorials. The Scouts (college servants) bring the food like waiters. The college has a closing time at night and you are fined if you don't obey it.

'Our room has two doors and when both are closed this is called "sporting your oak" i.e. Do Not Disturb. Most of the Men have been in the Forces but James hasn't, he said that's probably why the Bursar (the college organiser) chucked us in together. That's one big difference – those who've been in the Forces and the few of us who haven't. Some of them have been in action. One man on our staircase (Staircase Number 2) was in Malaya. James has an older friend from his school who was an officer in Kenya. Most of the men are from public schools or independent schools. And it is only Men, a bit like a monastery, I suppose, and very strange.

'The nearest bath is on Staircase 6 in the far corner of the quad! (Main square – with a bowling-green-sized lawn in the middle.) There's a don (lecturer) who lives in rooms on our staircase: he keeps a dog and gives it a bath on Fridays, I'm told. There's another who seems to me to have been drunk after lunch (dinner) the three days I've been here. He's supposed to have a brilliant mind. Oxford is a great place to walk around and look at. I bet you'll like the "dreaming spires" they talk about. I was wandering about late in the afternoon yesterday when there was a fog (or would it be a mist?) and it was fantastic to see those beautiful old buildings looming at you. They seemed to float in the fog. But to be honest – I know this is crackers – I prefer Wigton!'

—␣—

Rachel merely scanned the letter. She would read it more carefully when she was alone in her bedroom. He was unhappy and trying to hide it. She would dig up some Wigton gossip for him. She would pop in and see Mrs. Richardson on her way home.

Checking and finalising her figures at the end of the working day had become something of a pleasure. Rachel could not quite pinpoint the reason for this, although of course that it was the end of the working day must have had something to do with it. But there were subtler strands. She found the balancing of the numbers extremely satisfying. It was mundane, it demanded no great intelligence, some would call it boring, but when she arrived at the foot of long columns of numbers which balanced out precisely, sums which were dependent on scores of individual accurate transactions she had made throughout the day, Rachel experienced a distinct hum of pleasure. It was compounded by an ability she developed which was to pursue a parallel line of thought independent of the calculations she was making. At first she had worried that her mind was wandering recklessly and the calculations would suffer as a result, but that did not happen. It was odd. She even began to look forward to it. It happened in no other circumstances in such a sustained and calm way. She could think things through in an orderly manner while the tip of her pen steadily scanned the columns of pounds, shillings and pence.

So she thought through the letter again as she sat, head bowed over the ledger, her concentration on the job apparently absolute. There was something frantic about it, she sensed, something that disturbed her about Joe. She could be unnerved by his demands. But she missed him and wished she had the words to tell him that; the reflection made her melancholy, a mood she took care to shake off as she walked down darkening late afternoon streets to the Blackamoor just opened for the evening stretch.

She went straight into the kitchen, comfortable in the place now.

'I've decided I'm going to make a combined kitchen and sitting room out of that old parlour upstairs,' Ellen told her. 'I don't know why I didn't do it years ago. I suppose this kitchen was just too convenient.'

Sam had said,

'The brewery won't give us a penny towards it.'

'I'd rather have a kitchen than a car.'

'Why the sudden decision?'

'I don't know,' said Ellen. But she had to do something.

'Shall I tell him about the kitchen in my letter or will you?' Rachel asked.

'You can.' Ellen gave a tight smile. 'His dad writes. I just add a few lines on at the end. He seems to be enjoying it, from what he says. He seems quite settled in.'

'They get long holidays,' Rachel said, trying to help. 'He worked out there were more weeks off than time at university.' But three years, Rachel thought. Ellen's fears triggered off her own. Three years before they could make a move.

'It's not that he's somewhere else,' Ellen said. She looked at Rachel as if unseeingly. 'He'll be changed, you see. They'll change him.'

'Joe?'

'Yes. And maybe that's how it has to be. But I won't know him.' She paused and then appeared to come awake. 'Does your dad still shout?'

'Yes,' Rachel nodded. 'It's the only way he can talk.'

'Isaac was like that even when he was at school! This fat little boy with this big man's voice.'

'I'll tell him you said that.'

She would put the last bit in her next letter. She would say nothing about Ellen's sadness, maybe even lie, say she was cheerful.

—⁂—

William was rather ashamed to take advantage of Ellen's decision to switch the kitchen to upstairs. But it made it perfectly acceptable for him to ask to look at what she intended to do and so engineer a few moments alone with her.

They went upstairs together, the first time they had gone up the stairs together. Ellen felt uncomfortable. It took no time at all to point out her plans and she wanted to leave the cold room immediately, but it was clear now that William intended to say something and that was the purpose of this little expedition.

Very quietly, looking out of the window as he talked, his back to Ellen, William said,

'Alfrieda and myself are thinking of getting, maybe, engaged, Ellen, but I want you to know that this is, I don't know how to put it, because I know, well, I think I know, that I have embarrassed you enough. You've been very understanding. Likewise Sam. Not that I ever had any hopes. Never. I will marry Alfrieda.'

He turned and she saw a desperate expression she had not seen before, nothing approaching it. She took a breath to be calm.

'Everybody'll be pleased about that, William,' she said. 'Alfrieda's just made for you.'

'I'll still soldier on doing the washing-up,' William said. 'I enjoy that.'

—*m*—

Joe came back from playing rugby to find the sitting room he shared with James occupied by four newcomers. The air was a fug of smoke.

'Goodness me!' James, just a touch plump, voice a mite sepulchral, manner tentative but generous, stood up from his squat in front of the electric fire with toasting fork and crumpet. 'You look all in. Have some tea.'

'I'll,' Joe indicated his gear, 'thanks. I'll just . . .'

'Are you sure you're all right? You look bushed.'

'St. Edmund Hall,' Joe said.

'Teddy Hall,' a newcomer corrected.

'They're a big side.' Joe felt he had to explain his refusal of James's warm offer. 'Some of them played for the army. There's a full Scottish international – they murdered us.' And I funked, plain to see, at least two tackles on that Welsh centre.

'They lose their scholarships if they lose their games at Teddy Hall,' said the newcomer. 'The last of the Neanderthals!'

Joe nodded in appreciation of the attempt to help and limped to his bedroom. He had to be on his own for a while. He was sore, bruised on his thigh, his shoulders ached, and he felt humiliated by those failed tackles. One of the friendlier men had commented, as they walked back to college through the fields and the Parks, that Joe was rather lightly built for this level of rugby. Five foot eleven and a few pounds under eleven stone did not make for a fearsome forward. Joe had immediately suspected a tougher message behind the genial conversation. That was depressing enough. More, though, he was becoming worn down by this clamp of homesickness, love-sickness. It would not budge. He flopped on the bed. Counted the days until Rachel would arrive, sought consolation in the diminishing numbers. It was pathetic. He looked down the barrel of a Saturday night bleaker than midwinter. No way out.

'Do come and join us.' James's knock on the door was gentle but persistent.

'Just a minute.'

He let nothing happen for as long as was polite and then jack-knifed himself upright and went into the ample and classic seventeenth-century room with its deep window seat which overlooked the perfect seventeenth-century quad, a narrower window looking into the extensive college gardens, comfortable battered furniture, a two-barred electric fire.

'You must have met Roderick on the staircase,' James said.

'Room seven. Didn't know you were a ruggah buggah,' Roderick, blond, military cut, clipped voice, immaculately uniformed in checked shirt, school tie, sports jacket, flannels, brogues, 'I play the girls' game myself.' He saw Joe's puzzlement and smiled. 'Hockey.'

'The others,' three of them, 'are friends from school, I'm afraid,' said James, that gentle vicarage tone mocking himself. 'Appalling failure of imagination. Edward, Henry, George.'

'All kings,' said Joe. 'Like James.'

'Another appalling failure of imagination,' Henry said. 'It carries on from generation to generation. We are doomed.'

'All the crumpets have gone but I can recommend this fruit cake.'

James cut off a chunk, poured a cup of tea and brought them over to Joe, now sat or rather squeezed onto the sofa. 'It's almost time for sherry,' said James. 'But you probably need this more.'

'James always plays mother,' said Edward.

'I rather wish my mother did,' said Henry.

'You're from the North, aren't you?' George looked closely at Joe, who was instantly mired in self-consciousness. 'I think people from the North,' he said carefully, 'your sort of people, are much more real than we are.'

Joe felt flattered. Later, in recollection, he suspected that he had been regarded as a bit of a specimen. Yet his willingness to embrace what was offered him overlaid, at that time, any suspicions.

'Absolute rot,' said Henry. 'Well-meant rot. Perhaps rot because well meant. But rot.'

'I mean coal miners and steel workers, men in shipyards and the factories – the Satanic Mills,' George said, his face set in sympathy.

'I felt that about my school more than once,' Roderick said.

'But you were head boy, weren't you?' said James.

'That was the cover-up.' Roderick grinned: it was infectious; Joe followed.

'I suppose it made a man of me. Gawd help us.'

'I rather think,' James said, arranging his hands so that they formed a steeple, 'that the uniformity of our system which was originally designed to turn out leaders of Empire and men of Roman virtues has now lost its purpose and just churns out rather grey men.'

'Hold on,' said Roderick, 'did I hear a mention of sherry?'

'My turn,' said George and he took the bottle of Harvey's Bristol Cream to a pre-arranged line of small glasses and as far as was humanly possible filled each one full.

'Why has James, or Jim as we knew him down in our particular

Satanic Mill,' said Henry, as he handed out the brim-full glasses of sherry with the care of a magician demonstrating a very difficult trick, 'thank you, squire, why has he called up the notion of Grey Men?'

'What is a Grey Man?' Joe spilled only a little of the sherry.

'Oh,' said George, 'a Grey Man will try to get to the Bodleian or the Radcliffe or some such library as near nine o'clock as he can make it.'

Joe tried to do that.

'A Grey Man will always eat in Hall.'

Joe did that.

'A Grey Man will always get his essays in on time.'

Joe did that.

'A Grey Man will wear a college tie every day.'

Joe fingered his tie. Roderick noticed.

'I think you're rather tough on us Grey Men,' Roderick said. 'Salt of the earth. We've worked at being grey. Some of us have sweated blood in our Satanic Mills to be grey. We're proud to be grey and by God we'll stay grey.' He raised his glass. 'Good luck.'

Joe took too big a mouthful of the hated sherry and spluttered.

Over the next few weeks, Joe discovered that Roderick had been very successful at a 'grand' public school and that his father was a Major-General; Henry, who had fought in Malaya, was the son of a judge; George's father had just retired from the Foreign Office; Edward's father was something in the City and James was the son of a doctor in a fashionable part of London. He was impressed: with himself. He recounted this information to Rachel in letters of brittle cheerfulness and the tone undisguisedly said, 'Look what's happening to me.'

Emboldened by the tea and sherry party, and slightly tipsy after the second glass of sherry and the pint of beer over dinner, Joe decided to look for a dance hall. James and the others had been invited to parties. As Joe walked out of the college, other undergraduates were coming in, usually carrying a bottle of wine. Saturday night parties were the thing, he knew that. Peppered around the quad were rooms, lit up, windows flung open despite the chill autumn air, voices rising, snatches of laughter.

Oxford was sharply defined on that Saturday night. Joe was just beginning to be at ease among the daunting buildings, especially now he had found the lanes and narrow streets which threaded them together. He walked towards Carfax where there was a dance hall. Everyone who passed him by seemed full of purpose, spirited, on course, excited to be there, so pleased to be them. Why not him? This drag of homesickness on his energy, this stupid weep-threatening weakness of his must be a punishment, he thought, or was it just another face of his cowardice?

Carfax Dance Hall was just like the County Ballroom in Carlisle. The same ball of many colours suspended from the ceiling, the same fifteen-piece 'big band', the same styles and dances, even the same sized room. Joe felt like an alien. He knew no one. He stood out a modern waltz and a decorous Rock 'n' Roll medley and then asked for a dance. The girl had a faint resemblance to Rachel.

She was called Olivia. She worked as a secretary in a solicitor's office. She had just moved to Oxford a year ago. She liked it very much. She could not have been more pleasant and yet the longer they talked and the more they danced – they did two on the trot – the wider grew the gap between them and when he thanked her and led her back to the spot at which he had invited her to dance, both recognised an exhaustion. Joe made one more attempt, this time with a girl deeply absorbed in her steps and barely monosyllabic, and then he went to the bar feeling that he had betrayed Rachel and proved himself a failure.

He recognised the men but he was too diffident to go up to them. He had seen them together, the three of them, strolling around the quad, sitting with each other at dinner, tall men, bold looking, handsome, Viking stock, heaped hair not unlike his own, but so easy in their skin.

One of them raised his glass a couple of inches from the table, looked at Joe, tilted the glass a fraction, nodded and by this semaphore said – you're welcome. Joe joined them.

'Can I get them in?'

He could. Pints of bitter. It took time at the bar but the time he took at the bar put him in credit. When he returned, he was almost a friend. Harold had come over to help him with the four pints.

'Totty, is what they call it,' said Harold, 'that's what they call Talent. Totty. Good, isn't it? Seen much?'

'Well,' Joe sucked at his new pint having too quickly disposed of the old: he liked neither totty nor talent but joining in was essential, 'being new's no help.'

'Being new's a bonus,' said Frank. 'Being new gives you a real look in. See that over there?' Joe followed his gaze. Four young women were gathered around a small round table, conversing with seemingly exclusive intimacy. 'Begging for it,' he said, and took a manly draught of beer.

They talked on and included him. The constriction in Joe's heart relaxed: the common sound of their words, that burr of childhood, of certainty, calmed him. They spoke with northern accents, every bit as strong as his own but, perhaps because they came from old and powerful northern city grammar schools of proven and hard-nosed excellence, their speech had nothing of diffidence or apology in it. Joe's accent had started to behave as if it were on black ice. Whenever he braked the attempted pronunciation of a word to fit the governing sound of English, it slithered around helplessly. These Yorkshiremen stood firm.

Already Joe knew that accent could make a man. Accent and a few code words and a twang worth a life's mortgage to learn and hand on. But now, in the Carfax dance hall, for half an hour or so, Joe's voice was back home.

'I think we might have clicked,' Harold said, raising his glass to the table of girls. To Joe, 'Coming?'

'Oh no.' Joe's reply was so emphatic that they laughed. 'I have a girlfriend at home,' he explained, through the darkening alcohol. They laughed louder at that and then easily, confidently, the three Yorkshiremen moved off, moved in.

Joe was late. He dashed through the crisp, cold streets, the beer sloshing inside him, suddenly happy in anticipation.

—⟋⟍—

Rachel's Saturday night, the second since Joe's departure, had been even more dismal than the first. If you did not go out on Saturday night then when did you go out? On Saturday night you could dress up as on no other night, be later than all other nights, be the person you wanted to be not the person you had to be, go with your boyfriend, your girlfriend, have a laugh, drink a little, Saturday night was the climax of the week and gave it a shape. With Joe, Rachel's Saturday nights had been rich.

This time, for the second Saturday, she went with Linda to the Donaldsons' to play cards. Robert was the oldest of the Donaldson brothers, in his early twenties, as blond-haired as Rachel was dark, brown-skinned from the weather, thick forearms revealed by permanently rolled up sleeves. He invited them all to come with him to the dance at Silloth: they could all fit into his car: Rachel's brothers would be there, he said, catching her eyes full on, flirting. Rachel said no, quite severely, which made Robert laugh and repeat the offer as he paused at the door and surveyed the meek company around the table, cards held like fans. Rachel looked the other way.

She got back home by ten as arranged. Joe rang about fifteen minutes later. The phone outside the Junior Common Room had been occupied. And no sooner had he got inside than another man took his waiting place, thus ensuring that Joe could not be greedy with time.

Rachel's voice melted the lump of sick fear instantly. He felt so light he could have levitated. Just to hear her, whatever she said.

'The poem was good,' she said. 'Did you do it?'

'Yes,' he smiled at the relief of truth, 'it just came out of the blue.'

'I'll keep it,' she said. 'Your letters are good.'

'Yours are better. I liked the bit about your dad at the horse sales.'

'I saw your mother again, last Thursday. They're already getting on with the kitchen.'

'I don't know why she wants it. We've already got one.'

And nothing much continued to be said for the time Joe felt allotted him by the rather too obviously impatient man outside the box and the reticent girl at the other end of the distancing, clumsy phone, which brought you together and emphasised your loneliness at the same time.

'Had a couple of drinks with some men from Yorkshire.' He did not mention the dance. 'And you?'

'Cards at the Donaldsons'.' She did not mention Robert. 'Linda's getting warmer.'

'Less than two weeks,' he said, hoping that by declaring it he would dull the time, 'past half way.'

'Are you sure I'll fit in down there?'

'Why not?'

'It sounds' – Rachel had thought about Oxford a great deal and with apprehension before and more intensely and worryingly since Joe's letters; but she did not want to hurt Joe's feelings – 'a bit posh for me.'

It had proved a bit posh for Joe.

'It isn't,' he said. 'Everybody's really friendly.'

'And you're O.K. in yourself?'

'Yes,' he said, speaking accurately and warmly out of the moment, 'I'm having a great time. You?'

'To tell you the truth I can't pretend I'm not missing you,' she said, in a rehearsed and level tone. Rachel's flat declaration blew Joe's fears clean away. Less than two weeks!

The man tapped, politely, on the glass. Joe's reaction was that of someone caught at the scene of a crime.

'Somebody else needs the phone.'

'All right then.'

'I'll have to go.'

'Same time on Wednesday?'

He apologised to the man outside, who apologised for tapping on the glass.

Joe went back the narrow way, down the steps, past the Steward's bar out of which came the unmistakable sounds of ruggah buggahs on the beer. He went in. More than half the team was there and none of them accused him of cowardice. He bought a pint and sat on one of the benches against the wall. He was between the full back, one of the snootier and a big prop, one of the more amiable members of the team. Joe had not mastered all the names but fourteen faces had been familiar to him since the first full training session and he thought as he sank the pint that this was a company, one to which he belonged.

'Say something in your funny accent, Richardson!' Full back's sentence was delivered as an order. 'Something like "oop't'North like" or "Doon't'pit like".'

'Or Bugger Off, like,' said the big prop.

'Oh come on! Why don't we take Richardson's trousers off?'

For a tremulous moment Joe thought that this suggestion would be carried through.

'Oh grow up,' said a wing three-quarter, and to Joe, 'ignore him, the sad deviant in our midst.'

'A bit hard,' said Joe, 'when he's belting it out in my ear.'

Joe got up and followed the wing three-quarter to a small table. They talked about the game. 'Absolute bloody nightmare!' the rugby man said. 'Half the Blues there, I expect, but still. Absolute. Bloody. Nightmare. Another?'

He brought back two pints at which Joe looked with some concern. The early sherry had not gone down well. The number of pints was already way in excess of his usual intake. He lit a cigarette; remembered his manners; offered one; accepted.

'You're a bit light for open side flanker,' wing three-quarter said, raising his glass. 'Didn't you say you played blind side loose forward at school?'

'Yes.' Joe thought he swallowed the word but somehow it doubled back and came out whole. He raised his glass and took too big a draught to get it over with. 'I was blind side loose forward for two years.'

'I'll mention it to Dougie. Oh God! Absolute. Nightmare! They hammered us. They crucified us!'

As Joe walked, slowly and almost steadily, across the quad to his staircase, he still felt some of the stiffness and ache of the game, felt an uneasy turbulence in his stomach, felt as happy as he had so far been at Oxford, twelve days to go to Rachel. James above all was really a friend. Some of the ruggah buggahs were O.K. The full back didn't count.

He passed the chapel where he would go in the morning. It might be a good idea to join the choir, he thought, he liked singing in a choir, you could forget yourself in a choir, he would see if he could fit it in.

The stairs on the staircase seemed steep and he was glad that James was not yet in. He undressed unsteadily, got into bed, closed his eyes and then his mind became a sway boat, swooping up into his skull, up and up as if the skull were as wide as the sky and then rushing down again, whoosh, down, down the sway boat, then up, up, up and down again whoosh, whoosh. He got out of bed, clammy throated, his stomach beginning to move with a life of its own and just made the lavatory on the floor upstairs next to the lecturer with the dog. He tried to be sick quietly so as not to disturb the dog. It was the first time he had been drunk sick and after a while he thought he had heaved out all his insides. His throat was sore. His mouth stank. His stomach simmered and threatened still and when he got back to his bedroom and drank a glass of water, there was one last watery upheaval.

Joe spent some time wiping it off the floor. It would be terrible if the Scout saw it. The Scout looked a bit like Jack Ack who played the accordion. He used two handkerchiefs which he then rinsed in his sink. He felt cold and very shaky.

In the morning he could scarcely move for the aches and the trembling. He would still go to chapel. Outside he took several deep breaths. The cold air hurt. He was lucky, he thought, that it was not the eucharist – not bread and wine. His clerical grey suit felt too tight.

—ɯ—

'Dear Rachel,

'Thanks for what you said about the poem. I enclose another, not very good but maybe you'll like it. Everything is much as before. I can't wait for you to meet people here – I've told two or three of them about you. Good old Linda!

'You're always with people here, that means with other men. I suppose it's like being in the army or public school, but sometimes I'd just like to have a meal on my own, say, or walk somewhere without feeling that everybody around you was walking with much the same goals in mind. I want to say hello to people as we all do in Wigton, but whenever I try it they look through you or look as if I've done something to offend them. The gowns we wear make it even more conformist and when we take off the gowns there's still a uniform, of sorts, some variations, you can tell the more expensive stuff but a Martian wouldn't be able to. Some of them can be quite snooty about clothes. Remember that sports jacket Mam got specially made at Redmayne's? This man – I don't know his name – we were standing at the college entrance, rubbed his finger and thumb over the lapel and said, "Good bit of cloth, pity you didn't get it run up into a jacket." You can only laugh.' Though Joe had not laughed, felt put down.

'Breakfast is worst. It seems more intensive. Most of them read the papers – *The Times* is the favourite – and usually they talk about world affairs. It's been Eoka for days on end now, and Makarios and terrorism and the British Army. One of them had been an officer in the British Army in Cyprus and he reckons terrorism can never be beaten which seems very pessimistic to me and giving in. I mentioned the Algerians in the street I worked in in the Bois de Vincennes, but it didn't seem to add to the discussion. This ex-army officer just used it to bolster his own case and said Algeria would have to be given its

399

freedom soon. Look at Israel, he said. They know a lot; you have to give them that.

'Another time it was Germany's reunion based on what the Queen said. I disagreed with that but somebody who had a brother in the Foreign Office said it was the only way to make Europe a peaceful continent and we should join Europe as soon as possible. I disagreed with that as well but I didn't have a chance to get a word in. Sometimes it's best just to listen: you can learn a lot. Some of them talk like old men. Now that I've written this I realise that I probably enjoy breakfast more than I thought I did! But I do feel hemmed in, that's for certain. Only a week now! . . .'

Rachel felt even more anxious. There was a fearfulness creeping into her and she had not bargained for that.

—⁓—

The day before Matriculation and the photograph, Joe went to get his hair cut. There had been no more than a handful of remarks, not all disparaging, but he had made his decision.

'Just a trim, is it, sir?'

The young man, one of three, patted Joe's hair as if it were a favourite little dog. There was a prancing fun about him which made Joe feel good.

'No,' he said, 'I want it short. And flat. And no Brylcreem either.'

'Oh dear! Is sir absolutely sure? This suits you very well.' He flicked at it with a comb and looked admiringly in the mirror. Joe wavered, but only for a moment: he saw the rows and rows of other men, some long-haired but in a style different from his own, or a style that depended on wavy hair or a long face or a degree of self-confidence out of Joe's reach. Most wore short back and sides though now and then permitted themselves the extra inch.

'Short,' said Joe. 'Sorry.'

'Oh well. The customer is always right.' He winked. 'Cross your heart sure?'

'Sure,' said Joe and he wriggled a little under such pleasurable pressure of attention.

When it was done he looked at it very carefully. It looked just like almost everybody else's: flat, short, neat. He thanked him and wanted to say, 'Let's have a drink.' Joe's relief at not having to strain to fit in, the instantaneous closeness he felt for this – man? boy? – he would be about Joe's own age – persuaded him that he could have found someone who could become a friend. He lingered for a moment or two. The decision had to be made quickly. Outside on the streets short-haired undergraduates went to and fro. The boy smiled at him, openly, easily.

'Anything else, sir?'

What's your name? Why could he not ask? His indecision began to embarrass him. What's your name?

The boy smiled sympathetically. Yes, Joe thought, they could be friends.

'What time do you close tonight?' he asked.

'Six o'clock,' he replied, and waited.

Joe blushed. 'Thanks,' he said, and rushed out.

———

'Pity about the hair,' said James. 'I rather liked it as it was. It had character.'

Later Joe and James took tea together. Joe had been working at the desk, James slouched in an armchair with a book. James was just as open and easy as anybody could be, Joe thought, already a friend.

'You ought to read this,' James said, putting the book aside reluctantly. 'I just bought it in Blackwell's. *Saturday Night and Sunday Morning* by Alan Sillitoe. Wonderful reviews. Totally new world to me. I think you'd enjoy it.'

Joe nodded, looked carefully at James and then produced the lightweight pipe he had bought on the way back from the barber's shop.

'Tricky to keep those things going,' James said. 'I never mastered it.' He smiled.

Joe packed in the tobacco too tightly.

'If you don't mind,' said James, after pouring himself a second cup, 'I'll get back to my book.'

The pipe felt so awkward between his teeth, it seemed to rattle against them. He held onto the bowl, steadied it, and sucked in deeply. You needed to persist, the man in the shop had said, sometimes it could take weeks. Why had he not asked his name?

It was not until half past six that he felt in the clear. Where would they have gone? Would they be interested in the same things? Yet Joe had known him even though he was a stranger. He'd been so friendly, and in a way that had touched Joe so directly. He felt he had somehow let himself down. He would have to go to a different barber's shop in future.

'Let me buy you a pint of bitter,' James suggested, and snapped the novel shut. 'I don't want to finish this until later. Sometimes spinning it out like that can be . . .' – he was going to say 'exquisite' – '. . . quite exciting, you make your own cliffhanger.'

CHAPTER THIRTY-SIX

Joe went up the spiral of stone steps to meet his tutor feeling like a boy summoned from the lower deck to the captain's bridge. Matthew Turney's reputation was already vivid. It was claimed that he had written his first book while commanding a submarine in the North Atlantic; his second had been a hand grenade tossed into the cautious and patient scholarship of early Tudor history; his later books broke into local records of the gentry and with fresh evidence dashingly tilted at received opinions, delighted in fierce disputes over details, made history a war game.

When, later, Joe would reach the period of history in which Turney had pitched camp, he would find the weekly reading list of four or five books and an equal number of articles often quivering with debates provoked by the man who would listen to him every week at 5 p.m. on Monday reading aloud an essay, for about half an hour, and then fill out the hour with his own observations on the essay and on the subject. And the princely early seventeenth-century room bagged by Turney impressed itself on Joe almost as much as the man himself. When the ten 1958 intake of historians at Wadham had met Turney for sherry in their first week, the tutor had listed some of the scientists, historians, classicists, scholars of quiet fame and enduring importance in the chain of knowledge who had themselves over the centuries ascended those spiral stone steps and brooded on learning.

Many of the more artistically informed undergraduates had observed that Matthew Turney would have been a perfect subject for El Greco. He sat black-gowned in his high armchair facing Joe, similarly black-gowned, in an almost matching chair. Turney would settle himself deep in the chair, throw out long legs which managed to look bony even under his heavy cloth three-piece suits, the thin face, thinning black hair, somehow cowled by the top of the gown as he hunched up to listen – or, not to listen, who could tell? – to yet another essay on the same question asked by him of a similar band of novice historians during the past eight years.

For Joe so far this was the best bit. He felt secure, he knew how privileged he was, this was what he was here for. He delivered the essay at a steady pace.

Accepted to read Modern History, Joe had been a little surprised that it started in the fifth century, but now he revelled in that Dark Age richness. He knew so little about it. It was inhabited by Celtic Christians and northern warriors. Much of it was located in places he had visited – Iona, Lindisfarne, along the broken Roman Wall. He felt proprietorial about it and Matthew smiled at fulsome descriptions, amazement, panegyric.

'Well done!' he said when Joe finished. 'You put a hell of a lot into it, well done. You don't have to murder yourself over these chaps, you know. There's much more interesting stuff to come and frankly this will figure very small in Finals. I doubt whether you'll even bother with it. But well done, old chap!'

Joe flinched away from the compliment. He sought out the glass fronted bookcase, almost floor to ceiling, glistening with handsomely bound books, volumes of authority, and again he thought this was the best room he had ever been in. But though his eyes were reluctant to meet the enthusiasm of such an idolised tutor, inside himself Joe sang and for a while the song dispelled his homesickness. The work on the essay had numbed it but this was a lifting of a siege.

'You may,' said Turney, tactfully, burying himself even more deeply into the armchair, his face now all but shrouded in the gown and the large collar of the loose jacket, 'you may like to take a slightly different look at one or two aspects of this. Yes, those kings were fighting – when it suited them – for God and the cross, but they were the most terrible thugs. Think of Al Capone in Chicago, that's more like it.'

Al Capone? Thugs? Kings of Northumbria, Kings of Wessex and Mercia? Chicago?

'They're basically illiterate war lords – think of the Chinese war lords. The Roman Empire's collapsed, the Romans push off to defend their heartland and this place is up for grabs. There are the locals, there are mercenaries who've been in and out for donkey's years, the Germanic hordes see a chance to push across and snatch up the freehold, it's a good old-fashioned land grab. Nor is it so very unfamiliar to us today.'

Joe nodded but he was reeling.

'You're very generous about those Celtic monks – you are a Christian, aren't you? – and some of them were remarkable chaps. They came out of Ireland where the Romans had scarcely set foot – important point, uncolonised – then up to Iona – you wrote well about that, been there? I guessed so – down to Lindisfarne, then they'd go on to York over into Europe, sit at the centre of Charlemagne's attempt to make a Holy Roman Empire – some remarkable individuals. But are we to believe everything they said about themselves? The miracles, the prophecies, the healing of the sick? They're aping the

405

Apostles, you see, they want to beat the Apostles at their own game and all the mumbo-jumbo that went with it. We have to be a bit careful about the sources here, even Bede. There is a sense in which he's writing propaganda – for the Church and for the Northumbrian royal family. Serving two masters, you might say.' He smiled warmly. Joe needed it.

Propaganda? The Venerable Bede? The Founder of English History? St. Bede?

'And those Celtic saints, Richardson, they were far more worldly than you gave them credit for. Look at how they worked their way into positions of power by getting the women on their side. They arrive at the courts of these pagan kings. Nothing about the poor, here: they know their Bismarck, their real-politik, these chaps. They single out the Queen and her daughters and sisters. We don't know how they do it and imagination could run riot – but they convert them. The Queen stumps up for a church. More conversions. Their husbands win a battle or two after they nag them into planting the Christian cross on the battlefield. They're convinced the cross brings them victory and then *mass* conversions. Monotheism is in business. But these canny Celts saw that it was the women who could drive it. And when they built abbeys – like Hilda at Whitby – the women were staking claims to power because they ran these places and these Saxon women had independent inheritances. They could afford to be empire builders.' Joe concentrated hard. You did not take notes.

'At their abbeys the women trained the younger sons of the upper crust and probably one or two scholarship boys – not unlike this place today – and herded in a few earnest and privileged young women – ditto – and for a while Christianity gave these women a real power base. So who was using whom? We have Celtic cunning and feminine opportunism – a marriage made in Heaven!'

Turney had enjoyed that: not least seeing that the mind of the young man in front of him was being turned on a spit.

It was Joe's turn.

'Whether you're a Christian or not,' said Joe, '*they* were, and that's what matters, isn't it? Whatever you say about mumbo-jumbo and trying to beat the Apostles and roping in the women or being used by them, the fact is they did it, didn't they? They made these places Christian. They set up monasteries. They brought workmen from all over Europe to build and carve stuff. Bede wrote that first history and all his other books. There were the Lindisfarne Gospels – they're great works of art, aren't they? As well as being the Gospels. They used the Roman script to start writing in English. They wouldn't have been able to do that if they hadn't believed in God and if God hadn't helped them.'

'Other, and greater, civilisations, Richardson, take Greece, had managed well enough without a Christian god.'

'But they crumbled, they lost.'

'Not exactly. Not at all actually. The Greeks are still with us, thank God, despite Christianity's attempt to go it alone without them. It was the Arabs who took the Greeks over . . . seriously. The Arabs were coming on as the real boys at about this time.'

'But do you think that Northumbria would have been civilised without the Celts and Christianity?'

'Civilised? O.K. – the Lindisfarne Gospels, Bede, Hilda, yes, civilised. I confess to being rather worried when you say God was on their side. Lots of these saints of yours were martyred and once it had become the powerful court religion I suspect an awful lot of chaps just jumped onto the bandwagon and went into the Church. And they became every bit as greedy and often as bloodthirsty as their heathen warrior brothers.'

'But the monks still did it.'

As Joe tried to keep the argument alive, tried, in truth, to find some way of standing up to what he felt was an unfair and untrue reduction of the whole Celtic enterprise, he had to keep hypocrisy at bay. Despite the experience of Paris, his faith had dimmed to the point where he could even question the existence of God, the divinity of Christ, the facts of Heaven and Hell. Viscerally, especially at extreme moments, it could still be convincing but a growing and stronger voice was steering him towards the secular scepticism of Matthew Turney.

'But jolly good,' said the tutor as he stood up at the end of the tutorial. 'Well done.'

As he always did, he ushered his undergraduate to the door.

'I see you come from Wigton, in Cumberland.'

'Yes.'

'I get my suits copied there. The John Peel Tailor. Redmayne's?'

'That's it.' Joe felt a little surge of ridiculous pride.

'They do an excellent job. First rate. And jolly cheap.'

'My mother worked at Redmayne's.'

'Did she?'

'She made buttonholes.'

As soon as that came out, Joe wished very hard that he had not said it.

'Before the war,' he added.

Matthew Turney, Wykehamist Scholar, Officer, Gentleman, pressed his hand gently on the boy's shoulder.

'Well done,' he said. 'Don't work too hard on this stuff, Richardson, will you? Take time to have a good nose around.'

Joe had an hour and a half before dinner. He came down the stone steps exuberant, embarrassed, comforted and still intoxicated by the achievements of the Celtic monks. It was dark in the architecturally faultless front quad, dimly lit by yellow lights, shadowy men coming in and out of the black entrances to staircases, a misty sense of Sherlock Holmes about the place. Joe took out his pipe.

He would go back to his rooms and make notes on what Mr. Turney had said. After dinner he would start on the fortnightly essay which he had to write for his other tutor. He got his pipe going with just two matches.

James was at the desk and the two young men acknowledged each other in one of what was becoming a deeply companionable range of responses. Joe settled in the window seat. After a few minutes, James leaned back his chair and said,

'You don't have any Greek at all, do you?'

'None.'

'A pity. Damn!'

He stood up.

'I think I'll go to the bar.'

'I want to do a bit of work. I'll stay here, if you don't mind.' Part of him wanted to go, just to please James.

James nodded, as it were blessing Joe's diligence. He took his gown and then spotted that *Saturday Night and Sunday Morning* was still exactly where he had left it.

'Not read it yet?'

'I haven't had time,' said Joe. 'But I will.'

'Do. I'd greatly value your opinion on it.'

Joe was, guiltily, a little relieved to see him go. He could now be alone and luxuriantly burrow into himself completely and sift through Matthew Turney's comments. He had taken it for granted that Christianity was flawed, occasionally even something to be ashamed of, but still fundamentally the peak of human achievement in morality and in ideals of freedom and justice. However shaky his own faith was becoming, it was too early for Joe totally to abandon his belief that, for instance, the great Celtic preachers, Aidan, Columba, Cuthbert, had brought light to a dark world, hope to a miserable world, possibilities of truth and equality to a corrupt world. But Matthew Turney was the cleverest man he had met. Joe was excited to think he had the chance to take him on. He tried to relight his pipe with just one match.

—◊—

'Fancy a bit of Society Hunting?'

Roderick, who was also reading History, accompanied Joe, sometimes with a few others, on a grand tour of Oxford's beckoning societies.

The History Society was an obvious early stop. Joe was caught. Two dons whose books he had seen on the shelves debated and then led a discussion on the Jesuits in the Counter Reformation. Joe joined.

'Not for me,' said Roderick, rather enjoying, Joe thought, the fact that Joe so clearly liked and imitated his clipped way of talking – so he made it even more clipped – his brisk way of walking – more brisk – his quick-chop decision making. 'Too much like home. Next!'

The Literary Society. A critic from the *Observer* whose writing Joe revered was pitched against a woman novelist who chain-smoked through a cigarette holder. The subject was 'The Relevance of the Critic'. The room was packed. The speakers were only mildly funny. Joe thought they might be boozy. No sparks flew. Joe was puzzled. These were Titans.

'Alcos both,' said Roderick. 'And bloody egomaniacs.'

Neither joined although Joe took the programme and reserved himself the right to attend particular meetings. The Music Society. In the college itself. A recital of Schubert's songs by one of the new undergraduates, accompanied by a man in the third year.

'Bliss,' said Roderick. 'I'm on.'

Joe demurred. It would be easier, he calculated, and take less time to continue to listen to concerts on the wireless. He had brought his maroon plastic box and spare batteries.

Roderick marched off with school chums to two or three other societies: Joe went with James to the Philosophical Society where the discussion was so dazzling – and from men of about his own age – that he staggered out thinking the best thing to do would be to catch the next train home. James joined. There was a new society being formed to campaign against racial intolerance. All of them joined that.

The Politicals.

'We can always say we tried,' said Roderick.

The Conservative Club. 'Oh Gawd!' said Roderick. Labour. 'Gawd!' Liberal. 'Some very pretty girls there,' said Roderick, 'worth a sub.' Joe signed on for Labour but he was not sure he would stick it out. There was rugby, there was the Chapel, he wanted to summon up the nerve to audition for the college Drama Society. There were the societies he'd already joined and should he join the Jazz Society? There was the theatre, there were cinemas, there were rumours of an opera.

'All good men and true must go to the Union,' said Roderick. 'No getting out of that. Let's get it over with.'

Through the early winter streets of Oxford, in the yellow-lit dusk which always seemed touched with a river mist and curled around university buildings still too fine for Joe to take for granted, along the Broad and the High, up Turl Street and Merton Street, past the Martyrs' Memorial and across Carfax, like phantoms out of the mist, they came, the serious men, and serious women too, some cycling in from their more distant colleges, men in strong made-for-a-lifetime sports jackets, women in sensible warm coats, heavy and obliterating of all shape, puffing out the cold air like pipe smoke, college scarves slung around the neck in that precisely casual uniform style, streaming towards the Oxford Union. It was the place in which Prime Ministers had taken their first steps in public life, the place which had and would again breed Chancellors and Foreign Secretaries, leaders of newly liberated countries on several continents, statesmen, moulders of opinion in print, on air, masters of society or so it was thought and so it had often enough proved to be the case. Eagerly they came through the streets as a congregation to their temple of destiny.

'James said that he expected at least two or three of those we saw tonight would be in the cabinet, or running the civil service, maybe an ambassadorship, an important one, he said, America, Russia, France, India.'

This was from the last letter Rachel received before setting out for Oxford and everything in it fuelled her growing fear of inadequacy.

'It was great to see them,' Joe wrote. 'Most of them just two or three years older than me. Some of the main speakers in dinner jackets with black dicky bow ties. Others wearing white bow ties. And such speeches!'

What he really meant was such assurance, such aplomb, and a confidence beyond his understanding. He would have loved to stand up in the Oxford Union, as he had in the debates at school, and tell the world to be more just, argue that peoples of all races and religions show more tolerance to each other, demonstrate the need to work for a single world order and demand the end of all poverty. The schoolboy Joe had seen public and political speech as the essential platform from which to launch ideas which would sweep the world and change it for ever.

The Union tongue-tied him. He knew in the first few minutes

412

that he could not dress like that or speak or perform like that to an audience which he believed to be almost mythically intelligent and critical and itself packed full of the potentially great. The speakers in their evening dress, the speeches full of knowing, anecdotal embroidery, classical tags, the place so clearly a forum for those who would rule over us unnerved and paralysed him.

'That's my lot,' he said in a clipped, Roderick tone. 'Not for me.' He hoped his rejection was convincing.

'Seconded,' Roderick said.

'I thought that at least three of the speakers were really quite excellent,' said James, in that rather hushed clerical voice. 'Shall we have a beer?'

Was the train going up to Oxford or down to Oxford? Were her best clothes good enough? It would be an expensive weekend. Did he really smoke a pipe?

CHAPTER THIRTY-SEVEN

But when she saw him her fears fell away. He was standing too near the train but looking the other way. He should have been wearing his specs, she thought, affectionately, but when he turned and saw her and his face shone with a smile that brought out her own, she was glad, as she had been the first time at Wigton pictures, that he was spec-less. Even before she put down her case they attempted a hug, awkward because they did not want anyone to see them doing it, but vital because both felt they would have burst if they had not touched. He took her case and marched off for a taxi. He had it all planned and budgeted; he had dug into his savings.

Rachel decided to be generous as they waited in the rank.

'I think I like your new haircut,' she said. It made him look like a schoolboy.

Joe was relieved.

'It's just that this is what most men have,' he said, hoping to sound careless, even lofty.

'Just a bit too short at the back.' She paused. 'And on the top.'

He agreed. He scarcely dared look at her. Could just four weeks have made her even more lovely? The black hair seemed even blacker, more silky, more lush: her skin softer, sweeter, her eyes, her body. Joe peeked little side glances, aching to get to the small hotel he had finally settled on, a little more expensive than the bed and breakfast but convenient – in a street immediately behind the college.

'It's the first time I've been in a taxi,' Rachel said.

It was Joe's second but he did not quite know whether such a confession would be boastful or pathetic so he kept quiet.

The taxi was the right thing to do but Joe would have preferred to walk Rachel into the city in the eternally becoming dusk, to point out this and the other college, to stroll down the Broad in the Friday drift, to refer with casual grandeur to the Clever Men of Balliol, point out the Sheldonian, perhaps even slip around the corner to see the Radcliffe Camera, show off the little Bridge of Sighs, welcome her aboard this place in which her presence confirmed his own place. For the first time he felt that something of Oxford was him. And for the first time he knew that over the next three days and two nights he would not be mortified by homesickness. Or perhaps it had been love-sickness, because inside his composure, the successful straining to be the correctly anonymous Oxford chap, there was a rage to satisfy a desire suddenly unbearable.

He paid the taxi and calculated a ten per cent tip. Rachel stood on the pavement, her new suitcase in front of her, a sense of relief all but drowning her. It would be all right. Joe was tense and shorn and a bit distanced because it was in public but he was still Joe.

Mrs. Pryor, a woman whom nothing passed by, admitted Rachel to the hotel with, it seemed, reluctance. Rachel signed the book rather as if she were signing a confession.

'I'll help her up with her case,' said Joe.

'Gentlemen are not allowed in single ladies' rooms for more than five minutes. All guests are expected to be in by eleven o'clock unless special circumstances can be argued. Gentlemen are not allowed to

415

accompany single ladies into the hotel after 8 p.m. Your room is on the second floor, up two flights, turn left, along the corridor, right, down two steps, past the bathroom and the W.C., number fourteen, at the end. No more than one bath a day. No alcohol in bedrooms. Breakfast is seven-thirty to nine. No loud music.'

Rachel tried hard not to giggle but did not quite succeed, which was noted by Mrs. Steel-haired Pryor, who would keep a close eye on this one.

Joe dumped the case on the floor, took a look at his watch, did what could be done in five minutes and clattered loudly down the last flight of stairs into the tiny reception area. Mrs. Pryor looked up but without appreciation.

As they walked up Holywell towards the King's Arms, Joe could never remember being happier. Rachel looked excited, his arm was round her, they would have a drink in the King's Arms, then go back to his rooms while everyone was in Hall having dinner. James had pointed out he would not be coming back to the rooms until well after ten o'clock. Joe planned to go out to a restaurant picked after scrutiny of several price lists. Roderick had told him it was 'perfectly O.K.'

They were shy in the King's Arms and there was no one Joe knew well but two or three Wadham men waved or said hello, one even came across and was introduced. They were impressed, Joe thought, some of them noticing him for the first time. Rachel was relieved that the pub was her first step into Oxford.

'It's just a pub after all, isn't it?' she said as they left. 'I mean, just another pub even though it was full of students.'

'Undergraduates.'

Rachel took an unnecessary amount of time to look around the room, Joe thought. She was intrigued by the duties of Cliff, his Scout.

'Makes your bed, cleans the room, washes the dishes and the bed linen and the towels for you? What else? He's like your servant!'

Joe mumbled. At first he had found it embarrassing to have a Scout and had gone through contortions of over-politeness, of helping, making his own bed, washing his own dishes, but Cliff had said he was doing him out of a job. Nor did he respond well to matiness of any sort. Now Joe accepted Cliff. Soon he would scarcely notice him, even criticise him for not dusting for a week, and although he apologised for criticising him, he did it. But Rachel's rather scornful tone hit the nerve. He's like your servant!

'You can't do anything about it.'

'You're all spoiled. Put this gown on then.'

Joe did.

'Walk about.'

Which he did.

'You look like Mr. Braddock. I thought – undergraduates – would have different gowns.'

In the bedroom, in the dark, in the front quad of Wadham, it was, Joe thought, even better than he remembered it and God knew that had been often and intensely enough.

'Why don't we just stay here?'

'If you think I came to Oxford to lie in a single bed you're mistaken, Joe Richardson. Besides who knows when that Scout of yours is going to pop up?'

They took their time to walk the short distance to the corner of Turl Street, Joe compulsively playing the tour guide, Rachel soon switching off, relaxing into the ambling strangeness of the place, the vast street, the fine buildings, the monopolising presence of these polite young people.

'Are you sure it's all right?' Joe whispered.

'Yes. That's the third time you've asked.'

It was not confirmation he wanted for the third time but praise. To Joe the restaurant was more than perfectly O.K. There were prints of Oxford colleges on the walls, little lamps on the tables, not too long to wait for the menu, his glass of beer and Rachel's experiment with a glass of white wine served by an unsurly waitress – 'She's a bit like Jennie,' Rachel whispered, 'try to get a good look at her' – but most of all there were others like them just taking it for granted that you could eat quietly in a lovely room on the first floor overlooking Broad Street. Rachel was entranced by the men outside, walking singly or in groups, so purposeful, she thought, so confident.

'They're another breed,' she said, looking back from the window.

'Some of them are very nice, I mean, decent.'

'I suppose if you were out there just walking past I would think the same about you.'

'What's that?'

'Another breed.' She gave that quick smile, the nod, the clincher.

'Would you like another glass of wine?'

'No,' said Rachel, 'I'd like a beer but I'm not drinking beer in a place like this. Do you think they'd mind if I changed to a glass of red wine?'

They took it in their stride.

'That's better. It's red for me from now on.'

They lit up, leaned back, felt fully admitted. Joe had deliberately left his pipe in college.

They loitered back to the hotel by way of the High Street, taking a loop, Joe determined that not a drop of time be wasted. Both of them were tired, with Rachel's tense anticipation, the long and clumsy rail journey, the repletion, seeing Joe; his similar anticipation, the slog to

418

clear the weekend of reading and essays, an over-intense obsession with arrangements; and they were in a drowse of love for each other.

They reached the hotel.

Joe had been working out his five minutes.

'No,' Rachel said, as he turned in. 'Remember? "Gentlemen are not allowed to accompany single ladies after 8 p.m."'

'We could go back to my rooms.'

'Your friend will be there, won't he?'

'He wants to meet you anyway. He's giving us tea.'

'Tea!'

'Tomorrow.'

They found a dark slit between houses across the road from the hotel and stayed there for a while, although both of them felt a little uncomfortable, being in Oxford. They did not go as far as they would have done in Wigton.

He showed her the Singing Tower of Magdalen College and went up Merton Street, already one of Joe's favourite streets, small town, intimate, an intense seductive feeling of ancient scholarship, and from there into the bright vastness of Christchurch where Joe pointed out Big Tom the Bell over the main entrance and spoke rather inaccurately but enthusiastically about Cardinal Wolsey and the extraordinariness of the College Chapel being the city's cathedral. She peeped into the Radcliffe Camera, not allowed past the librarian, craned her neck looking at the cupola in the Sheldonian, saw the famous Uccello in the Ashmolean, had a drink in the Eagle and Child in whose back room, Joe had heard, men of unrivalled intellect spoke in impenetrable Old English. They landed up at George's in the Market for a quick, cheap, late lunch – home-made pie, mash, peas, and treacle pudding. Rachel went on strike after a walk in the Parks and insisted they sit on a bench and watch the ducks and do nothing else.

It was here he made his move.

'Not a pipe! So it's true! Oh, Joe! Not a pipe!'

Joe laughed at her outrage but stuck to it. There was a stiff north-westerly and it took three matches to get going and Rachel spared him nothing as she commented on his struggle.

'It'll be cheaper than fags,' he said, coughing just a little, 'in the long run. It's the wind that makes it difficult. You can get a little cap thing that keeps the wind off.'

'A pipe! Will you smoke it in Wigton?'

'Why not?'

'I hope not. I'll pay for your cigarettes.'

'What about tonight?'

'Is there a dance on?'

Joe had considered that.

'I know some men who went to one and they said it wasn't much good. I thought we'd go to the theatre. They're doing *The Seagull*. James says it's a very fine play.'

As with the haircut, Rachel made an immediate accommodating decision.

'We can always go to dances in Carlisle,' she said. 'Do they dress up for the theatre?'

'I'll wear my suit,' said Joe.

They went to the Playhouse to buy tickets before heading for Wadham for the encounter Rachel had dreaded for weeks: meeting Joe's friends.

—⁓—

'It's the first tea I've had where you start with fruit cake and end with sherry.'

It had worked. She was happy. Joe sipped at his glass of bitter. They had hit the King's Arms at opening time and for a few minutes the small saloon bar would be theirs. Joe was enjoying the post mortem much more than the tea.

'James's very kind, isn't he? You said that in your letter. And none of them was as snobbish as I'd thought.' Rachel said that to please him. There were bits of evidence she would weigh more carefully over the coming weeks. Joe suspected nothing. All he wanted was to listen to this proof that the two worlds had moved together. 'I liked his sister as well.'

A rather older sister in Oxford for the day to visit friends, and dragooned into service by James.

'She gave me one or two looks,' said Rachel, glancing down at the cigarette she was dabbing out in the huge red bowl of an ashtray: there was nothing she would say against Joe's friends, but the sister had made her aware that her tight skirt and high heels and hugging white rollnecked sweater and perhaps most of all the big buckled belt were worlds away from what she should have been wearing at an Oxford tea. And in the presence of this other woman the words she spoke suddenly sounded guttural, even rather coarse.

'Roderick's great, isn't he?' Joe nodded, happy as the smiling Buddha. 'Speaks' – she attempted an imitation – 'like officers do in war films. Tries to do it without moving his lips. He should be a ventriloquist.'

'He's –' Joe wanted to say 'grand', hesitated, stopped.

'Upper Class,' said Rachel. 'But nice with it. And he knows a lot about dogs.'

'He hunts,' said Joe, 'with a pack of beagles.'

'The fisherman was hilarious.'

'I don't really know him. He shares with Roderick. At the top of the staircase.'

'I thought I'd die when he told about going deeper and deeper into the river to get that trout. And just not noticing!'

Joe laughed as he had done then. He hoped he'd see more of the lanky, gentle zoologist.

'He may say he loves the trout but if Bob can't kill anything that moves in the countryside, it's not worth his getting out of bed,' Roderick had said.

'It was James kept it going,' said Joe. 'James made it. He liked you. I could tell.'

'He seems to like you, as well,' said Rachel.

Joe was surprised. That might be true.

'I was going to teach you to play shove ha'penny,' he said, 'but I think we'd better get ready for the theatre. We can play shove ha'penny tomorrow after we've been to St. Mary's.'

'It's still funny to think of a man coming in to wash all that lot up after we'd finished.'

'You are very lucky,' James had said to Joe, almost severely, as they left.

For the theatre Rachel wore her new dark blue close-cut dress, with another tight belt, only slightly less heavily buckled, this time in gold to match the great Parisian bracelet. Joe thought she looked sensational. Rachel glanced around the foyer and the bar in the interval and realised that she had dressed for the town dance. It did not bother her, as it had at the tea. There were many different styles on display and in that difference she found any extra confidence she needed, which was not a great deal, as she knew from the mirror, from Joe, and from the grazing gazes of the young men in scarves that she looked good enough.

Everything about both the theatre and the play gripped her. She liked the bustle in the foyer beforehand. She felt a shiver of expectation when the lights were lowered. The actors and actresses were wonderful, she thought, so real, and she could have cried for the girl. She loved the so good-mannered crush for drinks at the interval, the bells ringing them back, the meeting again with old acquaintances on stage. She hated the writer who seduced and then dumped the girl. Then the real shock of the ending.

As they walked back, Rachel said,

'That poor boy. Why did he have to do that? I still can't quite believe it,' and,

'What a bastard that writer was to that girl,' and,

'I'd like to see it again, even though I do know the ending.'

'I am a seagull,' said Joe, flapping his arms as the girl in the play had done.

'Don't,' Rachel said. 'It gives me the creeps.'

They approached Wadham. It was almost ten-thirty.

'James said he would be out late.'

'Where does he go?'

'I don't know. He keeps some things quiet.'

They turned into the front quad. Blotches of light from flung-open windows and little energies of sound indicated where the parties were. Joe, who had never been to a private college party, suddenly wanted to crash into one of them, Rachel on his arm. He knew you could. Especially if you took a bottle. He had an almost full bottle of dry sherry in his rooms.

'Eleven o'clock is closing time at Pryor's Prison,' Rachel said.

They went into his bedroom. The sound from the parties somehow teased Joe and distracted him.

'Careful!'

423

He fumbled with the condom in the dark and Rachel vaguely wondered why fitting it was so difficult.

'That writer in the play really was a bastard,' she whispered, 'wasn't he?'

—m—

They walked to the station later on the Sunday afternoon and though an observer would have guessed at their closeness, Joe tilting to Rachel with the weight of the suitcase, Rachel's arm loosely through his, the two of them in step, in physical harmony, there was unresolved agitation.

Joe had insisted on paying the bill at the hotel. Rachel had said nothing at the time but found herself blushing, she did not know why, as Mrs. Pryor made rather a meal of it. Outside, out of earshot, she demanded that she be allowed to pay. Joe would have none of it. Again without knowing why, Rachel became flustered. She worked, she said, Joe didn't. He had budgeted for it, he said. She did not want him to pay for everything.

The more she argued the greater grew Joe's obstinacy and the greater his sense of pleasure and perhaps of proprietorship that he could and had done this for Rachel. She knew that in such a mood she would not shake him, which infuriated her: but the obstinacy impressed her.

Yet it disturbed them, it raised the spectre of Joe's unpaid years ahead, it crystallised the visit as an intermission, became the hyphen between them, when what they wanted was to be joined.

When she got on the train which would lug her across country to Bletchley to meet the London connection for Carlisle, Rachel quelled all that. Joe looked miserable. He was trying to smile but that made him seem even more miserable.

'That was great, Joe.' She stood on the platform, her luggage safely stowed, the doors still open. 'That was one of the best times we've had.'

'Was it?'

'Yes. It was. And,' she gave him a proper kiss, not lingering, not slow, but no peck, 'thank you very much for being so generous.'

'You don't mind, do you?'

'No.'

The guard blew his whistle. Doors began to bang shut along the platform.

'I liked your friends. Bob was very funny.' She laughed, remembering the story of the fish that would not be caught.

'They liked you as well. At breakfast this morning they all said they liked you.'

Meaning – who wouldn't? Who couldn't? Who was he alive who would not like and even love you, as you moved away and waved until the train went out of sight.

CHAPTER THIRTY-EIGHT

'Did you understand much of it?' James asked.

They were still applauding. Joe felt that his brain had been taken over but by what he did not yet know. Nothing had prepared him for this.

'Some of it, I think. Just some.'

The young actors skipped onto the stage, in movement and gesture almost absurdly at odds with the movements and gestures which they had seized on to play *Waiting for Godot*.

'I suggest we discuss it back in our rooms,' said James.

Roderick: 'Beats me. Bored me, frankly. Two old tramps spending two hours waiting for Godot who never came. Who cared if Godot came or not?' He decided to 'push off and draw up guidelines for a P.G. Wodehouse Society, urgently'. Bob Romford, the zoologist, who had been a regular theatre goer in his school vacations, spurred on by a stepfather who was a critic, edged diffidently into the room clutching a bottle of sherry, 'Can't drink yours all the time.' James had asked along Brian Jacobs, a friend from his old school, described as 'brilliant', two or three years older, a major scholar at Balliol. Joe knew himself to be far and away the least qualified of the quartet and guessed he would have more to offer to the P.G. Wodehouse Society.

But he had to know what the play meant. His mind had now unfrozen, leaving only a question mark on a blank sheet of paper.

Sherry was poured. Joe was getting used to it. He was even beginning to develop a preference for dry. They sat down as if taking up positions. Joe had never before seen James as an acolyte but there was no doubt that Brian was to be deferred to.

'What we're talking about,' said James, after a glance at Brian, enviably long-haired, Joe thought, but intellectually long-haired, almost excessively slim, very white-faced, long fingers draped around the tiny sherry glass, almost chain-smoking, 'is clearly a play of ideas: the problem is, which ideas?'

'I rather thought,' Bob said, in his hesitant voice, gazing down legs which seemed to reach out for the skirting board, 'that if they'd done it as it were Charlie Chaplin, you know, music hall, we would have laughed a lot and not been so very bothered about meaning.'

James, infinitesimally, nodded.

'But you don't deny it has meaning? Why are they there? Who do those tramps represent? Why the sadism? Who is Godot? Why does he not come?'

'Godot's God, isn't he?' said Joe, hopefully.

'God is dead,' Brian murmured. 'Nietzsche told us that.'

Dead? God? Joe could not let that pass.

'He was never alive, was he?' said Joe. 'Except through Christ: and Samuel Beckett calls him Godot. It's got to be something to do with God, hasn't it?'

'So why does he not come?' James talked to Joe but still his glances flitted to Brian.

'Maybe they weren't good enough for him,' said Joe and felt his words fall on stony ground.

'I rather think,' said Bob, picking his way carefully, in build and

427

speech rather like a heron delicately picking its prey, 'that the Christian context is not necessarily the one we should be looking at here.'

'Godot's a blind?' James asked. 'What do you think?'

'So why call him Godot?'

'Irony, I presume,' James said and Joe was checked. What was ironic about that?

'It may,' said Bob, musing on his ankles, 'be one of those pieces subject to several interpretations. I do concede that it is tantalising.'

'Brian?'

Brian lit up again and spoke in smiling, nervous and rapid sentences, and in a manner that sounded familiar to Joe. He got it! Professor A.J. Ayer, whom he had seen on the Brains Trust and once thought he'd spotted in the High Street.

Joe took out his pipe to listen with full attention.

'I think the play has to be seen in the context in which Beckett wrote it. Here we have an exile, a man who writes in French and translates his own work into English.' Joe had not known that. He listened even harder. Brian was diffident but authoritative. He would glance up every now and then as if seeking permission to go on and yet he was enviably confident, Joe thought, miraculously at ease with names and ideas which were often just vague shapes on the far horizon of Joe's knowledge.

'We have someone, we are told, who was a member of the French Resistance and so we add war to exile and the deliberate distancing and disguises of a language not his first. He is in Paris after the war when not only Nietzsche but Kierkegaard and to some extent Dostoevsky – two plus two equals four is a wonderful thing: two plus two equals five is a more wonderful thing – have influenced the French, especially of course when Sartre came along.'

428

Joe wanted him to slow down. He wanted to make notes. He wanted him to go over it again.

'Sartre has become as it were the St. Paul of existentialism and it is his sparring partner Camus who tells us in *The Myth of Sisyphus* that each one of us is Sisyphus, we are all condemned to roll the rock to the top of the mountain only to see it roll back again which raises the question, the only question, why should we stay alive? Why are we waiting for Godot, not who is Godot?'

Joe was holding on for dear life and partly to give himself time to digest some of this, he said,

'I read *The Myth of Sisyphus*. I read *The Outsider* as well.'

And then he stopped. They waited. But his brain had clammed up. No words came. No thought gathered. They waited politely.

'But how does this bring us to Beckett and this particular play?' Bob asked, after a silence which seemed to Joe as long as the Lord's Prayer.

'Existentialism infuses the work, in my view,' Brian said, 'and one way to approach that is to note the prevalence of anxiety in the piece, anxiety being the pre-eminent creator of awareness.'

Was it? Joe wanted to know. How could you prove that? And awareness of what?

'I would still like a neater conclusion,' James suggested. 'What you've said is very impressive but we are still looking for a key interpretation, aren't we?'

'We are still – all of us here –' said Bob, laughing aloud, 'Waiting for Godot.'

Brian took another cigarette, the smallest sip of sherry, and a deep breath as if embarking on a risky venture.

'I believe that if it has a single root, then we can find that in the Holocaust, in what happened to the Jews.'

It was the first time Joe had heard the word Holocaust uttered.

'The Holocaust,' said Brian, looking ahead above the mantel-piece, and speaking more slowly, 'was an event of such significance or will prove to be, on the minds of those sensitive to its true meaning for humanity, that no hope, no answer, no speech will any more be adequate.'

'Was Beckett a Jew, then?' Joe asked.

'No,' said Brian. 'He was Irish. But the essential condition of all our lives has been disturbed, deeply and possibly permanently, by the Holocaust. An artist of Beckett's genius would recognise that, consciously and unconsciously, and this is his reaction. It may,' he looked benevolently at Bob, who, like the others, felt subdued by Brian's intensity, 'it may well "play" as comedy. But the comedy would be a travesty. Beckett's play is a call into the abyss and out of the abyss.'

Joe concentrated on trying to score into his mind as much of this as he could. When a few moments of silence had passed, Bob asked why it was that this particular event, the Holocaust, terrible though it was, should be so much more significant than other massacres, other exterminations of tribes or classes or peoples, and for the next quarter of an hour Brian, face even whiter, Joe thought, dark eyes even darker, haunted, responded patiently, gently, unyielding. Joe saw the door open and he had a glimpse of another world in which ideas about life and how it should be lived were central to any life worth living.

James walked Brian back to the gate and down to the corner of the King's Arms.

'Do you think your friend Joe has ever met a Jew before?'

'Not,' James chose his reply with care, 'not I suspect knowingly. Even though there are several in college.'

'I imagine he's sound.'

'Excellent.'

'I liked him. But a dangerous ignorance.'

'Innocence might be better. He knows other things.'

'I'm sure . . . but in the end, James, we all need to know the same things, don't we?' For a moment, their eyes locked and James felt that he had heard a great truth.

Brian waved and then glided off, almost a spectral figure, under the dim night lights on the Broad.

When James got back he found Joe with sherry poured. He handed him a glass.

'God,' he said, 'he's just brilliant.'

James nodded, curiously relieved. Things had gone better than he had anticipated.

'Brilliant,' Joe repeated eagerly and raised his glass.

'I hope you don't mind,' James said, 'but I'm rather tired. I'll pour this back into the bottle and then – bed. Good night.'

—⚹—

Joe walked slowly across the quad. There was light drizzle which made the winter lawn shine emerald. He had been to a lecture he regretted wasting time on and so he wore his gown but no coat. The quiet persistence of the drizzle matched the depressed persistence of his homesickness, which had lifted when Rachel was here, held off for a couple of days afterwards until the evening of the discussion he now looked back on with such respect, but now it was back, lodged, and he was again counting the days until he'd see Rachel again, fed up with himself, with this mood, evidence of weakness, proof of cowardice but not to be budged.

He concluded that he did not really know what existentialism meant. He had read parts of *The Outsider* again and knew that he felt like that but as to what it meant, if he was honest, he was all but clueless. When someone passed by and nodded it seemed as if a fish were swimming past, something which was wholly unlike himself. Was that existentialism? The buildings, so praised, oppressed him with their bare-faced stone, enclosed, cut off. Was that it? On this morning the college was like a prison for scholarship. Only men and so many so clever, the burden of their achievements, their potential, the certainty of their upward advancement. He would have stayed outside in the drizzle until he got soaked but knew enough to know that would do him no good, he would be seen to be merely eccentric.

Uncharacteristically, he decided to waste the hour before lunch in the Junior Common Room. He had looked in briefly, once or twice, when he had been working in the College Library and seen young men as absorbed in newspapers as the old men were in Carlisle Library. Joe could not see the point: books, yes, but newspapers were to be polished off over breakfast. He picked up the *Telegraph*, spotted the *Daily Mirror*, carried both to a corner and read the *Mirror*. He felt he could be in an aquarium.

Mike had spotted him and navigated his way down the room with many a 'Hi!' and a wave and eventually docked alongside. He tapped Joe on the knee.

'Hi!'

Joe looked up to meet a wide smile, merry poached eyes, a large head already bursting through its hair, and a magnificent black corduroy suit.

'Sorry about the audition.'

Mike's accent had been worked on but, Joe thought, still 'us', not 'them'. There was some camaraderie in that.

'It's all right,' Joe muttered, though why had he attempted that raving ranting speech of King Lear on the heath?

432

'It's just a three-hander. In fact I'd more or less promised the parts. We've all worked together before.'

So the audition had been a waste of time. Joe put his pipe down. A fix.

'I wanted to say,' Mike put his hand under the seat of the lightweight armchair and both he and the chair did a frog-hop forward, 'there'll be more. I'm thinking of doing something from the Mystery plays next term. Do you know them?'

Joe nodded, lying, he excused himself, in order to keep the attention of this star of the college's dramatic firmament.

'The Guild that interests me is the Carpenters. They made the cross. They actually made the thing. Then they did the crucifixion. They put Christ up on it – one of them actually played Jesus Christ! In the bloody Middle Ages!' Joe immediately saw himself on the cross. Mike had himself in mind for the part. 'We'll need good northern voices. I want to do it northern. We can all get near it but I want the real thing. At the heart of it. So keep that in mind, would you?'

'Yes.'

Mike glanced at his watch. Another three or four minutes.

'Do you read many plays? I saw you at *Godot* – isn't he a genius? – but as I always say first do it, second see it, but a good third – read it. A surprising amount rubs off. Oxfam has a good line in second hand,' he laughed, 'tenth hand! paperbacks. You can pick up a lot there. Sixpence a volume. The kitchen sink stuff's harder to get your hands on – Osborne, Wesker . . .' His smile grew enormous. 'You haven't seen them? Read them? I'll put something in your pigeonhole. Don't thank me. And,' he stood up, only, then, to lean down and whisper, 'don't lose the northern thing. They all want you to. They want to absorb you. They want to rub you out. Don't let them. Look what's happened to me! I was Manchester when I came up two years ago. Don't let them get you! Ta-ra!'

Mr. Tillotson was waiting in Joe's rooms. He had come to Oxford for a short conference and had an hour to spare.

—⁓—

'I had given him another twenty minutes,' he told the other two in the staff room. 'His friend had been very kind and made me a cup of tea. He left as soon as Joe got back. Nice touch.' Mr. Tillotson had thought he might not divulge this next observation. 'To be quite honest I had the impression he was going to burst into tears at the sight of me. He didn't of course. Nobody ever has to my knowledge. But it was an odd moment and it was consistent with our meeting in that he seemed more than a little – how shall I put this? – discombobulated.'

'Little fish in a big pond,' said Miss Castle.

'They should have reduced National Service to a year,' said Mr. Braddock. 'Abolishing it altogether –' he reached for his pipe, 'a big mistake.'

'The way he talked he was just longing to get back here.'

'But here will begin to be as strange as Oxford,' said Miss Castle. 'Does he still see Rachel Wardlow?'

Mr. Tillotson nodded.

'He'll never settle until he leaves her,' the Latin mistress said. 'Which he will.'

Mr. Braddock lit up.

'He's trying to smoke a pipe,' said Mr. Tillotson. 'He's making a terrible mess of it.'

CHAPTER THIRTY-NINE

'We come from the same place,' the young woman said and closed *Dr. Zhivago*. The train had just pulled out of Crewe, they were half way home. She had been reading all the way with commendably close attention. Joe, with his sixpenny volume of *Three Ibsen Plays*, had found it difficult to keep his eyes on the page: he could justify looking out of the window as a thought break, to digest what Ibsen was on about in *The Doll's House*, why it had caused so much fuss at the time, but, truthfully, he gazed out of the window to will on the train, take him to Rachel, take him home, flicking telegraph poles taking him home.

The young woman's remark, her first, surprised him. He had noticed her as they waited at Oxford Station, how tall she was, short blonde hair, that sort of easy uppery thing about her which he had begun to spot on the rare female sightings at Oxford, self-possessed and, he concluded, without any wish to chat, a wish for privacy in public which through painful snubs he had learned to respect over the past two months. He was learning not to take it personally.

'Just a few miles from Wigton,' she smiled, a sensible smile. 'You played rugby against my brother Archie when you were at school. We went to the Friends' School. We saw you at Brenda's party.' She laughed. 'I thought you were terribly funny.'

'What's it like to be a Quaker?' Joe's question was stabbed out to puncture the blush of embarrassment. Funny?

'It's what you must already know,' she said. 'We use the lovely Meeting House on West Street.'

My mother told me she used to clean that. Joe checked himself.

'They have the library there as well,' he said.

'My mother helped set it up. Archie and I used to help choose the books. Great fun.'

'But what's it like? Do you really just say something when the spirit moves you?'

'Yes.' Her head tilted up with seriousness and as she paused the regular consoling rhythm of the wheels on the track appeared louder in the crowded softly moving carriage. They were at full speed now, Joe thought, streaking back into the far North, leaving behind the farewell plumes of smoke.

'How do you know when to do it?'

'You know,' said Mary, firmly. 'It needs to come out of a particular quality of shared silence.'

Joe took this as a reproach and prepared to re-enter *The Doll's House*.

'Archie,' she said, 'thought you were very good as Elvis Presley. Do you still imitate him?'

'No.'

'Why's that?'

Joe shrugged and grimaced. There had never been an opportunity. He had never had the energy and boldness to make one. Classical music was O.K., jazz was O.K., even American musicals were O.K., but he had found no fertile ground for Rock 'n' Roll. There would be the occasional reference, but Joe had kept his peace. Once or twice he thought he had betrayed Elvis by not sticking up for him. Elvis was just one part of what he had done in Wigton which was not mentioned, which did not count, around which an embarrassment was beginning to fester.

'I suppose they might be rather stuck up about it at Oxford,' said Mary. 'Archie's at Manchester. They love pop music. They seem much less stuck up there.'

'But you don't wish you'd gone there, do you?' Joe was anxious that Oxford remain top, remain worth it.

'I find Oxford rather too pleased with itself,' said Mary, her calm manner now impressing itself hypnotically on Joe. He would love to possess that calm. How did you achieve that tranquil aura? 'Altogether,' she emphasised, 'too pleased with itself.'

Criticism! Of Oxford. He held his breath.

'But one meets some good people,' she said, 'don't you agree?'

'Oh yes.' He told her about James, about Roderick, about the unexpectedness of zoologist Bob, about Brian the genius from Balliol. She listened patiently and it was only when he clocked the willed smiling patience in her that Joe stopped.

'We must all meet up in the vac,' she said and raised up *Zhivago*. 'Isn't it dreadful what the Russians are doing to Pasternak?'

But she was reading and wanted no discussion.

—◦◦◦—

Joe walked slowly up King Street, past the Fountain and into the High Street, past St. Mary's, the school beyond, and down Proctor's Row past the Auction, into Church Street, back along Water Street and Birdcage Walk, down to the Tenters, back past Vinegar Hill, nodded at everyone, stopped to talk here and there, sought and found morsels of gossip, wove in and out of the alleyways, ambled into the Crofts, back

437

past the Quaker Meeting House, making absolutely sure it was all still there, now and then unconsciously reaching out to touch the sandstone walls, and finally to Alan's shop where he would wait until Rachel had her break – see her for the first time for twenty-seven days. All was well.

—m—

'Now tell me the truth,' she said as soon as she came into the new room, 'what do you really think of it?'

Ellen had planned this moment with some care. Sam was downstairs getting on with the morning's work. She had left Joe alone after giving him breakfast and he was wallowing in being home, relishing the privacy, the poached egg, the unlimited toast.

She sat down at the table opposite him. He looked around the new room determined to please.

'It's great,' he said, and meant it, and yet.

'Do you really mean that?' Her delight was only very slightly shadowed – she had caught the merest scent of his doubt. He in his turn sensed that and chased it away.

'It's terrific,' he said with conviction. Ellen nodded, smiled, poured herself a cup of tea.

The parlour had now become a kitchen and sitting room combined. The sink unit and cooker in one corner. The dining table next to the window overlooked Market Hill. A green sofa and two perfectly matching armchairs embraced the electric fire. A glass fronted cabinet for show: a small bookcase, and cupboards under and around the sink for cooking and utensils.

'Everything G-Plan,' said Ellen, 'everything modern.'

'It all fits in,' said Joe, trying his best. 'It all matches up.'

438

'I should've done it years ago.'

'But you have to come up and down stairs.'

'Keeps you fit.' She sipped and glanced at the clock. Sadie must not feel abandoned. 'Sure?'

'It really is. Great.'

'Good.' She stood up, hovered for a moment and then came over to give him a hurried kiss on his forehead. 'Nice to have you back.'

Alone again but now without the deep relish in it. Had he lied? He did like the new kitchen. He was even proud of it. It was amazing how much was in it and yet so compact. It was smart. It was modern. Yet there was a fidget in his mind. Too smart? He was developing the knowledge that it was, in some unfathomable way, better to cultivate a liking for the old, the used, the faded, even the battered grandeur of his rooms and the rooms of others at Oxford. How did the G-Plan fit that?

Downstairs to help, waylaid by Sadie.

'Your mam's pleased you like it,' she said, loudly as ever. 'But you couldn't not. I told her. It's a palace up there.'

'It is,' said Joe, stamping on the demons. 'It's lovely.'

He noticed as he had done on the previous morning that Sadie's accent was very broad. He liked it. He liked everything about Sadie. But he could not help noticing how broad it was and he wished he did not.

'Hey. Remember you asked me about gossip yesterday morning? Two of them's been sent down for pinching dynamite from the factory to blow up the becks for fish!' She gave the names.

'The usual suspects,' said Joe.

'And there's rats down the lonning up Longthwaite where they have the allotments. The council says they'll chuck the men off the allotments if they don't get rid of the rats but everybody knows the rats

439

comes because of the council men tipping the rubbish further down because the council won't make the rubbish dump up Kirkland bigger. There's always been allotments down Longthwaite. You should've kept your old haircut, Joe. It was smarter. You haven't lost yourself, have you Joe?' She looked at him keenly and Joe felt uncomfortable.

Joe brought up a couple of crates but it was midweek and the shelves needed little replenishment. It was good to be back behind the bar with Sam, but Joe was nervous. Perhaps old fears had returned, his father's thick white muscles like weapons bulged under the rolled up sleeves, the unflinching blue eyes.

Sam had to make an effort to hold back. What had they talked about in Oxford? What were they like? Are you keeping up? Is the competition too hard? What's it really like, this Oxford? How do you find them? How do they find you? Above all, what do you talk about?

'Still smoke?' He offered a cigarette.

'A pipe now,' he said, taking the cigarette. 'But thanks. Now and then.'

'I tried a pipe in the army. Too fussy for me.' He lit both the cigarettes and as he leaned forward, elbows on the counter, gazing towards the window, Joe was moved. He had seen his father there so many times, wreathed in smoke, adrift, seemingly contented, a man on his own.

'There's a lot of talk about Eoka,' said Joe. 'Some of them did National Service in Cyprus.'

'We'll clear them out,' Sam said.

'Some of them say that you'll never beat terrorism when the native population's behind it.'

'We beat it in Malaya,' Sam said, 'you can always beat it if you've a mind to.'

'But look at Israel. When is it terrorism and when is it people determined to get their rights and be free?'

'That's politics,' said Sam, crisply, turning to him now. 'I'm talking about the army. If the politicians leave you alone after the decision's made, you can clear it out and our lads will clear it out in Cyprus if they'll leave them be.'

'How can you leave politics out of it?'

'There's a point where politics has to end and action has to start. If you mix the two up you just get a shambles like Suez.'

'I'm glad they got mixed up over Suez,' Joe said, rather heatedly, 'we were on the wrong track.'

'We'll see,' said Sam. 'Have they got you more interested in politics, then?'

'No.' Joe did not reveal his funk after the visit to the Union. 'Not any more than I was already. There's an Oxford undergraduate just been elected for Parliament in Aberdeen. He's only twenty-three.'

'Stiff competition.' Sam smiled. 'I think that Berlin's where the real trouble will start. And not Germany's fault this time.'

Joe was about to leave to meet Rachel in her break. Sam said, 'Anything I should be reading?'

'I've got a novel a friend of mine recommended. It's just come out. I haven't read it myself yet. I'll go upstairs and get it for you.'

Joe was convinced that Colin had been waiting at the top of Market Hill for some time: it felt like an ambush. Colin was carrying a brown suede briefcase and a rolled up umbrella.

'Thought I'd forget, didn't you?' He held them out at arm's length. 'They'll have to do for Christmas as well.'

'Thanks.' He knew immediately that the briefcase would not work. 'That's really, thanks, Colin.'

'The briefcase,' Colin said, 'I daren't tell you. Top notch. Arm and a leg. But you're worth it.'

And for a brief moment, as Colin's eyes, so like Ellen's, focused on him with such pride and affection, Joe wished that it could be different with Colin, that he could like him, that Sam could take him back.

'Some of them thinks you're a traitor to Wigton, you know,' said Colin, 'but I tell them, that lad has always wanted to get out of Wigton and why shouldn't he? So would you if you had the brains.'

'But I like Wigton. I don't want to get out of it.'

'You don't have to pretend with me,' Colin said. 'I can see through you, remember. I'll walk up street with you.' Which he did, tugging Joe to a stop as often as he could, introducing him to people he knew so well, 'making sure,' he whispered in a slant-mouthed aside, 'that they know you're not stuck up. But the way you're talking sometimes – watch it.' The new umbrella felt like certain proof of betrayal.

'But it isn't even raining,' Rachel said.

Colin had surrendered him to the bank and then bowed out with the words, 'Remember. I'm the best pal you'll have.'

'And what are you going to do with a suede briefcase in Oxford?'

He asked Rachel to carry the briefcase to the new coffee bar behind the cinema, but she refused.

There was a jukebox, shiny, chrome-covered, flash, attention-claiming, irresistible. Joe fed it with his own hunger: not only Elvis, but the Everly Brothers, Johnnie Ray, Frankie Laine, Little Richard, Doris Day, Buddy Holly.

'Anybody would think you were a millionaire,' Rachel said, but she too was happy to be submerged in the sound, stir the milky coffee, smoke the cigarettes, and look at Joe, the long college scarf snaking proudly around his neck. He beamed at her, she thought, just as he had done that time beside the tennis courts when they first met at school.

—∞—

'Well?' said Sam, putting aside the new novel rather reluctantly.

They still spent the last hour in the old kitchen.

'He's different,' Ellen said, just as reluctantly turning from the dying fire, 'it'll never be the same – how could it be? But I like him back.'

'I think he's been jarred,' Sam said. Ellen's dreaming expression concentrated itself. 'He'll just have to get through it.' Yet Sam was not wholly sure he would succeed: maybe that nervy business when he was younger had shown up flaws that would always drag him down.

'I know what to get him for Christmas,' she said.

Sam waited.

'A duffel coat: they all have duffel coats. With those little wooden toggles.'

Ellen laughed.

'They're funny, aren't they, those little toggles.'

—∞—

As Christmas Day approached, Joe drifted around the town alone while Rachel worked, Alan worked, John at the factory, Edward now apprenticed at Moore's garage. He recognised but could not describe a different sort of solitude in himself, unthreatening but questioning. He felt too favoured.

He was remotely aware that he was playing at being a student –

he had given up using 'undergraduate' in Wigton. He was this altogether different person now, wasn't he? Nineteen years old and no job: living on scholarship money and help from his parents but still the means to smoke and go out. Most of all, though, he was a student. People became soldiers and different when they went into the army. People become miners not boys when they went down the pits. A student meant – what did it mean? You could no longer behave like a schoolboy. You were as yet of no use. You were tolerated.

Students were supposed to study and to think. That was the main part of it. The more they thought the better they were. You were supposed to make yourself think and about everything, not just wait for it to happen. Passing exams, he saw now, with mixed feelings, was just the start of it. Students were there to think things through and with his college scarf layered around his neck he tried to look the part. But how did you prove it? How could you prove you were thinking and had changed into a real student? Still not got a job yet, said the men around the Fountain, still no job, Joe?

—∿—

Joe was not invited to Brenda's party but two days afterwards he went with Rachel to a party in the grander home of Mary. Rachel drove them in Isaac's unbegrudged car and nodded happily to Joe as she pulled up in the drive of the small Georgian manor which dominated the deeply secluded hamlet.

'This'll show Brenda,' Rachel said.

Brenda came across the room to them as soon as they came in.

'I didn't know you knew Mary and Archie.'

Joe smiled. Without looking at Rachel, Brenda said,

'And good to see you again too, Rachel.'

444

'What did you smile at her for?' After Brenda had moved elsewhere.

'What else could I do?'

'Ignore her. Just ignore her. She ignored us. We weren't good enough for her party! I wanted to kick her ankles.'

Joe liked her saying that.

'If she asks you for a dance – and she'll have the face for it – say no or I'm off and you can walk home.'

That was not so comfortable.

'I mean it.' He knew it. 'Smiling all over you!' Which cheered him up again.

'I read a poem of yours,' Peter said, 'in the school magazine. My sister brought it back. I can't remember it. But I liked it. I paint.' He held out his hand. 'I was at the school many moons before you. And "hello" to you too! You're –?'

'Rachel. I'm with Joe.'

'I can see that, Rachel. Lucky Joe. You're the perfect artist's model.'

Rachel grimaced, but as the evening went on she forgave him. 'You couldn't not,' she said. Peter Carson – in his last year at St. Martin's College of Art in London – was very tall, very thin, long-haired, twirling moustached, a well cut brown velvet jacket, cavalry twill trousers so tight he could have ridden in them and did, and glistening brown boots made in Wigton for him by Ivinson the saddler.

Joe realised that although Peter was in another age group, another circle, and one of the better off, the man had been at the edge of his Wigton vision for years. And he was an artist!

'What do you think of Van Gogh?' Joe asked. 'I've seen his real ones in Paris.'

'I like his letters,' said Peter. 'It's moved on to De Kooning now. More Abstract-Expressionism.'

'But Van Gogh's great, isn't he? The colours and the way you can see what he's feeling – just by looking at a chair!'

'I'll grant you that,' said Peter. He smiled, at Rachel, it seemed to Joe, and his jealousy shot into her, an unwelcome warning. 'But things move on.'

'Not if you're good enough,' said Joe. 'What about Leonardo da Vinci?'

'The thing is,' Peter said, 'art's a mug's game but drawing is all I can do. I'd like to draw you,' he said to Rachel, exercising his pantomime wolfish smile.

'No,' she said, 'certainly not.' And was annoyed with herself because she thought she had to say this to appease Joe.

'You then?'

Joe was flattered. Peter rolled another cigarette in dark brown paper.

There was about the evening something both calm and sure which eventually spread contentment. Joe could not have analysed or even guessed how it came about. The Quaker annual family party for Mary and Archie was spacious and free, Joe felt the fine house was his for the evening; he liked everything about it – the simple furniture, the few landscape paintings, the ease of everyone. If ever he had a house he wanted it to be like this and he would give parties just like this.

Towards the end he tried to explain existentialism to Archie and refused to give up even when it was clear to Rachel that he was tying himself into knots and Archie knew much more about it. It took an effort from her not to refer to it on the way back.

It was a party which led to other parties that Christmas. Peter's own, a much smaller affair which Rachel thought was 'a bit weird' and

446

which Joe hoped qualified as a Beat generation party in which case, his first. There they met William Anderson who was training to be an architect. His family had just bought a double-fronted sandstone mansion near the cemetery overlooking Wigton and Joe and Rachel were invited as were other younger people to the house-warming.

'And Brenda got invited to neither of them,' said Rachel.

'That's understandable,' said Joe, hypocritically.

'It is! It's very understandable!'

'How do you know she wasn't invited?'

'Brenda? Don't be so soft. Sometimes you are soft, Joe.'

—m—

Alan gave him a lift on the motorbike. The dance was in Rachel's village.

'Who's that?' Joe demanded.

'Robert Donaldson. Michael's brother.'

'He's coming over to ask you for a dance.'

'You have this dance with Linda. She'll like that. You both will and Michael won't mind. He can't dance anyway.'

It was a slow foxtrot which allowed you to dance close to someone even if you were not going with them because the nature of the dance required it. Robert and Rachel did little more than shuffle. Robert was taller than Joe was, and handsome, the blond, curly hair already freed of the combing, tumbled about his strong weathered face. Rachel, there was no doubt of this, was being held very close.

Linda knew exactly what was going on. Joe's jealousy had always convinced her how much he loved Rachel as she had several times reassured a perturbed Rachel. 'Don't bother about Robert,' she said,

447

staring through him, glassily, 'he's got a girlfriend but she broke her wrist this morning. He dances like that with everybody when he's had a few.' She smiled: the effect of the poison lessened a little. They tried one or two bolder manoeuvres.

'You can't do much with a slow foxtrot,' said Linda when it finished, 'save sort of stick against each other.'

'Did you have to be so close?'

'Oh Joe,' said Rachel. 'I knew you'd say that! It's just a dance.'

He did not believe her.

'You're in a sulk,' she said, as they stood in the shadows, just inside the gate of the farm. Alan had given them fifteen minutes.

'I'm not.'

'You're a liar, Joe Richardson, and not a very good one.'

How could she be so casual about it? Clinging together.

'I turned him down when he asked for a second dance.'

'That was a quickstep,' said Joe, miserably. 'He has a girlfriend, you know. She broke her wrist this morning.'

Rachel kissed him, deeply, and he had to give in.

'Tomorrow night,' she said. 'In Wigton. I'll stay the night.'

'O.K.'

'You'd better go now.'

She watched him walk into the middle of the barely lighted road and stand to be seen. Alan's motorbike revved up a score or two yards away. Rachel waited until they were gone.

The truth was that Robert had pressed himself against her very hard and she had not resisted it.

As she undressed for bed she thought she would apply for that job in Carlisle and see if she could share a flat with some of the other girls. It was time to leave the village.

Peter Carson was funny now that she had cottoned on that his

448

propositions were never serious; William Anderson's bold free-standing house looked clear over the rooftops of Wigton right into the Lakes. He was as good mannered as anybody at Oxford, she thought, and spoke just as well as they did. But Joe so swaggering in that duffel coat! And sometimes his pronunciation just skidded away. Neither Oxford nor Wigton nor anything else. Talking to Archie about whatever it was, knowing nothing about it but going on and on, had been embarrassing. And imitating Roderick too often, even though it was funny. Yet he liked Roderick.

It took Rachel some time to get to sleep. Her mother would not want her to leave for a flat in Carlisle. Rachel smiled to herself in the dark: even Isaac might want her to stay. It was Joe, to be fair, who had sorted Isaac out, to everyone's surprise. She ought not to have danced like that with Robert. She would make it up to Joe. It was Joe she loved.

Aunt Claire was still away at her brother's and as Rachel had brought in her clothes for going out and also the clothes for work the next morning, Ellen said it was easier if she stayed the night with them.

They went to Carlisle to see *King Creole*. Elvis seemed distant. He did not hit the nerve. Joe felt out of sorts, even disturbed. It was only too obvious what it was, he concluded gloomily, as they swayed home through the black countryside upstairs on the last bus. He would be leaving for Oxford in the morning. Where was the happy anticipation other people reported? Why had it not infected him? Already he felt a certain dread, bracing himself for conflict.

They had a cup of tea with Ellen and Sam who sometimes seemed to get more chat out of Rachel than he himself did, Joe had observed. She would tell Sam stories about the bank and make comments he had not heard before. Rachel often told him how much she liked Sam and although he was pleased there was just a prickle of resentment.

449

Rachel's bedroom adjoined his own. It was where Colin had slept, for two or three weeks, until Sam had moved him out. It was separated from Sam and Ellen's room by the landing.

Joe lasted no more than a few minutes on his own. Rachel was waiting for him. Danger lent urgency and also Joe desperately wanted to kill this stupid fear of going, to lose it in the body of Rachel. They lay a while wide awake, listening, sharing a cigarette. Outside, Wigton wrapped around them in a quiet as complete as could be, no cars, no dogs, no sudden shouts.

Again they made love, this time with a languorous, even sleepy care not usual between them, more tender, more homely even, and fell fast asleep.

—m—

Ellen opened the door. For a while she stood stone silent, simply gazing on the two of them in the same bed. Joe appeared to feel her gaze and woke up to look at her, but he could not see her eyes: she stood with her back to the thin curtains which let in the morning light. Joe could detect the beginning of tears in her voice when she said,

'The sooner you two get married, the better.'

Then she was gone.

It took some time to coax Rachel out from under the bedclothes.

Breakfast was apologetic.

Joe walked her to the bank. He would be gone before her midday break.

'I'll never be able to look your mother in the face again,' Rachel said.

'She won't tell anybody. Except Dad.'

Rachel smiled. Sam would be all right. She looked around, very carefully, gave Joe a quick kiss on the cheek and went in to work.

—⁓—

He was packed to go.

'I'll see myself to the station this time, Dad, thanks all the same.'

'Quite right,' Sam said. 'Your mother?'

'Upstairs. We said – it, cheerio, upstairs. It's great, isn't it, upstairs?'

Sam raised his eyebrows. In the nervous state before this un-wanted departure, Joe felt a surge of affection for his father, as he had done in their first talk on his return. Yet they had talked so little since, Joe so often ducking a conversation, pleading work, appointments, fudging it. Now that he saw him standing plain before him, the quiet smile, the steady look, he said,

'You'll have to come to Oxford sometime.'

'Do you mean that?'

'Yes. Yes. You have to. You'd really like it.'

'Sure?'

'Yes. I'll show you round.'

'I might take you up on that, Joe, one day.' He looked at his watch. 'Time to move off. Make sure you look up to the window and wave when you get outside.'

CHAPTER FORTY

'Dear Rachel,

'I think that we should get married. I don't suppose I'll be allowed to while I'm living in college but next year (October that is) I can live in digs and I know at least one man who is married and lives in digs. Admittedly he did three years in the navy and is a bit older but it shows it can be done. And there are plenty of banks in Oxford!

'Why not? If we wait until I'm finished here and get a job that's more than two and a half years and what's the point? I just sit here missing you. It would have to be investigated and maybe they would cut off my grant but not if you weren't pregnant, surely? Even if they did cut off my grant I could get a part-time job in a pub. But I can't see why they should. It will have to be sorted out. You would be here: we would have the best of both worlds.

'All this must sound very practical. I don't feel "practical". I know that if I were with you all the time I would be very happy. I hope you feel the same. So why don't we do it? I love you and you say you love me. We've known each other more than two years and I'll be twenty next birthday. We're going to get married one day, anyway. It would be normal. It would be so good if we could do it now. So, Rachel, please, will you marry me?'

He took the letter to the main post office some distance away, giving himself every chance not to post it. But walking only stimulated him. To be with Rachel every day, to make love to Rachel every night, without a doubt that would not only be wonderful but it would take away this underdrag of missing, he would be able to belt into things as he should be doing, not dither around the edges, wondering what an undergraduate was supposed to do – he would do it, whatever it was, because Rachel would be there. Joe felt himself the beneficiary of a revelation. The more he thought about it the more euphoric he became and the sooted buildings and the anxious chilled faces of an Oxford winter January afternoon were exactly the contrast he needed to confirm his own mood, full of light and warmth and certainty.

Rachel read the letter quickly, stowed it in her bag and went to the Picture House coffee bar in her break, where she read it again, several times. She was thrilled. Married, away, living in Oxford, Joe, a new life, Joe's wife, married. The sensation filled her with a sense of boldness and a flush of happiness which she concealed rigorously as she took another cigarette and read, yet again, 'Will you marry me?'

Her letter arrived the next day.

'Dear Joe,

'Well, that was a surprise! I nearly fell off the chair at home and only dared peep at it in the bank in case my calculations all went mad. I went to the coffee bar to do it justice! The most important thing is to tell nobody. I won't. Nobody at all until we talk about it face to face when I come to Oxford a week next Friday. But I do love you and your letter made me realise how much. You're right. We've been together at least as long as most people who have a formal engagement. I suppose they'll make us have an engagement – I would want one anyway! The ring! Have you thought about that, Joe Richardson? I never thought a proposal would come in a letter, but there's something very romantic about it, I think. Am I supposed to say "thank you"? . . .'

So that's it, Joe thought. He folded the letter very carefully and put it in his wallet so that he could take it out and read it whenever he felt like it. It's all settled.

—⁓—

For the next ten days, Joe floated. The strain went and in the slack he prospered.

He even went to the College Labour Club and, where previously he would have been too strangulated to speak, took part in the debate and though he felt patronised by two expertly pipe-smoking men from Winchester who talked about Trotsky a lot of the time and implied that Joe's Labour Party values were little more than a form of conservatism which duped the masses, he managed to come away without feeling the need for self-flagellation. What did they know about Labour, he thought? They were supposed to be Conservatives. Why was what British Labour had done so much less, so insignificant, so dismissible, compared with what the Russian Trotsky had done? Joe had been on shaky ground with Trotsky and he would try to read up on him, but it was very annoying that these two from public school should virtually tell him he was not really Labour.

It was at this time that he decided he would play out the season in the rugby team but not pursue it after that. It took up too much time and, in the privacy of himself, he did not enjoy it. Both tackling and being tackled were no fun. Another load lifted.

He refused to join in a desperate raiding party led by the Yorkshiremen who were bound for a hospital dance in search of Irish nurses. He felt new clad in virtue: it wiped out Carfax.

454

Bob said that he had heard there was excellent fishing in the rivers of Cumberland and could he come and stay for a few days in summer to chance his arm? Joe felt complimented, both for the rivers of Cumberland and for himself.

It was at this time that he encouraged a shake-out of his societies, cutting down to the History Society and the College Dramatic Society. He found himself spending more time with the Joint Action Committee against Racial Intolerance and made a couple of obvious but welcomed points at their biggest meeting so far.

James seemed unsettled this term, there were two or three sudden visits to London, asking Joe to cover for him in the morning. Whenever Joe enquired, though, he insisted he was fine, just fed up with these bloody exams, the Prelims they all had to do at the end of their second term, as if getting in had not been proof enough, James said. It was childish to keep swotting for exams, James said, and he found that he resented it so strongly he could not bring himself to do it.

He left the choir but would, he promised himself, still go to chapel. What if they could get married in the chapel!

Roderick met him after a tutorial and they went to the King's Arms. Joe was becoming a regular. Perhaps the landlord would take him on if it proved necessary. Before they had taken a sip of bitter, Roderick picked up on a conversation they had started a few nights ago about the Impressionists in the Jeu de Paumes. Roderick was ecstatic, detailed, lavish in his adjectives, he out-boxed Joe several times on artist and painter, but the fact that Van Gogh was not his favourite gave Joe as he thought an unbeatable edge, a winning argument. Roderick put his money on Manet.

'Did you go to many strip clubs?'

Joe was totally off guard. The blush was the answer.

'Bloody expensive,' Roderick said. 'I trawled Pigalle half the night until I found a place I could afford.'

Joe's throat went dry.

'The Apache,' Roderick said. 'What a dump!' Joe nodded. 'Same again?' Joe nodded again. While Roderick was at the bar he rehearsed all the options and decided to confess nothing. Later, on his own, as he was walking along the street to the Bodleian, the recollection of it made him smile. Roderick! Gawd!

———

When Joe met Rachel at the station this time he thought that their new circumstances justified a deep kiss, but Rachel was having none of it. He was not offended: nothing could now disturb him, it seemed: his life was now fear-proof, afloat, ready for all comers.

'I'll pay for the taxi this time,' Rachel said, before it came. 'And I'll pay for the hotel. And we're not arguing about it. And when we have a meal we go Dutch.'

Mrs. Pryor unbent to receive a returning customer and Joe took advantage by spending almost three times the allotted span with Rachel in the narrow single bedroom. Neither by look nor word did Mrs. Pryor reprimand him, but neither did she smile.

Joe had worked out a new routine but Rachel wanted to follow the old. The King's Arms, followed by his rooms while the college ate in Hall, even the same restaurant, red wine from the start and then less tired than before to the White Horse where they had played shove ha'penny on the Sunday after church and where they queued to play again. Joe raised the issue, the chief, only, burning issue in the hotel bedroom, in his own bedroom, over the table in the restaurant, on the street outside the White Horse and each time with a different line or

456

manoeuvre though never hurtfully she put it off. 'There's no rush, Joe,' she said; 'I'm here all weekend. Let's just get settled first.' Even on the walk back to the hotel as eleven o'clock rushed towards them, she brushed it off and yet before they reached the hotel she gave him such an embrace that he shimmied back to Wadham.

'We'll talk about it tonight,' she said in the morning, 'after we've been to the theatre. We are going to the theatre?' He had taken her for coffee in the Kardomah, which James had suggested and called 'famous by Oxford standards'.

'It's *Hamlet*,' said Joe. 'Undergraduates. They're brilliant. They'll probably be the next stars of the London stage.' Some of them were known to come to the Kardomah. He waved, indicating limitless horizons. 'Writers and directors as well – they're all here. But *Hamlet*'s –'

'Do you think I'm too thick to go to *Hamlet*, Joe Richardson?' Her laugh was contagious.

'Now I come to think of it.'

'I'm not missing *Hamlet* at Oxford. We'll get tickets right away.'

'O.K.'

'Then – are those boats – on the river –'

'Punts.'

'– available at this time of year?'

'No.' Joe took the right swipe at a guess.

'I'd like to see one or at the very most two colleges. And no museum this time. Are we meeting your friends?'

'I thought some of us would have a drink in the Turl. You'll like that.'

'Good. I want to see them again. We'd better make sure of the tickets.'

Rachel paid for the coffee. As they crossed the café to leave, Joe thought he recognised one or two 'names' and 'faces' lounging in their young success, cloistered glamour.

'Let's not rush,' Rachel said when they went for a drink in the bar of the Randolph Hotel – another first for Joe. 'We can talk about it after the theatre.'

But the play was long and back in the King's Arms, Rachel said, 'Why did he not kill him when he could have done, when he was saying his prayers?'

Joe had a vague idea of how to answer that, was it to do with not killing men when they were praying? To do with stabbing him in the back being cowardly? To do with him being ready to go to Heaven because he was talking to God? To do with Hamlet's chronic indecision? He tried to bluff it out. It was not easy to be tested in the King's Arms on such a Saturday night, even in a corner of the saloon bar and especially when two or three came over to say hello to him and, as Joe saw it, eye up Rachel, which first pleased then began to agitate him.

'O.K. then,' said Rachel, 'if you don't know that one, here's another. Why did she kill herself? Ophelia.'

Once more, Joe struggled and in response to her persistence, tied himself in knots.

'I can agree with some of that,' Rachel said. 'But she needn't have killed herself. Her brother was sexy, though, wasn't he? Better looking than Hamlet.' She touched his arm. 'He was a bit like you. Last one. Why did the Queen let Claudius kill her husband in the first place?'

'Lust,' said Joe, firmly. 'Lust.'

'Yes.' Rachel nodded. 'That's what I thought. And he was very good looking. It's amazing to think that they are – "undergraduates" – as well. They were as good as real actors. You were good in that one at school.'

'*Our Town.*'

'The part you took was nearly as big as Hamlet's.'

'I didn't get a sword.'

'No. And it wasn't anything like as interesting.'

He decided that he would ask her if she wanted to see the final run through of the section of the Mystery play in which he had a part. Others were coming. He had mentioned Rachel to Mike who had been very welcoming. It would be at eleven.

'We have to talk before then,' he said.

'As long as we don't go back to that stuck-up place you took me to this morning.'

Joe was relieved. Rachel had received one or two caressing looks in the Kardomah. But they could find nowhere else open early on a Sunday morning and so they sat in Wadham's gardens on a bench beside the huge and famous old copper beech tree, both wrapped up like mummies against the frost which had crept in through the night.

They lit up, private face furnaces, and the smoke competed with their breath in the crystal air.

'Well, it's yes,' Rachel said quietly, rehearsed, steadily, and the tone restrained Joe, on whom the word 'yes' had the effect of a match lighting the blue touch paper. 'But I think we have to wait a bit before we tell anybody.'

'How long?'

She shook her head and drew hard on the untipped cigarette.

'I think we should do it before autumn,' he said. 'So I can come back married for the second year. So that means we should do it in summer at the latest.'

'I'm not eighteen until September. It'll be that much easier when I'm eighteen.'

'All right, September. But we have to tell them before then, surely. And I have to talk to everybody here and make sure it's all right.'

'It depends which comes first,' Rachel said. 'As soon as you tell them here, then the odds are it'll get back. If we start at our end then it'll get out and that could affect your scholarship money. I've thought I could apply for a job down here; that would be one way to get it going.'

'That's a great idea! Then you'd be here anyway. And –' he paused, 'but we have to get married. It's not just you being here.'

'I'm glad you said that.' Rachel looked at him, seriously. 'I'm very glad you said that. So,' she scoured the cigarette into the path, 'I was thinking of applying for a full-time job in Carlisle – it's counter work, not stuck in a back office and it would put me in a much better position to get a job down here.'

'Carlisle.'

'Don't worry. Garry's moved on; I made a phone call. So I'll try Carlisle. And then, I think, we have to choose our moment. Your mother won't like it, whatever she said, and my dad certainly won't – he's been waiting to get one over you and he'll take it. Some time in summer. We'll announce we're engaged.' She looked at him. 'And they'll just have to put up with it.'

He should have kissed her but he feared the eyes from dozens of the rooms with windows like his, overlooking the gardens.

'Until then – nothing?'

'Nothing and nobody. Except us.'

'So you accept?'

'Aren't you getting down on one knee? Joe! Don't you dare! I accept! I accept!'

It was not a good sequel to go to Mike's rooms and endure a run through of the crucifixion with no scenery.

Rachel thought it was terrible. Everybody spoke in fake flat northern voices including Joe, who had nothing to do but just stand

and tell the story that everybody knew anyway. The director, who was the chief actor, kept asking her opinion and she did not want to give it, but he would not give up. He also said she was 'totally authentic'.

She kept all this and more to herself.

—⁂—

She looked so like her. Had he carried on down Walton Street and just glanced quickly at the photographs outside the Scala Cinema he would have sworn they were of Rachel. The film was called *Summer with Monika*. The photographs of the star drew him into the cinema. He rearranged his timetable as he bought the afternoon ticket. He had not been to this or any art cinema before.

He came out shaken. The young man who had so desperately loved Monika had been brutally rejected. How could he live now? Joe wondered as he walked slowly back to his college. How could he possibly face life knowing that the incredible, sexy, unique, enrapturing woman who had been his was now angling for someone else, had cut him out of her life, just cut him out with no anaesthetic, nothing to do but bleed. What would he do?

And wasn't she so like Rachel? It could not be, it was not possible that Rachel could do that, but there had been a recognition of resemblance, and not only physical, on some level which Joe could not begin to unravel save he knew it was there. He had never loved Rachel as much as he did now, walking what might as well have been empty streets, nor had he ever felt such an engulfing sense of loss should she go.

In his bedroom he read again the letter she had written after her visit three days before and slowly he thawed to reassurance.

That a film could do this! Joe had been to films since he was a child, often two or even three times a week. He had cheered them on, he had danced to them, sung along with them, laughed hysterically, bitten his nails, found heroes, heroines, sex symbols, icons, people next door, followed adventures at sea, in deserts, in jungles, in war, in big city crime, on the range, and in the analysis and dissection of scores of crimes, and so it would not be true to say that this film affected him as no other had done. Yet there was a difference. Seeing a film would never be the same again.

He was to spend some time trying to define that difference. *Summer with Monika,* he discovered, was directed by Ingmar Bergman and the Swedish director became a passion as powerful as that which he had had for any novelist, any playwright. And through this director, and in the Scala, he was to meet other directors – and directors, not actors, were the stars now: the Italians, Fellini, Visconti, Da Sica, Rossellini; the French, Carné, Renoir, Godard, Truffaut; Buñuel from Spain, Wajda from Poland, Ray from India, Kurosawa from Japan. At school, Mr. Tillotson had said that great writers spoke to the human condition. For Joe, so did these film directors.

Perhaps the impact on Joe was so strong because films had been such an everyday, throwaway part of his life, and so to be confronted by films as immediately compelling as a work of art unbalanced him, made him think anew, made him think more clearly. Perhaps he was readier for the complexities in these films because of all the complexities absorbed without being aware of it in the films he had seen at the Palace Cinema, Wigton: he had been unknowingly educated in films. It was an education which only now came into play. But it was the vision of these directors that mattered most, a vision which bit into him and brought insights and a community of interest with others similarly afflicted that he was to find in no other arena throughout his time at Oxford.

'Dear Rachel,

'Thank you for your letter. Yes. I can't believe it either but now we're agreed I wonder why we didn't do it a year ago! I do love you. I was walking down Walton Street this afternoon and saw what I thought was your photograph outside a cinema. From a distance – and without my specs! – it looked exactly like you. It did honestly. She's Swedish and the film was called *Summer with Monika*. I've never seen a film in a foreign language before but I went in because of the photograph. There were subtitles. Rachel, you have to see this film. You have to. It gets right inside you somehow. It makes me remember how mad I was about *Snow White and the Seven Dwarfs* and how frightened I was of *The Hunchback of Notre Dame*, and dancing down street (trying to!) like Fred Astaire, but the difference is it's about people like us, now. I won't spoil the story for you. You have to see it . . .'

CHAPTER FORTY-ONE

The days were getting longer but all that Rachel could see from her bedroom window was a row of red-brick semi-detached houses. She hated the room. She hated being stuck in Carlisle with no real friends and nowhere she wanted to walk to on a warm spring night such as this. The two girls from the bank who had alerted her to the accommodation had gone to the Wednesday night hop at the County. Rachel had felt obliged to turn down the invitation to join them. She was, after all, spoken for now. Public dances without Joe were out. But the move to Carlisle had been more upsetting than she had anticipated, chiefly, she thought, because it coincided with this new self-imposed rule of non-availability. You had to get up and get out in a new place and it would not do to do that.

Joe had compounded her restlessness by taking an extra week to get back home. This 'authentic' Mike person had fixed up a 'tour' of the Mystery play in London schools, starting at his own old school. Joe was going to stay with James for some of the time. When he had originally written to her about the tour it was to tell her that he was not going on it. Rachel had immediately replied that he should, he would enjoy being in London, he would like staying with James, he

464

liked acting. She was a little disappointed when he wrote back saying that he agreed with her.

She got up for work in the dull, over-furnished room which she would never like. The heavy furniture was so unused it seemed to belong to a museum, she thought. Whoever could have lived in a place like this? It was dead and it made her feel dead. She made herself a minimal breakfast.

In the bank she was now at the counter, which had more interest than being stuck in the back room and she enjoyed being directly in contact with the customers. Rachel had no complaints about the work. It did not take long for some of the customers to act like old admirers. She brought sandwiches for lunch and ate them as quickly as possible in the tiny kitchen at the back. The three young women had agreed that they would take it in turn to make the evening meal but a combination of fads, sudden dates and forgetfulness made that an unreliable fixture. Besides, Rachel admitted, she liked the other two well enough but not enough to work with them, lunch with them, gossip with them, work again, eat again, chew over the same stale bank gossip and go to bed knowing that they would walk to work in the morning, all three, and do it all over again.

On one miserable night she wrote three long letters to Joe but in the morning she put these aside, too long, too mawkish, too sad when they should not be. A brisk cheerful note was substituted and posted on the walk into the mediaeval centre of the old city near the Cathedral where she worked. She supposed that her loneliness was proof of how much she loved Joe and how much she missed him. 'College'll be worse than him doing National Service,' Linda had said.

At weekends, after the morning stint, when she jumped on the bus which would take her straight through Wigton and back into the village, her spirits lifted. She could not wait to get back to the farm, to the busy house she knew, to her family, the village and the gossip from the kitchen of the Donaldsons. She had not realised how much she liked her own place.

—◊◊◊—

'I've one confession,' she said, 'and one surprise.'

She tried to sound happier than she felt. She found the location disagreeable. They were, yet again, on their 'island' on the Moss, the first time since last summer. Once a den of secrecy, a hidden cave for early forays into sex, glamorised, magnetised by the force of what they felt for each other. Now the den seemed to Rachel to be intolerably childish. But where else could they go to be as private as this on a Saturday afternoon? Especially in the Easter holidays: people out and about, taking time off.

'Go on then.' Was he taking her for granted? Straight back to this damp dump. He had scarcely been back for twenty-four hours but it seemed they had hit a routine as old as Darby and Joan.

'The confession is that I went to a party at Peter's.'

'Who was there?' He tried to sound calm.

'Only the people we met before. I thought, should I go? But' – I was lonely – 'it wasn't a dance' – it was better than a dance – 'and it was in his house' – but his parents had gone away for a couple of days – 'so it was all right, wasn't it?'

'But did you enjoy it?'

After the digs in Carlisle and the brooding on Joe and herself, the inklings of a too early sense of enclosure, a nagging spreading greyness in her life, the party had been like November the Fifth.

'Yes,' she said in a neutral tone, 'they're a nice set.'

'They are a set, aren't they? That's a good word for them.' Joe hunched himself around his knees and took out the unreliable pipe.

'And I suppose we're part of the set now.' Rachel was wary. He was trying too hard not to be seen to mind. 'What did they talk about?'

'Oh – I can't remember. Peter was very funny.' About going to the lavatory in France, that was all. About doing his backside business standing up or squatting down on what he called the gorilla's footpads and he demonstrated this with sound effects and all the miming. He had them in stitches. He had done it in broad Wigton dialect which made it even better. She did not offer this to Joe.

'The surprise?'

'Aha! I met your mother in the street last Saturday afternoon. To tell the truth I think she had been waiting to meet me because she came right across and started talking as if nothing had happened.'

'She's said nothing to me either.'

'But,' said Rachel, clearly pleased, 'you know what she did? She said we should go to the pictures together and when I said I was stuck in Carlisle all week she said she could come down to Carlisle one night and we could go to the early evening performance.'

Joe swelled with comfort.

'So she's got over it.'

'Looks like it.'

Joe wanted to take the opportunity offered, he thought, by the upswing in her mood and he moved to lie on her but she checked him.

'Not here,' she said. 'Everybody knows. It's become embarrassing, this place.'

'Nobody's around.'

'That's what you think.'

'Who cares? Especially now.'

'I care.' She got up and stooped her way out of their cave.

Outside, in the bright spring sun she stretched widely as if her whole body were expelling a deep yawn. Joe looked crestfallen.

'Tonight then?'

'Yes.'

'After the dance.'

'After the dance.'

She had hoped they might go out to one of those country pubs Peter had talked about: they sounded something new.

'I wish you would give up that pipe,' she said.

—⚍—

Joe and Sam were together in the bar just before opening time.

'Why do you want a job at the lemonade factory?'

'Good money,' said Joe.

'Have you got yourself into debt?'

'No.'

'I could put a bit more to your top-up,' Sam offered.

'You give me enough. I like working there anyway. I like doing the deliveries around the villages with Wally. We go to places I haven't seen since Alan and I went there on our bikes.'

Sam was not convinced. He had waited a few days for this conversation. This late Monday afternoon, Ellen in Carlisle, the bar empty, Joe just back, all conditions met.

'But what do you want this extra money for?'

'There's an outside chance I might be going to Germany for a month this summer.' That was strictly true.

'Germany?'

'They're taking a play and I might audition. If I got a part I'd need more money.'

'What does Germany want with a play from you?'

Joe beat his father to the draw and it was he who held out the packet of cigarettes.

'I don't know. Except this director, who's brilliant, he's had a review in the *Observer*, he says the Germans are mad on Shakespeare and somebody he knew at his school who teaches English in Heidelberg says he can lay on a tour of the university cities along the Rhine.'

'Well, I'm blowed!' Sam smiled. 'Will you have to learn German?'

'They all understand English.'

'Do they now.' Sam looked at him slyly. 'Is it *King Lear*?'

'*The Tempest*,' Joe said.

'Any good?'

'Not as good but it's famous because it's his last play. Mike says he knows how to stage it with a minimum of props. And he says it's the most significant of Shakespeare's plays for the state of European culture as he sees it today. Anyway – it hasn't happened yet. And it might never happen.'

'And that's what this lemonade job is all about?'

Joe paused, and to save him from a direct lie, Sam said,

'I saw some college lads on the television, with their scarves and their duffel coats, marching to Ban the Bomb.'

'I wish I'd been there,' said Joe and he braced himself.

'And I wish them luck,' Sam said, quietly. 'All the best. I don't agree, not a bit, but maybe that's what you lot should be doing and keep on doing.' He turned and leaned on the bar and concluded, quietly, 'But I'm afraid it'll never happen, Joe. Not in this world.'

—m—

Isaac liked to give Joe jobs to do and the boy was willing enough.

'I want you to tar that flat roof, Joe,' he said. Joe had joined Rachel's bus at Wigton as she came back from Carlisle for the weekend. Joe took the tub of tar, the thick-haired stiff brush, announced it the 'best job of the day', whistled 'Hey ho, hey ho, it's off to work we go!', put the ladder against the roof and tried to feel like Tom Sawyer.

Sometimes he enjoyed working on the farm and part of the enjoyment came in the associations it set off. He tried to turn the kitchen into the lair of the Brangwens. When they were down on the Flow he imagined it as Egdon Heath. Haymaking the previous summer he had felt like Tolstoy and explained Tolstoy's great happiness at haymaking to Josh, Rachel's more sympathetic brother. Now he was blacking the roof as energetically and hypocritically as Tom Sawyer had whitened the fence. Tarring a roof had no dignity to it, he thought, it was just a dirty job to be foisted off. He had planned to walk to the Moss with Rachel. The walk was still an erotic promenade despite the ban on the cave.

He must be thinking about that studying, Isaac thought: the boy's mind was certainly not on the tar. Isaac noticed but raised his fingers to his lips as Josh too saw what was happening. Robert Donaldson came into the yard with some bales he owed and he too was mimed to silence. The three men pottered about, doing some business, but never more than a few seconds away from looking at the young man on the roof, furiously lashing down the tar.

Isaac slipped into the house.

'Mother!' He managed to whisper a shout. 'Rachel! Come now! Come quick!'

The women came to the door. Robert concentrated a strong smile on Rachel which it would have been ill-natured not to return, though not to the same degree. Isaac's timing was perfect. Joe had tarred himself into the centre back of the shed top. He was marooned. He looked up, looked round, looked down, saw the crowd and swore silently.

'And you're supposed to be at Oxford University!' Isaac was delighted. 'Where's your brains now, eh?' The laughter was generous but it was laughter and Rachel was not altogether pleased.

Then Joe did a little presentation: as if he were a magician about to perform a trick.

'Does anyone have a plank? Josh – could you bring me that plank from the barn over there. Thank you.' Josh went across for it. 'Ladies and Gentlemen,' Joe said, 'you are about to witness your very own version of The Great Houdini. Bring the plank up the ladder, Josh.' Aware now and tickled to be part of the act, Josh took the plank to the top of the ladder and aimed it at Joe, who guided it to the small untarred patch. 'One moment,' he said, and he turned around and tarred the last bit.

'And now, Ladies and Gentlemen, I will walk the plank. So.' The brush in one extended hand, the tub of tar in the other, like a tightrope walker with a pole, he walked slowly, even delicately, up the plank, gave the implements to Josh, twisted himself onto the ladder, carefully drew the plank behind him and when he reached the ground, turned and bowed.

'Well, that beats the band!' said Isaac almost proudly, and Rachel sought out Robert to give him a victory smile.

—⟋⟍—

Linda had sworn total discretion. In her bedroom she played her new passion – Buddy Holly – low, but loud enough to prevent any

471

possibility of their being overheard. Rachel had been waiting for her when she came back from Chapel.

'The fact is,' Linda said, sitting on the bed in her Easter-new ruby-coloured coat, 'everybody will say why don't you wait?'

'I know.'

'Why don't you?'

'I've thought about it a lot,' said Rachel, lighting up. Linda turned down the offer: she was trying to give up smoking, cakes and sweets at the same time. 'Joe really wants to do it. I think he misses me a lot down in Oxford and he just doesn't see why we don't get it over with and get on with it.'

'They would still say "wait". What about you?'

Rachel laughed.

'It was nice to be asked!'

'But now?' Linda's questioning was close.

'I want to as well.' There was, Linda thought, a defiance in the tone.

'Well, do it then.'

'He'll have to find out if he'll lose his scholarship. I don't see why he should.'

'Has he found out?'

'We've done nothing yet. You're the only one, the only one who knows.'

'Why hasn't he found out?'

'I asked him to do nothing. I thought it was better to wait until nearer my eighteenth.'

'When are you going to stop doing nothing?'

'I don't know.'

'He must love you,' Linda said, rather wistfully, 'he must really love you.'

'He does.' To Linda's ears, Rachel's words sounded helpless.

'And you?'

'Love Joe? Of course I do. You know that. You knew that before anybody.'

'Marry him then.'

———⚬———

Joe could hardly contain himself on the way back to Oxford. Every mile was taking him nearer the place in which he would live with Rachel. The anticipation made him giddy with confidence and though he tried hard to concentrate on the books he had under way – *Justine* from the 'Alexandria Quartet' and *The White Goddess* – a general warmth of Rachel overwhelmed his senses and he was content to let it, and sit supine as England slid away behind him.

'You look extremely well,' said James, and Joe was far too self-absorbed to notice that James looked troubled.

'Are you anywhere near the Eden?' Bob asked. 'I've been looking up the rivers.'

'Why not try the Lakes?'

'The Lakes.' Bob looked down at his feet. 'You know, I don't think I've fished in a lake. A tarn. A pond. A reservoir. Never a lake. Yes.'

'I was talking to Andrew when that very clever indeed chap came up to us,' said Roderick. 'You know. Got a First. Black curly hair: too long. Published a short story in London. Needs a shave. Writes for one of the Sundays now and then. Hanging on for some American scholarship bung. Jacket always buttoned up one-two-three. Know what he said? Not quite straight off, but said it – "What I'm going to do," he said, this chap, "in my first novel, is cross Evelyn Waugh with Scott Fitzgerald and give it a contemporary twist." He actually said that! Gawd help us!'

473

Everyone agreed that the dullest and direst part of Modern History was the Gobbetts – where you had to translate from mediaeval Latin and comment on the constitutional importance in what you had translated. Joe's tutor was a boyish Welshman in All Souls who was mocked for his too perfect sports jackets, his immaculate suede shoes, his perfectly knotted cravats. Somehow, Joe thought, he made it all easy. He liked going to All Souls. He liked to imagine himself there one day, with a set of rooms for life, nothing to do but read and if moved write a definitive scholarly article. Love and the imminence of the total satisfaction of marriage tamed the terror of Latin.

He played no sport at all in these summer weeks. He did the things all Oxford undergraduates had to do in order to be an Oxford undergraduate. He learned to punt because you did. He drank Pimms, only one or two because of the expense, but Pimms had to be drunk. He lay on the lawn to read in any afternoon sun even though it was uncomfortable, stained your shirts and was too distracting to read anything properly: but that is what you did. He resented none of it.

With Roderick he went to a series of free lunchtime concerts in St. Peter's Church and discovered Bach. At first he could not warm to it. Joe wanted music to possess him, to overcome him, and Bach seemed to make few demands. But with unusual firmness Roderick insisted on Bach's virtues and Joe began the experience of learning to like somebody he only admired.

In his political philosophy course he had begun with Aristotle and the experience of hitting a wall of genius in a discipline for which he was so inadequately equipped was invigorating.

And now there were films. There was La Scala. Ingmar Bergman and what seemed to Joe to be his progeny called him down to Walton Street at every change of programme.

'I miss you but it's all right,' he wrote. 'Now that everything's settled I'm quite happy to wait. But not for too long! Next time I come home, remember, that's when we tell them. Oxford is such a fabulous place, Rachel, you'll really like living here.'

'I've moved out of those terrible digs,' she wrote, 'and I'm sharing a two-bedroomed, one sitting room, kitchen and bathroom (all quite roomy) with Alison Hargreaves whose brother was at Carlisle Art College with Peter! Small world. It seems he was mad as a hatter even then. All my love.'

'We stayed up all night and got a bit drunk and punted down to Magdalen Bridge for May Morning. We couldn't hear the boys' choir singing at the top of the tower but some of the men jumped in the river from the bridge. The truth is I was freezing cold all the time and it seemed a bit pointless at about 4 a.m. but everybody does it.'

'Alison is really very nice. We laugh together all the time! We go out together but you mustn't be jealous. She says she's my bodyguard! Not that I need one.'

'Only a week to go,' he wrote.

He walked around the college with a smile on his face and discovered, as summer brought people out of their rooms, that from the rugby and his brief time in the choir, from his own History set and the college drama society, and the new core of film addicts who had asked him if he would be interested in helping them set up a college film society, a network had grown up. Effortlessly relaxed, well able to withstand the few snobs, he was part of an unofficial company of men, he thought, leaderless and without any common strategy save that of being pleasant enough on a passing level, perhaps knowing that out of such unspoken unobtrusive connections, daily lives could feel secure and even reach the foothills of a kind of unaware contentment.

The promise of his secret fed Joe day and night.

CHAPTER FORTY-TWO

Joe was lucky to hitch a lift at the top of the Banbury Road which took him to Warrington. The driver apologised for dropping him off in the dead of night. But he only waited three-quarters of an hour for the next lift. By eleven o'clock he was on Howrigg Bank looking down over Wigton, the Italian tower, the church, confident sandstone buildings guarding the mediaeval huddle and the last of the Saxon settlement. He went straight to bed.

He overslept but phoned and took his bike up to Aunt Claire's and collected her Wigton gossip until Rachel arrived on her bicycle, furious, it was mad to depend on her father for the car, she had to save up for her own. Joe thought she looked perfect but he noticed she took more than ten minutes to get ready. They walked to Peter's. Her rather strained quiet attitude was not difficult to explain away – the bike ride had been into a strong wind, the lack of a car had been a loss of dignity. Joe was supposed to have come out to the farm that afternoon.

When they all met up, it seemed, to Joe's relief, that she relaxed. Peter could make her laugh whenever he wanted to. There were about a dozen of them and Peter's mother gave them tea while they all assembled and decided on their evening. Malcolm was there. Joe felt a surprising warmth towards him – they had not talked for months. Joe listened while

476

Malcolm talked about Dizzy Gillespie whom he had seen play live in Newcastle and Joe had to be told about it in detail. He enjoyed it, enjoyed Malcolm's obsession in a way he had not appreciated before.

They decided to make for Sour Nook, a tiny country pub on the back road to Sebergham, a pub with a landlord of the new kind, attracting groups such as this, knowing how to pander to them, unable any more to make a living from the dwindling number of farm labourers and locals. There were three cars. They piled in. Seven miles later they decanted into the saloon bar which they all but filled, like a private party.

Joe was separated from Rachel but he tried not to mind that too much. They were all friends together. When he glanced at her she seemed absorbed – for some time she was talking to William Anderson but Joe neutralised his jealousy by switching points of view, since for some time he talked to Malcolm's girlfriend, Ursula, who, like Malcolm, was reading Natural Sciences at Durham. They were, Malcolm observed, a little club of their own inside the pub, better-dressed, better-off, classy. Joe was uncomfortable at the accuracy of this.

William invited them back to his home for beer and sandwiches and though Joe was not keen, Rachel wanted to go. The billiard room had been completed and Joe tried his luck while Rachel sat in the adjoining drawing room deep in a three-seater sofa, talking to two of the women.

Peter gave them a lift back to Church Street.

'It really is becoming a set, isn't it?' Joe said as they walked the few narrow yards to Aunt Claire's which Peter's car could not navigate.

'I suppose it is,' Rachel said. 'Do you like that?'

'I do. It's something to come back to.'

'Yes,' said Rachel and she slid in the key very quietly.

—◊—

'I can't do it, Joe. I'm sorry. I can't do it.'

They walked their bikes down the twisting narrows of Church Street and under the arch which led to King Street. There was not a soul to be seen. The only life was the three lights thriftily illuminating the street. The town appeared like a rock, deeply settled, blending into the dark, not clinging to the land but dug into it, deepening in until it became like the oak from the ice age Flow which Mr. Kneale had given him. That tranquil sense of permanence temporarily eased the shock of her words. They got on their bikes and freewheeled past the Blue Bell, freewheeled down Station Road, could have freewheeled under Station Bridge but applied a steady pedal or two before turning towards the sea, the Flow, up the hill to Standing Stone.

Standing Stone had once, perhaps as long ago as Stonehenge, been the marker of the place that became Wigton. There were two references to the Standing Stones in unreliable histories but the name had been noted clearly in the first records and Mr. Braddock had pointed out the 'beauty of the location', how it commanded both the plain to the sea and the flat lands which led to mountains distant but fully in view. It was here that Joe and Rachel would usually change pace, here they would finally quit the town and dive into the full darkness of the country. But on this night Rachel stopped.

She had chosen a spot far from the single yellow street light to be certain of privacy, even in such a remote undisturbed place.

'Best to talk here,' she said, 'rather than you bike back.' She felt sick to her stomach. She did not know if she could go through with this. Perhaps she did not need to go through with this? Joe, and it was the only time she smiled to herself, Joe did not yet understand. It hadn't dawned. She pushed down the protective affection that this provoked in her.

They parked the bikes against the beech tree. Rachel leaned against its broad trunk on the other side. Joe faced her but did not touch her. The street light was barely a glimmer. The lights of Wigton were blocked from view. He began to fear the significance of all this.

'Well then,' his voice sounded over-loud, ringing with nervousness. He spoke more softly. 'What made you change your mind?'

'I don't know,' just as softly, very carefully, 'it seemed to decide itself.'

'But we'd worked it all out. You thought we would sort it all out about now.'

'I did.' She tried to think what to add. 'I did.'

It would be all right, he thought, it would work out, wasn't it usual for people to have second thoughts before marriage?

'Joe,' Rachel said, and she knew this was it, this was the seed of ending, this was what she had to say, the truth which would hurt, 'what I mean is it's *all* over. Not just us getting married. But us. Altogether.' She licked her dry lips and leaned, almost slumped against the tree, weakened.

'What do you mean?'

She said nothing. Joe's question was so forlorn she almost gave in. But she had guessed it would be hard.

'Not even seeing each other?'

Rachel needed a moment. It was painful to breathe.

'Not be with each other at all?'

Joe began to see the consequences of this and the shock was turning into panic.

'Not even like it was before we said we'd get married?'

Joe, oh Joe, if we, if you, if you had not suggested we get married then none of this might have happened, we might have gone along as we were. It was the marriage that made me feel so loved by you and I'll never forget that. But it was marriage that scared me, Joe.

'There isn't anybody else?'

479

'No.'

'Not Robert. Not Peter.'

'No. They're not a patch on you. I like them.' She was scrupulous. 'I like all your real friends – Alan, Malcolm, James, your other Oxford friends and the new Wigton friends.' I'll miss them, she thought. It was a new thought. Will I see them again? That was sad. 'They're a good lot, your friends, Joe.'

'Our friends.'

'Yours, Joe. I tagged along.' It was still difficult to breathe properly. 'Maybe that's all I did,' she said.

'No you didn't.'

'It began to feel like it to me,' her voice was thoughtful. How could she sound so measured, when inside her head there was such turbulence?

'But more than that.' She was tired again, but this, she knew, was as near as she could get and Joe deserved that, he deserved the best she could give him, he had done nothing wrong and he loved her, she loved him, maybe she was just a fool.

'I couldn't move without you keeping an eye on me. You were always watching me, Joe, wherever we were. And if anybody talked to me, let alone danced or had a drink or gave me a cigarette or just looked at me, I knew you would see it, you would be onto it and I would feel awful. I would feel guilty. I felt trapped, Joe. I knew that you were always watching me. Maybe I should have felt flattered but I just felt trapped. And it was getting no better, Joe.' This, she knew, was as near as she would ever get.

'What's wrong with looking at you?'

'Nothing.'

'What's wrong with making sure nobody else . . . You're my girlfriend.'

I was. She could not bring herself to say that.

'Anyway, I don't think . . . You're exaggerating.'

'Not from the way I saw it, Joe.'

It was over now. She had said it and she could not bear herself with Joe any longer. Yet you could not just run away. You could not just abandon him.

'I have to go now, Joe.' Her voice trembled a little. Joe took heart.

'Stay. Please. Just another five minutes. Please.'

It was real now. Joe could not bear it.

'Please, Rachel. Please stay.' A sudden gust of tears threatened and he drew in his lip, bit on it hard and checked them.

'I love you, you see,' he said, helplessly. 'What'll I do without you?'

Rachel felt the tears on her cheeks but forced herself to ignore them.

'You'll be fine.' It was so difficult to speak. 'You'll show them, Joe.'

'Please, Rachel.'

'I have to go now. I really do have to go now.'

With a great effort, she levered herself from the tree and took her bike. She wanted to kiss him but it was too much for her. Finally she said,

'I'd rather bike home on my own, Joe. And, I'm sorry, I really am sorry, but I mean what I said, Joe.' It should not be so hard. The tears were uncontrollable. 'And I won't change my mind.'

CHAPTER FORTY-THREE

'I've brought us a couple of bottles of cold white wine,' said James, in that almost clerical voice. 'I can't bear any more bloody sherry. I shall never drink sherry again.'

Joe was pleased to stop working. The windows were open onto the quad on one side, the gardens on the other. The light breeze of a late warm summer evening drifted happy murmured sounds through the rooms, like bees, Joe thought suddenly, like Mr. Tillotson's bees.

James looked in disarray, no jacket, no tie, shirt with two buttons undone, hair grown long, unkempt, shirt sleeves ineptly rolled up, loose and flapping.

'Not bad is it?' James asked after more of a gulp than a sip.

'No,' said Joe. 'Thanks.'

'Not that I know the first thing about wine,' James said, accepting the cigarette. 'Thanks. I'm glad you've dropped the pipe.' They lit up. 'That's one of the things that annoys me about this bloody place, people talking as if they were connoisseurs or eighty year olds when in fact they know damn all.'

Joe was surprised at James's language. Two bloodies and a damn so far.

'The snobbery doesn't seem to impinge on you,' said James, and

Joe, who was still cowering deeply in himself, nursing the wound of Rachel, saw enough to register the anger in James, more of a wildness, all the more disconcerting because it came in those precise tones and from that hitherto so well-poised friend. 'I don't mind the Tory Viscounts of Christchurch,' James said, 'and all that old snobbery of the Gridiron and Vincents and croquet on Merton lawn.' Joe had only the very dimmest awareness of what these references meant. Seeing that, perhaps, James clarified it for him. 'The *Brideshead* hangover is quite fun, another colour in the palette. As long as it does not predominate. It would be sad to see it go.' This time he took a sip. 'It's not much good, is it? It's what you get for six and ninepence. Still, it's cold.'

'I like it,' said Joe. 'It's the sort of stuff you could drink all night.'

'It's too obvious to list the glaring deficiencies.' Joe was happy to let James do the talking and James talked as one who has waited some time to talk. 'Remember the chap caught in flagrante with the girl at Somerville last term? She was sent down, permanently, possibly ruined for life. He was rusticated for a couple of weeks and I believe the University Jazz Band gave a party for him when he came back! And of course people like you are under-represented, to say nothing of women. But it would be hypocritical of me not to admit I could live with that because that is exactly what I have done. But it's all so intolerably bloody smug!' He drank more wine and a new mood came on him. 'I'm talking about myself far too much. You're not at all smug, Joe. Quite the reverse. And since you came back, you've looked rather rattled. I hope you don't mind my saying so. None of my business. Have another drink.'

So Joe told him. He had told no one else. He wanted to say, 'Rachel and I have broken up,' and leave it at that, but he responded to James's intense attention and his silence, steepled hands to his lips, eyes never making contact for more than a second or two. He talked at length. It was such a relief. He even confessed that he had proposed to her and found the guts to say that it was she who had turned him down. But why, he wanted to ask and did, into the silence. He went over her reasons and added some of his own – he showed off too much when he was talking to her and in her presence to others and she hated showing off. But he could not understand it. He told James about her father and her brothers, he told him about Linda and the dancing, he told him about the parties and their new 'set' and how they went for walks to the Moss and into the Flow. He did not talk about sex.

'I presume there was sex,' said James.

Joe nodded and left it at that.

'Well, I'm very sorry to hear about it,' said James. 'I liked Rachel very much indeed. We all did. Remarkably attractive and intelligent and unspoiled. She seemed very fond of you. Are you quite sure it's over?'

'Oh yes.' Joe was too ashamed to admit that he had rung three times and each time asked her to come back. The last time she had said the calls were upsetting her as much as they seemed to be upsetting him and would he mind not phoning again, it would be better that way.

'You're obviously cut up about it and I can't blame you.'

Joe wanted to say more but he thought that already he had said too much.

'I can't give you any consolation,' James said, and Joe noticed, once again and affectionately, in the latening evening that slight boom in James's voice, 'except to say – and of course this is meaningless – that in the very long term Rachel may have done you a favour, indeed she may well think that she is doing you a favour in the short term.'

'I don't understand that.'

A favour? When he felt worse than he had felt even on those very first mornings at Oxford. A favour? When he was crying inside and scared that the panics which possessed him would bring back the loss of himself, the wipe out, the terror of paralysis and disappearance

484

which he hoped he had conquered and left behind on a younger battlefield. A favour? When he so fiercely missed touching her, looking at her, making love to her, talking, joking, just being with her in the same room, in the same town, in the same country, and knowing that she was there for him as he was there for her. James noted his distress.

'As I said, meaningless. Ham-fisted. Have another glass of wine.'

James felt he had overstepped a mark.

'I came back tonight fully armed to tell you my own news,' he said. Joe looked up. 'Trivial. But there it is. I won't be coming up next year. It's having to re-take those bloody Prelims. Frankly I can't see the point. I'll take them but I refuse to do any work for them.'

'You might pass this time.'

'Not a chance,' James said. 'I've scarcely done a stroke since I won a place here – what? – eighteen months ago. Frankly it was a waste of a place. I have no interest whatsoever in the academic life on offer. I enjoy one or two of the societies. I like the theatre and so on. I love talking to my friends, Brian, yourself. But I don't need Oxford for any of that.'

Joe was dumbfounded and impressed. How could anyone give up being at Oxford? Seemingly out of the blue, he said,

'Is that the only reason?'

'Shall we open the second bottle? Before it warms up?'

The operation seemed to take a long time.

'You're quite right, of course,' James said, standing above Joe, pouring the wine. He put the bottle beside his chair. 'Very perceptive.' Yet he was pretty certain Joe suspected nothing. 'I just feel freer in London,' he said, 'and I don't find certain things easy here.'

James left a gap and Joe ignored it. Could it be innocence? James took a deep sip of the wine. 'The fact is that although I like women and I liked Rachel very much, I prefer men.' James took his time. 'I am, in

485

fact, homosexual.' The word was pronounced with great care, even reverence.

Joe nodded, somnambulistically.

'You are the only one I've told. Brian knows, of course. Others may suspect.'

Joe looked blankly at his wine for a few moments and then he lifted his eyes to meet James's gaze. He saw the pain there for the first time, the extreme nervousness, and even in that first glance he gleaned something of the tortuous route which had brought James here.

'I'm glad you told me,' he said. 'It was good of you to tell me.' He felt like a real friend now. And in some way, he could not analyse it, it made them equal.

He took out his cigarettes, tapped them forward in the packet so that they jutted over the edge, leaned across and saw that James's fingers trembled a little.

'That must have taken some doing,' said Joe.

'It did.'

Joe lit both cigarettes.

'We'll still stay friends even after I've left here,' James said.

'Oh yes,' Joe said, 'we will.' He raised his glass and then drank. 'We will.'

'It's very important,' James said, taking care not to slur his words. 'Friendship is the most important thing of all. Don't you agree?'

Joe liked to agree with James – but was that true? Friendship more important than love? How could anything be more important than love?

'Save of course for love,' said James carefully, 'though love is very difficult. Real friendship, I believe, though not as passionate, can be longer lasting and just as enriching.' He was tired, the fumes from the alcohol drugging his mind. 'Real friendship.'

Like ours, you mean, Joe thought, and he nodded, feeling warm in their friendship though on the horizon there was the chill realisation of an Oxford without James.

'You've been a good friend to me, James,' he said. 'You really have. Thanks.'

—ɯ—

In the summer vacation Joe came back home for as short a time as he could. Wigton belonged to the time of Rachel which was gone for ever, how could he ever accept and absorb that, and Rachel still came there and had to be avoided. Avoiding Rachel was the root of those days. Wigton belonged to boys from school who were working now, real jobs, their roads forked from his and inevitably growing more distant. It belonged to a time so near he could reach out in his memory just a finger length and touch it like rubbing his hand on a sandstone wall. Yet it was so far now with the intervention of university and more, so much more, since his abandonment by Rachel, which meant, he felt, the end of love itself, and of all the decisions and instances and accidents in his life that had intertwined and led to the amazing thing, being in love with Rachel and being loved by her, and through her, finding such a sense of rightness about himself in the little town, at the school, despite all his failings and vanities. Now Rachel, and that love, were gone. His heart ached. The wound was too deep. The thought of Rachel was so tormenting and so painful in his mind day and night and there was no one he could tell. He had to lock it in, afraid that he would seem soft.

No sooner had he got off the train and walked up to the Blackamoor than he wanted to be away again: it was all but unbearable.

487

CHAPTER FORTY-FOUR

They took the lead and the slates to Longthwaite Road and turned into the lane where the men had the allotments, kept pigs, hens, pigeons, ducks, bred finches, grew flowers and vegetables. Diddler led the piebald slowly pulling the flat cart to where he had moved his caravan. The other horse was hobbled nearby. He called out to his wife to make some tea. Sam and Joe had almost finished stacking away the first load in the shed Diddler had borrowed for a while. He and his wife would live in the caravan until he got a place. There was a dilapidated old cottage along the Syke road that he could rent cheap: there was a garth came with it for the horses. It was just a matter of haggling.

They were pulling down Vinegar Hill. The council had declared it unsafe and unfit for human habitation and the demolition men would be there on the Monday. Diddler had offered to help out by taking off the roof, and disposing of the slates and the lead. Since now and then he helped out the council with the dirty jobs, and also for the convenience of it, they had agreed immediately. Diddler knew that they had no idea of its value.

'My pension,' said Diddler, 'the roof off Vinegar Hill! It was big, Sam. "Unfit for habitation"! Vinegar Hill was good enough for us, eh,

Sam? That old roof would have lasted until Doomsday. But it's mine now, so.'

He had called on Sam for a hand. Joe was there, the last day of his brief visit before going off for a summer tour of Germany with the play. He was pleased to help, to get out of the pub, to put in time before he caught the sleeper to London and joined the others at Victoria Station in the morning.

Sam and Joe worked together steadily. Joe collected a neat pile of slates and carried them across the scruffy thistle- and nettle-infested ground. Sam took them into the shed and stacked them with care to get in as many as possible. When the cart arrived, they stopped and all three unloaded it. Then Sam and Joe set to work again. Diddler went across for the tea. It was a warm day, cloud closed in, listless.

They worked well together, father and son. To Sam it was a sweet interlude. He sensed it meant nothing to the boy other than a useful killing of time until he could leave and be as far away as he could be from what was hurting him. But there was a bond in the rhythm of the work, the passing of the slates, the handling of the lead; there was a nod of appreciation here, a touch of extra help given there. That was all, Sam thought, and it had to be enough. He wished it could have been more.

Joe had promised to go down and see Alan and when the tea came he was already overdue and yet he paused, not wanting to be one who walked away when needed.

'You'll be late, Joe,' Sam said. 'I'll see you.'

'Thanks, Joe,' said Diddler. 'Germany, Sam says.' He grinned, that wide gumless grin which almost engulfed his face and had always triggered a return from the boy. 'Germany it is.'

'See you then,' Joe said, and walked up between the allotments, gathering pace as he went.

The men took up the fine china cups and drank the tea.

'He's on his own now, Sam.'

'He's been on his own a long time.'

'He's still the same Joe.'

'Is he?' Sam looked to the end of the allotment path: Joe was gone. 'I can't seem to get through to him nowadays.'

'You're in him, Sam. You'll be there when needed.'

———

Ellen laid out the clean shirts on his bed. He had been home for so short a time and now away again for weeks and saying he might then find work in London for a month or so before the next term. He was taking every shirt he had.

Instead of going back into the new kitchen she stayed in Joe's room and went to the window. On Market Hill before her she could see the whole of her life. The big house over there in the cliff of a terrace, the house in which Grace now lay, often too ill to move. Ellen would go there later on, as she did every day, for an hour or more, to sit with her and to let Leonard get out, go up the street.

The Hill was empty now but Ellen could summon up her own life, the town's life, just by thinking on it. The traders with their fast talk, the fairground in October, the games she played as a small girl, silly games really, just excuses to run around and chant verses and numbers, and Joe had played there too, rougher games but much the same, much the same, and time had passed by so quickly. She saw herself come out of that door to be married and then the war and Sam coming home, after it was all over, standing on the steps, grubby, unshaven, that quiet smile, alight with love, and Joe thrown high in the air.